FRANKENSTEIN
A LIFE BEYOND

Book 1 of 3

The Resurrection Trinity

PETE PLANISEK

Book and cover design by Pete Planisek
Photos by Scott Coons

Frankenstein A Life Beyond
(Book 1 of 3) The Resurrection Trinity/Pete Planisek

ISBN 978-0-9850982-3-0 (print)
ISBN 978-0-9850982-0-9 (ebook)

Enceladus Literary is a registered trademark.

Book released in the United States of America
First hardcover edition, 2017

Published by Enceladus Literary LLC
Columbus, OH

10 9 8 7 6 5 4 3 2 1

www.enceladusliterary. com

For Mary

Characters

Ireland
*Ernest Frankenstein
*Robert Walton
Ailis Tierney Frankenstein
Tara Tierney Frankenstein
Quinn Tierney
Mr. and Mrs. Shaw
Mrs. Kelley
Padric Kelley
Dr. Martin

France
Abrielle
The Moon Shadow clan
*The Creature
Chloe

Geneva
Christiansen
*Caroline Frankenstein – deceased
*Alphonso Frankenstein – deceased
*William Frankenstein – deceased
*Elizabeth Lavenza Frankenstein – deceased
*Victor Frankenstein – deceased
*Justine Moritz – deceased

Salzburg
Jack Clerval
Costanza Clerval
Ingolstadt
*M. Waldman
*M. Krempe

The Wild Rose clan

Jal Nalie
Baseria Nalie
Espen Nalie
Nasi Nalie (Nagyanya)
Mayte Nalie – deceased
Patia Nalie – deceased
Jucika – deceased
Etolie

The Moon Shadow clan
Nicabar
Tasaria
Pias

*All characters from Mary Shelly's novel Frankenstein, or The Modern Prometheus. Not listed but also referenced/appearing are: Henry Clerval and Robert Walton

“The being who patiently endures injustice, and silently bears insults, will soon become unjust, or unable to discern right from wrong.”
– Mary Wollstonecraft

CHAPTER 1
GHOST STORIES

from the journal of Ailis Tierney Frankenstein

I had just finished tying a piece of dark lace around the end of a braid when I first heard the sound. It was a throaty grumble of protest and warning. I moved from my dressing table towards the window, and as I did so, the light from it faded. The air was dead and oppressive. A storm was coming. I resumed my seat and studied my face in the mirror. The knowledge that our plans would likely be broken weighed on my spirit and dissipated my energy. We'd been dressing to attend a dance in Louisburgh, a much needed diversion. When Ernest first mentioned the idea, my mood was so black that I protested vehemently against it. But he'd quietly overruled me, and as the day drew nearer, my mood improved, and I even began to look forward to it. In a few days August would arrive, and my self-imposed deadline would compel me to inform Ernest of my medical condition. The dance had come to represent an oasis of sorts, a last perfect moment of innocence together before shared knowledge altered us forever.

A sudden flash of light, reflected off the glass, broke the spell. Ernest was humming a waltz as he entered my chamber. Our reflections regarded one another until I felt his gentle touch upon my shoulder.

"What are the odds?" He grinned as I reached up and rested my hand atop his.

"With us …?" I managed a smile.

Before I could finish, everything in the house seemed to jump. My perfume bottles rattled in sympathy with the glass in the windows. The discussion was over before it had begun. It might not last long, but this storm would be bad.

"Did you get the clothes off the line?"

"No, I went out front and closed up the barn. I thought we'd have more time."

I went back to the window. If it was already raining, I'd just have to let them get soaked. As I returned to my seat, the unexpected sound of knocking halted me in mid-motion, and we exchanged identical looks of surprise. Who would be out calling in this weather? Perhaps Dr. Martin had been making a call and realized he'd be unable to reach his destination before the storm hit. Or maybe the Shaws or one of the other neighbors needed urgent help. The authoritative knock repeated itself but louder and with a more pressing beckon. Rain began to sting the roof.

"Check that the other windows are closed. I'll see to the door," your father called over his shoulder as he took rapid strides down the steps.

A quick circuit of our relatively modest-sized upper floor revealed no surprises, and it wasn't until I fully descended the steps that I heard two male voices arguing.

"No, I'll not come back!" The voice was deep and carried a commanding tone.

At first, all I could see of the stranger was his tall hat, which was higher than my husband's head. A hand suddenly clamped it downwards as the winds and rains began an outright onslaught. I was hesitant to interfere. I had no desire for this visitor to be caught in such an angry tempest but knew Ernest well enough not to attempt to directly intervene, so I waited until completing my check of the downstairs windows.

"Darling, all the windows are now shut so unless you intend to invite the storm in through the front door …"

Torn between mutual sources of disapproval, he relented, and grudgingly granted the stranger entrance before rudely slamming the door behind him.

Though it had been brutally hot that day, our guest was enshrouded in a rather heavy looking and soaking wet, traveling cloak. Beneath it, he wore the garb of the officer corps of the British Admiralty. Undoubtedly, this was reason enough for my husband's extreme reluctance to speak to the man.

The stranger set his sturdy cane aside as he removed his waterlogged outer garments.

"Madam, I am in your debt." He hastily acknowledged my presence as he resumed his grasp on the nearby cane and abruptly turned to face my husband.

"And you, sir, are Ernest Frankenstein?" Both men's faces could have been chiseled in stone for all the emotion they betrayed.

"Brother to Victor?" Ernest's face remained impassive but the tension in the room grew. "Once a resident of Geneva?"

Just as I began to fear that our unwelcome guest would not relent, he suddenly smiled. "Relax young man. The British Navy does not seek you, only me. Captain Robert Walton at your service." His head bowed a degree as he extended his hand, which Ernest ignored.

Walton waited a moment then decided to try a different approach.

"I assure you, sir, I'm here of my own accord on a personal errand," he stated, withdrawing some papers. "Your solicitor ... M. Christiansen's recent request for your purchase of these lands from my family is immensely fortuitous. Indeed, had it not been for this transaction I might never have known you were here, as unlike many absentee landlords, I pay little attention to the details of our Irish holdings. My work for the Admiralty keeps me far too busy. Still, I have been searching for you for some time. For you see, I was one of the last people to see your brother, Victor, before he died."

Only the rage of the inhuman winds and ceaseless waves of rain dared to fill the silence following this statement. Ernest turned his face from both of us. My own emotions surged with confusion. I was suddenly aware that I was sweating in the humid, sealed house.

"You have proof of this?" My tone was much harsher and challenging when I spoke the words than they sounded in my head. Walton looked uneasy.

"I do. I mean I did … but … well, it's rather a complex story."

"So you don't have any proof?" I angrily pressed.

Details from Christiansen's letters flowed through my memory, the litany of unsavory characters who had tried to exploit the remnants of my husband's devastated family. And despite his uniform and forced politeness, this Walton seemed no different to me. He was just another sycophant trying to take advantage of my love, who'd already suffered enough for one lifetime. I moved behind Walton and opened the door to a rush of rain-cooled air and mist.

"Leave," I ordered.

It's hard to tell who was more surprised. I said the word through clenched teeth, which altered the sound of my voice and startled me to a degree.

"Madame?"

Walton looked affronted that I, a woman, and technically still his land tenant, would dare to demand he resume the road in this type of weather. Ernest finally turned to face us, his visage still unreadable.

"You will tell us your tale, Captain. And then you will leave as my wife has requested and never set foot in this house again."

It was my turn to slam the door. The tailing swirl of winds snuffed the remaining flames from the candles in the hallway and plunged the room into twilight. Tersely, we followed Ernest into the front room. Here, the soft glow from a dying fire competed with lightning flashes. Walton hobbled in on his cane and claimed the chair my father had passed in for himself, and began a tale that was at once terrifying and outrageous.

He paused a long time before beginning, grinning slightly as he did.

"It is fitting," he quipped. "It's fitting that we should meet in this fashion, Monsieur Frankenstein."

He did not wait for us to inquire about this statement before he continued.

"Ten years ago, I was a much younger man: an adventurer, a poet, and a fool. You see I set sail from the port at Archangel, intent on reaching the elusive northern pole, and if possible, finding a way through the ice to the other side of the world. My dreams of personal glory, I justified by touting the enterprise as an advancement for science to be marveled at through the ages. My own life and the lives of my crew were a secondary consideration, and I've paid a small price for my uncharitable attitude."

This said he removed his right boot and revealed the reason for his cane.

"Forgive me, but you cannot imagine the pain of first the frostbite and then the gangrene. Fortunately the surgeon managed to save the back half."

I shuddered to think of them cutting through his decaying flesh and bone. He replaced his boot and continued.

"The Arctic has a unique beauty, one that defies description. It is a singular place with treasures beyond imagination and terrors to freeze your soul. My ship became encased in sea ice not long after we penetrated the frontier. It was while we lay trapped within that sea of ice that I encountered your brother. He was alone, half-mad, exhausted beyond reason, and driven by a singular obsession—to destroy a foe he had pursued there."

Rain pulsed against the window panes and threatened to drown out Walton, so we were compelled to move closer together. Our faces were a ghastly blend of frantic highlights and deep shadows in the shifting frenzy of the storm. At some point, your father and I clasped hands, and though his face still betrayed little emotion, the heavy beat of his rapid pulse left little doubt of his true feelings. The foe! Walton could not begin to comprehend what these words meant. Hearing them justified the brothers' paths of flight from Europe and quieted ancient doubts while simultaneously igniting new fears. Could one person truly be responsible for all the pain Ernest had suffered? Time seemed to dissolve as Walton continued.

"Understand me, in the short time I knew your brother, I grew to feel both friendship and pity for one who was so obviously gifted but so fatally flawed. While he lived, I was compelled to record the details of a most fantastical, and for a time I felt, unbelievable tale."

Again he flashed a wistful smile.

"Yes, it is fitting that we meet in this fashion because the roles have been reversed. For you see, I am now the stranger with the story no one will believe, and you are the doubting audience."

He paused suddenly and sucked in a deep breath as he considered the storm still hammering the house. Slowly he fumbled in his jacket, removed a pipe, and began to fill it with tobacco.

"Madam, do you mind if I smoke?"

I gave permission, and his hands trembled slightly as he went through the ritual. It was then that it struck me that this man somehow seemed prematurely aged. He smoked, and we waited. Ernest would apparently have to tell him if he wanted to hear more.

The great temptress, Passion, whispered to us there in the dark. The language it used was both familiar and seductive. It penetrated our minds and caressed our emotions. I suddenly felt as though we stood upon the edge of a great and terrible abyss. I wanted to hear no more of this story. Victor was dead. What more could the man have to say of relevance? As if fighting to release his words, my dear husband spoke again.

"And did you see this foe?"

I've never witnessed such a shift in a man's demeanor as I did Walton's. He seemed to shrink, as if he carried a great burden within, the difficulty of which had finally been noticed by another. The pallor of his face dimmed, framing his eyes as orbs of sadness and fear. The slight tremble in his hands became a pronounced shudder. Words were unnecessary. Yes, he had seen the foe.

"Do you believe in mercy, Monsieur Frankenstein?" Walton's eyes again sought comfort in the raging tempest outside.

"For whom?" Ernest studied the man, as he finally turned to face us.

"For all, of course. What man can say he lacks need of mercy?"

"Are you such a man?"

"I am a man in need of your mercy," Walton insisted.

"I don't understand."

Upon hearing these words Walton's countenance again transformed.

"He lives. The Devil lives! He stalks upon this earth. I have seen him. God help me I have seen the wretch with my own eyes … but I did not destroy him."

The intense conviction and despair in Walton's voice frightened me. What had this man seen that could affect him so?

"You speak of my brother's enemy," Ernest breathed.

"I speak of the demon that boarded my ship and claimed your brother's body."

The man's breath grew thin, compelling him to calm himself by attending his pipe.

"And yet, I must remember, you are an innocent in this. You know not the great crimes of your brother and his … creation."

Ernest stood, his eyes afire.

"You would come to my home, Walton, and speak such words about my brother? Slander the dead, who cannot defend themselves?"

Walton seemed to recover and with the aid of his cane also stood.

"I come to you because I fear your brother's foe is not dead. He vowed before he left us that he would end his misery and spare humanity the burden of his existence … but he lives. I know he lives! And now families suffer anew."

"Well, who is he?" Ernest hotly demanded.

The adventurer shook his head and resumed his seat.

"He had no name."

"All men have names …"

"I told you … he is not a man. But he hunts them. He kills them," Walton attested.

"And how would you know if this … if it still exists?" I interrupted.

"You speak of a ghost, Walton," Ernest agreed as he coolly sat back down. "You said this voyage of yours was ten years ago. Have you returned to the Arctic since?"

The man squirmed in his chair and cleared his throat.

"No. But I have advised three expeditions for the Admiralty since that time. All have met disaster."

Ernest and I looked to one another. Walton's story was beginning to collapse.

"Forgive me, sir, but is that not a common occurrence in the face of the unknown?" I did my best to sound dispassionate.

"Agreed." Walton sensed the trap.

"Then how can you blame their misfortunes on anything other than fate?" I persisted.

The captain flashed me a cruel smile.

"Witnesses."

"Survivors?" Ernest rejoined.

"Yes. Not from the first expedition, but the last two …," he shook his head again. "Four survivors, all with a similar story; their ships became trapped, just as mine did. One was crushed, and the other was abandoned by her crew. All four spoke of being hunted, pursued; their companions were killed or vanished as if they'd never existed."

This was becoming ridiculous. I threw up my hands in disgust. It was my turn to stand, and I wandered towards the smoking fire, paused before it, and then rounded back upon the man.

"So it never occurred to you that in the wilds of the Arctic they might have been hunted by polar bears or fell through ice, got lost, wandered off, went mad …"

"Of course it did!" Walton fired back as he leaned forward in his chair. Our false niceties were strained to the breaking point as we stared each other down. Ernest's voice broke our stalemate.

"And?"

"What?"

"My wife's suggestions occurred to you … and?" Ernest's glacial smooth voice mirrored his demeanor. Walton leaned toward him and gripped his hand.

"This thing murdered your family, your friends, stole your world, and yet you will not believe me?" he passionately demanded.

"What of this record of Victor's story you claim you wrote?" I asked.

Walton sighed, his head momentarily hung downward.

"I had to surrender it to the Admiralty during my hearing, to validate the events during my voyage after I returned. Some years ago there was a building fire at the Admiralty. The building was destroyed."

Ernest removed Walton's hand from his and stood.

"Unless you can offer some further proof, I'm afraid that there is very little I do believe about your story, Captain. But I believe our business is concluded."

I can only describe our intractable guest's reaction as stunned. He gathered his meager possessions and departed into the storm with a final plea.

"Monsieur Frankenstein, because I know you have suffered tremendously, I have already instructed my solicitor to negotiate the sale of this land with your representative in Geneva. Here is my card should you wish to contact me. Remember, dear man, if I can find you, your brother's foe can find you. Even if you don't believe me, do not stand idly by while more lives are lost. Redeem the fallen."

He favored me with the briefest, cursory nod, and then vanished into the gloom of the rain-choked night. For a long time, your father stood in the open doorway peering at the spot where Walton had long since disappeared from sight.

"The only devils on this earth are men like him, to come here and say such things," I averred but my anger was quickly abated.

When Ernest finally shut the door, he literally slumped against the wall. Was it with relief, heartache, or a pain so deep, his spirit was simply overwhelmed? In that moment, all I wanted from him was some reaction so I knew what to do. None was forthcoming.

"Are you all right? Speak to me," I finally whispered.

"Yes, I'm fine," he answered in a voice completely devoid of emotion. He silently left our hallway. Late in the night, I tried to speak with him again but to no avail. Eventually I lost myself gazing out the window, adrift in the relentless storm.

CHAPTER 2
GENEVA

from the journal of Ernest Frankenstein

20 September 1809

I am now only a matter of hours from the city of my birth; yet, all my thoughts tend upon you and your mother. I am homesick and ashamed. I can justify this black pilgrimage to others but find it difficult to convince myself. Your mother understands. She always has. I have no love for the life I abandoned here long ago and do not fully understand the strange circumstances which have conspired to draw me back to this mountainous land. In her wisdom, your mother bade me to keep a record of my journey, and I've no doubt that she will do likewise for you while I am away. She has always been more disciplined in both her desire to write and in her devotion to the needs of others. My poor words could never hope to do justice to the deep and abiding love I feel for her and for you. This is the longest we have been parted since I've known her, and the absence of her presence haunts my steps. A great dread stalks my soul, enabled by a fear I cannot name. And the lonely hours invite regret. She will never know how close I was to not coming.

The days have been hot, but the nights are quite cold. For the sake of speed, I have traveled by horse, alone. I have tried not to think too much about the task ahead, but have spent my hours reconnecting to the once familiar landscape. How strange that mountains and valleys, which are found throughout the world, should vary so widely. Each assemblage brings a unique presence: an echo of ancient times, a rugged secrecy, and the promise of rewarding challenges. It's not just the landscape, of course; the people and creatures that inhabit the lands also alter one's perceptions of a place. As I leave the unmarked boundaries of the French proper, the very scents in the air have awoken long forgotten memories.

I write these words on the shore of a nameless mountain lake, tinged with a blue-green surface, one similar to those my father would often take me fishing in. Though he was primarily a man of public service, he had rough calloused hands from hours spent outdoors: hunting, hiking, fishing, climbing. He introduced me to the subtle joys of nature, especially after the loss of mother and Victor's departure for university in Ingolstadt. My God, it has already been twenty years since mother's death. I am uncertain if I will be able to bring myself to look upon her tomb, to say nothing of the others. The veiled shadows of the mountains have begun to banish the light from this valley, so I will sleep now, and dream of all those I love who are far away.

21 September 1809

I've had the good fortune of locating a hot spring near my campsite this morning. The long days of harried travel across Napoleon's domain has afforded me little time for simple routines, such as bathing. I startled a red fox that was hiding behind a rock near the spring. The nervous animal hissed then vanished from my sight in three great bounds; however, the ibex that were picking through the food at my campsite were not nearly so skittish and left little behind. Hopefully I'll find some farms in the lower altitudes who'll sell me some food.

*

I've arrived at Geneva. It was dusk as I entered the ancient city by the western shoreline of Lac Léman[1]. I've managed to secure rooms near Christiansen's office and have sent word that I will meet him tomorrow. I am glad that darkness has obscured most of the surrounding landscape. For after all my travels and sufferings, I am now back to the one place on the Earth I have fervently hoped never to return to. In some ways, it is not the same city I left. Time, the dubious French occupation, and my own personal perceptions have marked the place, but in my weary state, my senses shudder in the presence of Geneva.

I will find little rest or comfort here. The great tragedy of our existence is our inability to escape the past. It infects us, bleeds our hearts, and shapes our futures. At this moment, I would gladly play the role of Faustus, if the bargain meant true freedom from the horrors I have outrun for ten years.

---

1 Lake Geneva

*

Why? What mortal sin could justify this? The fatal obsession of my days seems to be fixed. Is it possible? Before leaving Ireland, your mother and I argued about the wisdom of this trip. Now that I am here, I no longer know what to think.

For my own benefit, I will begin with Christiansen's urgent message, that I must come to Geneva for a particular letter, which has been sent to his offices for me. It was unaddressed and must have been hand-delivered to have arrived in such a fashion, but no one apparently witnessed the messenger. The message this letter contains is simple and brief, but those few words have shattered my world:

Brother,

Join me in Geneva.

Victor

**

"I would not have bothered you with such a thing had I not noticed this," Christiansen exclaimed as he held up paperwork regarding the arrangements of the Frankenstein estate.

For a moment Ernest's eyes failed to see the significance or his heart did not want to acknowledge it. The handwriting for both was identical. Even the letters of the signatures bent and swayed in matching fashion. An icy hand crept up his spine, electrifying Ernest's nerves, freezing his mind.

Christiansen pressed a glass of brandy into the younger man's hand before settling into the chair opposite him. Ernest numbly took a sip from his own glass and gazed out the window towards distant peaks. The brandy helped, and when Christiansen felt his visitor was ready, he continued.

"It was fate," he shrugged.

"What do you mean?"

"Well, I only had those estate papers out due to your inheritance request from April," Christiansen explained.

"When did this arrive?" Ernest asked as he held up the letter.

Christiansen rubbed his balding head.

"Early August," he decided. "It probably sat on my desk a day or so and when I discovered …well, I contacted you as quickly as I could."

His brother's face seemed to float before Ernest. No, not his face; it had been years since he'd been able to recall it clearly. In some ways, it was as if Victor had never truly existed. He'd grown so accustomed to seeing him as nothing more than a shade or faded memory that when Ernest really tried to resurrect his visage, it was like trying to paint upon a canvas with sand. The form was essentially correct, but the details were blurred and obscured.

He firmly set down the glass on Christiansen's desk and studied the letter wordlessly.

"Is there any chance…?" The words left before he could complete the question. Ernest did not even want to look upon his companion's face. As he stood, the bass of Christiansen's smooth, even voice refused to let the thought go unanswered. Ernest smiled inwardly at this well-remembered trait. Maybe it was his lawyer's pride, but he never did allow a question to pass unanswered.

"To date, aside from this letter, there is no conclusive proof. I have made inquires around Geneva, sent men to your father's house, and posted notices in the local papers. If he is here and, if you will forgive me, wishes to be found, as is alluded to in this letter, then he will reveal himself to us. But I will tell you this, my boy."

His hand settled firmly upon Ernest's shoulder.

"I've learned never to underestimate a Frankenstein."

The paternal grin elicited one from Ernest who relaxed as they chuckled softly. Christiansen took both glasses back to his server and refilled them.

"Imagine," he quipped as he returned Ernest's glass to him, "that anyone would have the nerve to come to my office and claim to be you, as if I'd fail to recognize my own godchild."

He vigorously shook his head as he took a hasty sip from his glass, continuing before his guest could interject.

"Of course, I was more than a bit surprised by your original letter.

Well … that is to say … I never would have given you up for dead," he amended brushing at his large, white mustache nervously.

Was this thoughtlessness genuine relief that his godchild was alive or the rantings of a brain unaccustomed to such a generous dose of brandy this early in the morning? His last words resonated within Ernest for he had given Victor up for dead. So was it morbid curiosity or hope that had compelled him to come?

"Have you ever met a man named Robert Walton?"

Christiansen's facial hair enveloped his lips, as he pursed them in thought.

"Walton?"

"He came to see me at the end of July, an Englishman, attached to the British Admiralty, claimed to have been a captain with links to Arctic exploration," Ernest explained, dutifully describing Walton's appearance to Christiansen but unable to bring himself to reveal the nature of the narrative the man had told back in Ireland.

"Ernest, with the number of people who've contacted me over the years regarding your family and its estate … who knows; I could have spoken to him eight years or eight months ago. I've even had a few people come wearing a disguise … but why should a wealthy British naval officer go through all that trouble?"

And here was the basic paradox of Ernest's life: only questions, never answers. Christiansen did not press the matter.

"What will you do?"

Ernest finished his drink.

"I would like to proceed with assessing the value of my estate. My wife …"

"Yes, the family," Christiansen broke in as he returned to the seat behind his desk. Godchild Ernest might be, but this was business. He smoothed his remaining hair and stowed his brandy glass.

"I take it you'll want to inspect the property firsthand?" His left eyebrow rose slightly. Ernest nodded in affirmation. And just like that, he committed to return home but turned down Christiansen's repeated offers to accompany him to the Frankenstein's family's country estate in Belrive. Ernest was unsure how the place would affect him and did not wish to subjugate another to his inner turmoil. Only Ailis engendered enough trust for that.

The men remained together for some time, even taking dinner together in the offices as they reviewed legal documents, traded stories of Ernest's travels, and recent local history. They largely avoided the topic of Ernest's family history, though he knew Christiansen longed to talk about his parents. He'd known Ernest's father for most of his life and had served as a type of step-uncle to both his godchild and Ernest's brothers.

As he finally took his leave, Christiansen pressed the keys of Ernest's family's former home into his hand.

"I've tried to keep things up, but with the French occupation and … well," his voice broke only slightly.

His ties to Ernest's family ran deep, as did his devotion. Whatever the estate's condition, he knew Christiansen had done his best. They exchanged a few more pleasantries with Ernest vowing to return in a day or two.

As he walked the streets back to the inn, Ernest was relieved that darkness held the familiar sights of Geneva at bay. It was not until he'd nearly reached his rooms that Ernest realized he'd been unconsciously studying the face of every man he passed looking for his brother, wondering if Victor be there, waiting for him when Ernest returned home?

**

23 September 1809

I was beyond the city walls by the time the sun caught up with the world. Sleep had been only a notion, so rather than indulge my hours in worthless while, I abandoned further pretenses and tried to focus my mind on what was to come.

I plan to remain a day or so, alone, at the house. I call it a house, but to me, it is no more than an extension of a vast tomb, one which houses memory, time, and the lost hope of my family and friends. I have seen the worst of humankind in my travels, spent untold hours in the cemetery where Quinn Tierney now sleeps, and in my journeys faced my own death untold times, but the thought of entering the house made my spirit tremble and my senses dull. Fearful that my resolve would fail me, I dressed and roused the innkeeper to pay my bill. The cool darkness of the slumbering city revived me. The blackness provided a sense of anonymity, and for a few precious moments, I was unshackled and my mind replayed the vast star fields I witnessed in the night sky during my years at sea. Strange how such an unyielding environment can harbor such beautiful treasures. Some nights the cold comfort of the stars has been my only solace, the only calm place of order in a life of chaos; their mystic fires burn undisturbed by the passions of our brief existence.

Though I left Geneva early, I did not manage to arrive at my home until quite late. I deliberately traveled a winding path, one which over the course of the day, afforded me long forgotten views of the ancient peaks of the Juras chain to the north, of Mount Selve on the city's southern boarder, and of the towering Alps of the Savoy. The majestic, frigid heights of "the white lady," Mount Blanc, held me transfixed for some time.

I walked through a land of shadows: the rock where my mother once gave me an early reading lesson, the trail to the boat docks near Cologny, the field in Plainpalais where William's shattered body was discovered. The image of my brother's blue eyes and curled hair passes unbidden before my eyes. We'd been at play, some sort of hiding game, when he vanished. We parted vowing that neither would ever find the other. And that was the last time I ever saw him alive. After a lengthy search, Father discovered him and then bore his body to the house early the next morning. Though the land is now clearly in autumn's withering embrace, my mind only replayed that summer day so long ago, and all I could smell were wildflowers.

When I finally arrived at the house, we silently regarded the changes to one another. Windows were broken or patched, decaying curtains hung asunder, an assortment of ivy, weeds, and grasses choked the lawn as well as Mother's once prized flower beds. The deplorable sight of my once safe and familiar home holds little emotion for me now. It is an empty shell, as I feel I have been for most of my life. My only interests in it lie in using it to secure the financial future of my family. It is ancillary to the true purpose of my visit. I turned my back to it and made for a small, gated plot of land near the woods.

The graves stood in long shadows as the fading light cast them into gloom. The headstones, or what I could see of them beneath the heavy growth, stood as silent sentinels adhering to their macabre duty. They have remained faithful. I have not. The corrupting effects that time worked upon the stones portends to what it has done to those at rest in the soft earth below. There, alone in the shadows, I, the last living Frankenstein, tended to the dead.

One by one, I cleared the stones of the decaying, encroaching debris, and allowed my heart to embrace each name my efforts revealed: Caroline Frankenstein, Alphonso Frankenstein, William Frankenstein, and Elizabeth Frankenstein. I paused a long time before clearing the fifth and final remaining grave. I could not even bring myself to look upon the name etched into that stone. I have never approved of its inclusion, and its occupant still arouses painfully intense feelings of love, anguish, and shame within me. Befittingly, briar rose bushes have encamped themselves nearby, ensuring that my hands were pricked and bloodied by the time I finished my grim task.

The light was vanishing rapidly now. I knelt before the graves, my surging emotions blending with a silent prayer. My senses turned inward to a rush of images, sounds, smells, and sensations richly preserved in long buried memories. All the people who had made my life real, who'd shaped and created my sense of purpose in the days of my youth, lay massacred beneath me. Here, before them, the silence was deafening. Tears mingled with blood as I passed my hands over my face. The man before them bares little resemblance to the boy who failed them and fled so long ago. Do they know that I died and have been resurrected by your mother's love? And what of Victor? Has his destiny been fulfilled in a frozen Arctic wasteland as Walton contends? Or is he here, alive, hidden for some as yet unknown purpose? I crave your mother's gentle spirit for no answers can come from the dead. Still, I hope that my pilgrimage will allow them to relinquish their grasp on me.

The stress and fatigue of the day finally overwhelmed me. With the last muted hints of daylight, I returned to the house and stole a quick glance at the family crest above the entry. The door was locked, but that formality had apparently been overcome many times. Inside, the dust lay as thick as snow in some places, while others attested to the recent presence of both man and beast in the house. I managed to locate an odd candle or two and began to explore the dark, musty chambers.

Rats and field mice have picked the kitchen clean. Some rooms are ransacked, while others remain as pristine as the day I abandoned them. At some point (I'm guessing French soldiers) used one of the larger fireplaces as a privy. Fortunately, the only occupant I found was a raccoon, though I've heard bats flapping about in the darkness around me. I discovered my old room was basically intact and sank mercifully onto my rank smelling bed. It shifted to the left and broke almost immediately. I tried to sleep on the floor, but incessant insect bites, most likely fleas, made this a rather uncomfortable option. Finally, I returned to the listing bed and became one with the darkness.

Dawn was grey and brought no comfort. I set about the task of assessing my property. Perhaps it was the unresolved matter of Victor or maybe the nearness of my family's graves, but as I moved from empty room to empty room, I became aware of a presence—watching me. I tried ignoring it, confronting it, and finally with no evidence that it was anything more real than my imagination, simply banished it from my thoughts. This task I must complete is for you and your mother. I will not allow phantoms to deter me; at least, none from the present.

As I encountered them though, certain objects and spaces took on a life of their own. My father's writing desk still smells of amaretto flavored pipe tobacco, and the top left-hand drawer still contained his journal. A journal he will never write in again. He'd been doing so when Victor returned with Elizabeth's body. I turned to the final entry and noticed how the last words trailed off, as the small sense of normality we'd fought so hard to regain was obliterated in that horrible moment. I left the room and took his journal with me, though I doubt I'll ever be able to bring myself to read it.

My mother's spirit still resides in the small bedroom, at the back of the house, where she passed, quietly of scarlet fever. The bed she died in was never used again, and oddly enough, it was one of the few rooms uncorrupted by either thievery or time. The floorboards near the bed still creak, and the dried flowers that Elizabeth brought her remain on the nightstand. My mother died while far too young and left all but her oldest child with a loss from which we could never recover. All of us mourned her, except Victor, who left for university in Ingolstadt not long after her death and immersed himself in study. He rarely returned or corresponded until William's death brought him home. It was as if we did not exist to him all those years. He never saw how the loss of Mother affected the rest of us. And he seemed mostly indifferent to the fact that his prolonged absence from our lives caused additional sorrows; though in the end, his own return resulted in nothing but heartache and death.

With William, I feel the strongest connections, either when I am outside or among the myriad of hiding places we used over the years; my poor, dear brother who never had a chance to grow up. He would have been brilliant, and his stubbornness unrivaled, except perhaps by Victor's. Thank God for Elizabeth's maternal presence. I don't think Father and I could have handled William by ourselves.

The library was by far the coldest room I entered. When I tried to draw back the curtains and allow the scant daylight into the room, it resulted in the final disintegration of the aged, decorative cloth. It was here that I felt the strongest connection to Elizabeth. She spent untold hours here, immersed in the minds of Dante, Milton, Plato, and Virgil. She was raised as my sister, though no blood tie existed. Her romantic nature flourished among the pages she read, and it was she who finished my schooling. Her gentleness, love, and strength of spirit kept our family going through the dark years after Mother's death. And it was Elizabeth's loss that shattered the Frankenstein household forever.

When I realized that the daylight would be gone soon and I'd brought little in the way of food, I decided to save my survey of the outer buildings until tomorrow. Three rooms remain for me to visit here in the house also, but I must admit, I dread the demons each of these might hold. Still, they wait for me, and despite my misgivings, I know they too will be visited tomorrow. With limited options, I headed for the nearest residence I could remember.

The LaShalls were once close to my parents but grew more distant after the death of my mother. So it was no great shock when they found my purported identity more than a little ostentatious. In the end, we passed a pleasant but equally awkward evening together. I left knowing they did not believe that Ernest Frankenstein had come to visit. They both well knew that he and everyone else in that cursed family were long since dead. But at least they were willing to feed me. I think the money I paid them for the food helped.

I returned to my mirthless estate and attempted to pen a letter to your mother in the murky surroundings. Were it not for the light of the full moon and flickering candles keeping the phantoms at bay, it would not be hard to imagine that I've joined my family in the grave. Dark thoughts tend me in those lonely hours. And I ponder how this house ever felt inviting. Several times noises have cried out from the dark, unseen corners of the house. I dismiss these as best I can, though with a growing sense of unease.

Man's worst enemy is often his own imagination, and as such, only nightmares found me last night. I remember few of them, but one image fixes itself to my mind, as it has often done for many years. The most repugnant aspect of this image is that it once greeted me in life before it crossed into the realm of nightmare. I witnessed it in my youth. The image of Justine Moritz's eyes before the gallows's door opened beneath her feet. Right before she was hung for the murder of my dear brother, William. She is the first woman I ever loved and the final grave I uncovered in my family's cemetery.

Chapter 3
Beginnings

May hope spring eternal in your heart and soul

November 1809

My darling child, I write these words praying that you will never see them. A life motivated by fear is no life, and I am ashamed to admit that fear now drives my words onto this page. Your father has always accused me of seeing with my heart instead of my eyes. Perhaps we both do. I hope that one day you will possess the wisdom and passion to follow and trust your own heart as I have followed mine. But now I feel compelled to leave you an account of who I am, who your family was, and to give you a sense of belonging in case my terrible fears are realized.

I am alone in the house (except for you—getting larger within me by the day—my how you kick) and have been for several months. Your father left for Switzerland, and I am too sick to accompany him. If I have died by the time you read this, I know your father has been loving and supportive of you. Never blame him for leaving me (us) for we are children of tragedy.

Whatever our fate, I will always love you, and all the fears and darkness of this world can never erase that.

Your loving mother,
Ailis

from the journal of Ailis Tierney Frankenstein

You are of the clan Tierney, whose ancestral home is here in County Mayo, near the town of Clauain Cearbán (Louisburgh). A vibrant land of mountain and river, wood and bog, ocean and green grass; it is a place I did not come to know until I was twelve.

Not long after my birth near Kinsale, my mother grew weak and developed mysterious lumps, an affliction which has been passed to me.

She would have good days when we would play games in the parlor or she would brush my hair and sing me lullabies. A bad day would find her too weak to get out of bed, insane with fever or in extreme pain. Though she suffered, I never remember her being unkind or distant, and I have felt her absence in my life for many years.

Before my birth and Mother's illness, Father intended for us to return to our ancestral home and live there. I love the sea and cannot imagine a life without it. Father reassured me, many times, that our new home sat very near the great Atlantic and that I would be able to hear the selkies[2] sing in the foam from my bedroom window. I've never seen my father's selkies, though I often tease your father that he is one, but several times I've heard what could have only been whale song. Their melodies are hauntingly beautiful. Almost as haunting as the spectacular mosaic of orange, red, and purple, which often graces the ocean skies at sunset.

My parents were both gifted storytellers, as is your father. It was my mother's stories which began my interest in Celtic history. I would curl up with her in bed, and she would read me tales of our heroes and myths of magic and struggle. She would tell me of ruins we would visit together one day, and I would spend hours imagining or drawing these places. My dreams of these trips always included my mother. I truly believed she would one day get well. But it was not to be.

My relationship with my father was always complex and became more so as I grew older. As children, we tend to think in very concrete terms. We put our faith in the ordered worlds we are raised in and cannot conceive that life, or our family members, could ever have been different than they are. During the difficult year we spent in France after my mother's passing, I was compelled to learn this basic truth. As a young man, and indeed through a significant portion of his adult life, my father was a traveler who embraced the new and challenged the old. He would never admit it, but I think your aunt Abrielle's rejection of him broke his spirit. We never returned to France, and he was never the same afterward. Still, he recognized the need to establish a normal life for me.

After years of uncertainty and sadness, born of Mother's long illness and our failed quest for Abrielle, the promise of a home devoid of these things bound us to a lovely, shared dream. Here in the West Country, our spirits were cleansed by gentle spring showers; they feasted on the hum

2 A seal in Irish folklore that can shed its skin and take human form for a time.

of life around us and were utterly transfixed by a countryside that was both familiar and wild. Even Father became more relaxed when he, at last, again set foot in the family home, a place rich in both the memories of the past and hopes for a bright future. The rehabilitation of the house and farm seemed to mirror the rebirth of my soul.

When we first arrived, spring showers and neglect had caused everything surrounding the house to grow lush and wild; some of the windows were missing, but the two-story house looked sturdy enough, even after eight years of abandonment. It possessed an aged but proud look. There is a slight rise in the main road which curves just before the house and barn. The main fields for our farm lay across this treed lane. Our home is west of Louisburgh and sits near the mouth of Clew Bay. This affords one a spectacular view of three things: the bay, the fortress-like Clare Island, and the expanses of the Atlantic Ocean.

In time this place of happiness and peace caused the general uncertainty of my early years to ebb with the cleansing pulse of the waves outside my bedroom window. Even today I love to sit in the window seat of my room reading and listening to the restless sea. And now I pray for it to return your father safely to us.

from the journal of Ailis Tierney Frankenstein

Your grandfather instructed me in Gaelic, our true language. British edicts have banned the open teaching of the tongue of our ancestors. Thanks to my parents, however, the stories and language of Ireland and her rich history have filled my heart, and I pray that one day, my child, I will be able to share them with you.

I have always intended to honor my mother by preserving our stories and legends. My plans have not been looked favorably upon by certain members of Irish society. Some want to adhere to the will of the British, and after their Act of Union 1800, the divide within our society has deepened even further. Early after our return from France, Father declared that I was to be tutored and not put into an educational system run by the British. We would not let Ireland be educated out of me. Never forget, my child, that hate is taught; you are not born knowing it, and it lessens whoever embraces it.

As I grew older, I began to take trips to various historical sites all about the county. Standing stones, ancient castles, old abbeys, craggy peaks, rocky rivers, and monuments of antiquity intrigued me to such a degree that I eventually announced to Father my wish to open a museum in Louisburgh dedicated to local history. Much to my dismay, he neither embraced the idea nor rejected it.

Fate is an odd companion because you never know when it will suddenly invest itself in your life. It is a changeling, one that does not separate good from evil. It takes on many forms: acquaintance, fool, idea, whim, spirit, the common, and the extraordinary. Fate works in your heart and in the souls of others long before anyone is aware of its presence. It challenges us toward moments of abhorred perfection and merciful insight. Fate crept into my life subtly. Its chosen means was a book I arbitrarily selected from my library shelves on an unusually cold winter's eve in early 1806. This book would turn my passions towards obsession and eventually lead me to my destiny.

**

Ailis sat on a bench by the Bunowen River letting the fresh air fill her lungs and the sound of running water sooth her senses. It was as if a ghost from her past had risen from a grave and clutched her soul. No, the store clerk must be mistaken. Ailis' mind was a symphony of the images of faces, smells, and jumbles of conversation. How had she arrived at this bench some distance from the store? Could she have fainted? She hadn't even cried when a horse stepped on her foot and broke several bones. Still she could only clearly recall a surge of emotion followed by blackness.

Though she could feel the weight of the object she held, it took an eternity for her to look down at it and confirm that her sister's name and a French postmark did indeed grace the envelope. Why after all these years would Abrielle send her a letter?

Just before leaving the orphan's convent in Bayonne, France, her Father had scribbled down addresses in both Kinsale and here in Mayo, and left the paper with Sister Annette in the hope that this letter would one day come. While the hoped-for letter had arrived, it was not addressed to him; it was written for Ailis. She tried to force a surfacing memory back to the dark corners of her mind by closing her eyes and turning them towards the blinding spring sunlight.

But it refused to be silenced, and Ailis replayed the only memories she had of her half-sister: the beautiful, tall, seventeen-year-old with the slight limp. She could still feel the sense of shame and embarrassment as Abrielle slapped their father's face and vanished. Wait. Had he cried when she slapped him? No, Ailis was crying. Over six years later, she was crying alone on a stone bench and couldn't stop it. She didn't want to stop it. She wanted to destroy this letter. Ailis felt stained by the look in Abrielle's eyes as she stared into her sibling's just before she'd cruelly fled. How could she do this?

She tore the letter in half and stood, intent on consigning it to the rock choked stream below, to watch as the paper absorbed the water and the ink became obliterated. But when the moment came to release it, her hand did not open. Abrielle's soft brown eyes again flashed in her mind but this time the memory was different. She saw her sister's eyes alive with fear, curiosity, and underlying both, ardent need. Ailis suddenly felt hollow inside as tears of anger turned to ones of shame. She wanted to destroy her wayward sister's words to her but couldn't. The thought of Abrielle's absence in her life plagued Ailis.

"Oh, there you are." The sound of Doctor Martin's voice behind her returned Ailis to the present. Her hand secreted the envelope into the pocket of her dress as the other worked to dry her face.

"Are you ready to go?"

"Yes, yes."

The doctor studied her as she stood still wiping her eye.

"You look a bit flush. Is everything all right, Ailis?"

Ailis waved her hand dismissively.

"Oh, it's nothing, Doctor; something about the spring air always affects me. It's worse when it hasn't rained. The breeze coming off the river sometimes helps."

His gaze held a moment longer.

"Well, I'm sure crossing the bay will give you plenty of fresh air. But if you're feeling infirm perhaps you should remain here. Much as I appreciate your help, I'm sure I can manage or Mrs. Kelley could come."

"No, I'm … I'm fine. See?" She smiled reassuringly as she pushed a strand of blonde hair from her eyes.

Dr. Martin raised his hands a measure in both a sign of resignation and as a directive that it was time to board his cart. For a time they journeyed quietly, neither minded. Ailis had been volunteering with the local surgeon for years, and they were used to long hours spent traveling together around the countryside seeing patients.

"How many days do you think we'll be gone?" Ailis finally asked.

"Depends," the doctor barely managed to get the word out as he yawned. "Excuse me. The Krendells' second is due any day so I'd prefer not to be gone too long. But it seems like every time I finally make it out to Clare Island, the trip takes longer than I'd anticipated. Most residents don't make it back to the mainland often enough or when they do, I'm out seeing other patients. Actually I'm a little surprised you wanted to come with me this time."

"Why?"

"What? Oh, just something your father said the other day … or was it Mrs. Kelley?"

Inwardly Ailis cringed as she glanced at the doctor, certain she was all too familiar with the subject he was trying to raise. She was grateful they arrived at the dock before the conversation could go any further. The doctor was one of the more sensible men she'd ever met, but Ailis doubted he could fully understand how trapped she now felt.

They boarded a small vessel, and as the pilot cast off, Ailis was greeted by the familiar and, by now taunting, presence of Clare Island, silently waiting for her out in the bay. Her apprehensions about home faded momentarily as she returned the sightless gaze of the island. What secrets did it long to share? Ever since the winter's night she'd randomly picked up a book about the history of Oileán Chilara, Clare Island had become an increasing source of fascination. A living presence beckoning to her from across the bay; one rich in history, this former realm of a pirate queen was one of the few local areas she'd never managed to visit. Ailis was more than aware that with an undesired marriage proposal awaiting her when she returned from this trip, this might be her last chance to embrace a fate of her own.

*

Doctor Martin crumpled the missive as he turned to Ailis.

"I've got to get to the Krendells," he declared as he reached for his jacket.

"Go," said Ailis, "I can finish up here."

They'd spent the last three days traversing the island, dealing with a host of patients and ailments, thankfully, primarily mundane ones. Doctor Martin hesitated.

"Do you want me to come with you?"

He shook his head.

"No, no, you'd best be getting back home. The Krendells are a fair bit from here, and you know how these things go. Could take an hour, a day, or be over with before I ever get there. Besides, I think the only thing left to do here is to deliver those powders. I'll … uh ...," he reached for a piece of paper and began to scribble instructions.

Ailis tried to conceal her excitement as he wrote.

"Now please, don't go stoppin' at every rock or ruin you come across. Just deliver these and get back on the boat," the doctor directed as he repacked his bag.

Ailis nodded but offered no protest as he began to pat his pockets and swivel his head.

"Oh, and if you get … get a chance … where did I put ...?"

She picked up the watch he'd been searching for off the table and handed it to him.

"Ah, thank you. If you get the chance, when you get back, check in on Shannon, see how her eldest daughter's toothache is."

"Of course."

Dr. Martin completed a final check of his possessions and snapped his bag shut.

"There. I think I'm all set."

He placed a hand on Ailis' shoulder.

"Remember to send me a note when you get back."

"I always do."

He grinned as he put on his hat and gave a brief tug of the brim as he reached the door.

"Kindly give my regards to your father."

"Good luck."

With the doctor gone, Ailis was at last free to fully indulge in her curiosity involving both the island and her mysterious sister.

*

The deliveries did not take long, and while she was engrossed in this task, Ailis pondered her sister's life. Abrielle had grown up alone during a time of great upheaval. First, the ruling French monarchy fell, then the revolutionary forces swept murderously across the land, and now Napoleon Bonaparte was attempting to reinvent her nation. How had these events affected her? Where had she been all these years? Had she found love and family? How old was she now? Probably about twenty four, but not knowing exactly when her birthday was, Ailis couldn't be sure. What would Abrielle think of her nearly eighteen-year-old half sister? If they ever did converse, what would they talk about? Would they simply lapse into an uncomfortable silence? Did they have the same sense of humor? Was Ailis an aunt?

Several times during the last few nights she'd risen and taken out the torn envelope but always shied away from reading the contents inside. The revelation of her sibling's existence had been shocking, but Abrielle's rejection of her family had been devastating. Should Ailis confront her past or continue trying to deny the pain it caused?

Ailis' final delivery took her near the island's remote southwestern shore and to a rare artifact she'd discovered a day earlier but hadn't had an opportunity to examine. She wandered away from the road and sat before the moss adorned, engraved Celtic cross, which stood abreast the edge of a cliff that plunged dramatically down into the sea. From the road the relic was almost hidden completely from view. The book she'd read spoke mostly of the island's primary family clan in residence: the O'Malleys. Ruling the island since the Middle-Ages, the colorful family had fought British landlords, annihilated the shipwrecked crew of a Spanish Galleon from the infamous Spanish Armada, and under the leadership of the legendary pirate queen, Gráinne Uaile, served as a major irritant for Elizabeth I. Most of the island's principle ruins were tied to this family's history. But what of this cross?

As she began to eat the food so thoughtfully provided by the household of her last delivery, Ailis pondered the cross. It was reassuring that something seemed so permanent. These crosses were rare, usually centuries old, and had often been used as markers. But why place one atop this lonely pinnacle overlooking the Atlantic? What could it mark?

Ailis stood and hazarded a glance below. Only a small rocky beach was visible, though there did appear to be a recessed area under the cliff. She delicately stepped back, sat, and resumed eating. When she'd finished, Ailis retrieved the by now much abused letter from her pocket.

It could take a long time to translate; she hadn't used her French language skills for many years. She frowned. The name of the town provided as the return address was entirely unfamiliar. Ailis would have to consult a map when she returned home. Removing the contents from the bisected envelope, she reunited them into a single page. It was an extremely brief letter, written in a blend of English and French. Perhaps her sister couldn't decide which would be easier for Ailis to read. The thought comforted her.

Fully translated the letter said only this:

10 January 1806

My dear sister,

Do not think ill of me. We have been too long absent from each other's lives. Write me. I implore you not to tell your father.

Yours,
Abrielle

Ailis read the letter several times to be sure that she'd translated it correctly, then returned it to her pocket and stared absently across the sea: 'Your father,' not 'our father.'

By now Quinn Tierney would be waiting for his youngest daughter to return home. What would she tell him? After all these years of silence, should she honor her sister's request or tell their father that Abrielle had finally reached out? What would the knowledge do to him? Her sister already felt betrayed by him; if Ailis told her father about the letter would she feel the same towards Ailis and disappear forever?

Some of these feelings Ailis could understand. After her mother's passing, when she'd first learned of Abrielle's existence, she'd felt betrayed by her parents, uncertain about her place in the world, guilt, embarrassment, but also a curiosity to learn more. Perhaps her sister's feelings were the same. Cheered by the thought Ailis made her decision. She would write Abrielle back.

She knelt before the cross and ran her fingers over the worn carvings. She'd never fully mastered reading ogham or other symbolic variants, and many of the crosses were irrevocably damaged by time and nature. Ailis gazed bravely back over the ledge, her fingers clutching the stones as a powerful gust of wind startled her. Again she retreated. Maybe there were relics below, the cross positioned here to mark the inlet. Or could the ancient cross possibly mark the location of Gráinne Uaile's unknown grave? It was a tantalizing thought, but there was only one way to be sure.

*

The third pass would be her final attempt. For over an hour now, Ailis had struggled to land her sailboat in the rocky inlet above which the cross stood. In fact the entire venture was proving to be more trouble than it was worth. But several of the O'Malley clan's families had expressed interest in her museum and that alone was enough for Ailis to keep trying. She'd never been someone who gave up easily as demonstrated by her ability to sail.

Living by the sea and being the daughter of a former mariner, she'd learned how to sail not long after their arrival in Mayo. Not that these had been formal lessons. When she was younger, she convinced her father to take her sailing, posing innocent questions while carefully watching everything; then she'd persuade Padraic, to whom she was close in age, to take her out in the Kelleys' boat, which inevitably she'd talk him into allowing her to sail. Her father had been quite vexed the first time he learned she'd taken a boat out by herself. But she kept doing it until he relented and gave her a more formal training, though he still discouraged her from sailing alone.

Sailing could be terrifying, exhilarating, but above all, exhausting. It did not help that since she'd left Clare Island's main harbor dark clouds now marched across the Atlantic towards her. Still, if she could make landfall and discover something of value, her dreams for the museum might gain new validity and protect her freedom.

The shifting winds from the incoming storm, combined with the narrow channel of the inlet's rock strewn waters, kept forcing her to make larger circles to align her boat. Time was becoming more important. As she tensely commenced her last effort to make landfall, Ailis began to sing a song her mother had taught her. The winds buffeted her sail; rocks scraped the haul, which moaned under the stress but survived the nerve-wracking passage. By the time she struggled out of the freezing water, Ailis was numb with cold and additionally taxed from dragging the boat ashore. The rocks that comprised the beach of stone still held the warmth from the faded sunlight, and she sat huddling, shivering upon them as she attempted to restore feeling back into her thin limbs.

She turned, her eyes tracing the imposing cliff, but it was impossible to detect the position of the cross from this vantage, though she was certain it was there. The recess into the cliff was murky, the towering walls daunting. The dismal setting breathed with the echo of waves that Ailis could tell were increasing in strength as the storm drew near. She retrieved the matches and candle she'd had the foresight to bring then began to explore the confines of the recess. It held more branches than she would have guessed when she'd stood atop.

She waited to light the candle until it was absolutely necessary, afraid the wind would too quickly abate the flame, which it repeatedly did. Ailis also became aware of the sound of a modest waterfall further back. Despite the poor light, she was able to locate some pottery fragments and metal jewelry. Unfortunately she had little time to celebrate her discovery.

A harsh scraping sound intruded, repeated itself and, within seconds of realizing what it meant, she was up and running back to the stony beach. Any moment now it would be too late.

This was going to be unpleasant, but there was no alternative. She cast off her shoes, bit her lip, plowed into the frigid surf, and began to swim. The ceaseless tide had plucked her boat from the beach, and only a few cragged rocks in the inlet prevented it from drifting away. When she reached it, Ailis struggled with the boat only to discover that it was stuck fast on some unseen obstacle beneath the surface. Her hand was almost crushed between the rock and the boat as she tried to free it. In pain and defeat, she returned to shore. Salt water burned the cuts on her hands and feet, from which rivulets of blood flowed. They stung horribly but paled in comparison to the knowledge that she was trapped. The boat could break free at any point or remain stuck on the rocks and eventually break up; it was all just a matter of time and tide.

With the noise of the surf and the incoming storm, no one could hear her scream for help and who would know to look for her here. A mangled, grime encrusted lock of hair flopped into her eyes as she fought against the urge to panic. She angrily shoved it away and headed back inside the recess. The boat would be no place to be in a storm. Perhaps deeper in the recess there was a way back up to the top. Ailis returned to where her extinguished candle lay and retrieved the jewelry she'd found. The rest would have to wait. She proceeded toward the sound of the waterfall closer to the recesses' entrance.

She thrust first her head then salt-stung limbs into the cascading fall. Sputtering cold but fresh water, she began to scrub at the grime on her hair and skin. Ailis was so angry and engrossed in her cleaning that she failed to notice the man at first. In fact she nearly tripped over him in the gloom as she began to walk away.

Her initial instinct was to scream, followed instantly by the urge to run, but Ailis quickly realized this would not be necessary. He was dead. Well, he looked dead. He wore no shoes; every item of clothing on him was ripped and filthy. He had unruly long brown hair and an unkempt beard. He was lying face down and had apparently crawled there from the beach. All this she discerned after noticing the blood-soaked wound in his left shoulder. Curiosity and compassion supplanted fear, and she knelt down beside him. Before she left, Ailis had to know if he was dead. By the look of the wound and the stench of the man, he should have been—but he wasn't.

He turned slightly at her tentative touch. He made no sound, but his eyes slowly opened and fixed on her. For an endless moment, his blue eyes fixed upon Ailis' grey ones. Finally his lips moved and with a rattling breath, he uttered a single plea in French, "Please … don't kill … me."

Chapter 4
Of Unions and Loss

As he slipped back into an unconscious state, Ailis stood and backed away gasping for the breath she hadn't realized she was holding. A noise somewhere between a repressed scream and uncontrolled laughter tried to escape, but she forced it down. Her body was quaking with the effects of both fear and cold. The recess echoed with the sound of breaking waves. Ailis knelt again to examine the wound. She ripped one of his pant legs and used the fabric as a bandage, wrapping it over his shoulder and under his arm. He barely seemed to notice. His body felt quite warm, and undoubtedly, an infectious fever had set in.

As she completed her task, he regained a degree of consciousness and began muttering. Ailis leaned him against the wall, cupped her hands, captured a measure of the falling water, and applied it to his lips. It had the desired effect and calmed him. She fervently wished she felt the same. What could she do? She probed the dark corners of the recess but they appeared to offer no other escape. The prostrate stranger had already lost a lot of blood. If they remained, it was likely he would die, and she could not abandon him to that fate. Their only hope was the sea.

Ailis was still considering the problems when the man's hand reached up and brushed at one of the silent tears she hadn't even realized was upon her face. It startled her, but she did not draw away. Even in his semi-conscious state, his look of soft reassurance warmed her spirits. She could do this. They slowly, awkwardly staggered out of the recess, onto the barren shore of rock. The wind was howling, rain flew all around them.

Ailis gritted her teeth as she swam to the pitching boat and retrieved a line of unused rope and some spare boards from the deck. Returning one final time to shore, she tied one end of the rope beneath the stranger's arms, partially affixed him to the wood, and dragged them both back into the sea. The strategy nearly drowned them both, but finally Ailis managed to pull herself aboard the unstable boat. By now she was far too weak to haul the man from the water, and he continued to drift in and out of lucidity. If she didn't find a way to get him aboard soon, he would drown.

"Hey, hey!" She screamed down to him, slapping water in his face hoping to jolt him awake.

His eyes opened with a start as he looked up.

"Did you find William?"

Was there someone else injured who'd been with him? It didn't matter. She needed to get him in the boat.

"Yes, he's up here. Climb up to us," she cried out in crude French as she held out her hand.

Their efforts combined, she was finally able to draw him to safety. Ailis cut away the rope and boards, and both collapsed in the narrow, rocking boat.

"I knew you'd find him, Justine. I knew you would."

His senses faded to oblivion again, and she was a shivering, exhausted wreck. With no other heat source, Ailis drew her body as close to his as possible. And then she waited.

For hours they were knocked about by the tide and rocks. The sky darkened, the rains increased, forcing her to bail, and still she waited; by now if the boat shattered, she was too ill, frozen, and tired to save the stranger or possibly even herself. After the mast broke, a new, terrible thought occurred to her: if they did break free, the strong currents around the island might seize the boat and carry it into the Atlantic. The end seemed so near. Still Ailis struggled against the urge to sleep. If it came, she wanted to meet death awake.

When it finally happened, she must have been very close to passing out because it took a while to realize that they were no longer scraping rock. The tide had freed them. Ailis raised her head, but there was nothing to see. All the world's candles had gone out. There was no destiny to steer towards, only murky, fog-choked darkness.

The sea was tranquil, the motion of the boat soothing. Her senses stretched out into the void, and she gradually became aware that her companion's breathing had changed. He was awake. Maybe he would simply fall asleep again. Ailis was suddenly acutely conscious of the closeness of their bodies. She must have tensed for he abruptly attempted to give her more room.

"Where are we?" he asked in a voice layered with a thick French-

Germanic accent. Until she knew his state of mind, Ailis decided honesty was the best option.

"Adrift near the Irish coast."

Tense moments passed.

"Are you all right?"

It was a simple question but hard to answer. She knew nothing of this man aside from the fact that he was injured. Would he take advantage if she admitted her weakened state? Was he asking her or was he having another conversation with this Justine?

"Yes," she whispered at last.

"Good," he sighed and some of the tension in his body eased. Even in this pitiful condition he sounded genuinely relieved. For a long time, they silently lay in each other's presence in the darkness. There was an exciting and enticing intimacy beyond anything Ailis had ever imagined or experienced. She'd never laid this close to a man. An unfamiliar sensation began to pulse within as she sensed that the small hairs on their exposed skin seemed to carry a charge where they met. Their breathing fell into sync, and the world around them disappeared.

The spell was finally broken by the first rays of a red dawn. It would storm again. As light abolished the darkness, his face took shape before hers. They were very close, but neither tried to move. The backs of their hands were rubbing together with the motion of the boat. At some point their legs had entangled and remained that way.

"Who are you?" she asked from her dreamlike state. He blinked and seemed to consider this question very deeply. When his eyes returned to hers, they shone with some deep personal victory, as if he'd discovered the answer to a question he'd long asked of himself.

"Ernest Frankenstein." He smiled slightly as he spoke his name.

The sudden, jarring sound of waves smashing against coastline very near the boat interceded. Ailis rose and pivoted about, seeking her bearings. Joy surged through her. She grabbed her companion's hand as she realized that the currents had carried them towards land near her home.

"We're going to make it."

He was drifting back into unconsciousness, but a smile played across his lips.

Ailis' aching muscles loudly protested her efforts to row them into shore by issuing sharp, shooting pains. Behind them the promised storm was gathering. She knew her home lay further down the shoreline, but she didn't know how far. The first rumbles of thunder issued from the storm as she beached the boat. Time was running out, and she could not carry him. There were no structures nearby to ask anyone for help. The sand absorbed her toes as she leaned down to check for Ernest's shallow breathing. With a last look in the boat and a silent prayer in her heart, Ailis began to run along the shoreline.

Events became surreal. Utter exhaustion hounded each painful step as she collected new wounds on her feet. Her lips and throat were parched. Soon rain began to pelt her skin. It fell so steady that she was repeatedly forced to shake it from her eyes, the motion of which made her dizzy, and several times she became disoriented. But she kept going.

*

"It was still in his back?"

"No, it entered through his back and lodged itself among his ribs, about here, ruptured one lung quite soundly. I may have done more harm than good removing it, but we'll see." Dr. Martin shook his head. Ailis had been present for several childbirths or the odd resetting of a bone but never witnessed surgery to remove a pistol shot. And from what she'd heard, she was glad. It sounded brutal, and the procedure further drained the remaining strength from Ernest's body.

"Will he heal?"

"As I've told you many times, Ailis, the body is secondary to the mind. If he wants to heal, he will. If his mind gives up, the body will follow," he observed.

"And what of the spirit?" Ailis asked, her eyes fixing upon the sleeping figure on the couch.

Dr. Martin paused packing his instruments.

"I'd say that's the only thing holding this man together right now. I've rarely encountered anyone with a body so traumatized."

"What do you mean?"

The doctor measured his response as their eyes again met.

"He's been whipped; there is ample evidence of fractured bones throughout his body, burns, scars from knife wounds, and obviously shot, actually more than once. Frankly, I don't know what's kept him going: spirit, hatred, fear?"

Shaking his head, he finished packing his remaining medical supplies. Gratitude swelled within her, and suddenly, Ailis was hugging him.

"Thank you for our lives."

After a moment, he cleared his throat and stepped back a bit embarrassed.

"You chose life, my dear. And without you, he wouldn't have stood a chance. No matter what happens now, never forget that."

But at what cost, she wondered. She'd managed to find help when she fled the boat but soon fell to exhaustion, and then a fever set in, one so severe it had nearly claimed her life. The doctor felt it likely that it had ended her ability to have children.

"I'll stop by tomorrow," he promised squeezing her arm reassuringly as he left.

Ailis lingered in the front doorway intoxicated by the rich scents of the sea air, damp grass, and honeysuckle. She had not set foot outdoors since the onset of her illness eleven days prior, and for a long moment after exiting the house, she stood still and simply absorbed the delicious feeling of freedom one can only experience by being outside. She stooped and picked some wild mint leaves for tea in the warm May sun.

Wandering to the property's edge, she discovered her father hard at work struggling to affix a rather large rock into an empty space in an existing fence line. He must have heard her footsteps because there was only a slight reaction as she knelt to assist him. Despite their efforts to manipulate the stone it would not stay and both were panting when he finally gave up and stretched out on the ground.

"Would you like some water, Da'?"

"Later," he panted. "Later. Did Martin leave?"

She nodded. They'd spoken little in the past few days. He seemed older somehow. Perhaps it was simply the additional, unanticipated strain of caring for her and Ernest.

"You shouldn't have tried that," he admonished. "You've only been outta that bed a day."

"What should I have done? Watch you collapse trying it yourself?" The comment did little to lighten his mood. "At least get Padraic to help you."

A look crossed his face but it was quickly hidden beneath a piece of cloth as he wiped his brow. They sat in silence for a moment.

"Well, best be getting on with it," he declared. "Go on inside and rest."

She touched his arm lightly.

"I'm strong enough to go to the Kelleys' for …"

"He ain't at the Kelleys'," her father replied abruptly as he hung his head. "Padraic's in jail."

This was not the first time such a thing had happened, but it was always unwelcome news. He was strong, loyal, and dependable, but the young man possessed a lightning fast temper, which had increasingly led to problems for him.

"What…," the word was barely out before Ailis' father confronted her.

"He got into an argument and nearly beat a man to death." She could feel the blood completely drain from her face. "He was fighting to defend your name and your honor, which apparently you care nothing about."

The accusation stung, but Ailis tried to remain calm.

"What's being said about me?"

"Nothin' I'll be repeatin' here," Quinn crossly asserted.

Ailis sighed as she sought the right words.

"I know I've made some mistakes …."

"Mistakes."

"… but I saved a man's life."

"By nearly getting yourself killed. Do you have any idea what you've put me through, your friends? Ailis, you're a brave child …"

"I'm not a child."

Her father's voice grew soft.

"You're the only child I have left. The only family."

They looked away from one another.

"Who was that letter from?"

"What?"

"The one with the French postmark that caused you to faint before you left.

Ailis' head felt light. She'd completely forgotten about the letter.

"How did … I can explain."

She stared at her father feeling helpless and vulnerable. Did she tell him the truth?

"Was it from that man in there?"

"Is that what you think?" she incredulously demanded. "Because he speaks French? That I went to the island for some, some secret rendezvous? Is that the story people are telling? Why Padraic is in jail for fighting?"

"Ailis, I need to know you can still be honest with me because you're right. You're not a child. But I'm still your father."

Ailis cleared her throat as she struggled to look at him.

"I know he's like a son to you, and he does have some admirable qualities but … I don't love Padraic, Da'. I could never be happy with him."

Quinn said nothing as she continued.

"I was trying to collect artifacts for the museum when I found Ernest. It was an accident."

"And the letter?"

She hesitated. His gaze, though stern, sought hope in hers. Did he suspect Abrielle had written to her? If so, how could she tell him that his first born must be denied him a third time? That his prayers must go unanswered because of Ailis' choice to save a stranger. How could she wound him further?

"It was destroyed."

After a moment, her father's lips parted but the words in his heart were left unspoken. He turned from her and renewed his labors with the fence of stone.

*

Ailis lay down her flute on the window seat and listened to the tranquil rhythms of the waves as they caressed the rocks below. Her fingers traced a portion of the necklace she wore down to the small, silvery pendant she'd cleaned and attached to it. It was one of the metal jewelry pieces she'd discovered. The piece possessed a beautifully etched five fold design. Her eyes rose from the pendant and were involuntarily drawn to the stoic silhouette of Clare Island, which was rapidly dissolving into the night.

She felt melancholy. Her decisions had brought nothing but misery to herself and those she cared about. She had betrayed their trust; worse still, after all the collective suffering her family and friends had endured because of her choices, there still remained the real possibility that Ernest would die.

The past several days he had slept a fitful and often feverish slumber, reliving what she could only imagine was a nightmarish existence. He would cry out to lost loved ones, desperately yell orders as if he were fighting for his life at sea, and fervently speak to imagined phantoms in languages native to many distant lands.

These manic fits had made forcing nourishment into him almost impossible, which only increased the likelihood that when Ernest finally did sleep, he would never awake. If that happened, the story of who this man was would die with him. All Ailis would ever learn of him would come from the maltreated journal she'd discovered abandoned upon the hearth of the parlor fireplace. Probably left there when Ernest had first been brought into the house, it had been wrapped in oil cloth to protect it from water. The tattered, musty pages contained few entries and were difficult to read; still they intrigued Ailis.

from the journal of Ernest Frankenstein

18 August 1798

There is nothing left. Tomorrow I leave this house forever, leave the shadows to whisper, leave the ghosts to haunt all that was once safe and familiar.

22 September 1798

Oh Christ, I am alone, two weeks removed from the Italian coast. I have become a rover of the sea, a nameless sailor on the English merchant vessel Habes. They call me the foreigner, as I speak almost no English and shun all company. I spend hours in the crow's nest, isolated, shivering, my eyes always to the northern horizon. I often refuse to be relieved and have already felt the cat-o-nine tails for insubordination. I care little of physical discomfort. If they only knew true horror as I do.

September

Stars caressing a silent sea; oblivion never seemed so close.

18 October 1798

We have landed somewhere along the African coast for supplies. Have I left my pursuer behind or do I run from a phantom? Nightly, I have seen Victor in my dreams and cannot banish his last look or words from my mind. He is a madman—set out to murder "the devil." Devil take him. Madness take me.

1803

I died today.

Ailis closed down the window, stretched, and then pulled on a worn pair of slippers. It would be her turn to watch over Ernest soon, and she did not want to keep Mrs. Shaw waiting.

If Mrs. Kelley had played the role of surrogate mother, then the more elderly Shaws were Ailis' grandparents by default. Always ready to help their neighbors, Mr. Shaw and his jovial wife possessed a simple wisdom about life and they always seemed to take everything in stride. During Ailis' illness, they'd practically moved in so they could help. Mrs. Shaw had remained to help the Tierneys care for their mysterious patient.

As she paused by her cramped writing desk to retrieve a shawl, Ailis noticed the unfinished letter to Padraic she'd started composing three days earlier. At the time, it had seemed a simpler alternative than going to the jail to talk to him. She sighed but left it undisturbed. Perhaps tomorrow she would be able to finish it.

Descending the stairwell, she began to perceive low, male voices coming from the parlor. Was something wrong? Had Doctor Martin returned already? She quickened her pace, taking care not to drip candle wax on her hand again.

Only two men were present in the room: her father and Ernest, who seemed alert and lucid. They were holding a hushed conversation in

French. Her father's back was to her, but upon perceiving his daughter's presence, Quinn rose and closed the parlor door behind him. Ailis caught only a fleeting glimpse of the man she'd worked so hard to save.

"He awoke about an hour ago," Quinn said without preamble. "James Shaw's already gone to find the doctor, and we've got dinner waitin' for you in the kitchen."

"Is he …?"

"Ssshhh. He's doin' fine for the moment but best to take things slow."

Ailis anxiously looked past him to the closed door. Was he really going to live? Her father kissed her cheek.

"Go on, child, there'll be plenty to do soon."

She nodded and left the candle burning on the table in the hallway.

"Have a seat, girl," Mrs. Shaw ordered, pointing to the kitchen table as she bustled to the pot over the cooking fire. "Did you have a fair sleep this afternoon?"

"Yes," Ailis said as she placed her napkin on her lap.

"Good."

"Why didn't anyone come get me when he woke up?"

"Bit of a surprise I suppose, and I have a house to keep fed. Here, and mind you, it's hot." She ladled a generous portion from the pot and handed the bowl to Ailis who sniffed the contents.

"Lamb potato stew?"

Mrs. Shaw enthusiastically nodded as she began to sit with her own bowl.

"My children used to love when I'd make them this recipe. Oh my, where is my mind…almost forgot the bread. There we go. Afraid we've run out here but I have some more jam at home. Remind me to ask James to bring some back. Well, then again, I'll probably be going home with your patient on the mend. Still you should have some of that jam."

Ailis couldn't help but smile as she ate.

"Peculiar…," Mrs. Shaw mused, "a British sailor from Geneva."

"How do you know that?"

"It was one of the first questions your father asked him. Fortunate it was you who found him; not many 'round here would have saved him with that uniform on. Course I tend to forget you came here after the slaughter of the last rebellion."

"Hello?"

Mrs. Shaw hurriedly finished swallowing her food.

"In here, James. How are you tonight, Doctor Martin? You look like you could use some tea."

"The man needs something, slept in the back of my cart the whole way here," Mr. Shaw exclaimed as he sat down.

"Bless me. It's been a day," Martin affirmed as Mrs. Shaw made him tea, "Nothing but unscheduled house calls. The Connors lost their son to smallpox; Mrs. Tate's new baby girl was three weeks early; O' Macklin broke his arm, and Miss Cross … well best not discuss Miss Cross."

"Mentally feeble that one," Mrs. Shaw stated, handing him a mug.

The doctor chuckled as he sipped at his drink.

"I think I need to let that cool," he stood, paused only to retrieve his bag near the front door, then entered the parlor.

Ailis followed but patiently remained in the entryway while Dr. Martin performed his examination and held a brief, quiet discussion with Quinn Tierney. The men kept nodding to each other as they spoke. Engrossed by the scene playing out before her, Ailis was startled when she noticed that Ernest's eyes were following her every motion; embarrassed, she hastily attempted to smooth her rumpled clothing.

The doctor cleared his throat as he turned to Ernest.

"You'll have a prolonged recovery, but welcome back to the land of the living, monsieur."

CHAPTER 5
LEARNING TO HEAL

"Incarceration of the defendant will continue for a period of one year as of this date. This court stands adjourned." Quinn Tierney rose as soon as Magistrate Kendrick did. He was more than ready to leave.

Within moments, he was surrounded by the shuffling crowd of judicial attendees as they joined his exodus out to the street. He felt beset by eyes of suspicion and judgment. Quinn had come to act as an advocate for the young man, relating to the court his more favorable traits and actions. But Padraic's cursing tirade had not only condemned him but publicly given voice to the whispered, unflattering rumors regarding Ailis and Ernest. Despite these, his daughter had done the right thing in rescuing the man, however extraordinary the circumstances. Quinn was certain of it.

His arm was seized from behind as he began to resume his hat.

"You must stop this, Quinn," Mrs. Kelley cried out in Gaelic. "He is going to jail for defending your family's honor. Please. Talk to the magistrate …."

He turned as he removed her hand.

"There's nothing more I can do, Ena. Padraic's temper almost killed a man, and his insulting outburst towards me nullified my efforts on his behalf. Had my testimony stood, his sentencing might have been more lenient, but he's made his choices. He'll have to live with them."

The damage was done, and suddenly the lines between the past and the present blurred.

"So, you reject me again." Her voice was rich with bitterness.

"Your son has made his true feelings about my family abundantly clear this day," he responded in kind.

"Why shouldn't he? He's been spurned by your daughter as you once spurned me."

Quinn stiffened.

"I was young," he protested as the old argument was reborn.

"So was I," she shot back. "But I loved you. Before you ever knew what you wanted. I loved you. After you left, what choice did I have but to marry?"

He looked away. She'd always wanted something that could never be. If he had stayed, he would never have gone to sea, never met either of his beloved wives, been blessed with his children.

"We each made our choices just as our children have made theirs."

"And you trust your daughter's choices? Ailis is still a child. She can't possibly know what she wants. Don't let her …"

The argument died as she met his eyes, perceived his body language, heard his words, rich with a tone of finality.

"She is not a child. And if you or your son truly loved her you would respect her choices … and mine."

It was as if she had never really seen him before.

"Quinn?" She issued her final plea.

He said nothing as he turned and walked away. Endings are never easy, and both he and Ailis would sincerely mourn the loss of their friendship with the Kelleys, but it was for the best.

*

Ailis drew in a deep breath as she opened her eyes and blinked. It had happened again. How long had it been this time? Still recovering from illness, her body kept betraying her senses by embracing the lure of sleep. She turned her attention to the clock on the mantel and noted the passage of hours. Her neck hurt. She sat up straighter in the chair.

"Parlez-vous Français?"[3]

The deep voice startled her, as did the book that fell from her lap onto the parlor floor. Ernest had been asleep when she'd come into the room.

"Un peu,"[4] she demurely replied before bending down to retrieve her book, which contained a collection of Perrault stories such as "La Belle au Bois Dormant" and "Barbe Bleue." Between Ernest beginning to recuperate and her recent experience with Abrielle's letter, Ailis felt the need to revisit the French language.

---

3 You speak French?

4 A little.

"C ést bien."[5]

"Merci," Ailis smiled at the compliment before asking a question in her native language.

"Labhraíonn tú Gaeilge?"[6]

This time Ernest smiled but could only shake his head. Ailis was not deterred. She felt drawn to him and did not care if he fully comprehended her offer to teach him Gaelic.

"Ansin beidh mé ag múineadh agat."[7]

Each was transfixed by the other; the sense of intimacy created by their shared struggle was both compelling and confusing.

"Oh good, you're both awake," exclaimed Mrs. Shaw as she entered with an arm load of clothing, half of which she deposited on Ailis' lap.

"Monsieur Frankenstein can't go through the rest of his life living under that old blanket. Fortunately you and James seem to be about the same size. Could you be a dear and thread that please," she requested, handing Ernest a needle and a measure of string.

"How do you know they're the same size?" Ailis asked her in Gaelic.

"I measured him while he was asleep; used to do it to my three boys all the time. Much easier to get the alterations done … ah, thank you, dear," she said to Ernest in English and chuckled at Ailis' expression.

"Afraid we didn't have a choice but to burn your former apparel … and Ailis' bedding and sick clothes as well."

"Good," said Ernest pointedly, "I never chose that uniform."

"So Quinn mentioned," replied Mrs. Shaw as she perched her glasses on the end of her nose, eyeing the stitching on a pair of trousers. "Ailis, those shirts are almost done; you just need to double stitch the right shoulder sleeves on a few of them."

For a few minutes, the only sounds in the room came from the sea and bird song carried on the wind entering through the open window.

Ailis and Ernest would steal glances as she worked. He seemed to be particularly interested in her necklace with the pendant. This activity did not go unnoticed.

"Any thoughts, Monsieur, about your plans once you've recovered?" Mrs. Shaw asked Ernest. "Do you think you'll stay in Ireland?

---

5 It is good.

6 You speak Irish?

7 Then I will teach you.

Return to Switzerland?"

"Mrs. Shaw," Ailis began in protest.

"Oh I'm just making conversation, Ailis, the way us old ladies do," she calmly asserted. "Besides, I think Ernest and the British Royal Navy have permanently parted company."

He nodded darkly.

"Not surprising given the way you were treated," Quinn Tierney noted as he sat down on one of the parlor chairs, drawing on his pipe.

Ailis forgot herself.

"What did they do to you?"

Mrs. Shaw halted her work. Ernest's eyes gazed downward.

"Last summer I was serving on a merchant ship in the Atlantic. It was boarded by the British Navy, the crew forced into conscription with the promise we would be freed when no longer needed."

"They enslaved you?" Ailis asked in disbelief. "How could anyone be so cruel?"

Ernest and Quinn greeted her incredulity with a haunted look of certainty; each had experienced enough to have no such qualms about the nature of mankind.

"It was common," he answered. "The British needed men and materials to ensnare their prey. Throughout the summer we fought a series of engagements with Napoleon's Combined Fleet but Admiral Nelson wouldn't relent. He pursued them to the Spanish coast."

"Good heavens. You were at Trafalgar?" Mrs. Shaw gasped.

"Yes," Ernest answered. He'd experienced plenty of battles before but nothing as massive as the now well-publicized culmination of hostilities last October between the British and the combined French and Spanish fleets; the most epic sea battle since the defeat of the infamous Spanish Armada.

The carnage was unimaginable. Men died by the thousands on both sides as ships raked one another mercilessly with cannon and small arms fire. Nelson died during the fight but so had Napoleon's ability to control the seas or to invade Britain, now the predominate master of naval power.

Ernest closed his eyes, his fingers rested against his temple.

"I served on two ships during the battle. The Mars was decimated under the incessant pounding of French guns. Nearly a third of her crew was slaughtered outright. I don't know how many were maimed under the onslaught. As we floundered I was taken aboard the nearby Swiftsure, which survived the battle intact, but suffered damage during a storm the following day."

"Between repairs and crew replacements, we didn't leave Spain until a few weeks ago. Captain Rutherford refused to release me from conscripted service as promised. That's all I can say right now," he concluded seeing Ailis' horrified expression.

"Mercy, you must have angels on your shoulders, lad, to live through all that," Mrs. Shaw said.

He managed a brief, awkward smile.

"I need some water," Ailis stated as she rose and quickly vacated the room, one which lapsed into silence.

"I upset her," Ernest lamented after she'd gone.

"That girl's got a thick hide and a heart of gold. She'll probably walk back in here with endless questions for you, so don't be worrin' none about her," Mrs. Shaw advised as she returned her attentions to sewing after wordlessly rebuking Quinn.

Again it grew silent as they each lost themselves to smoking, sewing or private reflection.

*

She was sitting alone on a bench by the water when Ernest found her.

"Are you cold?" he asked.

Ailis turned to respond, paused, and then burst into laughter. He smiled.

"So I'm not the only one who thinks the hem of these pants is too short?"

"No," she shook her head. "You … you must have had your legs bent when she measured you."

"What?"

"Never mind," Ailis said, wiping below her eye.

They continued to chuckle as Ernest sat down on the bench, but they soon lost themselves to the gentle ministrations of the sea.

"I did not mean to disturb you …."

"You didn't …," she said quickly before looking down at her hands.

"I mean you did but not because … I found your journal before you woke up. I read it."

"Ah," Ernest leaned back on the bench. "I was not aware that had survived."

"I'm sorry," Ailis said. "I shouldn't have, but your story this afternoon … those entries they were so sad. You've suffered so much, and they reminded me of …."

She swallowed, unable to finish. Ernest's fingers softly drew her hand into his.

"Thank you, Ailis Tierney, for restoring my life to me."

There was such tenderness in his steady, rich voice, in his gaze as he delicately kissed the back of her hand.

"Do not suffer with the sorrows of my life for it is mine again because of you."

She hugged him, allowing Ernest to hold her a moment before they resumed a respectable space between them, but their fingers remained laced. The sun was traveling into the sea.

"That is the island where you found me?" Ernest asked.

"It's known as Clare, in English."

She hesitated a moment.

"What happened after that captain said he wouldn't release you?"

Ernest looked to her, but Ailis' eyes remained fixed on the distant landmass. He drew a deep breath.

"As we neared the Irish coast, I pleaded with him again. The captain chose to address my insubordination with the whip, a punishment I've endured before. This time I fought them when they tried to clasp me in irons. I managed to jump overboard, freeing my manacles as I swam toward shore. Then they opened fire. I don't remember much after that until we were together in the boat."

Ailis said nothing but her fingers clasped his hand more firmly.

"Your father said you found me in a recessed area of cliff, accessible only by sea."

With her free hand, she pushed the loose strands of blonde hair away from her eyes, tucking them behind her left ear, hoping he didn't notice her blushing.

"What were you doing there all by yourself?"

*

"Bhfuil cabhair de dhíth ort?"[8]

"What?"

Ailis heard them before they fell off the barn roof and dodged the wooden shingles and straw that clattered to the ground. At least he hadn't accidentally hit her with a hammer. She could hear Ernest cursing to himself.

"Rá cad a rinne tú?"[9]

"I asked if you needed help," she replied as she finished picking up the shingles. His Gaelic was improving, as was her French.

"Qu'est-il arrivé à Quinn?"[10] Ernest's tone held both irritation and concern.

"He got tired again," Ailis said ruefully as she climbed the ladder and handed the shingles back to Ernest. "I told him I'd help you finish. He's probably asleep in his favorite chair by now."

Ernest wiped sweat from his brow and nodded. These last months had been difficult on all of them. With Padraic's absence and Ernest's slow recovery, almost all of the strain of running the farm, caring for their animals, and maintaining the property had fallen on Quinn's aging shoulders. To make matters worse, the poor growing season this year had caused additional financial hardships.

Despite his earlier misgivings, Quinn Tierney and Ernest had developed a genuine friendship, the bond formed by their shared understanding of life at sea, Ernest's determination to restore and repair the property, and their relationships with Ailis. Even during this demanding period, Ernest and Ailis had managed to cultivate their feelings for each other, growing closer with each day, though not without difficulties.

"No, Ailis, don't climb up here."

"Why not?"

"I don't want you falling off the ladder again when you try to get back down."

"That was one time, and I didn't fall … I nearly fell," she asserted but remained on the ladder's rungs. "Besides, ever since you moved out

---

8 You need help?

9 What did you say?

10 What Happened to Quinn?

here, it's been leaking on you every time it rains. You were right. We need to get this done."

Ernest was a far better carpenter than her father, Ailis mused, as he hammered several more shingles down and glanced at the winter sky.

"I don't think it's going to happen today. We got most of it reshingled, but I don't think there's enough daylight left to finish," he decided.

"That's fine. I started dinner before I came out," she smiled as he drew closer.

"What, you don't trust me to do it again?"

She leaned forward.

"I don't want to have to spend another afternoon chipping the burnt remnants of your cooking out of my pots."

A slight tremor shook her frame as his lips kissed her forehead then lingered near hers. They kissed briefly before she reluctantly pulled away. He really would make her fall if she didn't. His eyes held trepidation as she withdrew.

"I thought you weren't going to wear that anymore," he said, referring to the necklace with the small pendant that had slipped out of her dress, then shawl.

Her tone grew serious.

"I was, but I like it, and until you decide to tell me why it bothers you, I'm going to keep wearing it."

She waited.

"I told you I don't want to talk about it," he muttered, leaning back on the roof and looking away.

It seemed to bother him even more if she played with it between her fingers, which she occasionally did when she read, eliciting a pain, even a darkness within him that he worked to hide. For eight years, he'd served on various vessels, braved the far corners of the world, even the distant Pacific, his travels changing him until even his real name had been abandoned, all to escape his past. She wanted to understand him, but also knew by now that if she pushed too hard, he would only become moody and distant, or avoid her by throwing himself into another project.

"It's getting dark. I'll wait while you get this cleaned up," she said calmly before descending the ladder. Ailis also now recognized, as her father had earlier, that in spite of his reluctance, Ernest needed to talk.

As the weeks passed and their sense of trust and friendship deepened, he'd begun to open up to her more readily about a number of topics, with one key exception. They'd spent many hours together in quiet conversation talking about the beauty and dangers he'd encountered during his voyages. She'd introduced him to the stories of her homeland, an experience that had been enriched by his desire to learn Gaelic from her. But he would never discuss his family or life in Geneva. As she'd pursued this vulnerability, Ailis began to realize that Ernest was not the only one in need of reconciliation with their past.

"Ernest?" The air was becoming colder. She called after a few minutes.

"I'll be along," he answered. She only left when she could hear him putting the tools away.

Her father was resting peacefully before the fire in his favorite chair in the front room, his noxious pipe still smoldering away on a nearby table. Ailis hesitated. Should she wake him first or check on the food she'd left cooking? As she stood in the hall for a moment trying to decide, her breath abruptly left her. Suddenly she was ten years old again, discovering her mother's lifeless body in her bedroom, the icy air from the open window biting at Ailis' skin. She took his cold hand and tried to look upon those now sheltered eyes to no avail before sinking to the floor beside him. Initially no tears flowed, only two whispered words, spoken as if she was scolding him for teasing her.

"Oh Da'"

*

With the ceremony concluded, the assemblage of mourners laid their flowers and departed the graveyard on the slanted hillside. The solitude was peaceful. The sun still drifted among the towering clouds as if to reassure Ailis that her father would not be denied light in this place. Quiet winds gently broke over the cemetery grasses as they did over the surrounding chorus of rolling hills. Ignoring the cool air, she wandered the grounds reading the epitaphs which graced the stones. The memory of another graveyard far across the seas of water and time flooded her senses, the one she'd spent hours alone in translating the French on the stones, anxious to learn the language so she could speak to her sister when they found her. She'd never told him about that day. What else had she failed to tell him?

Her father was strong. This wasn't fair, wasn't right. How could his heart simply have given out? Had she told him she loved him often enough? Probably not. We trust others to know our heart when too often we don't understand it ourselves. Death's raw arrow had taken him too quickly from this world. She should have told him about Abrielle's letter, that for a brief instant, the possibility of their family's reunification had lain in her hands. It had been selfish not to. If she'd done so, he might still be alive, his heart made strong by the real hope that his eldest child would finally forgive him.

A lone figure remained standing over her father's grave. Ernest did not stir when Ailis drew close; his eyes remained fixed on the freshly turned pile of pitiful dirt. She delicately touched her fingers to one of his damp cheeks. Comforting another made the moment bearable. Wordlessly, they laced their fingers together. Ailis' voice trembled.

"He should never have died alone."

Ernest's final inner barrier crumbled as his troubled soul reached out to hers.

"My father died of a broken heart. I think yours died because his heart was so full of happiness."

She turned to him. Finally giving voice to his family's tragic past, Ernest's self-perceived weakness granted strength and absolution to Ailis in her hour of need, and as they embraced, love and hope breathed anew there among the vanquished.

CHAPTER 6
FAMILY PASSAGES

"Ailis Tierney … Frankenstein …?"

She absently tapped quill against damp paper as she leaned back against one of the ancient oak trees of Brackloon Wood. These woods were old and full of feeling. Being within this stand of trees felt like a birth rite to her; it was a singular place, one that forever enticed her imagination. Stories purported that they were riddled with unexplored caves and buried treasure, hidden during the reign of the ancient Celtic kings. It certainly was rich with ruins like the monument she was sketching, or trying to. Her mind kept drifting.

Ernest was still standing near the wood's boundary, studying the features of the diverse landscape. Plains of grass, crisscrossed by rivers, vanished among a growing number of mountain chains whose spines stretched out in all directions. Their words to each other had been spare today as each remained immersed in their own contemplations.

Soon their time together for the day would end; she'd return to the Shaws and him to her father's home. In the weeks since her father's passing, this had become the arrangement; staying at home was too difficult.

It was just as well. Until they married such an arrangement in Quinn Tierney's absence was inappropriate; however, separations such as these served to make them further appreciate their stolen hours together. It also gave them both the time to evaluate and gradually reveal their pasts and dreams to one another.

"Ailis." She rose to Ernest's beckon.

He stood behind her, enfolding Ailis in his arms as the persistent fogs abated at last to afford them a glimpse of the Twelve Bens. They waited, but the dominating heights of Croagh Patick remained hidden above the mountainous range of mist-shrouded sentinels. Her nerves exploded when he kissed the top of her head, and she turned to face him.

"I'm glad you brought me here," he said.

She smiled.

"At least the weather's cooperated this time."

They returned to the monument ruin, reposing together; his fingers traced paths through her hair.

"Maybe we should move here and spend the rest of our lives searching for gold," he suggested after a time.

Ailis laughed lightly as she sat up.

"What?"

"You sound like my Da' the first time we ever came here. He told me an ancestor of ours found Brackloon gold then hid it in our house, and if I heard any knocking in the night, it was just the ghost looking for cursed gold. Kept lecturing me not to look for it"

"Did you ever hear anything?"

"Yes, the first few nights after we moved in. I'm sure it was just Da' teasing me, especially after I complained about hearing noises."

Ernest grinned.

"Sounds like him."

Ailis' smile faded, she shook her head.

"He was always doing stuff like that. It used to drive Mother crazy … but they always seemed to know how to deal with each other."

Ernest's gaze became distant.

"I've come to believe that my mother was the only one of us my father could relate to. After she died, I don't think he knew what to do, none of us did. We were all left dealing with the legacy of her choices, trying to fulfill her dreams as best we could. Maybe if things had turned out differently … so much should have been."

Ailis was silent a moment.

"You were only ten when she died. Maybe your father did the right thing trying to keep your lives similar to what they were. After Mother passed, nothing in my life was the same; roaming France for almost a year in search of someone I never knew existed. I hated him for that."

"At first you did," Ernest reminded her.

"Yes." Her voice was dull, emotions given to the sins of memory. "I was angry at him for leaving Mother, Ireland so soon after her death. That he'd been married before … all of it."

They were quiet for a time.

"I wish my father had known someone like your mother."

"Why?" Ailis asked in that vulnerable tone he'd come to adore.

"Something your father said to me a couple of months ago." Her gaze begged him to continue. Ernest took a breath. "He said after losing his first wife, then Abrielle, if he hadn't met your mother when he did, if she hadn't been the strong person she was, then his life could easily have become the one I've lived."

Their fingers shifted awkwardly for a moment before Ailis kissed his hand and clutched it closer to her.

"She saw his pain," she said quietly. "You know…when I was very young, he would take those trips to France, and whenever I asked why he was leaving, my parents would always tell me he was looking for a lost treasure."

Ailis leaned forward and pulled her arms in close to her chest.

"She taught him to confront his pain," Ernest said after a long moment. "If she hadn't, you and your father probably wouldn't have forced me to confront mine."

Ailis turned to him, their souls full of love and gratitude for acceptance from the other. Ernest stood and walked a short distance before returning, genuflecting upon one knee, and taking her hands into his.

"I've told you about my parents, Ailis, but not of my siblings' fates, and before you agree to marry me, I must.

She felt weak, humbled, and frightened. Trust was fragile; it required mutual sacrifice for actions and words to remain consistent, intimacy, strength. It was a gift in others Ernest had believed himself no longer capable of until he met Ailis.

Her fingers reached out, delicately touching his face.

"Tell me," she bid softly.

*

"My God ... you're really gone."

Ailis sat alone on the bed. Mrs. Shaw's gracious offer to help with the alterations to Ailis' mother's wedding dress required Quinn's daughter to enter her father's room to retrieve it, a place she'd not been since the departure of his soul from this world.

Being here felt like a violation like she was sneaking behind his back, stealing something that didn't belong to her. She'd spent so little time in this house since his death, it had been easy to pretend she'd fully accepted his loss. She often went to the cemetery, laid flowers, uttered soft benedictions, even talked to his tombstone about her life, but holding the aging, scented fabric of the dress once worn by another person she'd loved and lost made it all real. They would not see her in this dress, exchanging vows. They were gone, truly gone, just like Ernest's family.

"Ailis?"

There was a tentative knock from the other side of the door. After waiting in silence for a time, Mrs. Shaw entered.

"Are you all right, girl?"

Ailis nodded her head but did not look up.

"Do you want me to wait downstairs?"

With no directive forthcoming, Mrs. Shaw sat down beside Ailis and put her arms around the young woman. They sat together for a time before Mrs. Shaw stood and began to open the room's windows.

"What are you doing?"

"Airing this place out; room's been closed up for months. Believe me you don't want to move back in with it in this state."

"No, no. Close them. We'll live in my old room."

Mrs. Shaw sighed, sat down, and took Ailis' hands into her own.

"We honor the memory of those we love by living, not locking them away in the past. The purpose of any marriage is for two people to build a shared future, and you cannot do that until you've accepted the present. This is now your room, just as this is your wedding dress and this is your house."

She kissed Ailis' cheek and patted her knee as she stood.

"Besides, at least you have a fireplace in here," she said.

Ailis smiled demurely.

"Now, do we have everything we need? Any jewelry we should take for Friday?"

"Yes," Ailis replied, rising and going across the hall to her old room where she kept her mother's jewelry. She opened a drawer and withdrew a pair of earrings.

"Oh my, yes, lovely," Mrs. Shaw beamed as Ailis held them up.

"I think that's everything then."

Mrs. Shaw bustled back to the other room, while Ailis lingered in her own. She withdrew the necklace with the silver pendant from her pocket and fingered the metal for a moment. She'd not worn it since Ernest explained how it reminded him of the woman who murdered his youngest brother. Ailis looked upon it one last time before setting it in the bottom of the drawer. She never wore it again.

*

Ailis was in a world set aglow. The words she spoke felt alive, as they touched her lips in the cool air of early dawn. The light was so brilliant, as if the gates of heaven itself stood open; every sense in her tingled as Ernest's warm fingers gently slid the ring onto Ailis' finger. As he repeated the words of ceremony, all she could see of him was his silhouette against the bright light of the sun, reflecting off the water below. It gave him an almost angelic quality.

They stood with a small gathering of friends on a wind-swept hilltop devoid of all but a ruined abbey and a mass rock, a singular place, graced with the duality of destruction and uncounted beginnings. One of Ailis' earliest discoveries after settling in Mayo, the powerful setting had always provided her with a sense of familiarity, of security; this was the only place she'd ever truly envisioned the unconditional joining of her soul to another. Ailis was in a state of grace, the emptiness of prior years seemed but a dim memory in that beautiful moment, her heart overwhelmed by joy as she answered the most important question she'd ever been asked.

"I do," she said without hesitation.

Their love was destined; it had been earned. And now with two words, all things seemed possible.

*

Ernest kissed the back of Ailis' neck as he rolled toward her.

"Good morning," he breathed sleepily.

She smiled at the sensation of his hand tracing her side.

"Morning," she said, turning her body as each enfolded the other. They kissed tenderly.

"Everything all right? You were restless again."

"I'm sorry. Did I keep you up?"

"For a little while," he admitted. "Another bad dream?"

"The same one," she said quietly.

For the past three nights, she'd been visited by the disquieting image of a man whose broken body lay trapped in a vast wasteland, his arms frozen to the ground.

Ernest kissed her.

"What happens in it?"

Ailis paused before answering.

"It's … I think I'm dreaming about Victor."

Ernest withdrew a measure.

"Why?"

Her fingers laced with his beneath the cover.

"Ever since we started trying, I've been thinking a lot about what kind of life we can provide for our child. When you told me your fears regarding Victor's fate, it made me begin to reconsider the status of my own family. He's your last potential living link. My immediate family and grandparents have all passed. I know nothing of the whereabouts of any other relatives. My last true link is Abrielle. I want to find her but… I'm not sure how or even if I should."

It was a difficult admission. With all the changes in her life, she'd once again consigned Abrielle to the past. The dream, though disturbing, had reawakened Ailis' fears and desire for Abrielle to be a part of her future.

"Because you worry she's still angry?"

Ailis shook her head.

"I'm embarrassed," she confessed. "It's been over a year since she sent her letter. I don't really know the first thing about her. What if she was reaching out to me because she needed help and I never answered?"

Ernest was quiet for a moment.

"You might not know much about her adult life, but from what you've told me, you probably know more about her origins than she does."

A poor sailor when he landed in France, Quinn Tierney had secretly courted and wed a young woman whose family was of the French aristocracy. Their clandestine union was initially supported and then betrayed by the woman's youngest brother. A clergyman, he'd agreed to file the paperwork necessary to legitimize the marriage after the couple compensated him with either a portion of her dowry or an equivalent sum provided by Quinn.

Desperate for money so they could begin their new life, Quinn left on a voyage that took him from France for a year. Upon his return, he learned of his young wife's death and also the birth of Abrielle; however, he could learn little else before the family had him incarcerated. An embarrassment, the existence of his child was immediately concealed upon her birth. The family did not want her nor were they willing to allow Quinn his daughter. His wife's brother never filed the marriage document, leaving Quinn no legal claim and separating Abrielle from her own inheritance.

The clergyman vanished soon after his sister's death and remained hidden throughout the Revolution, during which, most of Abrielle's remaining family had fled France or been killed.

"Father spent years trying to find that vile man and Abrielle. I still can't believe her uncle knew where she was all those years, and he simply left her in that orphan's convent. He never wanted anything to do with her, while our lives were so incomplete without her."

Ailis was literally trembling with anger.

Ernest's fingers squeezed hers reassuringly. She cupped her chin over his shoulder as they held one another.

"How can I find her without the letter? I don't even know if I can recall the name of the town on the postmark correctly."

"Well, how did Abrielle find you after all these years?"

Ailis began to open her mouth to answer, but instead, covered it as she gasped.

"Oh my God! Father's note, the one he left at the orphan's convent with the nuns. It had our addresses. She must have actually gone back there at some point and gotten them."

*

Locating the address for the convent among Quinn's papers took time. But when she finally beheld it, Ailis released a deep sigh of silent gratitude. The paper it was written on was yellow with age, dusty, and at some point in the past had been crumpled, as if her father meant to throw it away. She stared at the sheet.

"Do you think he ever tried to write to the nuns?"

She asked the question aloud as much for own sake as to hear his insights.

"What are you thinking, Ailis?"

She shifted slightly before responding.

"What if …what if he …," she frowned, uncertain if she wanted to finish the thought. "Abrielle requested that I not tell Father about her letter. Do you think she said that because he'd mailed letters before and never told me?"

The thought troubled her, as did the length of time it took Ernest to answer.

"Your father never struck me as the type to give up."

"But how could he not tell me?"

She stood and began pacing furiously. Had they been in contact for a time, before having a second falling out, one he'd never mentioned? Were there other letters from her here in the house?

"We don't even know that he did, but it's possible. Ailis, if you're going to write her, you might discover any number of things you wish you hadn't."

She halted.

"What are you saying, that I shouldn't write her back?"

He considered his words carefully.

"Family's have secrets, Ailis. Some are more dangerous than others. I just think you need to be aware of that before you write."

The sadness in his eyes cooled her temper a degree. Still both knew there was really no choice; she would write her sister.

*

"No, no, I'm sorry, we have to get going. I'm sure your mother won't mind telling you some stories until I see you again. Be sure all of you take good care of your brother." There was a clamor from the assembled children of the Walsh household as Dr. Martin and Ailis took their leave.

"My goodness. How they live with all that noise I'll never understand," he remarked, shaking his head. "Thank you for keeping the kids busy, Ailis. You're so good with children, I never would have been able to complete the examination without you."

The compliment both pleased and pained her, a reaction that did not go unnoticed by the doctor.

"No problem. Did you figure out what he has?"

"Seems to be some variation of the flu that's been going around since winter; the good news is he hasn't got pneumonia yet. Well, I think it's time to get you home."

They journeyed through a kaleidoscope of light as brooding clouds from the Atlantic clutched at the landscape, the sun and the sea trading shadows over Clew Bay. Towering above it all was the mist-adorned presence of Croagh Patrick. The brooding, mysterious air of the mountain helped to reinforce Louisburgh's charm.

"Any news about your museum?" the doctor asked as they crossed the Bunowen River, which whispered peaceful songs to the town's vibrant array of neat stone buildings.

Ailis perked up.

"Yes, actually, I'm going to submit those local history journals I started writing last summer for publication soon, to try and raise money for the museum."

"Really? Good. I didn't know you were so close to finishing the editing."

"It's been difficult with Ernest's mood lately."

"Still won't tell you what's bothering him?"

Ailis' eyes drifted downward a moment. She could guess. So could Dr. Martin.

"Ailis, you're not the first couple to have problems conceiving."

"But we've been trying for almost two years. Maybe you were right. Maybe I can't have children."

Dr. Martin drew the cart to a halt.

"Ailis, look at me. Just because I suspect that doesn't mean I'm right. I've been wrong before, and I pray I'm wrong now. I don't want to give you false hope because I do feel, given your past, that it will be very difficult for you to conceive, but it is not impossible. If you and Ernest intend to keep trying, I'll be happy to tell him the same thing."

She nodded.

"Thank you, doctor. I appreciate it, but give me a little more time before you talk to him."

"Of course."

He tapped the reins lightly, and they began to move again.

"If things get really desperate, we can always try having both of you sleep on top of the Reek during the harvest festival," he said facetiously.

The ancient belief that sleeping on Croagh Patrick during Lughnasa would encourage fertility was one Ailis had already considered long ago but next August was months away.

"We'll see," she sighed.

*

Ailis cradled the slightly damp envelope, bearing a French postmark, in one hand for a moment before greedily tearing it open. Dated two weeks prior, the pages inside contained a hint of perfume. She smiled; Abrielle's letter was on time. Traveling ceaselessly across France, and even to other parts of the Continent for her profession, Abrielle's letters always contained instructions as to where Ailis should send her reply. On occasion, however, Abrielle's plans changed, and Ailis' letters would not reach her sister in a timely manner. Ailis was always relieved when this was not the case.

She studied the pages within. The shape and form of the handwriting betrayed haste with Abrielle merely scratching out mistakes rather than rewriting pages as she sometimes did. Their mutual decision to teach each other their respective languages often made communication more difficult as each was still prone to making mistakes when using the other's dialect. Depending on circumstances and time, the resulting missives commonly evolved into a blend of French and Gaelic.

Once translated, the contents of Abrielle's letter, as usual, were at once revealing and cryptic. Since their initial correspondence over a year earlier, Ailis had learned much about her sister's life, but other aspects remained in shadow.

Abrielle had wandered the streets for months after Ailis and Quinn's initial disastrous encounter with her, eventually finding employment in various venues of entertainment: salons, theaters and dance halls. Graced with an aptitude for music, she played several instruments, and from time to time, the sisters wrote and exchanged sheet music for the other to learn. Naturally gifted with the ability to master languages in short order, Abrielle occasionally alluded to using this talent in some type of service for the French government, but never really provided any detail about the work.

Her sister was a woman of great talent and passion, but in many ways, she continued to be guarded and distant. Still, her letters, and the colorful stories of her journeys, revealed both her cleverness and fierce sense of independence. Instinctively Abrielle needed the connection to her family as much as Ailis, but she also clearly feared it. Ailis' determination and patience were slowly beginning to diminish Abrielle's fears, with one notable exception. The subject of their father remained a sensitive one, and on occasion served as a genuine source of tension between them. It seemed, even in death, Abrielle was unwilling to forgive Quinn Tierney.

Fortunately, Ailis' relationship with Ernest enabled her to understand her sister's feelings better. After adopting a life at sea his existence had taken a narcissistic turn, one driven by doubts and fears, by a victim's guilt and anguish; he'd traveled until he literally lost himself. The better parts of humanity such as love and friendship were distant memories by the time they met. He had become a survivalist of not only his past but of wars, starvation, imprisonment, the cruelty of man, the relentless sea, and the misery found in the soul itself.

Despite all of this, the warmth of his spirit had remained intact, buried deep within, sleeping through those dark years, waiting for them to find each other. Now love was renewing their spirits, allowing them to explore untold dimensions of self and even beginning to heal ancient wounds.

Like Ernest, Abrielle was a survivalist; however, unlike him, she had never found true love so the walls to her soul remained difficult to breach. Trusting anyone, including herself, was complicated, just as it was for Ailis' husband. She prayed Abrielle's love would one day overcome her doubts and allow her to fully embrace her family. Until then Ailis knew her desire to again meet with her sister in person would, unfortunately, come to naught.

As she studied the musical composition Abrielle had included, Ailis rubbed her eyes. Was her flute upstairs or in the front room? The evening grew late. This could wait, she decided, as she stood, massaging her stiff back as she walked away from the parlor's writing desk.

She found Ernest in the front room sipping a glass of whisky, staring vacantly at the flickering embers of a dying fire, lost in thought. His fingers absentmindedly turned a piece of paper over and over, and it wasn't until Ailis sat next to him on the sofa that he finally noticed her entry into the room. She drew a blanket over them but said nothing, knowing by now that whatever was on his mind, Ernest would speak when he was ready.

Ailis closed her eyes and began to drift towards sleep. When the words came, her mind had a difficult time deciphering if they came from the dusk of consciousness or from him.

"I'm going to write home."

The words hung between them as her eyes slowly opened. Prior to this moment, he'd never once expressed any desire to reestablish any contact with Geneva. In fact, he'd flatly refused the notion. The demons of his past and the unspoken fear that he might still be a hunted man always prevented such thoughts. She sat up straighter.

"Why?"

He did not meet her gaze.

"Because of Abrielle," he cryptically stated.

Her sense of puzzlement only deepened. Any notions of sleep evaporated as Ailis delicately turned his face to meet hers, the question repeated in her grey eyes.

"I've been considering this for some time," he finally confessed. "Ever since you began writing your sister, I've thought more and more about Victor. Perhaps he isn't dead."

So that was it. The realization was sobering. Ailis had never really reflected on how her success in reconnecting to her last living family member might have affected him. She pondered this new reality for a moment.

"Who will you write?"

Ernest sighed deeply.

"Victor and I left our solicitor, an old family friend, named Christiansen, in charge of our properties and inheritance. If there is news of Victor, he will know."

He paused.

"I have to try," he asserted, almost apologetically.

"I know."

She squeezed his hand as they kissed, silently pleased there was still someone from his past whom he trusted.

“It may take some time. Before we left Switzerland, Victor, Christiansen, and I took the precaution of working out a series of coded questions to verify our identity in case we ever attempted to return. Knowing Christiansen and his sense of duty, I’m sure he’ll ask me all of them before accepting that I’m alive and who I claim to be.”

“You were that worried of being followed?”

Ernest swallowed hard.

“Yes … because of Justine’s trial and father’s role in the community, by the time we left, our family’s story was quite well known to the public, and we wanted to ensure that no one could steal our inheritance by posing as us or by claiming to be an agent acting on our behalf. Maybe we could send the letters through Abrielle, make it harder for anyone to trace me here,” he suggested.

“Do you think that will put her in any danger?”

“She moves locations often enough, it should be safe, but I’m not going to make either of you do anything you’re uncomfortable with. You found her letter on the desk?”

“Yes.”

“How is she?”

“She came across a bit more stressed than usual,” Ailis reflected, “but she seems to be fine. Wanted to know if I had any family news, how my journals were coming … any pregnancy updates.”

He drew her closer, his fingers caressing her shoulder.

“We’ll keep trying,” he promised.

Ailis kissed him deeply, her hope renewed. His face broke into a mischievous grin.

“Speaking about the inheritance money, you’ll love what I want to use it for.”

“What?”

Now she was smiling.

“I want to invest in some local property.”

“Do tell, Monsieur Frankenstein,” she said playfully as she kissed along his neck.

“If it’s not too much of an imposition, I was thinking of purchasing this farm from your English landlord and perhaps a building in Louisburgh.”

"That's very generous of you," she said in mock seriousness. "What would the building be for?"

"I was thinking of funding a local history museum, but I'll need an expert to help me design exhibits. Know anyone interested in starting one?"

Her gasp of surprise and the hug she wrapped him in were nearly simultaneous.

*

By March, Christiansen finally accepted that Ernest was both very much alive and who he claimed to be. Sadly, he'd heard no credible news regarding Victor, but did disclose that a number of people had made inquires into both men's whereabouts over the years. Christiansen loyally dealt with each situation as it arose and seemed to be genuinely moved that one of Alphonso Frankenstein's sons still survived. He promised not to reveal to anyone in Geneva that they were in contact and that he'd see to the paperwork regarding Ernest's inheritance.

The letter had a calming effect on Ernest. Far from being upset that Victor had never been heard from, it seemed to grant him a sense of closure. His silence appeared to confirm his long held suspicions that Victor Frankenstein was indeed dead, his soul released from the anguish and loss he'd suffered in this world. A specter from the past could now be put to rest, and the new future he and Ailis were creating fully embraced.

*

from the journal of Ailis Tierney Frankenstein

Not long after Christiansen's letter, our lives took an unexpected and miraculous turn. In April, I learned that I was pregnant with you, my darling child. Beyond all hope, God had seen fit to bestow such an astonishing gift upon us. Though we still worked on its preparation, the museum was placed on hold, as we adjusted to and planned for this new reality for our family.

I didn't notice it at first. With all the changes in my body due to the pregnancy, it was easy to explain away. Even later, when I was reasonably sure, I did not mention it to anyone, at least not directly. I'm sure your father and the doctor have their suspicions, but I managed to conceal it fairly well before Ernest left.

It began as mere fatigue. It was unusually warm all this past summer, and as May and June progressed, the weariness grew worse, but still I considered it a normal part of pregnancy. I told myself that it was caused by the stress from the heat, a result of changes to my constitution or drained by my vacillating emotions. Even the occasional shooting pains which would awaken me in the night could be explained by the pregnancy. The appearance of the first small lumps, however, could not. Still I did not see them for what they truly were. Perhaps I simply couldn't accept what they represented. I dismissed them as a rash, which I was convinced would fade, and said nothing to your father, but my doubts and fears grew. By July, I was certain that the affliction which had claimed my mother was now my burden to bear. I also knew it was infecting me much more rapidly than her.

I felt numb and betrayed. I wanted to be close to your father but pushed him away at the same time. One moment my soul raged that it could defeat this silent foe; the next I felt ready to lie down and submit. I was angry. And I was terrified of what this disease might do to you, my angel. Learning such things about one's self is not easy, but accepting them is something entirely different. I had to accept what was happening as fact before I involved your father or the doctor. My bitter feelings over the loss of my own mother wrenched my heart anew. I did not want to imagine even the possibility that you would grow up knowing this eternal loss yourself. July was slipping away, and I resolved to try and make my personal peace with the situation before the beginning of August. Then I would tell Ernest. But my plans were corrupted, by the arrival of a man on our doorstep, one storm-plagued evening in late July, a failed English adventurer named Robert Walton.

Since his departure, your father and I have both suffered many dark nights of the soul. For several days we lived in the imagined safety of a shared lie as we tried to pretend that nothing had happened, but to me, our lives felt increasingly fragile. I awoke several nights hearing my dear husband calling out to some phantom in his nightmares. Our inner demons and secrets began to separate us emotionally. In the blackest recesses of my mind, I feared we were waiting for something worse to happen. Walton was an unwelcome surprise, but his final warning left me badly shaken. Worse still, I knew Ernest could not dismiss it. And that truly terrified me, as did my still unspoken confession regarding my condition. The tension finally broke one afternoon, a week later, when Christiansen sent word, an urgent communiqué, which contained the realization of his worst fears and hopes and again put to question the true fate of Victor Frankenstein.

I could have told him then, could have revealed to him that his wife was dying a little each day. I know that grim knowledge would have kept him here with us. But I was seized by a new and powerful thought: could all of the loss and suffering I've endured in my life have led me to this moment? Graced by this perfect clarity, I realized that your father was not meant to know. Not yet.

I will die but so would your father if he didn't go to Geneva. This was something he had to do, if he was ever to be a complete person, and a sacrifice love demanded I must make. And so in early September, he left us, and from that day to this, I have not told him how near the end is. And now my blessed child, it is only a question of time—for all of us.

CHAPTER 7
AMBUSH

from the journal of Ernest Frankenstein

24 September 1809

The door to the conservatory proved exceedingly difficult to open, and I finally resorted to kicking it in, the hinges issuing a final groan of protest before relenting. Dust roiled from the floor in great clouds and obscured the room. When it finally settled and I could enter without choking, I slipped past the ruined door and crossed the threshold of what had once been Justine's sanctuary. Of all the rooms I've visited, this appeared to be one of the most heavily damaged.

Almost all of the glass panels in the three outer walls were either cracked or broken. A large, collapsed beam from the ceiling was primarily responsible for my difficulties with the door. The piano had been cannibalized of most of its parts, and Mother's older, antique harpsichord was missing completely. Tangled masses of ivy, which had crept inside, were winding their way towards the ruined and leaking ceiling. The only music left in the room was the ghostly whistle of the wind through the assorted holes in the glass panels.

My hands were sweating as I rubbed the grime off a section of glass so I could gain a view of the outer buildings. I slept poorly through the night and then much longer than I'd intended into the day. Daylight was again becoming a precious commodity, so I resolved to visit the outer buildings at once. Besides, I could not bring myself to face the final two rooms in the house: Justine's room and Victor's.

The outer buildings are a blend of storage, stables, livestock barns, and boat docks. We turned our horses and other animals loose before fleeing, so I was not worried about finding their remains. It's amusing to think about the LaShalls trying to capture one of our pigs. The decaying hay in the first barn was rich with a scent reminiscent of honey. Surprisingly, most of the harnesses and even one of the carriages remained untouched, but filthy. The work wagons have vanished, but Father's family carriage remained. Here it has rested since our last day together; Victor drove it back from Christiansen's office, packed up a poor assortment of supplies, harnessed our best steed, said his final, morose farewell, and then disappeared to meet whatever fate found him. As I rubbed my hand over the dust on the driver's seat, I pondered the notion that dust might be all that now remained of the seat's last occupant.

In one of the storage buildings, I uncovered a treasure trove of items from my childhood. My first sled, the old crib, Father's favorite tool box, a steamer trunk worth of Mother's old hats, a sketch book of Elizabeth's, some foul smelling beakers of Victor's, a set of handmade toy soldiers, old paintings, which used to hang in the main hallway, and a camping lantern were just a few of the items I found. Their discovery had me smiling for the first time since arriving at my old home. Unlike so many of the house's contents, these are from happier times, long forgotten.

A fresh wave of nostalgia overwhelmed me, and for a moment, I was really back home. Briefly, I considered loading some of the objects into Father's old carriage and toting them across France and back across the sea to Ireland. But I need to return to you and your mother as quickly as possible, and hauling so many additional items will only hinder that goal. Perhaps Christiansen could have them shipped for us. I was in a much better mood as I proceeded towards the stables.

Ironically, I never learned to ride a horse until the day I left here. Well, learned might be overly generous. The horse and I fought each other for dominance in our relationship all the way to the Italian coast, where I boarded my first merchant ship. Later in my travels, I became a skilled rider both in peace and war. I walked right past the empty stables. The roof has more or less collapsed, and the building still reeks of manure. Perhaps the stables had still been standing when French troops temporarily occupied the grounds. I also did not bother to stop at the docks for long. There are too many memories here. And I really don't care what, if anything, is left in the boathouse.

So I settle in for my final night in the house in much higher spirits than last night. I've decided to leave the ghosts alone in the last two rooms. Tomorrow I will head back to Geneva for a final conference with Christiansen, and then home, to you and your mother. How I miss Ailis; our separation has pained me. Her health concerns me greatly, and I am anxious to know if you are both all right. The thought that a letter from her could be waiting for me in Geneva cheers me further. I am certain tonight I can fall asleep almost peacefully.

**

He awoke from a dead sleep, confused as to his surroundings, and uncertain as to why he'd suddenly started. What time was it? The mosaic of light and shadow adorning the room suggested that the moon was still high. The realization of where Ernest was had just entered his consciousness when he saw him. Though he wasn't certain at first, his mind still partially in the world of dreams, initially the momentary image of a face in the window did not disturb him. The laughter that accompanied its disappearance did. Victor?!!

Ernest ran to the window and looked about frantically. No trace of the wraith remained. There was a narrow ledge outside and a tree nearby, but there was no easy way to gain access to this second story window. He rushed to dress properly for the damp night air and managed to remember to grab the loaded gun he'd taken to carrying since Walton's visit. Ailis and Christiansen had also insisted that he travel armed at all times. With a silent prayer of thanks to both of them, he fled into the dim, moonlit corridors.

He lit one of the few remaining candle stubs beside the main door, then charged out onto the lawn. There was a hard frost upon the ground, and a thick mist enshrouded all but the closest objects. But even ten years removed from them, he knew these grounds and easily reached the corner of the house below his former bedroom in less than five minutes after the mysterious visitor had vanished. No swirl of mist betrayed movement, no prints fled across the frost laden grass, and absolutely no sounds broke the silent night air, but Ernest knew he was being watched.

"Victor!"

He waited, as the beat of his heart measured the seconds.

"VICTOR!!!!" He whirled frantically, probing the black mist for any sign of life.

The third time he yelled his brother's name, a large stag broke from the nearby woods, only to disappear seconds later. Angry and frightened, Ernest suddenly realized how vulnerable he was. He quickly extinguished the candle and waited for his eyes to adjust.

When he finally returned indoors, Ernest searched the rooms nearest to his own, not wishing to venture far from his chambers. He did his best to seal the door and took up a defensive position, which would afford him a clean shot at any intruder should they attempt entry through either the door or window. As he settled in, he abandoned any thought of leaving. The risk of an ambush was too great. He'd have to wait for daylight.

As the endless hours crept towards the promised return of the sun, Ernest replayed the image of the face over and over in his mind's eye. The more he concentrated, the more blurred the true image became. At first, it was a pale face with penetrating yellow eyes, but in time he could only evoke the image of his brother's gaunt face. In the end, Ernest began to doubt he'd seen anything.

Despite the fact that he was tired, hungry, and emotionally drained, he did not leave when the sun rose. Doubts had cooled his fears, but he decided to wait and see if his invisible adversary wished to attempt contact a second time. Nothing happened, so he began packing his meager possessions, only hoping that the phantom had not diverted his attention just to steal his horse. If so, another visit to the LaShalls might be in order. He'd intended to survey the hidden family safe before departing, but the night's events subdued any further notions of doing so. Nothing seemed out of place, at first, as he exited the house without incident, locking the useless door behind him.

Ernest soon discovered that his mount was not where he'd tethered him. The night's fog still clung heavily to most of the nearby landscape, but his shoed hooves had left visible depressions in the lawn. He located the animal tied to a tree near Ernest's family's burial sites. He did not seem harmed in any way, but again, no trace remained of whoever had moved him. Ernest was eager to leave this place, but also resolved to say a final blessing over his sleeping loved ones. As he approached the cemetery he noticed a sight both thrilling and sickening, again he drew his weapon and surveyed the obscuring fog.

"SHOW YOURSELF!" he demanded to the air. Nothing.

The act was a violation. He angrily stooped to remove each of the red roses, which had been deliberately and mockingly laid upon his family's graves during the night.

Daylight backlit objects across the open landscape and created numerous shapes and shadows. If Ernest's unbidden phantom still followed, he would have little warning before the other struck. He offered one last, albeit, hasty benediction to his family then cautiously began the return journey to Geneva, opting to take a local ferry across the lake, rather than attempting the, now seemingly perilous, journey by land. He gained the ferry in short order and was soon safely outside the city wall.

By the time he reached Christiansen's offices, fatigue blurred his vision and weighed down each of his steps. After a brief conference, the two departed for Christiansen's home, where Ernest could safely rest.

"This arrived at my offices for you yesterday," the solicitor stated as he handed his godson a letter from Ailis.

"Could you post these," Ernest asked, handing Christiansen several he'd written before opening Ailis'.

Ernest,

My dearest love be assured we are well and pray for your safe return to us. Mrs. Shaw has been stopping by to check in on us daily. The oppressive heat has lessened but not left Louisburgh and sleeping is still problematic. I received correspondence from my sister several days ago. She is well and her ensemble will be staying in Autun for a week or so.

After reading the loving, intimate end of the letter, he placed it on his chest, folded his hands, closed his eyes, and dreamt of her.

*

By the time he awoke, it was quite late and dark. The Christiansen household had already taken their supper, but kindly provided Ernest with a late repast. As he ate, Ernest and Christiansen discussed the day's strange events.

"I never should have let you go alone," he shook his head. "You know, for a time, I did have an older couple maintaining the place, but they quit rather suddenly, and then with the French occupation, I just never imagined …"

Ernest pushed the potatoes around on his plate.

"No further word from my brother I take it?"

Christiansen suddenly found an urgent need to clean his spectacles.

"No…unless you believe that the man you saw was him."

It was Ernest's turn to find a distraction, while his mind attempted to rationalize the issue. He returned his attentions to his meal, unwilling to comment on Christiansen's implication.

"Ernest, there is something I need to discuss with you."

The younger man met his gaze evenly.

"Have you considered the possibility that your brother may be alive, though not himself?"

Christiansen paused a moment before plunging the conversation forward.

"I do not mean to speak ill of the man, but can you really say you knew him in the latter part of his life? Might not the terrible losses he suffered have brought about some sort of brain sickness? I mean, what do you really know about his time in Inglolstadt? Your father spoke to me at great length about how worried he was about Victor after he left and his emotional instabilities after he returned. Ernest, what if Victor simply went insane?"

This was a notion Ernest had considered countless times, but one his heart refused to believe. Yet, many of Christiansen's words held true. After Caroline Frankenstein's death, Victor had left almost immediately for university, practically vanishing for several years. When he did resurface, he was a haunted man, whom spent little time trying to reconnect with his family.

Granted, his return was prompted by William's murder and Justine's subsequent execution, but his emotions and actions had been erratic long before those events, nearly the whole of his time at university, in fact. Later there was the unexpected and mysterious, journey first to England and then later to Scotland; the unexplained murder of his best friend, Henry Clerval; Victor's drug use, Elizabeth's tragic, unexplained death on their wedding night. His brother's impassioned ravings about a mysterious foe, a man from Ingolstadt; Victor had claimed he was responsible for the murders, but refused to explain why this man, who no one had ever seen, possessed such an unmitigated hatred towards Victor.

"Then you think that I did see him? That he's toying with me because he's insane?"

Christiansen nodded sympathetically as Ernest pondered the implications.

"Disturbing as your night was Ernest, I'm afraid that my thoughts tend toward an even darker place," he continued.

Ernest knew.

"It's not possible," he said rejecting the notion before Christiansen could utter the unthinkable.

"Ernest, you loved your brother, I know but …"

He tried to silence him with a bitter glare, but Christiansen was determined to articulate the hateful thought out loud.

"What if he murdered Henry and Elizabeth?"

"Victor may have been many things, but he was not a killer," Ernest resolutely asserted.

Christiansen seemed unmoved.

"Love can blind us to truth," he observed.

"Or inspire us to seek it," Ernest retorted.

Christiansen's voice rose a degree.

"And are you truly prepared for what you might find?"

"I've been to the other side of this world and back. I have few illusions about mankind."

"You speak of the many," the older man said quietly. "I speak of one man. Are you prepared?"

Ernest leaned back in his chair and looked away. No, he wasn't prepared. Victor was a man he'd long since given up for dead. This trip was raising questions and memories he'd once nearly annihilated himself to escape. The need to forget these things once caused him to witness and experience events that nearly destroyed him forever and, were it not for Ailis' love and devotion, very nearly cost Ernest his soul. For the first time in years, he was truly happy. How far should he pursue this?

His eyes rose to his godfather's.

"You've done enough, Ernest," he said.

He rested a hand upon Ernest's shoulder, for a moment, before exiting the room, leaving the younger man alone to decide his course.

In time Ernest's senses yielded to the soporific effect the myriad of dancing flames in the fireplace placed upon his senses. As he began to doze, his mind again replayed the image of the piercing yellow eyes at the window. His last thought before falling asleep was that somehow, he'd seen them before.

*

He remained in Geneva for two more days while he and Christiansen poured over the details of the Frankenstein estate and drew up various papers. No further dangers presented themselves during this time, and Ernest began working towards making yet another uneasy peace, within himself, regarding his brother's fate. If, as Christiansen postulated, Victor had suffered some type of crippling mental incapacity, it would explain many mysteries. It even validated Walton's story—to a degree.

If madness had driven him into the far north, and his exposure to the elements was as severe as the captain indicated, then the wild story he'd ostensibly told Walton might have seemed perfectly plausible to Victor's diseased mind. The foe, who Victor claimed to seek, could have been nothing more than a fantasy created by guilt or madness. That Walton had so readily accepted the tale at face value simply reinforced Ernest's judgments about the man. He still did not believe his claims of having set eyes upon Victor's "foe" either. Of course, the elements, stress, and the ultimate failure of his voyage may have affected Walton's state of mind in a similar fashion. Whatever the truth regarding Victor, Ernest could never bring himself to believe that his brother was capable of murdering both his best friend and his wife.

"What about the letter in Victor's hand?" he asked Christiansen.

"Yes, that's more difficult to reconcile."

"I mean, if Victor didn't perish and his madness drove him back to Geneva after all these years, why go through all of this trouble and then not contact me while I'm here?"

Christiansen sighed.

"Ernest, madness has no purpose."

"All right then, what about a goal? What might my brother's goal be in luring me home and then taunting me with bizarre actions?"

The two men silently regarded one another. Over the past several days, Ernest's sense of paranoia had grown steadily as he confronted the truth of his situation. Had he endangered all those he loved by coming here? Was Victor waiting for him, beyond Geneva's walls? The longer he dwelt upon these thoughts, the more eager Ernest became to leave. Perhaps he'd underestimated the trap he'd walked into all too willingly.

Ernest leaned back over the desk in Christiansen's study and returned his attentions to examining maps. They'd decided that Ernest should take a less direct route home to Ireland, hoping this might expose any latent threat.

"Are you certain you won't take me up on the offer?"

Ernest shook his head.

"They'd only slow me down."

"Being dead or injured might slow you down too," Christiansen quipped.

Ever since he'd learned of Ernest's intention to leave, he'd begun urging his godchild to travel with armed guards.

"If they'd been willing to move to Ireland and watch over us on a permanent basis, I might be interested; otherwise, their protection will be short lived at best, and their presence might attract unwanted attention or questions," Ernest explained.

"Well, at least allow me to hire someone to guard the house until we finalize the matter of your estate," Christiansen bristled.

Ernest wanted to point out that if their efforts to draw out and confront his tormentor were successful, then a guard at the house would be unnecessary. However, one look at the sour expression Christiansen wore prevented this.

"Look into it." He sighed inwardly as he shuffled the maps.

After his own experiences at the house, Ernest was reluctant to needlessly endanger someone for a property he would soon be rid of, but he also understood that Christiansen's need to feel he was doing something to protect his godson, even if it was really just protecting his decaying estate.

"Are you still considering this route," Christiansen's finger traced lines across the French countryside.

"Actually, I think I've settled on this: southwest towards Lyon, then north to Orleans, and finally west to Nantes."

"Hhhmm," Christiansen frowned slightly though it was not immediately clear if it was to Ernest's proposed route or from the knock at the door.

A second letter from Ailis arrived, again assuring Ernest that she was tired, but otherwise in good health. For a brief moment, the vexation of his spirit was soothed by the lovingly crafted words; however, they also reinforced the sense of alienation he felt here in Geneva.

Kneeling before his family's graves had touched a deep and vast emptiness within, an emptiness he knew Ailis felt every time they visited her father's grave. And now she was alone, while he tended upon his selfish errand. The only comfort Ernest allowed himself was that the Shaws would not neglect their promise to watch over her.

He re-read both letters, committing their dear lines to memory before burning them, unwilling to chance that they might be stolen and used to locate his home, his family.

Ernest sat down to compose a brief letter explaining to Ailis the delay and the timetable for his return

"Could you please post this five days after I leave?" he asked, drawing Christiansen's attention away from the maps.

"Of course, Ernest, though if time is a factor, I really think our first route works much better."

His godson nodded but said no more. The course selected afforded him a singular opportunity. As he turned north for Orleans, he'd pass through Autun, a town steeped in ancient history. But it would not be the past he sought there, but a beginning. For, according to Ailis' letter, Autun was the most recent location of her sister, Abrielle. If no threat presented itself before Autun, he would attempt to see her. His trip may have failed to grant him peace regarding his brother, but there was a chance that by reaching out to Abrielle in person, he might at last reunite Ailis with her mysterious sister.

That evening he and Christiansen exchanged farewells, and long before the sun rose the next day, Ernest Frankenstein once again fled the city of Geneva.

*

By the following day, the French frontier lay behind him and the road to his beloved stretched beyond the horizon. He doubled back, switched horses and clothing, and varied his patterns as often a possible, but as threats failed to emerge, Ernest began to feel as if all he was doing was needlessly wasting time. He never should have come. As his temper steadily darkened, the bone-chilling drizzle which began to fall did nothing to brighten his spirits. By the fourth day, mere hours from Lyon, the ambush he dreaded happened.

Rounding yet another rock-hemmed corner, lost in thought, distracted by the steady rain and lax attention, he almost didn't notice the weeping child until the horse was on top of her. The horse jerked back at her sudden appearance. The girl, no older than eight, was dressed in a green coat with a colorful, patterned scarf upon her head. Her tears were indistinguishable from the rain, but her sobs were unmistakable. She looked as startled to see the horse and rider as they were to see her.

"What's the matter?" Ernest demanded.

At this the sobs ceased, and she slowly turned her head up to face him fully.

"Great work awaits." Her shrewd grin was unnerving.

Ernest was still puzzling over these strange words when he perceived the first sound of a pistol's hammer being pulled back, followed immediately by others. He turned to find nearly a dozen men, who'd been hidden among the trees and rocks, pointing various weapons. They were a motley sight. Some appeared half-starved, while others were clearly well fed. All were dressed in a blend of modern French apparel and tattered, colorful bits of cloth. Their appearance, and the few words they spoke, left little doubt, that if these men held any allegiances in this world, it was to some rabble band of gypsies.

They efficiently covered one another as they forced Ernest down from his mount and disarmed him. These were seasoned, hardened thieves who would not hesitate to shoot if their intended victim caused them too much trouble. Offering no protest or resistance, Ernest's reward was a harsh blow to the head, which struck him senseless for quite some time.

He awoke bound and gagged in the confines of a rocking cart transporting him. The motion, combined with a sudden wave of double vision, made Ernest very ill before passing out again. The second time he awoke, rough hands were pulling him from the back of the cart. One of the bearded highwaymen cut the rope around his ankles then yelled in a harsh, unfamiliar language, gesturing behind Ernest towards a dark hole in the rock face.

As he entered, the darkness enticed the darker corners of his mind. He was returning to the womb in a sense—into the dust and the rock, the minerals from which he was comprised. It was a good place to meet death, this natural tomb. Perhaps these gypsies meant to hold him for ransom. Or would his fate be sealed here while his loved ones fought a useless battle to retrieve Ernest alive? For a moment, he imagined Ailis explaining to their child how her once loving husband had abandoned them both: how he'd failed them, just as he'd failed all those he'd loved before and who were now gone.

Ernest suddenly felt old, disconnected from life here in the womb of Mother Earth. Was he ready to join them, those souls in Geneva?

But these were whispers in the dark. Something within him knew that being here had a purpose greater than ransom or fear. The earth seemed to be holding its breath in anticipation of what was to take place.

The light from the surface faded. The scoundrels halted, motioning him forward with their weapons. When he was far enough away, they threw a lit torch at him, seeming to confirm his original fears. He was destined to die here. But as it arched and clattered to the floor, Ernest realized that the torch was not meant to harm, but to help. It was clear that he was to proceed deeper into the caverns, alone.

How many human eyes had ever witnessed this place? The subterranean is apart from the world in a way that even the ocean depths are not. It echoed silence, breathed lusty gasps of musty air, and kept the secrets of the earth safe from the curiosity of man. Thankfully, no cave dwellers appeared—no bats, bugs, or common vermin strayed into the light, but he was being watched by eager eyes. The knowledge of unseen eyes was unnerving enough, but the accompanied sensation of intimacy made it worse. Ernest was watched—pace by pace. He halted, uncertain if what waited ahead could be worse than trying to sneak up and waylay the gypsies.

He'd stopped near a large chamber off the main passageway. Perhaps another way could be found to escape. Maybe his captors had not explored these caverns thoroughly. Hope coursed through Ernest and seemed to warm his chilled bones. The realization that the damp cold had begun to caress him with unseen, embracing hands frightened him. Ernest broke from the main tunnel and entered the large chamber to his left, only to halt after a few steps. A motionless mirror covered the floor, and mist hung thick in the echoing darkness. A fathomless lake stretched before Ernest, mocking his feelings of hope.

A voice both harsh and familiar shattered the solace of the place.

"At last you have come."

The damp cold embraced him again, and his grip on the torch momentarily faltered. Ernest swung it round, but the mist and the echoes obscured the speaker.

"Who are you?"

The voice seemed to shift locations and surround its victim in the echoing chamber.

"One who has known you and your family for some time."

Ernest fought to process these words, but in the end, allowed the silence of the cavern to fill his head. He gave no response. This seemed to please his captor.

"You are not here to die, though it would present no challenge if I chose otherwise," the voice starkly promised.

"What am I here for then?"

The voice seemed close but far. Ernest peered into the gloom, but only the disembodied voice answered his pains.

"You are here so we can help each other."

"Help? A voice in need of a body; I can't be of much help."

"I am flesh."

Ernest cast the torch away. It would be easier to find the devil without it.

"No, you are an echo of pain from a time long since past," he cried.

"Then you do remember me."

A brief flash of cold, yellow eyes in the window entered Ernest's mind.

"I remember you. Show yourself and I'll help you, fiend."

Ernest was reaching for a rock when one struck his hand. The voice seemed to dance through the gloom.

"How alike you are."

Ernest hurtled a rock to where the sound seemed to emanate, but it clattered uselessly against the wall of the cavern. As he reached for another, a massive hand gripped his. The stupendous strength easily overpowered Ernest's resistance. He could not turn to see what grasped him, but knew the other's earlier threat had not been an empty boast. The hand drew him closer to a giant being, and in harsh, hushed intonations it declared:

"You will help me, and in return, I will help you. I will assuage your doubts and your fears. I will grant you the peace you seek. And I will provide you the means to discover the answer to the question which has plagued your existence for ten years: the fate of Victor Frankenstein."

CHAPTER 8
CRUSADES

"He's dead."

The words were barely uttered before the crushing pressure on Ernest's hand became excruciating.

"You do not believe that. If you did, you would not have returned to Geneva. Do not lie," the vile speaker commanded, brutally twisting its victim's arm.

His body's momentum carried Ernest into the unforgiving wall of the cavern, as his tormentor backed away and once again became one with the mist.

"The letter was a forgery to lure me back," Ernest coughed.

There was no answer to this challenge, only the brooding silence of the cave.

"You came because you love him. Will you now abandon him?"

Ernest cradled his injured hand.

"I cannot save the dead."

"And what of the living?" the voice asked.

Several moments passed before Ernest realized the full impact of these words.

"What of the living?"

"Can a man who's only half alive truly be a good husband … or father?" the voice wondered thoughtfully as Ernest frantically searched the darkness for the demon.

"You will never truly be alive until you understand," the fiend continued.

"What am I to understand?" Ernest implored as he relented his futile efforts to locate the hideous speaker.

"Only with trust between us can there be understanding."

"I am not interested in trust, only your destruction."

Gruesome hands were again upon Ernest; held fast, he was unable to see his attacker's face.

"Victor Frankenstein has injured us both. I understand your need for vengeance. I have walked your path and know its bitterness. I do not seek your destruction or the destruction of your family, only our mutual salvation."

"How do you know about my family?"

"I have watched and listened to your words ever since your arrival in Geneva … the stories of your travels, of your family."

"By God, you will not harm them!" His struggles proved fruitless.

"I will not harm them … provided you assist me in my quest," the other said.

Breathing heavily, Ernest ceased fighting, a part of him even anxious to listen.

"Your brother is guilty of crimes too terrible for you to know. These were chronicled in his journals. I must have these if justice is to be fulfilled," the voice rasped.

"And what would you know of justice?"

"I know that without it, humanity serves no greater purpose than to live and die in selfish abandonment. Justice is a chalice from which all must drink or thirst eternally."

"So I am to find these and then you will deliver this justice upon him?"

"No, I will merely ensure that it is well served; another shall pass judgment."

Ernest paused before his shaking voice could utter the word.

"Who?"

"You will."

Victor's sibling laughed bitterly.

"I am not fit to be my brother's judge."

The ruthless voice spoke directly into his ear. "Very soon, you will be."

The menacing shadow projected by the flickering torch, which now burned uselessly upon the cave floor, roughly released Ernest. Though it did not flee into the mist, Ernest trembled to face it.

"Once this task is complete, you will trouble me no more?"

"There will be no need, for either of us, to concern ourselves with the other."

For a moment, Ernest considered fighting the hateful fiend to the end of his strength, insuring that neither would ever leave the earthen tomb.

"Think of your family, of the child you will never know, of your wife's sorrow before you take any action against me," the other spoke into Ernest's transparent thoughts.

If they fought and Ernest lost, would this creature locate them after he was gone, and exact some terrible vengeance for crimes they knew nothing of?

"What must I do?" he relented.

"You must return to your home in Geneva and find the journals," the mirthless voice commanded.

"How many are there?"

"Several, but I am interested in only two of them."

"What do they contain?"

Ernest waited, but no answer seemed forthcoming, he turned and with a mixture of relief and anger, discovered only the burning torch. He took it and backed towards the entrance to the chamber. From the far reaches of the endless cavern the voice returned.

"You will know them when you find them," he assured. "And Frankenstein, you will be watched."

There was no mistaking the menace in his voice.

As he left the chamber, Ernest fully expected to be assailed again by the man's gypsy cohorts, but his fears proved unfounded. He managed to work his way back through the tunnels and to the surface without incident. It was dusk, the rain continued to assault the landscape, but he was free of that accursed chamber and the beast it held. No sign of the gypsies remained; however, they had, surprisingly, left his horse tied under a nearby tree. From what little Ernest knew of gypsies and their reputations, this was nothing short of a miracle, which left two disquieting possibilities: this might demonstrate the power the man in the cave held over these people, or the "watchers" had already begun observing their prey.

Regardless of the circumstances, he needed to find shelter. The ordeal had left him emotionally shaken, physically fatigued, and ceaseless rain afforded no reprieve from these discomforts. Uncertain as to his location, the miles became a march and the wildness a vast absolute. The temperature began to drop, and soon, the damp cold penetrated all but bone.

*

He paced until the floorboards seemed to shine anew under the ceaseless pressure of his boot heels scraping them. He ordered food, but did not eat, and eventually, even the hours ceased to register within Ernest's reality.

Should he keep his word or flee? How would he know these journals the man sought? What secrets might they contain? Where was Victor? Was Ernest truly being watched or had this been an empty threat? What of home? What of Ailis?

At last decisions began to emerge. He could not go home, no matter how much he longed to. If Ailis was indeed well, then Ernest's return would only put his family's lives in danger. He held few illusions as to the lengths the man in the cave would go to in order to achieve his goals. Ernest would have to return to Geneva. With luck, the journals could be rapidly located and turned over. But what then? Should he pursue Victor's whereabouts on his own? And what of this talk of justice?

These questions brought a new sense of sadness and fatigue to Ernest's soul, and he soon abandoned them, settling on two primary goals: finding the elusive journals and insuring the safety of his wife and child. He feared any letters he attempted to send would be intercepted. Should he write Christiansen and demand that he not send the letter Ernest had left for him to mail. In the end, he decided such a letter would probably be equally dangerous. Instead, he opted for a more time-consuming, but meaningful, way to serve his love. Before returning to Geneva, he would find Abrielle.

**

Autun, 1809

Her hands shook as the iron gate shut with a ruthless clang. But then again they always shook after she turned someone over to them, for what was most likely to be a harsh and violent fate. She wondered what she would use to silence the screams tonight: drink, meaningless sex, sleep deprivation … perhaps all three. She breathed deeply. This was business, and this one had taken her a long time to track and capture. Business she could live with, but the questions were something else. Did she still believe in what she was doing? She never really had power before, not like this, and was she not now a part of something greater than herself? But what had she become?

The woman presented something of a mystery to the casual observer. She walked with the grace of a dancer, her fine clothes attuned to rhythm of her motions, and acted as a natural extension of her exquisite beauty. Long brown hair framed her slender face and highlighted her petite frame. Her delicate hands betrayed nothing of the brutal life she led, but her eyes held little of the happiness, which by appearances, should have been hers. Though she radiated beauty which sought attention, she could vanish as stealthily as a cat when needed. She'd been trained, too, both by life and later by the necessities of her profession. Beauty was a weapon, identity a mask, and increasingly she cherished less and less.

Abrielle had never taken a last name; to do so would have corrupted one of the few real things she possessed in this world. Her parents had abandoned her. Why should she adopt a traitorous family title simply to suit society? She found the conventions of society of little use, for she lived well outside its norms. Paradoxically, it was thanks to her efforts, and the efforts of others like her, that society, and its valued boundaries were maintained. Besides, the lack of a last name made slipping in and out of various roles easier to deal with, and certain memories associated with them easier to forget.

Here in Autun, she was known as Isabelle, a member of a traveling ensemble of players who entertained with a variety of dance, music, theatrical performance, and song. They stopped biannually in the town, ostensibly to perform shows for members of the town's Ecole Militiaire. The true purpose for the visit was much more complicated.

Abrielle was just placing the francs from the bounty in her handbag when she came across the small child in the street. A brief conversation ensued and concluded with the amazed girl being rewarded with a generous sum from the strange woman. The girl was the daughter of a local baker and possessed the good fortune of being blessed with both attentive ears and a detail-oriented memory. On occasion, Abrielle had found certain facts the girl recalled invaluable to her own investigations. The reward, though it had not been called that, was more than just compensation. She paused briefly before rounding the corner and regarded the child who was running rapidly in the opposite direction. Soon the girl would be too old, too inquisitive, and would no longer be such a safe and ready source of information. Yes, this would be the last time Abrielle used her. She wondered briefly if the child would ever realize that she'd unwittingly worked in the service of a spy for Emperor Napoleon Bonaparte.

Did the man she'd turned over tonight have a little girl? One who even now expected a father who would, most likely, never return? For a moment, the look of fear in his eyes burned brightly in her mind. She shook the thought away and concentrated on enjoying the cool, early November air of Autun. After being shut indoors for performances, secret meetings, and finally by five days of unyielding rain, tonight was truly a gift. Actually, she'd grown quite fond of the historic little town. Augustus Caesar had christened the town with his own name, and evidence of Roman culture and occupation were everywhere. It was a walled city with huge, decorative archways; the Theatre Romain had once been the largest arena in Gaul. The great Romanesque artist Gislebertus' sculptures still adorned numerous facades, and even the Emperor and his brother had studied at the academy. Yet, Autun, a place significant to history, was easy to overlook, much like Abrielle.

At first, her work had been merely a means to preserve her own life, but now it was by choice, an increasingly uncomfortable decision. There'd once been as many as twelve members of her company during the early years; now the group numbered only five. Some broke their oath, others concluded their service and supposedly retired, and then there were those who had mysteriously vanished. None of those remaining spoke of it, but at least two former members had been killed on orders by superiors. Every six months they returned to Autun for debriefing and new orders. Over time, the group had become increasingly paranoid, selfish, and ruthless, even towards each other.

And so it had been for years: orders, lovers, admirers, missions, and lives came and went, while she tried to forget or ignore her actions. She'd learned to find solace in the study of art and architecture, through her own gifts with music, and of course, in the secret correspondences with her younger sister. She'd hidden her past and passions so effectively from everyone that those she worked with or met knew nothing of her true heart, her fears or plans. Her one time mentor, the great spymaster, Bellange, had once praised her as the perfect spy: no apparent ties to family, no mixed loyalties, professional, seductive, dangerous when needed, and blessed with inexhaustible talents. She had, at great effort, managed to keep and maintain a few real friendships. This too she kept hidden from her compatriots. Secrets kept her alive and powerful, but brought little real joy or comfort to her life.

Without meaning to do so, she'd retraced her path twice, an old habit useful in exposing tails. Five minutes later, she stood before the back-door of the inn the performers were using. Abrielle almost never entered through the front door anymore, not since that night two years ago when a man with a pistol had been waiting for her in a darkened entryway. Yes, the back, generally speaking, was much safer, and with the hurried lives of most innkeepers, few took time to ask why she entered or egressed using such an unconventional route. Besides, if time permitted the luxury of inquiry, a few francs rendered the habit quite acceptable to most proprietors. She glided through the back without incident, at least until she reached the rear hallway.

As usual, she smelled her before she saw her. Chloe possessed the most atrocious sense of what a fashionable perfume was. Moments after smelling her over-powering scent, Abrielle was grabbed from behind, and Chloe began kissing her neck and clutching at her body. But this wasn't about passion, it was about control, and Abrielle was in no mood to deal with her tonight. She may have been Chloe's junior, both in age and time in the profession, but she was the superior spy. They both knew it, and they both despised each other. This game was about power. Chloe needed power and sought to exercise it over others anyway she could. She was as corrupt as they came, and her vices knew few limits. Abrielle didn't need power; she simply used it.

Chloe began to rub her hands over Abrielle's body and was instantly smashed against a nearby door. Their faces were now mere inches apart and for several heartbeats they glared at each other. Then Chloe began to laugh.

"I was just checking to make sure it was you."

"And if it hadn't been?"

"Keeps things interesting," she leered.

"First night off in three weeks and the best you can do with your evening is skulk in the hallway," Abrielle taunted.

"It's Sunday, have to make my own entertainment," Chloe grinned coyly waiting to see what she would do next.

Abrielle wanted to lean into Chloe's body and breathe hot, lusty words in her ear. She wanted to tease her, play with her emotions for a moment, and then when she least expected it, disjoint Chloe's fingers. But to do so would mean she'd shown fear, weakness, and Chloe would win tonight's struggle, and Abrielle would not give her that satisfaction.

Besides, Chloe was dangerous. She'd been the one to carry out the elimination of the two former members of the spy ensemble. To blatantly retaliate was to invite a potentially unwelcome end. The game, and the unwanted attentions which fueled it, did ensure Abrielle a degree of protection from such a fate. And she had survived worse while living on the streets. She relaxed her grip on Chloe, who immediately moved closer again, and reached for a strand of Abrielle's hair.

"Did you catch him?" she inquired as she ran the hair and one of her fingers over Abrielle's ear. She removed Chloe's hand and began to walk away.

"One day you won't walk away," Chloe cried with a tone that was both gloating and threatening. Abrielle paused and rounded back upon the obnoxious woman.

"My money."

Smirking, Chloe wordlessly returned the francs she'd stolen from Abrielle's purse. Whatever shortcomings Chloe possessed, her skills as a pickpocket were not among them. Abrielle also knew that Chloe was right, one day she wouldn't back down, and then what?

Two sets of doors and one flight of steps later, Abrielle began to relax. After savoring a glass of Pinot Noir in her room, she was surprised to hear the town bells announce that it was only eight o'clock. It felt much later. Tonight did not feel like a night to celebrate. Her spirit was weary and the choice of destination simple. A few minutes later she'd altered her attire appropriately and was just about to descend the stairs when she heard her name, her true name, being discussed in a conversation below.

"Look I've been all over this town, she has to be here," a man's voice insisted.

"But sir, I've told you there is no one registered here by that name."

"Check again."

"If you could give me a last name …"

"Abrielle, that's all I have. She's with the acting troupe you said was staying here."

She didn't recognize the voice, and any of the locals would have called her Isabelle. The accent was wrong for the Burgundy region as well. The curvature of the staircase and orientation of the innkeeper's registry desk made identifying the speaker from her present location impossible. Of course, she could just as easily take the back stairs, slip away, and question the innkeeper later, but if this visitor was a result of her most recent bounty, then she was better off confirming this sooner rather than later. She took a moment to confirm that the knives she respectively hid around her ankle and waist were present, and then she sedately descended the staircase.

"I've checked three times, monsieur; there is no one here by that name nor has there been anyone by that name in the past three weeks." The innkeeper slammed his registry shut.

Abrielle paused as she studied the stranger. He proved rather difficult to place, but she was certain that he was not a local and doubted very much that he was French. Humbled and obviously out of favor with the innkeeper, he resumed his hat and exited the inn. She waited a handful of seconds before following him out the door.

"Monsieur," she called out, "Monsieur, you seek a woman named Abrielle who is an ensemble player?"

The look the man gave was a blend of wary annoyance and questionable hope. Actually, more than anything, he simply appeared to be exhausted.

"Yes."

"I believe she is in the cathedral. I am going there myself if you wish to accompany me."

"Thank you," he nodded in gratitude and the two began up the winding stone streets to Autun's primary monument and spiritual home, Cathedrale St-Lazare.

For several minutes neither said a word. Both were silently grateful that the other did not ask a lot of questions; nevertheless, a nonverbal conversation was occurring as each sized up the other. It was Abrielle who spoke first.

"You are not French?"

"No," he agreed.

"Are you here to visit her?"

"Yes, hopefully," the stranger added with a faint smile.

"Are you old friends?"

"In a manner of speaking. Are you?"

"I know her," Abrielle evasively responded.

This one was bright, his answers guarded, but she sensed no duplicity in him. Perhaps he really did just want to speak to her. It would be nice if the knives she perpetually kept on her person were unnecessary, especially in the cathedral.

The Cathedrale St-Lazare began its colorful existence as a church dedicated to St. Lazarus, the brother of Mary Magdalene whom, according to Biblical texts, was raised from the dead by Jesus. Sometime during the Dark Ages, the town had inherited a collection of religious relics, and even supposedly the body of the revered saint. The church was established partially as a tribute to its namesake, but primarily as a tourist destination for religious pilgrims. Centuries later, various canons had slowly transformed the church into a towering, brooding Romanesque-Gothic cathedral, filled with highly-detailed, decorative carvings by Gislebertus.

In more recent decades, most of these had been entombed in plaster, as the current canons sought a more classical appearance for the cathedral. Ironically, the plaster probably saved most of the artwork from angry French Revolutionaries, who had stormed the church and destroyed the tomb of Lazarus and the carvings of the north tympanum. It was not the largest nor most ornate of the great European cathedrals, but it was accessible without being overwhelming. Abrielle made visits to this cathedral a tradition during her visits to Autun. She was not overtly religious; her life did not permit such luxury, but she always derived a degree of inner peace from her pilgrimages to this place. The hour was late, and soon the clergy would shutter the doors. For better or worse, this meeting would not take long.

The man removed his hat as he followed the woman into the living stone monument and attempted to absorb its offerings in short order. Unlike Abrielle, he'd visited only one of the Continent's great cathedrals. The brooding stone arches towered far above them and disappeared into the shadows of night. Undoubtedly, the windows on either side of the aisle, imbedded in the high walls and soaring beyond the altar gave the structure a much different feeling during the day. Incense perfumed the air, and candles dressed the interior in a blend of light and shadow. The more recent plaster additions, which now hid most of the impressive sculptures, appeared as brighter scars upon the dark stone. A soft, cool breeze swirled between the pews and up the main aisle, which made the building somewhat uncomfortable to be in. This, combined with the lateness of the hour, meant few visitors lingered in this impressive testament to faith.

Their eyes met.

“Perhaps she is in one of the chapels,” Abrielle grinned reassuringly and began to make her way up the main aisle. The man paused for a moment then moved quickly to catch up.

“Why don’t we try this one,” he indicated a small, slightly dingy looking chapel on the church’s left hand side.

Abrielle’s adrenaline rose though her demeanor did not change; she merely altered her course towards the indicated chapel. If there was action to be taken, at least it would be out of the general public’s view. As she entered the obviously empty chapel section, Abrielle began to reach for the hilt of her hidden knife.

Without turning she remarked, “There is no one here. We can try another chapel, perhaps.”

“Perhaps we could pray together here first.”

Before she could react, the weary man brushed past her, lit two prayer candles to add to the symphony of those already burning, and knelt before them. This was Abrielle’s opening. With the aid of her knife, she could ambush and interrogate him, if she wished. He’d left himself completely exposed. But it felt wrong, so she chose to trust her instincts. Without comment, she settled onto the kneeler, just out of arm’s length, and knelt before the candles, though she did not light any. Neither spoke or moved; the man kept his eyes closed. For a short time, Abrielle wondered if he’d fallen asleep.

“You know,” he gently intoned, with his eyes still closed, “you and your sister have very similar smiles.”

“Monsieur, Abrielle is not my sister.”

“No, but Ailis Tierney is,” as Ernest spoke these words, he switched to Gaelic, opened his eyes, and stared at the shocked expression on his sister-in-law’s face.

Though Gaelic had become a regular feature of her sister’s letters, the only words that Abrielle truly heard was the maiden name of her dear sibling.

"You are the husband?" she deduced.

"Ernest," he moved a little closer.

"She is not here?"

"No, has she told you that I was on the Continent?"

Abrielle searched her memory for a moment. It had been weeks since she'd had any contact with her sister. She never requested that she mail letters to her in Autun; with such a strong military presence and key superiors in the town, it seemed an unnecessary risk. It was also her habit to memorize the contents of the letters and then destroy them. Her transient lifestyle and the distrustful nature of her companions made keeping them a liability.

"She mentioned you'd be traveling," her eyes narrowed.

Ailis hadn't mentioned anything else, had she?

"I'm sorry if I frightened you," Ernest apologized. "It's taken me some time to locate you."

Actually Ernest had spent the better part of several days canvassing two towns, due mostly to conflicting information in order to find her. Abrielle said nothing. Her emotions were a whirlwind of fear, joy, and annoyance.

"Why have you come?"

"I need your help," he answered directly. Abrielle's pulse quickened.

"Is Ailis all right? The baby?"

Ernest winced at the questions and began looking over his shoulder, back into the central part of the cathedral. By now he knew that the threat he'd be followed was not an empty one. For several days, he'd been more than aware of the fact that a network of gypsy spies hounded his steps. Some remained hidden, while others blatantly made their presence known. He wanted to answer Abrielle's questions, to explain what he could, but feared they would be overheard and his plans undone. He now realized that he'd been so focused on finding Ailis' sister that he hadn't really considered how he would explain all of this to her. A sudden inspiration struck him and he leaned over and whispered a question into Abrielle's ear.

"Why?"

Her puzzlement was more than understandable.

"Can you?"

Abrielle considered the request. Over the years, both women had tried to teach the other their respective native tongues through their correspondence. He knew that several times Ailis had sent letters to her sister written entirely in Gaelic.

"I'll try," she promised at last.

Ernest took a deep breath and continued the conversation in Gaelic. He could only hope that his pursuers were ignorant of the dialect. He also hoped that Abrielle's reputed skills with languages were true. In the end, the hushed conversation developed into a hybrid of Gaelic and French, but should have been sufficiently confusing to anyone who might have been listening.

"We need your help. My time is limited and I'm not sure how much Ailis has told you about my family's history, so I'll be brief. For several reasons, I was compelled to leave Ireland and travel to my ancestral home in Geneva. It was to have been a short trip, and I was on my way home, but complications have arisen."

Abrielle lit two candles as she listened, but both she, and Ernest paused when a swirl of cold air wafted through the chapel. An elderly clergyman appeared from behind the archway to remind them that the cathedral was closing. His task complete, he shuffled out of view. Her eyes fixed on Ernest's.

"Complications? Does my sister know of these things?"

"I left a letter in Geneva with an old friend and asked him not to mail it for several days until after my departure. It's probably on its way to Ireland. I wrote it before I was ambushed near the French boarder," he explained.

"Ambushed by whom?"

He paused and looked over his shoulder again.

"Gypsies."

Abrielle openly scoffed at this ridiculous statement. It was true, on occasion, certain gypsy clans had attempted to settle in France, but they'd always been repelled. Once she'd even helped to infiltrate a small group of Romani and successfully framed several members for crimes, forcing them to flee. It was impossible to believe that with the Emperor's ever increasing sphere of power that any clan would be foolish enough to try to settle within the Imperial French proper. Ernest didn't even seem to notice her disbelief as he pressed on with his narrative.

"Their leader blames my brother for some misfortune he's suffered. If I can fulfill a promise to him, he has vowed to leave my family alone. If I fail to go back to Geneva and do as he instructs, I will put Ailis and our baby in mortal peril."

Abrielle's patience was growing thin.

"Why cannot your brother handle this?"

Ernest's expression grew more strained.

"He's dead, as is every other member of my family."

Mentally Abrielle kicked herself. Yes, she was certain Ailis had mentioned that fact at some point. Still, there was no reason for her to trust any of this.

"If he is dead then his crimes died with him," she snapped, "you, Monsieur, belong with your family, not chasing ghosts."

She crossed herself and rose to leave. Ernest sprang upwards and raised his voice to Abrielle's retreating back.

"He may not be dead. My brother may not be dead."

She spun on her heel back towards him.

"You expect me to believe such things? You leave my sister, my dear pregnant sister, alone, then come here and tell me these lies and…," she shook her head and backed away.

"I don't know you well enough to know what you'll believe," Ernest confessed as he pursued her, "but she believed it was possible that he lives and so I'm here."

"What is it you want?" she demanded.

Ernest paused. He'd fully expected Abrielle to leave.

"I don't think anyone knows about our relationship. It should be safe to send you." He gazed meaningfully into her eyes.

As he did, the enormity of what he wanted began to dawn on Abrielle.

"You want me to go to Ireland."

For the second time that night, her hands began to shake. The image of that young blonde girl at the orphan convent with her father swam before her. Their encounter still haunted her. Had it not been for them, she might never have faced death or committed the hellish act that made her…

No, had it not been for her father, such things might never have been.

Ailis was innocent; she was family. In Abrielle's mind, Ailis had also become a moral compass, an ideal, something pure that she herself could never be, but deep in her heart wanted desperately to become. She'd reached out to Ailis after the darkest chapter of her tragic life, when she'd felt incapable of love, and Ailis had accepted her, unconditionally. The relationship with her sister had saved Abrielle. Could she now deny Ailis or her unborn child in their hour of need?

"She tries to hide it, but I know the stress of the pregnancy has made her ill," Ernest continued. "Please, Abrielle, there is no one else I can trust."

When their eyes met, Ernest knew his trip to Autun had not been in vain.

"I will go to her," Abrielle vowed.

Inwardly he breathed a sigh of relief.

"You will need to take precautions. They will try to follow you."

"They will not be a problem." Her declaration held such a degree of resolution that Ernest never doubted it. As long as Abrielle was with her, Ailis would be safe.

A few words were said in parting and instructions were hastily exchanged; then Ernest left. Abrielle lingered for a few minutes, memorizing the addresses he had written, and then she ignited the paper using a nearby candle. It flashed into ash before her eyes. This task completed, she exited the cathedral and began to head back down the hill toward the inn. Her emotions were again under control, her mind was clear, and she began plotting key decisions she must make. She pondered how she would slip out of the Napoleon's spy network unnoticed, the safest, most direct route to Ireland, and how she would deal with the man, in gypsy apparel, who had begun to follow her as soon as she left the cathedral.

*

<u>*Hungary, 1809*</u>

Baseria Nalie found herself in a mist-covered graveyard following a man. He cast about searching aimlessly. What did he seek? Suddenly a great shadow swirled up from the fog and issued a soft, bitter laugh. Her heart turned to ice upon hearing the distressing sound. The man she'd been following seemed unaware that the shadow now stalked him. She must warn him. As Baseria opened her mouth to speak, the menacing shadow suddenly turned upon her, the yellow eyes it possessed burning into her very soul.

She awoke screaming a name over and over again.

"Frankenstein! Frankenstein!"

Baseria's senses slowly began to return. Breathing hard, her nerves still dancing, she cast about the empty tent before pressing the heels of her palms against her eyes. The nightmare was fading.

She'd grown used to nightmares, ever since the deaths of her sister, Patia, and cousin, Jucika. But this felt different. For a moment she considered going to Nasi's tent and asking her for advice, but the old Seer was undoubtedly asleep. Besides she did not want to disturb her beloved nagyanya[11] over something so trivial. Baseria pushed back her dark hair as she again lay down. At least her brother and father, with whom she shared the tent, were still out patrolling the perimeter of the Wild Rose clan encampment. The less her father knew the better.

---

11 Hungarian for grandmother

CHAPTER 9
AGE OF ARROGANCE

Geneva, 1790

"I believe you," I said.

In that strange, surreal moment, my only thought was how this shared knowledge would change us. I had never been told something this dark, this intimate. Her black shoe tapped the foot pedals of the old piano, forcing air to hiss through the interior chambers of the instrument. Justine's brunette hair hid her pixie face, but I knew there were tears flowing from her brown eyes. Should I hold her? Ask her more questions about it? Sometimes when I went climbing with my father, I had accidents, which literally left me hanging hundreds of feet in the air. The only thing securing me to this world was the rope tied around his waist. In those moments, the fragility of life itself became a living presence, as I was reminded of my own mortality. This news evoked the same feelings.

"Say something." It was a command, not a plea.

My mouth and mind worked to fulfill her request. But I felt frail and scared. I knew anything I said would come out wrong. I looked down at her hands. I'd come to the conservatory because I'd heard her playing. I loved to listen to her play. She was due to leave in a few hours, and I wanted to hear her one last time. How often had I slipped through the door behind her and listened to her talents? The music she played and the notes she sang always seemed so pure and genuine, as if her spirit could only find breath by sharing her gifts. Justine's vile mother had recalled her, not out of love for this child she had cast aside, but out of fear and guilt. God had punished her mother's rejection of Justine by claiming Justine's three siblings and Madame Moritz's husband. Alone and God fearing, she'd contacted my father and demanded her only remaining child's immediate return.

One of my hands reached for her mass of hair and began to pull it back from her face; the other sought her fingers and laced my own among them. Justine was brought to our home as a servant by my mother, but as had occurred with Elizabeth, the young girl quickly became much more. She became not only a servant but a sister, friend, and daughter to us. Her vivacious spirit had dimmed these last months after the death of my mother. Justine attended her for endless hours as the scarlet fever Elizabeth had originally contracted worked on her. When my mother died, she lost not only her benefactor, but the only true mother she'd ever had. Justine grew very ill not long after the funeral, and Elizabeth and I took turns watching over her.

During one of those feverish nights, she broke into a hysterical fit. We'd packed ice from the lake around her in the bed, in an attempt to break the raging fever. I was alone in the room at the time and had begun to drift off. Her body was drenched in sweat. And her labored breathing attested to the doctor's contention that her windpipe was nearly swollen shut.

Her sobbing awakened me a moment before she began shrieking.

"No! Don't touch me again! Don't touch me!"

"Justine?"

"No!!!"

She threw back the covers, her bloodshot eyes looking frantically at nothing. I tried again to calm her, thinking it no more than the effects of the intense fever.

"Justine, you must try to relax."

I reached out a hand to try and get her to lie back down. She began screaming. She punched my hand, but still didn't seem to realize where she was or to really know that I was even there. Elizabeth rushed into the room.

"What did you do?" she snapped as she tried to cover the struggling Justine.

"Daddy, why are you hurting me? Why are you hurting me?" she sobbed uncontrollably.

Elizabeth snatched her into her arms and held her as if she'd never let her go. She held her so tightly; I wondered how Justine could still breathe. She stroked the girl's damp hair and rocked her gently.

"Ernest, go," Elizabeth commanded.

I was too startled to argue, too startled to move really.

"Ernest, you need to go. Shut the door behind you." Elizabeth did not seem surprised by Justine's outburst. Had she known? I crossed the small room in three steps.

"Ernest," Elizabeth fixed me a gaze I'd never seen before. It was a mixture of regret, sympathy, and threat.

"Say nothing of this to anyone." I nodded in agreement and left. We never spoke of the incident again.

I'd tried to forget it, even half convinced myself that it was just the fever. But now her confession a few minutes earlier had confirmed the worst of my fears. Why hadn't she told me this? My hand finally succeeded in clearing the mass of brunette locks from her face, and our eyes fixed upon each other. And in that moment, as we sat together in the conservatory, she was the most beautiful, perfect person I'd ever seen. The shared knowledge established a new level of trust between us. She took my hand from her hair and managed an awkward smile.

"My mother hates me. She thinks I chose …," she looked away, "and now having to return to her …"

"We all want you to stay," I finally managed, "Father even talked to a lawyer."

Justine swallowed hard.

"She used to beat me and …"

I didn't want to hear anymore. This time I held her tightly. Because of the differences in our ages, Justine had always been more of a big sister, like Elizabeth, than anything else.

"I believe you," I repeated.

"I'm sorry," she sighed, "but after that night with the fever, I needed you to understand. In case we never see each other again."

"Is that what you think will happen?" I pulled away.

"It's what I fear," she said simply looking into my eyes.

A few hours later she was gone. More than two years would pass before I saw her again.

**

from the journal of Ernest Frankenstein

October 1809

My dear child, I can only beg from you some degree of understanding for what I am about to write. I do not know if I write these words for your benefit or for mine. Perhaps it is a confession, perhaps it is something else, but the past eight days, since I returned to Geneva have forced me to challenge thoughts and memories I had long ago consigned to the dusts of the past. I have never written of them, and they are so painful, I have only spoken to your mother about them once. I ask your forgiveness for all that now follows.

***

Geneva, June 1794

After so many days in the cell the brightness of the sun brought tears to her eyes. She'd vowed she could cry no more for herself and wished for nothing more than to leave this world of eternal torment. Still, the tears traced silent paths over the curvature of her face. She was innocent, whatever else she may be; she was innocent of the crime for which she was to be executed.

As she was being led to the gallows, the mob, which had assembled to witness justice, assailed her with dehumanizing, hateful words. She was a beast for show, a wild hunted thing that would now be rendered forever harmless to mankind. She had never known hate could be so powerful. Some pulled her clothing, her hair, they scratched her, spat upon her; there was no dignity. It would be a hollow death, one perhaps she had earned, through the hatred and cruelty of others. Where had this vaulted sense of justice been when her father had raped her or when she'd been beaten by her mother and treated as a harlot. The only place she'd ever known real love had been in the Frankenstein household, and now, even that was gone. There was nothing left.

Though not exceedingly tall, the gallows platform and steps shuddered and swayed alarmingly as she ascended them. Time was moving too fast; life was not supposed to reach this unnatural conclusion. How could one prepare adequately for this moment? She wanted a pure heart, a peaceful soul to accompany her from this life, but both were alive with fear.

Rough hands gripped her and forced her body to a fixed location on the platform. The cries from the crowd were deafening. She was being asked something? She was being asked something by a priest, one of an order who had forced a false confession from her. One who, instead of serving as a champion for her innocence, had held her at sway with fear for her very soul—to die excommunicated.

What was the question? Last words? What had her first words been? The man dimmed in her vision; air was no longer reaching her lungs. She staggered as she fought to keep them working. Her bound hands made regaining her balance difficult, and her shoulder slammed into the abrasive surface of the platform. This drew cheers from some in the mob. Her face had been cut by the fall, and blood poured freely from the wound. She tried to remember anything that would grant her solace. Dirty hands grabbed her hair and began to haul her to her feet. It was in that instant that she saw him.

His face was agony. She could have blamed him. Where had his voice, once so full of love, been in her defense at the trial? His utter lack of kindness when she'd been shackled in a cell, forced to sleep on putrid smelling straw. His silence.

They had her back on her feet now, and apparently were willing to forgo further formalities. The noose slipped over her face, smearing the blood, then settled about her neck.

"Don't bother with it," she heard someone say.

For a moment, the crowd calmed, collective bloodlust held them at bay. No hood was placed over her face. They would see her last moments of agony. The murderess deserved that. But for Justine, the world had vanished. The only things left in it were the eyes of Ernest Frankenstein. Would he now look away? This is what he wanted. Now time did seem to stop. No, this is not what he wanted. Despite his harshness, this is not what he wanted.

She knew his heart was broken, that his love for both her and William had overwhelmed him. And the forced confession was her ultimate betrayal. Would he understand? If only there was time to explain. It was then that her final thought took shape, the last words she would utter in this life before her lips grew cold and lifeless. In her isolated agony and fear, the words brought the comfort she'd longed for, but they would be words Ernest never heard, for as they formed on her lips, the trap door dropped and her body plunged into the void.

Mercifully the end was instantaneous. Her last thought, a final gift she could bear before her in the darkness, ebbed through her dimming consciousness. If there had been time for a second thought, it would have been regret, that Ernest would never hear her final words to him: "I forgive you."

**

from the journal of Ernest Frankenstein

By the age of fifteen, I knew my future. Father did not approve, nor did Elizabeth, but I was confident it was the right choice. Father wanted one of his sons to follow the proud, distinguished traditions of my family and serve the public as a counselor or fill some other government office. He'd given his younger days in service to our country, and his reputation was renowned. In those days, he still served as a consultant and elder statesman to Geneva, and since my mother's passing, he'd allowed himself to become increasingly involved in this role. So it was that we began to spend various amounts of time at home, in Belrive, or in residence in his old home inside the walls of Geneva. But I knew I would never be happy as a public servant, tied to one place; mine was a restless spirit. Nor could I ever be satisfied with a life of study like the one that had consumed Victor. I would chart my own destiny, while serving my country in the Swiss Foreign Service.

The challenges and opportunities of a military career excited my imagination. Public service and school could come later. I would see the world, and could use the knowledge and experience I gained to serve my nation more effectively. Besides, the French Revolution and subsequent removal of Louis XVI, had destabilized the whole of Western Europe, and an era of change was beginning. I didn't want to passively watch it happen; I wanted to participate in whatever was to come. Elizabeth and Father gradually realized their attempts to dissuade me only increased my commitment, and eventually they would yield to my wishes. It was not that I was unhappy at home, but I knew I wanted more in my life. But I would still have to wait for Victor to return from Ingolstadt, if he ever did.

Victor's total disappearance from our lives added only unwelcome uncertainty. He had long since ceased to write either to my father or Elizabeth. Was he well? Did he ever intend to return? His absence, and later his silence, was particularly difficult for Elizabeth. For so long they'd been inseparable, and though she did not dare to speak it aloud, I know she feared that Victor's silence indicated that he'd found another while at university. Though I doubted this was the case, I could not banish the possibility from my mind. It was not until early in the winter of 1792 that news of his condition finally arrived in a letter from his best friend, Henry Clerval.

Henry had only recently gained the reluctant blessings of his father, an influential Genovese merchant, to attend university. Several of Henry's letters alluded to some debilitating illness which had affected Victor's health. The tone was always positive regarding Victor's recovery, but the contents consistently lacked any real detail. These granted us a collective sense of comfort, but also added to our frustrations. Father had married late in life, and with his advancing years, the long journey north would have been a great strain upon him. Elizabeth was eager to go to Victor but needed an escort. Raising William, keeping up our estate, and Father's business affairs took a great deal of time and effort, and even with our servants, my absence for a prolonged period would cause difficulties, to say nothing about Elizabeth's. And so we stayed.

It was during this time that I took to the habit of exposing myself to harsh conditions and environments, in order to better prepare myself for my chosen vocation. I spent hours rowing on the lake in all types of weather. I climbed great peaks and rappelled into plunging depths. Several times, I even spent nights alone on various glaciers. The frigid temperatures and moaning ice offered no quarter. Here one survived on skill and wit alone. My earliest attempts ended with nearly disastrous results, so I never told my family when I undertook the later trips. I would lie and tell them that I was merely going hiking with Jack Clerval. Jack, very much the opposite of his older brother, often used me to cover his own secret activities. It was during my absence on one of these trips that the impossible happened. Justine Moritz returned to us.

*

Actually, the circumstances surrounding our reunion were no less improbable than her unexpected return. Jack and I were once again using each other for cover, but his plans fell through, so my secret endurance camping would have to wait. I arrived home well after midnight to avoid unwelcome questions as to why I was returning purloined camping equipment to the storage buildings instead of being in Villeneuve with Jack to visit his cousin—the publicly stated goal of the trip. As it was nearly two in the morning when I completed my task, I decided to use a trick Victor had shown me for sneaking in and out of the house.

The drain pipes along the south wall, near his old rooms, were re-enforced in a manner which allowed them to hold weight with relative ease. Also, they did not shake or make other unwelcome noises as one climbed. From the pipe, it was a simple matter of either navigating the narrow ledge, which encircled the second story, or clambering over the roof and descending a short pipe near my room. Victor never really mentioned how he'd discovered all this, and I never asked. I considered it a Frankenstein brother's secret and looked forward to the day I could share it with William.

In a matter of minutes, I was easing the sash of my bedroom window upwards and slipped silently into the warm room. To my surprise, a dull, dying fire sputtered in the room's fireplace. I always assumed that they left the room unheated in my absence, but perhaps the winter chill had begun to permeate beyond it.

I took off my shirt and removed my boots, then considered the fire for a moment. Should I leave a note in the downstairs hallway to let the household know I'd returned? No, they'd find out in a few hours anyway. I fumbled across the dimly lit room to my bed and began to roll myself into the covers. They seemed to be stuck on something. I gave them a bit of a tug and to my great shock, they suddenly jumped with a reactionary pull from the opposite side of the bed. I assumed it was William. For some reason he'd always wanted to switch our rooms. I knew he liked to stay in mine when I was away. I think he felt safe here. Our rooms were close together, and on more than one occasion, he'd taken refuge here when storms had rolled through during the night. The sound of thunder, echoing off the Alps, was less pronounced in my room, and he typically calmed down in short order once he was safely inside. I briefly thought about going to his room to sleep, but the cold of the floorboards argued against it.

A low moan greeted my next attempt to gain more of the blankets, but I managed to free a little more when the bed's other occupant shifted positions. Moments after shutting my eyes, I felt an arm drape itself over my chest.

My mind froze.

It wasn't William's arm, nor his leg, or his soft breasts pressing into my back. The next thing I knew I was looking into a pair of brown eyes and then came the shrieking. We both flew apart and jumped from the bed, screams of surprise erupting from both of us.

Locks of brunette hair hid half the face, but the grin, which began to play across her lips left no room for doubt. Without thinking we mutually leapt back upon the bed and began to embrace each other. The initial shock turned to surprise and now joy. It was impossible, but she was here. Justine whispered my name, and I longed for our embrace to continue. That is until Elizabeth barged into the room, candle in hand. Justine and I parted immediately.

"What do you think you're doing?" Elizabeth demanded.

"I … well," I stammered uselessly.

"He didn't know I was here," Justine interjected, laughing slightly as she wiped her cheek.

"Well, I knew someone was here, but …"

"Uncle Alphonso … I mean your father, suggested I take your room since you'd be gone tonight. I've only been back a few hours," Justine explained.

"How did …?"

"Ssssshhhh. Let's leave the rest until morning," Elizabeth suggested, "we'll be lucky if William doesn't wake up from all this racket."

It had always been extremely difficult to get William to bed, to say nothing about his habit of being an early riser. Justine and I exchanged humored glances, and even giggled a bit, but did not protest. I was escorted from the room by Elizabeth who smacked me on the back of my head before gliding off towards her own room.

"Where should I sleep?" I whispered at her retreating form.

"Anywhere but here," she bit back.

I could have slept in mother's old room that night, but the thought of doing so was unbearable. It had not been occupied since the day she died. I ended up on a sofa, which was far too short to support my frame and passed a more uncomfortable night than the one I'd planned out on the ice. But as I tried unsuccessfully to sleep, I pondered my feeling about being reunited with my friend. That I was pleased to see her again was obvious, but there was more.

I realized that her fear had become mine; I'd all but given up hope that we should ever meet again. Elizabeth was the only family member permitted to visit Justine after she returned home. Elizabeth said little about the encounter to me, but she'd locked herself in Father's study for several hours upon returning. I remember several times hearing their voices arguing. Father looked quite pained when he left the room, but would not talk to me about either Elizabeth or Justine. I now remembered that he visited mother's grave for a lengthy period of time that evening.

For two years, Justine had been removed from our family after M. Moritz and all of Justine's siblings passed. Her mother recalled her out of the fear that God was punishing her for rejecting Justine. But Madame Moritz was a hateful woman, and not long after Justine's return the verbal abuse began. How far the corrosive mixture of bitter love and thoughtless abuse extended I never fully knew, but the longer she was with us, the more scars both physical and otherwise, I discovered. The pain she'd worked so long to bury while my mother was alive, and before she was forced to leave us, was much closer to the surface. The months to come would demonstrate this in a variety of unfortunate ways.

*

Justine's blackest secrets became known to me mere hours before her departure. Would she now regret telling me? Did she even still remember? Perhaps the intervening years had erased the significance of that moment. The memory of her body's touch against mine confused and excited me. Justine's role in our lives was always complex: a servant and family member who was, in actuality, fully neither. She was my elder by three years; at least that's what we thought since Justine never knew her true date of birth. As children we played together, teased each other, she even tried to teach me how to dance. Her laughter warmed my heart; her music tamed my soul, and her innate kindness brought cheer to all of our lives.

Apparently, her mother passed only a few days before her sudden return to us. At first Justine said little about her death, and we all tried to resume our lives as they'd been during the two years prior. I'd missed Justine terribly, and the first weeks of her return were happy ones, though we all adjusted to her arrival differently. Elizabeth, for instance, had not shown such joy and energy in months. To Elizabeth, Justine was her sister. When the news of Victor's illness first reached us, I'd feared for Elizabeth's own health. But now the weariness of her spirit seemed a dim memory. Justine's old room had been filled with items to be put into storage, so it took several days to return it to a habitable state. Fortunately, Elizabeth volunteered to share her bed with Justine, so I didn't have to spend another cold, painful night on the sofa.

It seemed to take William the longest to adjust to her return. He'd been deeply wounded by her sudden departure, so soon after mother's death. I think he felt betrayed. For the first several days, he practically shunned her, and eventually, Elizabeth was compelled to intervene.

"William, Justine couldn't help that she had to leave us."

"She didn't have to come back," he replied in a matter-of-fact tone, "she never even used to let me help out in the kitchen the way Aggie does."

Aggie was the senior servant and had actually worked for my father before he was married. She always scared me, but she loved William.

"Well, you were much younger then. I'm certain she'll let you help now," Elizabeth said reassuringly.

"Aggie didn't want her to come back," he stated as he continued to play with his toys.

"I'm sure that's not true. Why would she say something like that?"

"You know," William favored us with an accusing glance.

Elizabeth and I exchanged puzzled looks.

"Know what, William?"

"Because she murdered her mother," he declared bluntly.

This stinging, and wholly surprising assertion, stunned us both.

"William! How could you even think such a thing?!" Elizabeth asked after the initial shock abated.

"Well, that's what the servants are saying," he answered defensively.

"William," a deep, authoritative voice interrupted us.

"Yes, Father," William practically jumped up from his toys.

"Lies will not be tolerated in this house," his stern tone and withering stare left no room for argument, but William decided to try anyway.

"But Aggie said …"

"I've already spoken to Aggie about this. I also told her that you're banned from helping in the kitchen for the next two weeks."

William momentarily considered further protests, but one look at our father silenced him.

"Yes, sir."

Over the next several days, a fuming Elizabeth took every opportunity to berate the servants behind Father's back. Elizabeth's assimilation into our family occurred fairly early in my parents' union, so her full inclusion into the household had been quietly accepted. Justine was a different matter.

Her role remained more ambiguous. Those servants whose services my family had retained for a number of years did not accept her amongst their ranks. They thought she saw herself as more than she was and could not understand my mother's infatuation with the desperate child. It was charity run amuck, and after mother's passing, this sentiment began to make itself more publicly known, at least among the servants.

Justine's outbursts during her subsequent illness and mysterious departure had further damaged her reputation in the household, and so the rumors began. In the end, their mere existence would prove immensely destructive. With such burdens from her past and present, I often wondered how she kept herself together as well as she did. I think one way was to embrace my mother as a fallen saint.

It was a slow process, and one that really took hold after her return to us. She would not tolerate anything negative ever being said about Caroline Frankenstein. She cleaned mother's room, as if she would one day occupy it again. At some point, either consciously or unconsciously, Justine even began to adopt certain mannerisms similar to my mother. This delighted Elizabeth, but hurt my father. And she would spend lonely hours, hovering over Mother's grave in all types of weather. Their bond during Mother's lifetime had been undeniable, and it was this ardent devotion, which had inspired Justine to attend my mother day and night during the illness that would claim her life. They adored one another, and I have no doubt that had she lived, Mother would have pushed Father into legally adopting Justine, as they had done with Elizabeth. And it is here that my father's feelings must be questioned.

Before Justine's departure, he did make legal overtures that might have kept her at our house, but he was to serve as a legal guardian, not her adopted parent. Though I was aware of tension between them, I did not know the depth of the guilt and resentment, which existed mutually between my father and Justine until it was too late. He was always kind and polite to her, and never said an unkind word about Justine, but he did not see her as a daughter, the way he did Elizabeth.

I think looking back that he felt trapped by circumstance. I knew that her presence pained him. Perhaps it was the knowledge that his wife had died under Justine's care or the unrest among the servants regarding her. It might have been her ardent worship of his deceased wife. Or it could have been guilt; he'd failed to protect her from her abusive mother, and in doing so, had failed both Justine and my mother. Could it have been this rarely acknowledged anger towards my father that provoked her to murder William? Or was it perpetuated by all the years of heartbreak and hatred?

Hatred does not require courage, only clarity. It is single-minded in purpose, and a relatively simple thing to understand. Love is mystery, and it is often misunderstood, even by those who claim it as their own. Pleasure and pain make it, and courage sustains it. It is created by a thousand motivations, some with names, and others barren of thought. It can blend with hate or destroy it, and even fools need it. Before Justine, I'd had few experiences which could have prepared me for the astonishing powers and consequences of love. Her return brought new feelings, as well as an awareness that part of what I was missing in my life was a love of my own.

*

The first months of her return were joyous and challenging. She often took to her room ill for days at a time, with only Elizabeth to tend to her. Of the continuous rumors surrounding her mother's passing, she said nothing, and some days would not even meet my eyes. Other days she was cheerful, her wit and talents on full display for all to enjoy and admire. Our romantic relationship began simply: the exchange of a casual touch, pleasant hours spent in quiet conversation, and a marked attentiveness to the moods or emotions of one another.

One night in May, I was again sneaking home rather late having lost track of time while spelunking with Jack. After stowing the equipment in one of the outer storage buildings, I found Justine alone in the garden by the conservatory. Elizabeth was playing the piano, her silhouette dancing to the flickering candles she had burning inside. Justine was barefoot, sitting on a bench beneath a willow. I heard them before I saw the tears. At first I thought she was reacting to the somber music Elizabeth was playing, but as I drew closer, I saw the bloody knuckles of her right hand.

"Go away," she muttered.

"What happened?"

"I punched the tree. Go away."

"Hhmm."

I sat down on the bench, unwilling to leave her. She slid away and turned her face. Wordlessly, I took her hand and examined it by the dim light from the window. She did not protest. I ripped fabric from the lining of my jacket to stop the blood that was dripping freely from the wounds. I waited for her to speak after this task was completed but she said nothing. After a time I stood to leave.

"You don't believe them do you?" she asked suddenly clutching my arm. "You don't believe what they say … that I did … you don't believe that …?"

Her face was hidden by shadow.

"I thought they'd stopped talking about …"

Her head swung away.

"No! I just … you people, your family can't always fight my battles for me."

I turned to sit back down but she shrank away from me. I slowly eased myself onto the bench beside her. She held her breath.

"No, I don't believe them."

A short, harsh laugh escaped her.

"I wanted to. Dear God, there were days when I should have … it would have stopped it you know; I fixed her food I could have … it would have been so easy … but I couldn't." Tears began to flow. "I couldn't, I couldn't become her, become them. Isn't that sad?"

She leaned into me, heaving breaths shaking her body.

"You could have stopped it … why didn't you stop it?"

Through the tears she wailed these words over and over. And she was right. I'd known when Elizabeth returned that something terrible was happening; Father knew, and yet we'd done nothing. She hit at me, she held me, and the tears continued until she was nearly exhausted. I never felt more ashamed in my life.

Finally we stood, and I helped her into the house.

"Is this all there is? Is this all life is?"

"No," I choked, "no."

Fortunately we did not run across anyone during our journey, and soon I'd escorted her to her bed. When I tried to leave, she held onto my hand. I knew further scandal awaited if I stayed, but felt it was the lesser of two evils to do so. Several times I thought she'd drifted off, but the moment I stirred to depart, her grip tightened, and I resumed my seat. Later her grip slackened, and I moved quietly to leave. I paused to blow out the candle by her bed.

"Ernest?" Her eyes were shut and her voice was thick with the twilight of conscious thought, "Am I beautiful?"

I leaned forward, kissed her forehead tenderly, extinguished the flame and left.

Of all places, I ended up going out to our boat dock. The lake's water was black, but the reflection of the stars blazing silently above me shimmered upon it. The motion of the water had a calming effect as I tried not to think.

She was filled with so much pain. And I'd played a part in causing it. How does a victim find closure in this life when the criminal is at rest? My own sense of guilt pulsed at a dizzying pace. I wanted to talk to Elizabeth about this, but it was too big, too much. It was in those desperate hours that a new thought took hold of my heart. It was hope. At least, that's how I saw it at the time. I decided I would open myself to hope and offer it to her. I would embrace my feelings for her, and in so doing, I would show her that there was more to our lives than hate, hurt, and anger. I would love her; I would save her. It was a hope born of innocence and arrogance, and it would lead to the end of my family.

*

While there was attraction and desire, I was lacking one key element to a successful courtship—experience. My early attempts were painfully inadequate and even comical. They also added to the awkward mixture of attraction and shame we felt for each other. Pity was an outcast in her world, and my efforts were either met with a soft grin or unspoken anger. Though my efforts bore little fruit, I could not help but hope that the hand I extended would one day be seen as something more than guilt or pity. Still, I found cheer in the small details of our exchanges: a lingering glance, a dish I relished being served more often for dinner, a tune she knew I enjoyed being hummed while she worked nearby. I took these small signs as an indication that, though the secretive courtship was fraught with inadequacies, some part of us had forged a true connection.

As autumn descended to quiet the world in preparation for the unyielding clasp of winter, I became aware that one of the ceaseless rumors regarding Justine was true. I first overheard it from two of the servants. While their conversations were typically entertaining, if not highly inaccurate, I rarely put much faith in the "facts" discussed. It was not until early November that I was compelled to take more than an idle interest in the rumor.

I kept my feelings and hopes for Justine a secret from my family. If nothing ever came of them, then the loss would be my own. I'm sure Elizabeth could have guessed, especially in the early days, but to her credit she said nothing. William was too young to understand, and I doubted Father would approve. Had Victor been available, I might have confided in him, but he remained a distant enigma. Though fully recovered, news reached us that he would remain in Ingolstadt to study foreign languages with Henry. This sounded like an uncharacteristic departure from his previous interests, but regardless, his decisions continued to shackle me to Geneva.

What began as rumor, translated into fact, when I again overheard a conversation between two people; only this time the exchange was between Elizabeth and Justine. I'm not certain who was giving the piano lesson, but as was my habit, I paused to listen to the melodic art. The door to the conservatory had been left ajar, and when the music ceased abruptly I began to move on, at least until I overheard the intense argument that suddenly erupted.

"And if I did?"

"Then it's true?" Elizabeth's shocked voice asked.

"Does it matter?"

"How many times?"

"It doesn't concern you," Justine affirmed.

"It does when I have to defend you to the others, to say nothing about Father if he learns of it."

"Elizabeth, I need this. You can't understand, but I need this."

"You can't sneak out at night anymore. Please, promise me."

Sneak out? To where? I'd heard about this rumor before, but the idea had seemed ridiculous. Geneva was miles away. Where would she go if she left the house at night?

For some reason this made me angry. I felt betrayed. My imagination swirled with any number of unwelcome reasons for her nighttime ventures. The rest of their conversation took place in hushed tones, so my attempts to gain further details proved useless. Was she being courted by another or was it something worse? I was repulsed by how quickly my mind turned Justine and her unexplained actions into fears. If Elizabeth was so passionately advising Justine against her choices, then they must be bad ones. Despite Elizabeth's pleas, for several more months, Justine continued to disappear at night. There was no pattern to it, and my casual attempts to gain further information about what Elizabeth knew proved useless. The answers I sought required direct questioning, which might lead to new problems. I would have to trust Justine.

*

For a time, I did withdraw from her, while I decided how I felt about both Justine and the current status of my life. It was during this period that I resolved to fully commit to joining the Foreign Service the following summer. I loved my family, but knew I could not afford to remain much longer, regardless of Victor's absence. I was hungry for challenge and adventure, and yearned to prove I was a man.

Again I embraced the rigorous physical training I'd come to enjoy, but also began to take an interest in educating myself to speak a variety of languages. Elizabeth helped to tutor me in several of the Romance languages and was pleased that I'd finally dedicated myself to some form of study. Though I have never undertaken the formalized education Victor chose, my choice to study language did open my eyes to new realms of thought and learning. I would never be a great student, but I was now eager to pursue studies and topics which personally interested me. I began to take an interest in carpentry, mathematics, geography, and even history. My love of stories and storytelling would come later. In February, I decided to travel to a nearby portion of the French Alps, but this time the trip would not be undertaken in secret. Justine wished to visit her aunt in Chene, and I was to escort her there.

Chene was more than a league from Geneva, and at the time, my family was wintering in our estate in Belrive. I did not know how to feel about the prospect of such a trip. Justine and I were pleasant enough towards one another, but the months of tension between us had created discord. Every time the separation between us began to heal and draw us closer together, forces seemed to conspire to drive us apart. We both felt smothered and restless at home, so our journey would offer a brief respite from the mundane, but I also feared it would bring either unwelcome revelations or a final end to my hopes.

**

CHAPTER 10
THE SORROWS OF ANGELS

Geneva, 1794

The snow began falling when they were still several miles away from the city gates of Geneva. A look between them was all that was needed to answer the unspoken question. They would proceed towards France. An enticing sense of anticipation had sprung up between them, almost as soon as the house had disappeared from view. This trip meant more than either was willing to admit, even to themselves. They spoke little as they crossed the familiar miles between Belrive and Geneva, but the silence was agreeable. The world slowly began to fade beneath an ever thickening blanket of white. The scene cast a sense of utter tranquility, added to by the rhythmic motion of the cart and hushed hoof beats from the horse.

"Should we stop in town for dinner?" Ernest asked.

The question hung in the mist produced by his breath.

"No, I know a farm not far beyond town. It'll be faster if we eat there," Justine replied.

Ernest was secretly glad they'd avoid the crowds in the city, their trip having started much later in the day than planned. Darkness would soon attempt to shroud the suddenly iridescent world, and the temperatures would likely begin to plunge.

"So how do you know the farmers?"

"Oh they have one of the best produce stands at the market. Your mother and I used to see them every Saturday morning. She always liked to come with me on shopping trips for the household."

"I remember," Ernest smiled and returned his eyes to the road. Justine had always liked his smile. It never failed to reach his eyes.

The route to the farm proved to be more distant than Ernest had counted on, so they ended up saving little of the precious daylight; however, upon arriving at the farm, both the company and the fare proved hearty and inviting. Justine's demeanor was calm and happy as she spoke with the farmer and his family; there was a real bond between them.

This was a seldom-glimpsed view of Justine's life beyond Ernest's own world. The younger children especially loved her, and they ended up remaining until it was time for them to be put to bed. As he watched her, Ernest wondered, as he often had, if Justine might not be happier outside the Frankenstein household.

As they resumed their journey to the west, the weather took a turn for the worse. The snow was heavier, the winds more biting, and the temperatures increasingly frigid. They tried to sing to keep their spirits up as the torturous miles slowly passed by, but in the end, the chattering of their teeth prevented them from uttering more than a dirge-like hum. Justine wrapped her blanket around them as they both sought whatever warmth they could.

It turned out her aunt did not live in the village of Chene, but nearly three miles beyond in a remote, wooded area. By the time they reached the village, travel was almost impossible. Still they pressed on. Several times Ernest clambered down from the cart into the powdery, eight inches of snow to push it from behind, while Justine minded the reins. Both were quite exhausted when they finally arrived at the dark, cold cottage.

Justine knocked several times, but no aunt came to greet them, and finally, she simply shoved the door, which surprisingly swung open without protest.

"Is this normal?"

"I bet she had a call."

"Huh?"

Justine's aunt, it turned out, was a midwife, often compelled to leave home spontaneously to aid in deliveries. Though she had a family, her children were grown and her husband had been killed before the French Revolution. A note confirmed Justine's suspicions. In it, her aunt apologized for her niece's inhospitable welcome, and insisted they settle in and eat whatever they wished.

"The snow must have started after she left," Justine surmised. "She never mentions it, sounds like this delivery is going to be a difficult one though."

"I'd better take care of the horse and cart," Ernest decided.

"I'll make us something warm to drink."

The snow and winds continued to assail the cottage, which proved to be extremely drafty. The flames of the candles on the dinner table swayed to the icy rhythms of the winds outside. Both of them realized that Ernest's planned camping expedition would come to naught on this trip, so sleeping arrangements would have to be made. In order to delay this conversation, Ernest volunteered to go and clear a path to the outhouse from the back door.

The snow was nearly a foot deep now, and it took quite some time to free a path from the one-room cabin. If the snow continued to fall at this pace, he very much doubted he'd be able to get to the barn in the morning to feed the horse. In fact, this much snow might keep them isolated for several days.

Ernest could barely feel his extremities by the time he stomped back inside. Justine had lit a warming fire and poured him some type of strong drink to help ease the effects of the cold. It was surprisingly sweet.

"Do you think your aunt will return soon?"

"Doesn't look like it," she commented as she continued to brush her hair.

"We could be stuck here for a few days."

She put the brush down and turned to face him, and with an amused smile, nodded her head.

"Does that bother you?"

"No. It's … no, I'll just take the floor then?"

"As you wish," her smile deepened, and she turned to finish brushing her brown locks. Ernest felt the need to lighten the conversation.

"Is it always this drafty in here?"

"I haven't come here as much since my mother died, but, yes, I think it is. If we are here for awhile perhaps you could help her out and fix the holes. You've taken an interest in carpentry, haven't you?"

"You know about that?"

"Elizabeth mentioned it," Justine said casually. "My uncle's tools should still be in the barn."

Ernest didn't bother to voice his estimates about reaching the barn, but instead busied himself with making a place to sleep on the floor before the fire. He also pulled the cabin's lone bed closer to it, so Justine could be warmer. It would prove to be a long night: sleeping in a strange place, the alternating silences and forceful blasts from the on-going storm, and the emotional storms swirling within. He tried to sleep, but kept focusing on the sounds of Justine's breathing. Was she asleep? He felt tense and sleep eluded him for many hours.

They both slept unusually late, at least until the cabin's other occupant made itself known. Ernest awoke to a set of claws over his eyes, accompanied by a hiss.

"Oh, bad Calbit," Justine intoned as she scooped the cat off Ernest's face, "I forgot all about him. He must have been too scared of us last night to come out."

She kissed the cat and set him down.

"Thank goodness he got over that," Ernest remarked as he gingerly touched the scratches.

"He really is a nice cat, I'm sure he's just hungry."

Everything hurt after sleeping on the unforgiving floorboards, and Ernest's mood failed to improve when he stood up and looked over at one of the windows. A wall of snow filled almost half of the pane. He resumed his clothes and opened the backdoor, only to discover that at least another seven inches had fallen into the pathway he'd worked so hard to create. One thing was now certain, they would be alone.

A good portion of the day was spent re-clearing the path to the outhouse and beginning one to the barn. After several hours invested in this seemingly endless chore, Ernest's mood was truly foul. Tired, freezing, and by now starving, he paused to catch his breath. A snowball hit him squarely in the face, rapidly followed by another. Momentarily stunned, he didn't react until Justine started to giggle.

"You're dead," he grinned, and soon there was nearly as much snow inside the cottage as outside. They ran in and out, firing snowballs at each other as they went. Calbit again vanished and when a truce was declared, they decided it was time to eat something. It was during this late lunch break that Justine again surprised him, though this time with a question.

"Why are you still here?"

Ernest was about to state the obvious when he realized what she meant.

"Victor," he chewed the name with his stew. "Until he returns, the family's care is my responsibility."

Justine rolled her eyes.

"That was well-rehearsed," she shook her head. "I don't understand you."

"Why?"

"They'd manage if you left. And you'd be a lot happier."

"You think I'm unhappy?"

Justine studied him a moment then reluctantly turned her eyes to her own stew. Her insight was true enough on many levels, but the thought of abandoning his family as Victor had repulsed him. His plans to leave in a few months were linked to assurances that Victor would return, finally, from Ingolstadt. He'd said as much to Elizabeth in a recent letter.

"Are they the only thing keeping you in Geneva?" Justine's voice was soft.

Ernest met her eyes and spun the question back upon her.

"And why do you stay?"

The questions hung in the stillness of the snowbound cottage. They both knew the answer, but embracing that reality was difficult, and if it did not work between them, what then? Their gazes parted, and the meal was finished in brooding silence.

After dark, Ernest managed to finish the path to the barn and feed the famished horse. As Justine had surmised, there were tools, some very good ones in fact, that he could use to patch various holes in the cottage. He selected a choice few and hauled in an assortment of scrap wood. Before going inside for the night, he also managed to clamber onto the roof and free it of the unwelcome burden it bore. At least they wouldn't have to worry about the roof caving in now.

The tension between them grew worse after he returned inside. Justine was mending some of her aunt's blankets and clothing. She quietly hummed as she worked but would not look at Ernest, who also tried to find something to keep himself occupied. He finally decided to take an inventory of their supplies.

"We'll need more firewood if we stay through tomorrow," he noted.

Justine merely nodded and continued to her ministrations. They hadn't looked directly at one another since lunch. Ernest began to patch some of the holes, but soon found that it would take more than the scant supply of wood he'd located in the barn to really make much of a difference. With little else they could do, they decided to retire early. The heavy silence was broken only by the crackling logs being consumed by the greedy flames in the fireplace. The hours would go by even more slowly tonight and then what would dawn bring? He couldn't face the prospect of another day like today.

Ernest's thoughts were suddenly interrupted by the sensation of his blankets being pulled back, as a warm body came to rest tightly against his. He did not speak. At first he did not even move; the moment was all too delicate to disturb. Her arm curved over his body, and her hand came to rest over his heart. She sighed gently as she began to rub his chest. He released a deep breath he hadn't even realized he was holding. The doubts and fears were melting. Their breathing became rhythmic. They bathed in one another's scent and the sensations created by the unadorned contact of parts of their flesh.

After a time, she sat up and he turned over to face her back. She unlaced the nightgown and exposed her slender shoulders and the upper portion of her back. There, by the light of the fire, Ernest saw the scars and the seared burn marks forever imprinted on her body by horrific cruelty. She hung her head.

"Am I beautiful?"

Gently his hand began to turn her face towards his. She did not resist, and he rose to meet her. He wiped away her tears with one of his thumbs and fervently gazed into her eyes.

"You're amazing."

And then he kissed her deeply. Her arms encircled him and their kisses blended with her tears. She arched her back as his hand delicately traced a path up to her still knotted hair. She helped to free it then guided their bodies back down upon the blankets. Their hands and lips began to make memory maps of each other's form.

"Love me," she pleaded as they kissed. And then their passions knew no bounds.

*

"Tell me a secret."

"I could die happy right now."

"I could have guessed that," she smiled and emitted a low moan of pleasure as he kissed her neck. The first very dim rays of morning light were beginning to illuminate the cottage. A new world had been born in the darkness, one created by them and neither wanted to leave it.

"I'm serious. Tell me something no one knows."

Ernest shifted his body so they were once again eye to eye and thought for a moment.

"I plan to leave Geneva before the end of summer."

Her hand caressed the side of his face, but she made no comment to this pronouncement. He took her hand, kissed it, and let the idle minutes pass.

"Your turn. Tell me something true."

Their fingers laced together as she tried to select a secret to expose. There were so many. But there was only one simple, profound personal truth she wanted to share with him.

"I don't want to die anymore."

"You wanted to die?"

"I've thought about it." This was a vast understatement. During the dark years of abuse, she'd done more than contemplate it. "Sometimes at night I'd go to the edge of the lake and think about drowning myself. Elizabeth knew, but she can't understand."

Suffering the abuse had been bad enough, but living with its legacy was worse. Their hands separated.

"Why didn't you?"

This was a question she'd often asked herself, and it took time for the words to come.

"Because I would have failed my angels," she said.

Ernest searched her face for meaning. The confession was a difficult one, but she wanted him to understand. She needed him to.

"Your mother watches over me from heaven, but in this world … in this world it's you. It's always been you, my darling Ernest. You're my guardian angel. Your kindness, your willingness to see something good in me, my dream for this moment kept me going. Because I needed you to know that I love you. I love you."

She buried her face into his chest. She was embarrassed and relieved to have spoken the words to him at last. Ernest was stunned. He'd never suspected her feelings for him were so strong. The level of trust and openness she'd shown him was frightening and humbling. His arms wrapped around her and his hands touched the scars on her back.

"I love you, too."

"Thank you," she whispered.

For a long time, nothing in the world existed outside of them. Finally, he kissed the top of her head, and she turned her eyes up to his.

"Where should we go when we leave Geneva?"

She smiled at the question.

"Italy."

"Why Italy?"

"Because it's warm."

They laughed as they disappeared beneath the blankets. The sun was ready to set by the time they re-emerged.

**

from the journal of Ernest Frankenstein

We left the cottage several days later as changed people, ready to embrace a new life of shared destiny. When I finally met her feisty aunt, we said nothing of our days alone together. In fact, we planned to say nothing of our intentions to anyone, lest they should try to dissuade our union.

The next months were truly joyous ones. Actually, the only sadness came from feeling one way and having to act another. For all appearances, Justine and I needed to behave as we always had, so secret rendezvous became the norm. We found seemingly innocent excuses to disappear from my father's household for overlapping periods of time. Several nights we tempted fate by dancing together outside the conservatory while Elizabeth played. On one occasion, we snuck over the rooftop and fled across the lawn so we could walk in the moonlight together. We spent long hours discussing the course of our new lives and even decided where we'd settle in Italy. Our hopes and dreams became one, and we decided to leave Geneva at the end of June.

I was happy, but the closer our planned departure came, the more nervous we both grew. The changes and responsibilities we were about to assume filled us with wonder and fear. I began to rethink the wisdom of not informing my family of our plans. If we left under false pretenses, would we ever be welcomed back or our love accepted? We had no real proof that our relationship would be seen as a negative, but we still both feared this possibility. We'd struggled too long for our love to be judged as inadequate.

For the time being, I put thoughts of a military career on hold and worked to develop my skills as a carpenter. I hoped they were up to the challenges that lay ahead. I felt guilty that we planned to leave just after Victor was to finally return to our family. I was keen to learn what kind of person he had become. In this I was not alone.

Elizabeth grew increasingly agitated as the time of Victor's return drew closer. I knew her nerves must be on edge. How would Elizabeth and he adjust to one another after so many years of separation? After all Elizabeth had done for us, it seemed cruel to abandon her in what could be her great hour of need. I was also new to the experience of a romantic relationship and desperately wanted to confide my thoughts and feelings to someone before taking the monumental step we had planned. Justine and I loved one another, that was never in doubt, but would it be enough or were we being too rash? Sleep became elusive and the questions harder to answer.

Justine, I know, shared many of my concerns, and we tried to reassure one another that we were doing the right thing. But the stress of it all began to manifest itself in her as well. Her mood began to fluctuate, sometimes wildly, throughout the course of a day. Her stomach was often upset and she began to speak to me of nightmares or of waking in cold sweats. She also became obsessed with the post, sending a series of letters out and growing increasingly frantic with each reply, but she refused to disclose anything to me. This mystery only added to my general sense of unease. It is easy now to say we should have slowed down, or told others of our plans, but at the time, our choices made sense to us.

That fateful May would open with love and end with a legacy of hate. Time, prayers, tears, the loss of self, rebirth, and even love; none of these have given me the wisdom to understand it all. That month was to be our last spent in Geneva. Victor was to come home.

In late April, an elderly magistrate passed away unexpectedly, and it was requested that my father come to Geneva for a time, so that he could fill the post until another could be installed on a more permanent basis. As he had done his whole life, my father decided to answer this call to public service.

We left Belrive and temporarily moved back into the townhouse my father owned in Geneva. Most of the servants remained behind, except for Justine, Aggie, and Jolie. At first the change of setting had a strange, quieting effect on all of us. Elizabeth, Justine, and I had all been quite tense at home, waiting for Victor's return. The move kept us busy for several days and changed the focus of our energies. Even Justine's mood swings abated for a time, but it was not to last.

*

What should have been merely an unfortunate incident served to portend darker days. A passing series of storms kept us shut in the house for the better part of four days, and one afternoon, I heard raised voices from the hallway downstairs. As I descended the steps to investigate, I realized that it was William arguing with Justine. She'd apparently snatched a letter out of his hand and was holding his shoulder in a very firm grip.

"I said I was sorry," William stated as he tried to free himself of her grasp.

"What did you see?" Justine demanded.

"Nothing. You took it too quick." William tried to look away but she forcibly turned his face to hers and looked into his eyes; she was not convinced.

"You know, you know, you little devil, don't you?" William said nothing to this bizarre accusation, only stared at her,

"William, you must never say anything about this, ever!"

She shook him slightly. William had never seen Justine this angry, and neither had I. Over the past couple of days, she'd seemed more relaxed than I'd seen her in weeks. This unexpected turn caught us both by surprise, and William and I were each momentarily shocked into silence.

"Here now," Aggie called as she approached from the dining room.

William used the distraction to break free of Justine's grip and ran right past Aggie. I must have made some noise, before Aggie reached her because Justine suddenly looked up and saw me on the staircase landing. Her glance dropped instantly from mine, and she fled into Father's study. Aggie yelled something after her, saw me approaching, and then fled in the opposite direction in pursuit of William.

As I entered the crimson-adorned study, I saw Justine ensuring that the letter she'd taken from William was being fully consumed by a small fire alight in the fireplace. This task complete, she immediately crossed herself, and began to pray frantically to the mural of my mother, which graced the area above the mantle. She was muttering Hail Mary so rapidly I could not even identify it at first. Her guilt-fed prayers only added to my confusion. Too torn to immediately confront her, I left without saying a word.

"It's a bad business, sir," Aggie affirmed when she greeted me in the dining room.

"How's William?"

"How do ya think? I can't get a word from him."

I paused to consider the situation.

"The Master ought to know about this," Aggie declared haughtily.

"I'll handle it," I began back towards the study.

"Sir ..."

"I'll handle it," I cut her off before she could mount a full protest.

When I returned to the study, Justine was looking out one of the windows, absentmindedly twirling the silver necklace with the small cross she always wore. I'd come to understand that this was a habit she indulged in when she was either deep in thought or abundantly stressed. Both seemed to apply to the current circumstances. She must have recognized my footsteps for she did not turn around before she spoke.

"I have to leave."

"Why are you angry with William?"

"I have to go and see my aunt," she insisted.

"Justine ...," the words died on my lips as she turned to face me. I'd never seen such a hard, troubled expression on her face.

"What's wrong?"

Justine paused a long time before responding, her breaths escaping in short, labored huffs.

"He knows. He knows about us, what we've planned, he knows ...," she trailed off as if she were about to say too much and had just managed to cut herself off in time.

I remember feeling several things at once. A part of me was glad someone outside of us finally knew. It might remove the worrisome decision of whether or not we should be open about our love from our hands. Another part of me was filled with dread, that William's discovery might enable our worst fears to be confirmed. If that were the case, Justine might be banished from our house forever, and our futures destroyed before they really began. But I also knew that if she was right, then the damage was already done.

"So he knows. He'll either tell now or he won't."

Justine began to pace.

"Why did you destroy that letter?"

She clutched the cross so vehemently that the thin necklace she wore it on, broke from her neck and fell to the floor. For a protracted moment, she stared at it in disbelief, and then slowly reached down for it, as if she were retrieving some long-lost treasure. She picked it up and took it back with her toward the fireplace. As she gazed up at my mother's portrait, I realized who had given Justine the necklace.

"Do you love me?" she asked without meeting my eyes.

This unexpected turn caught me off guard, and she repeated the question before I could respond.

"Do you love me?" Anger had crept back into her voice.

"You know I do," the question exasperated me.

"Then you'll have to trust me. I need to go and see my aunt." She finally lowered her eyes from the portrait to meet mine. I knew that she was using her anger as a shield, but nevertheless it had the desired effect. I backed off. Our years together had taught me that she would reveal her secrets when she was ready. I could accept this up to a point, but shouldn't our love be changing this? Shouldn't it be engendering a deeper level of trust and openness when we were troubled about something? These questions must have been obvious by my expression, for sensing a change in my demeanor; Justine reacted quickly to seize the initiative.

"I need you to trust me." Both her features and voice softened and worked to cool my doubts. I should have thrown the issue of trust back into her face, but I didn't.

"When you return, you'll explain all of this?"

She approached me, took up my hand, and kissed it.

"I promise. I promise I will. I'll apologize to William, too," she vowed as she hugged me. I did not return her embrace. She was hiding something and using my feelings for her to evade honesty with me. But then again, I was letting her do so.

Apologizing to William would prove a difficult matter. She had frightened him badly and Aggie, ever my brother's protector, refused to allow Justine to see him. I decided patience was the best option. I promised to convey Justine's sentiments of regret in her absence.

The next day proved equally frustrating as Justine refused to allude to the purpose of her visit to her aunt's cottage, nor would she tell me how long it might last. She kept pleading for my trust, though she seemed unwilling to show any in return. She made arrangements for M. Haute, the farmer from the market whose home we'd dined at during our winter trip to Chene, to take her. She wrote two letters the night before her departure and took both of these with her when she left. I slipped out of the house not long after she'd gone and we met at a more private location to say a proper farewell.

As we held one another, I was seized by a sudden thought.

"When you return, we should probably meet someplace where our discussion won't be overheard."

She continued to hold me, but said nothing to the suggestion at first.

"The Haute's barn? Would that work?"

"Do you think they'd mind?"

"I know they normally turn in very early. I could wait for you there. They wouldn't even have to know."

"When do you think you'll come back?" I asked softly into her ear.

She pulled away so that we could see each other's eyes.

"Give me two days. We'll meet in the evening, maybe eight o'clock?"

For a moment her eyes danced before me, and we kissed tenderly.

"I love you, Ernest," she whispered before giving me one last, brief kiss on my cheek. And then she was gone. It was to be the last peaceful moment we'd ever share together.

*

The day of William's murder began as an exceptionally beautiful one. It was a Thursday and the storms, which had recently plagued the area abated, and the sun shone, clear, and warm, perched high in a pure blue heaven. By midday, no traces remained of the previous deluges, and the world seemed to revel unabashedly in the tranquil powers of that temperate spring day. Justine's departure allowed tempers in the house to cool a degree, and William and I were once again on speaking terms. He'd said nothing to anyone about Justine and me (if, in fact, he knew anything) and refused to say anything about the incident regarding the incinerated letter. Though uncertainty remained, we were brothers again. High spirits proved infectious, and by late afternoon Elizabeth had planned a spontaneous outing for us to the parklands beyond Geneva's walls known as the Plainpalais. Father's long hours at work afforded him precious few leisure hours, so we decided to wait for his arrival.

"Look what Lizzie gave me," William crowed when he entered the front sitting room. He was fingering a miniature, which contained a likeness of my mother. I recognized it as the one she'd given to Elizabeth for her First Communion. It was not a thing that Elizabeth would have parted with easily.

"She gave it to you?"

"Yes," he stated proudly as he held it up for me to see.

"That's pretty expensive, William."

"I'll be careful with it. You're the one who always breaks things."

Well, that much was true. I'd broken any number of ornate lamps throughout the house as a youth, to say nothing of all of the bowls, glasses, and other assortment of odds and ends. Elizabeth came in with an armload of items for us to take on our picnic. She dumped them onto an empty chair and dropped unceremoniously into another beside me with a mischievous grin on her face.

"William, why don't you get your kite," she suggested.

This idea sprung him into instant action, and he raced back up the staircase to find it.

"You sure about giving him that thing?" I asked casually.

"Not really, but I don't think I have much of a choice. He was helping me clean out my dressing room drawers and found it. Once he discovered Mother's picture in it, he wouldn't leave it alone. You know how he is. I'll get it back tonight."

"You hope."

"I feel bad for him. William never really knew her." She looked up the stairs as a series of thuds were heard overhead.

"Maybe I could convince Father to make him a portrait insert for a pocket watch or something when his First Communion comes," I suggested.

Elizabeth nodded in approval.

"Are you ever going to give him back that drum?"

Actually I'd forgotten that I'd hidden his drum. By the third day of storms, his incessant pounding on it was all too much for us to handle. I'd made a game out of hiding it for a time, but the incident with Justine had driven the instrument from our thoughts.

"No. Maybe we'll do a hostage exchange later if he won't give the miniature back."

Elizabeth laughed and playfully hit my arm. I would miss her. Regardless of the situation with Justine, I knew that our world was changing. If she and Victor did marry, it was very likely they'd move back to Ingolstadt so he could continue his studies. Elizabeth would probably love a more scholarly environment, I mused. Suddenly William tore back into the room, kite in tow, just as Father arrived home. Without pausing, he flew past him and out the door shouting how we were leaving. Shaking his head, my father offered no protest as he good-naturedly followed suit, and the four of us left the house.

It was a relatively short trip from town to the Plainpalais, and we walked the distance in pleasant, jovial companionship. When we reached the park, we spent another hour or so just wandering among the blooming wildflowers, by the lake shore, and even gazing in contemplative wonder at Mount Saleve and the alpine peaks beyond. William and I even skipped a few stones across the lake. I let William win. Our efforts to get the kite to fly met with mixed success, and a final, destructive crash halted our attempts altogether.

We used this as an opportunity to eat our evening meal, and it was not until Elizabeth casually mentioned her name, that I remembered that both the hour, and ironically the location, where I'd arranged to meet Justine were quite near. The spontaneity of the day suddenly turned into a mixed blessing. How could I slip away from everyone? In town it was easy, but out here in the park with my family, it seemed nearly impossible. I couldn't use Jack as an excuse because his family had been traveling abroad for nearly two weeks. It was not far, but no normal, even last minute, errand would take me in the direction of the Haute farm without arousing suspicion from my family.

"Ernest, let's play hide-n-seek," William suggested.

"It's getting rather late; shouldn't we head back soon?" I diplomatically inquired of my other companions.

Elizabeth and Father exchanged looks of strained patience with me.

"It's a nice night, play with your brother awhile," Father smiled and laid back on a blanket, content to let the evening play out where he had settled.

"Come on, Ernest," William implored. I loved my brother dearly, but his games of hide-n-seek either lasted forever because he hid too far away or were over too quickly because he made no real effort to hide. I hoped this round would favor the latter.

"All right," I sighed. At this William shot up and began to run away.

"We might hike a bit more after I've cleaned up so don't be gone more than an hour," Elizabeth advised.

I needed to be on my way to the Haute barn in just a little over an hour, but I merely nodded and trotted off after William.

The first two rounds of the game were over very quickly. He hid in obvious places and laughed when I passed him. I grabbed him and wrestled him to the ground when he tried to escape the second time, and after a brief struggle we ended up with our backs flat on the ground, laughing, and looking up at the gold-tinted sky. For a long time, we let the world spin beneath us. I was lost in deliberation regarding my problem when William suddenly broke into my thoughts.

"Why did Mother like Justine?"

I weighed my answer carefully before responding.

"Because she always looked for the good qualities in people and she liked what she found in Justine."

"But she's a liar, that's not good," William asserted.

I sat up.

"William, does this have something to do with the letter?"

It was his turn to think.

"Yes," he admitted, as he reached for the precious miniature around his neck.

"Do you want to talk about it?"

The answer came quickly this time.

"If she were still alive I don't think Mother would think Justine's good anymore."

He was studying the miniature's portrait as he spoke these words. So, he had discovered something. Did I want to know what he'd learned?

"Perhaps you should talk to her before you judge her?" I finally advised. "She really is sorry for the other day. People make mistakes; show her some trust. It will make things better between you."

I said this as much for William's sake as for my own. Whatever this secret was, she'd promised to explain it tonight. I intended to hold her to that promise; the future of our relationship and our happiness depended upon it.

"Maybe," William muttered in response.

I decided to put off assuming the weight of the world for a few more minutes.

"I think we have time for one more game," I declared, sitting up.

William seemed happy to leave the topic of Justine and was quickly on his feet. He started to run away then turned.

"Don't follow me right away. Let me find a really good spot this time."

"Just don't wander too far," I requested. "The others will be waiting for us."

He nodded with a grin. The last thing I wanted to do was spend time hunting for him in the gathering darkness. Justine and I needed to have our talk and make it back within Geneva's walls before the guards sealed the great gates of the city for the night.

"Count to thirty," William ordered as he vanished from view, down an overgrown pathway, vowing I would never find him. I sighed and counted out loud as I watched the vegetation that surrounded the area he'd fled through finally cease to vibrate. After thirty, the only sound in the woods was made by two doves, cooing ancient songs towards the fading sun.

**

Geneva, May 1794

"You there! Any luck?"

Startled, Justine fought to catch her breath. She'd been hurriedly walking down the road, lost in the depths of her own contemplations and emotions when the man with the torch abruptly appeared behind her and bellowed these words.

"Wh … what?" she stammered.

"The boy," he answered by way of explanation. "Have you had any luck finding the boy? Figured I'd ask just in case. Gonna be cold tonight.

I was thinkin' of heading home to get my heavier coat in case we needed to stay out here. Never thought it'd take this long, ya know?"

Justine tried to smile politely. She was not really interested in this man's problems. She had too many immediate ones of her own to confront, not the least of which was the fact that she was already over an hour late for her fateful meeting with Ernest.

"Sir, I'm returning from Chene, and I'm not sure what you're talking about," she clarified. He grunted and set the torch down on the dirt road as he fumbled in his pockets for a pipe and tobacco. He either had missed her body language or simply didn't care that she was in hurry. It was obvious she would not escape without hearing some part of his story.

"That's all right, Miss. You just go on home. Isn't safe for a young lady, such as yourself, to be alone on the roads this late anyway," he observed.

He stared at her expectantly. She nervously brushed stray locks of hair away from her eyes.

"The escort I'd arranged sent word he'd be delayed until tomorrow, but I couldn't wait," she patiently explained, eager to resume her travels.

"Oh?" he asked casually as he paused before lighting his briar.

"You mean you walked here, all the way from Chene, alone?" he asked incredulously as smoke began to emanate from the flavored tobacco.

Justine didn't like the way he was studying her. She bowed her head, but didn't quite meet his eye and took half a step before he spoke again.

"Heading for Geneva then?" he persisted, arms crossed.

"Yes, the family I serve is in residence there," she stated through a false veneer of calm. How long would Ernest wait for her?

"Are you lost then, Miss?"

The question was only met with a puzzled, drained look from Justine.

"City's back that way," he pointed with the pipe as he bent to retrieve his torch.

"Ah … yes … I know … I, my friends, the escort who couldn't come … I wanted to let them know I'd returned. I thought I might sleep there if the gates are closed."

The man nodded, but suspicion remained upon his countenance.

"Would you care for an escort to your friends then?"

"That is most kind of you, sir, but indeed, I have already delayed you far too long. It is but a short distance to them now, and I must try to return to Geneva before they seal the gates. Thank you for your thoughtfulness. "

"Very well, Miss," he tipped his hat slightly and began to stalk away into the darkness. Though she could ill afford further delay, Justine felt guilty that she had not returned his kind offers of assistance. With a silent, inner sigh, she made the only possible choice her generous nature would allow. She called after him.

"Sir, is there anything I might do to help you?"

He paused at the question, then rounded, closed the distance between them a measure and began to describe the child he sought and the circumstances of the boy's disappearance.

"Was out with his family it seems and just vanished a couple of hours ago," he explained. "Family's frantic. Can't blame 'em though. Lots of folks lookin'."

"How dreadful," Justine stated earnestly. "I will keep my eyes alert for him. What's his name?"

"Named William, William Frankenstein. He's old Alphonso's youngest."

William! Justine's blood chilled as she mouthed his name. Suddenly the man was inundated with questions, a few of which he could answer and many that he could not. This unexpected change in the girl took him aback until she revealed that she was Justine Moritz, a loving and faithful servant to the house of Frankenstein. The girl's sincerity quickly erased the man's suspicions, and he again offered to escort her, but she refused. Her mind and spirit, which had already been very troubled, were now cast into utter turmoil with the news that William was missing.

Should she proceed to the Haute's farm? Would Ernest be there? Did he know? She thought of poor Elizabeth, either alone at the house awaiting news or canvassing the darkness in search of her brother. Unconsciously, her right hand touched her abdomen as she sought to control her emotions.

No, if Elizabeth were at home, she would not be alone; Aggie and Jolie would be there to keep vigil with her. If William had not been found, it was unlikely that Ernest would be waiting for her at the barn as planned. But perhaps William had vanished after he'd snuck away from the others, and he knew nothing of his brother's disappearance. She was also closer to the Haute's farm than she was to Geneva. Justine bid a hasty blend of thanks and farewell to the man, then resumed her journey towards the Haute's.

When she arrived, the house was dark and the barn was empty. For a moment, she sat upon the straw and held her head. She had been walking for hours. She was so tired. The physical demands had been preceded by a series of emotional shocks over the past two days, and now with William's fate uncertain, she knew there would be no reprieve. She wanted to explain everything to Ernest; she needed to, though she feared how he might respond to her news. His love meant everything to her, but she'd needed to be certain before she told him anything. Her aunt had informed her it was still too early to be absolutely positive, but she also felt Justine was correct about the signs. A new life now grew within her, one created by her and Ernest's love.

The enormity of this unexpected gift was both indescribably beautiful and wholly terrifying. She'd refused her aunt's attempts to learn the name of the father. Justine possessed a deep faith in Ernest's love for her, but if he became frightened and rejected her, she would flee to a foreign land to raise and love the child on her own. She prayed this would not come to pass but needed to prepare herself for either possibility. But now another child needed her, and she could not afford idleness.

For hours, she wandered about the darkness, in an ultimately vain effort to locate William. Guilt from their last confrontation dogged her steps, as she traversed grounds both familiar and unknown. It hadn't been his fault. Could she be responsible for him running away? If something had happened to him, she'd never be able to forgive herself.

Justine's winding paths finally drew her close enough to the grand walls of Geneva to realize that the gates had been shut for the night. Her body and mind grew increasingly weak. At points, it was as if she were sleepwalking across the countryside, with no sense of self or purpose to her actions. The damp chills of the spring night numbed her limbs, made her hair and skin clammy. The bottom of her dress and her shoes were sodden. Still she searched.

It was with a profound sense of relief that she greeted the sight of the Hautes' barn, the only plausible refuge this close to the city. Yet, she did not sleep. For several hours she remained near the doors, watching the darkness for any sign of movement, any sign of William. Several times she believed she did see something, but every time she rose and investigated, her efforts only established that nothing was, in fact, there.

Time ceased to have any real meaning, and it was in this twilight state of consciousness that the waking dream occurred. She was asleep, of that much she was certain, but exhaustion prevented her mind and senses from connecting. Had she heard footsteps? Perhaps William had found her, she smiled at the thought. Ernest's relieved, beloved face swam before her, and suddenly, he was in the barn, bidding her to awaken and bless him with her loving gaze. She wanted to open her eyes, but her brain was numb with fatigue. Her body cried out for rest, but her spirit bid her to awaken to her lover's embrace.

When she finally forced sleep from her body, dawn had arrived, but the barn remained empty. Justine felt ill when she tried to stand. By now she suffered not only from exhaustion, but also from the many hours since she'd last consumed even a single drop of water. Every part of her body hurt; the gentle light of morning seemed harsh. It stung her slightly swollen eyes. In spite of all of this, Justine, propelled by love, struggled to her feet and resumed her search.

She resolved to attempt to retrace her earlier path. Now, in that grey daylight, she might notice something she'd missed in the darkness. Justine's spirits were low as she quit her asylum, and the world soon became nothing more than a blend of dull colors and shapes. Her body protested every step and pleaded with her to rest. She felt increasingly raw and feverish. She wandered in this state until she became aware that someone was yelling at her. She turned to see a woman, laden with goods for market, gesturing and barking harsh words at her. It took her a moment to realize what she was looking at, and even longer to comprehend that the stranger was upset about something. Was she trespassing on her property? Her dry throat protested her attempts at speech, and finally, after a few unintelligible syllables, Justine simply shuffled away in the opposite direction.

Had she become turned around somehow? Her eyes searched the landscape for familiar sights to guide her home. Yes, it was time to go home. She could do no more here. Before she rejoined a recognizable road, she happened across a stream, which fortunately was not very deep. She drank enough to quell her immediate thirst and splashed icy rivulets upon her face. The cold water revived her senses for a short time and with renewed purpose, she began to head back towards Geneva.

Her ragged appearance and blank visage drew unwelcome attentions once she entered the city, but she took little notice of them. She looked like what she was — an exhausted traveler, desperate to reach home. She was so tired when she arrived at the townhouse that she took the unusual measure of knocking on the door, as if she were a stranger. She was practically leaning on the door when Jolie answered it. A look of surprise spread across her face as she surveyed Justine's decrepit condition, and she quickly ushered her inside.

"You look a fright," Jolie exclaimed as she shut the door.

Justine was certain that she heard crying from the front room.

"Where have you been?" Jolie asked, recalling Justine's attention.

Justine ignored the question.

"Has William been found?" she asked breathlessly.

Jolie bit her lip and gave a pained nod as she momentarily closed her eyes. Justine's heart wept.

"I have to see him."

Was she talking about William or Ernest? She resisted her companion's suggestion that she rest first. Reluctantly, Jolie took Justine's hand and began to guide her towards the closed pocket doors of the front room. The sounds of sorrow from within grew louder. She recognized that it was Elizabeth crying. She had no illusions about what sight would greet her when the doors opened. Even before they did, she felt dizzy. She did not want to go inside, but knew that she must. Jolie was talking to her, but Justine was deaf to her words. The door opened, quietly. And there they were.

They did not notice her when she entered. There was a surreal, dream-like quality to the scene. It was all so perfect. So tragically perfect. Ernest held a sobbing Elizabeth near the window. The frame of the window and lighting within made it appear as if they were a painting brought to life. As she moved forward, she saw Alphonso Frankenstein sitting in the blue chair by the sofa. She studied his face as she approached. He had never looked so old, not since …

Her eyes followed his vacant gaze down towards the sofa. The object of her torturous hours of searching lie there: silent, ashen, dead. His head was set in an unnatural position, the cause of which could be traced to bruises upon his bare, exposed neck. Dark imprints had been left by the fingers that had crushed the life from William's body.

For a long moment, she stared dumbly at the bruises and the body. The scars on her own body felt aflame, and unconsciously, one of her hands passed over the life growing within her; the other groped for the necklace Caroline Frankenstein had given her. The air in here was thin. The world was collapsing. The room began to spin, and she began to scream. William, who had never harmed anyone, was dead, just like her siblings, all of their bodies marked by violence. He was dead. Maybe her screams could wake them all from their eternal slumber. The sensations of hands guiding her body and voices trying to calm her only agitated her more. The room spun faster, and she shut her eyes against the fury. The screams only stopped when the fever and stress finally overtook her, and she sank into merciful unconsciousness.

CHAPTER 11
SECRETS AND SILENCE

from the journal of Ernest Frankenstein

The clock measured beats to its own patient count. I listened to its march but had no interest in the passage of time it marked. The noise filled the void, filled the silence of the house. The calm was a facade, but a precious one to be sure. My brother had been laid to rest next to Mother at the family estate in Belrive the previous day. The ceremony was not a quiet family moment, but a large, drawn-out and very public affair. The people of Geneva turned out for the Mass in untold numbers as a show of both support and respect for our family. Many even walked the miles to our home, far outside the city, following the funeral procession. One of Geneva's finest citizens' sons had been brutally, shamefully murdered, and it sent the residents of the city into a type of mad fury. Hysteria grew rapidly regarding the capture and elimination of the vicious killer, and suspects and searches abounded. But my concerns were inward.

I was not concerned with the guilt of others. Elizabeth blamed herself as soon as she learned of William's death. The precious miniature of my mother was missing, and it was presumed that the killer had taken it. She maintained that its theft must have been the reason for his death. Aggie reminding Elizabeth that she'd counseled against allowing William to wear it in the first place did not help, but Father had absolved Elizabeth of her recriminations. The fault was not hers; it was mine.

It was a sentiment I shared. I was the last one, other than his killer, to see my brother alive. He had been my charge, my responsibility. Elizabeth attempted to comfort me and denied that I was to blame. It was a kindness I was not ready to accept or return. I wasn't aware of how deeply Father felt, until I offered to go to Ingolstadt to retrieve Victor personally.

"No," he said evenly, as he shuffled papers on his desk, "I will write him."

He would not meet my eye. He'd been unable to since discovering

William's body. My very presence seemed to pain him. I didn't want to be here anymore. I couldn't stay.

"Father, please," I begged, "I only want to help. I need to do something."

"You've done enough!" he roared suddenly, as his fist pounded the desk.

The accusation, conveyed in both his words and the glare in his eyes, burned into my soul. Our relationship would never be the same. I left without a word, and from that moment, spent as little time as possible in his company. The family alternated between Geneva and Belrive over the next several days, so avoiding him was not difficult. Our confrontation only added to the profound sense of loss and isolation I already felt; it was almost unbearable.

Through all of this, Justine slept. Jolie kindly attended to her while our family was occupied. I visited her room several times, but she did not wake. She slept as though she were some fairy tale princess, awaiting only the kiss of her one true love to awaken her.

Jolie informed us that during her few lucid moments, Justine claimed to have been out all night searching for William. During my own efforts to find my brother, I stopped in the Haute's barn, but Justine had not been there. Frustrated and frightened, I never returned later to check. I now claimed Justine's fragile health upon my guilty heart.

Several days after William's burial, Elizabeth arrived from our house in Belrive. Father was to come later in the day. Even before the news of his impending arrival, I'd decided I could no longer tolerate being shut in the house and resolved to leave. I passed Jolie on the staircase, who was hauling a filthy mass of clothing in her arms.

"They're Justine's, from the morning she arrived," she explained in answer to my inquiry. "I had quite a time getting her out of them when she took sick and haven't had a moment to clean them since."

I nodded in understanding.

"Is she feeling any better?"

"I believe so, sir," Jolie smiled and continued down the stairs.

I paused in Justine's doorway, but she still appeared to be asleep. Since no one was immediately present, I took the opportunity to enter and kiss her forehead, and then slipped back out of the room. I informed Elizabeth that I'd return later, and then quit the house.

I spent most of the day wandering the streets of the city. I wanted to feel alive again and hoped that reconnecting to the outside world would help me to do so. I had no destination in mind, so finding points of interest did not prove challenging.

I listened to a chorus practice their harmonious arts in a church. I visited the docks by the lake and struck up conversations with strangers covering any variety of topics. I bought books from a shop, then sat in some café and lost myself in their pages. I even spent a few idle hours in a tavern listening to random conversations while sipping ale. None of it helped. My sense of loss and isolation only seemed to be reinforced, as I tried to blend into the normal rhythms of life. My life was not normal. It had been corrupted. The world seemed wrong, unbalanced. I felt guilty for trying to embrace life, while my poor brother would forever be denied its most basic pleasures.

Such was my frame of mind when I ended up lost in thought on a bridge over the Rhône River, watching the dark waters swirl and flow. I'm not sure how long I stood there, but I remember being startled when the voice spoke so close to me.

"Not thinkin' of taking a swim are ya?"

I jumped slightly and turned to observe a middle-aged woman, whose attire left no questions as to either her profession or purpose in starting a conversation at this time of evening.

"No, just thinking, thanks," I said evenly, allowing my gaze to drift.

"'bout what, darling?" she persisted.

"Family matters," I answered, gripping the rail.

"Family, yes; trouble at home is it then?"

I nodded numbly and turned my eyes back to the mysteries of the water.

"Won't find no answers down there, but I might be able to help." She edged closer to me. "If it's a few comforts you might be needin' to ease your troubles?"

"Unless you can raise the dead, I doubt it."

She did not waver in the face of this statement.

"The dead. They be the will of Providence, child. When you do what I done for as long as I have, you learn to live with His will. Not to question it."

For a few minutes, we said nothing, only stared together into the river, each consumed by our own thoughts. Finally, I cleared my throat.

"Well …?"

"Call me Sophie."

"Well, Sophie, thanks for the conversation. I'm sorry if I've wasted your time."

"Think nothing of it."

She held up her hand in parting as a lady would and I took it.

"Ernest."

"Reaching out to others is never a true waste of time, Ernest."

I bowed my head a measure and began to walk away.

"Ernest," she called, "I am sorry for your loss."

Again I nodded and again my steps were interrupted by her voice.

"You wouldn't be related to the boy that was killed by chance, would you?"

I stopped. Neither of us bothered to close the distance now between us.

"Why?"

"If it be the case, I may be able to offer you some comfort after all then. Have you not heard the news?"

"What news?"

"They arrested his killer today."

*

"How did this happen?" I demanded of Jolie, who was too upset to speak. She shook her head, unable to contain the tears in her eyes, and fled into the kitchen. I thought about pursuing her but doubted she was in any condition to help me.

I needed answers. I was vacillating wildly between sheer horror and stunned disbelief. A quick survey of the room upstairs had validated a part of Sophie's story, and now I was truly frightened. It was then that I spotted Elizabeth, in the darkened front room, seated before the fire, sipping tea. She wasn't blinking, and even by the dim light, I could tell she'd been crying for some time. I entered the room, but it was a long time before she noticed my presence.

"Oh, Ernest," she said in an emotionless voice I'd never heard her use before, "you've returned."

"Is it true?" I held my breath, my heart trembled.

She stared into the fire and sipped her tea. I repeated the question.

"Is it true, Elizabeth?"

Her gaze did not break with the fire when she answered.

"They took her," she said but could say no more.

My mouth worked to say something, to form words that would make sense of all of this, but failed to do so. Angrily I began to leave the room.

"You can't see her. I tried. They won't let anyone see her."

"Why?" I asked sharply.

At this Elizabeth dropped the cup, which promptly shattered. She began to berate herself as she stooped to pick the pieces up. As I bent down to help, I noticed her hands were shaking uncontrollably. I took them, and she released the broken fragments of the cup, which clattered back upon the floor.

"Elizabeth," I whispered.

When next she spoke, she wasn't seeing me. She was reliving the images of the moment in her mind.

"They hauled her away … like an animal. We were praying; she'd only been awake a few hours, and she kept asking about you and William and then … they took her and said she'd … that she's the one who …"

Her voice went dead, her emotions too vexed to complete the horrific thought. I helped her rise from off the floor and sat down with her on the sofa. We said nothing, only clung to one another in the darkness.

I felt shattered, broken inside. What if it were true? No, it could not be true. Then why had they arrested her? She loved my brother. She loved me. She was incapable of such brutality. Had I missed something? The image of her shaking William by his shoulder blazed across my mind, followed closely by her smiling, laughing face. Much later, I fell into a dreamless slumber, hopelessly lost.

The full story came out in starts and fits. Jolie had discovered Elizabeth's missing miniature among Justine's clothing when she began to clean them. Without knowing what to do, she'd shown it to Aggie, who had seized the portrait, and Justine's clothing and immediately fled the house. Frightened, and uncertain about what to do next, Jolie said nothing to either Elizabeth or Father when he arrived. Aggie had gone directly to a magistrate and offered a deposition.

Upon further investigation, witnesses were produced who had seen Justine in the vicinity of the murder scene, both the night of the crime and the morning that William's body was discovered. The woman who came across her in the morning attested that Justine had behaved strangely and would not answer any of her questions. Armed with this information, the authorities arrived and confronted Justine while she and Elizabeth were praying together. Justine's inability to explain how the miniature found its way into her pocket and her general confusion over the collective details only exacerbated the situation. They'd bound her, roughly, while she continued to protest her innocence. Father said nothing as she was led away, and all of Elizabeth's pleas fell on deaf ears.

A large crowd formed around the prison not long after Justine was brought in. The city now had a focus for its rage over the murder. Soon word spread, and the authorities had, for a time, literally become prisoners in their own jail. They feared that if they opened the doors to admit anyone, the mob would take justice into their own hands. So for several days, they barred any entries into the facility. It was during this time that I sought out the advice of my godfather, Christiansen.

With this new, hideous revelation, my family ceased to interact amongst ourselves. Elizabeth closed herself in her room, and Father spent his days in the study. Each of us was wrestling with our hearts and minds. We were emotionally drained, and the thought of discussing the disastrous issue at hand was repugnant. Still I needed to reach out to someone, and Christiansen offered my best hope.

**

Geneva, May 1794

She was not really asleep. It was nearly impossible to achieve that here, so she felt the approaching footsteps before she heard them. The pile of straw, which had served as her bed for over two weeks, did little to impede either sounds or vibrations. She wondered dimly if any of the rats, dead or otherwise, that members of the ever-fluctuating crowds outside the prison threw through her window had taken up residence in the pile.

The guard entered her cell and nodded his head towards the far wall.

By now this routine required no conversation, other than the silent one they'd just completed. She approached the manacles hanging from their dangling chains and wordlessly locked one of her slender wrists into the cuff. The man, who spoke as if he were reading everything from a manual, recited the standard speech as he shackled her other hand.

"Visitor comin'. No more than an hour's time together will be permitted. No physical contact whatsoever. Misbehavior of any type will not be tolerated."

"Thanks, Jean," she muttered without really looking at him.

The man had never engaged in any conversation with her, so she had no idea what his actual name might be. She'd decided to call him Jean. He looked like a Jean. If nothing else, at least the name added a sense of normalcy and familiarity to life, in such a stark and uncomforting place.

As usual, Jean had no reaction to her words, and after a brief inspection of the manacles, he vacated the cell, but left the door open. The chains were long enough that she could still manage to reach the pile of straw and sit while bound. This she did while she waited for her visitor. So far only her inept, young legal solicitor had come to see her. No one from her family had come, not even Ernest. How had life become so terribly wrong? Her lawyer provided few details regarding the evidence against her and seemed more concerned about his reputation and future in the legal profession than in actually helping her. She couldn't blame him. All the world seemed to have given her up for guilty. Why should he be any different? She hung her head and waited.

It was some time before her visitor arrived, but when he did, he was quite flustered.

"Imbeciles, complete imbeciles working here," Christiansen railed without preamble, as he whisked into the room. It took Justine a moment to recognize the man.

"They actually confiscated my glasses. Said they could be used to pick locks! Ridiculous nonsense. I can think of ten things within this room that would work just as well. And I'd be able to see them."

He threw up his hands in exasperation then knelt down. She did not know him well; they had only met on a few family social occasions and secretly several weeks ago in his office, but the very sight of Christiansen brought a new lightness to her spirits. She seized one of his hands in both of hers and kissed it. His initial surprise at this greeting was quickly overcome, and he gently rested the other hand on her shoulder.

"There now, how are you my dear?"

Justine released his hand then looked at her own iron bound ones. He nodded in understanding.

"Are you to be my new solicitor?" she inquired hopefully.

"Have you fired M. Eltbrandt?"

"No," she said meekly, "I just …"

Christiansen rose as a guard brought in a chair for him and remained silent until the man was once again out of earshot. A deep sigh escaped Christiansen, and he paused in careful consideration before answering the question.

"No, Justine, I have not come to serve as your solicitor. I cannot represent you in this matter. My connection with the family and the other legal matter you retained me for prevent it."

Justine searched his countenance, and then sat up straighter. She felt certain he had news to share.

"You found him?"

Again he paused before answering. Unable to find the right words, he finally shook his head in self-disgust, reached into the inner pocket of his jacket, and withdrew an envelope. Justine stared for a moment then snatched it from him. Her fingers fought clumsily for the paper inside. And suddenly there it was before her. She could not remove her eyes from the signature at the bottom of the page. For months, obtaining this had been her sole concern, as the sins of her past had threatened to deny her future. A short, laugh and bittersweet smile were her only celebration. This was to have been her proclamation of freedom, but when she looked to Christiansen, his troubled expression silenced any genuine happiness. Something was terribly wrong. Still he said nothing, as she worked to interpret the nearly life-weary sadness, which had overtaken him. And then the full, horrible realization came to her.

"He knows," she gasped.

The unthinkable was confirmed when their eyes met.

"He knows," Christiansen said needlessly.

Her heart trembled with the knowledge. She felt tired, as her nerve-racked hands embraced her suddenly pounding head. She tried to think.

"You said no one would ever know. You said we'd handle it."

"And you deceived me. Both you and Ernest," his voice cracked with barely restrained emotion, "you deceived me. You deceived us all."

She shook her head and moved away from him. Her worst fears had come to pass, but the chains held firm. She could not escape this. In a flash, the anger, fear, and frustration she'd fought against for weeks could no longer be contained. She unleashed it in a desperate but entirely futile effort against her bonds. Her frantic cries quickly brought the alarmed guards, who arrived ready to pacify her, but Christiansen held up a hand of warning and they slowed. He motioned them back and shut the iron door, sealing himself inside the cage with Justine. The others remained on alert outside, until her wild energies finally fled, and she sank to the floor in exhaustion and defeat.

Though they waited several minutes, Justine made no attempt rise or speak. The guard's interest waned, and they left without taking any action. Christiansen resumed his chair and waited quietly. The minutes passed, but the pain within her did not diminish.

"I'm sorry," she finally whispered, "I'm sorry."

Tears were silently caressing her skin. Christiansen said nothing. Emotional attachment of any kind in his profession was often viewed as a liability. In fact, he'd worked most of his career to avoid it, but this was different. This case and his relationships with those involved made it so.

He did not know if Justine was guilty of the monstrous crime she'd been accused of, but he could not leave her in such a state. She'd lost nearly everything. He truly pitied the poor girl, regardless of her deception, which he could now almost understand. Under normal circumstances, the news he'd borne would have been joyous to her, but nothing was normal now. Her trial would begin in less than two days, and she could not defend herself bereft of hope. He must work quickly to restore it to her.

He quit his chair and knelt beside her. She barely seemed to notice the proximity of his presence.

"I had no choice," he began, "Ernest implored that I serve as your defense attorney. I tried to explain that there would be a conflict of interest, but he would not hear it. He was frantic to prove your innocence. He grew enraged and announced his plans to marry you. I had to tell him of your status, before he did more damage. I had to tell him that you were already married."

Her expression did not change, but the tears seemed to lessen as she listened. Encouraged to a degree, he continued.

"He didn't want to believe it, of course, accused me of all types of things. I told him everything you told me about how your dying mother forced you into the union with your second cousin. How neither of you desired the match and had never embraced it; that the marriage existed only as a legal contract. I even told him about the letters you'd sent, seeking your husband's whereabouts so the divorce could be settled. But you never told me, Ernest was your intended."

When at last she spoke, her voice betrayed the weariness in her spirit.

"We never told anyone. We were afraid to."

Was this the moment for total honesty? She thought of the child she was now certain grew within her. She thought of the incident with William and what the boy had learned shortly before his death. No. Much as she liked this man, he could not help her, not now. She held her silence. Christiansen continued.

"If any of this were come to light now, it would be fatal. The prosecution in your trial is relying primarily on circumstantial evidence. It will build its case against you on those points and personal character. If I file these papers with the court, they'll destroy the image of your character in this community. I'm sorry, but we cannot finalize your divorce."

"It doesn't matter. Ernest will never …," she trailed off unable to complete the thought. She'd lost him. Christiansen gently touched her arm.

"He got them signed."

At this simple statement, Justine finally turned her head and faced Christiansen. A blend of shock and disbelief etched upon her features. Ernest had done this?

"He demanded the name you gave me and spent nine days combing the countryside in search of your cousin. He only returned with these earlier today."

The numbness in her soul began to abate. Ernest had done this. Her guardian angel had done this; he had not abandoned her in their darkest hour. For the first time since her arrest, a real sense of hope kindled in her heart. He still loved her. He would not have helped her if he believed her guilty, if he'd stopped loving her. Suddenly, the only emotion in her world was one of gratitude, and without thinking, she hugged Christiansen, inadvertently banging his head with one of her sagging, iron chains.

She was not alone anymore.

A nervous, endearing laughter erupted from her, and she smiled as Christiansen helped her to her feet.

"Thank you! Thank you!" she breathed.

"No touching!"

They hastened apart as one of the guards re-entered the cell with a pistol in is hand. This second infraction was certain to result in an extended period of time in her manacles, but it hardly mattered.

"We will proceed as you have counseled," she declared after collecting herself. And with that, the meeting was over. The guard had already taken the liberty of removing the chair to further emphasize to all that it was time for Christiansen to leave. The lawyer followed the guard, who immediately locked the door behind them.

"Sir," she called after the departing solicitor.

He paused.

"Would you kindly inform M. Eltbrandt that I will see to my own defense at the trial and that his services are no longer needed?"

Christiansen was torn by this request. Part of him took this to be a positive sign, that his news had rekindled some sense of purpose in her, but another part feared she did not truly grasp the full reality of her situation. She was going into a very public trial, for the senseless murder of a child, a trial which had aroused a very black and terrible side of human nature within the city's masses. The prosecution and city elders were desperate for a conviction in this case, and Christiansen feared the lengths they might go to in order to ensure one. He was to appear in another courtroom the morning of her trial and would not be able to attend her proceedings. Hesitantly, he nodded in affirmation of her request, and looked, for what he hoped, was not the last time into those mild, warm eyes.

"I shall pray for you," he said in parting, then vanished from sight.

Alone again, Justine took several minutes to kick more of the foul straw closer to the wall, then sat upon it and pondered her future. She imagined the courtroom and what might be said of William's death. She envisioned those who would rise to her defense, compelling the judges to realize that she was incapable of committing such a brutal crime. Then she would be free. How would she live when this was all over? She was innocent, and the murder of William truly grieved her. She would mourn him forever, but there was a chance for a new future.

Her previous marriage could now be dismissed with the paper she'd held in her hand. She and Ernest could at last leave Geneva, to begin a new life together, heal their wounds, and raise their child. With her angel, she would finally be lifted from her dark and tragic existence. Though they left her shackled until dawn, for the first time since she'd arrived, Justine slept soundly that night.

*

from the journal of Ernest Frankenstein

"The name, Christiansen. Give me the God-forsaken name," I demanded.

"I haven't been able to locate him," Christiansen crossly replied.

"Give me the name," I repeated accentuating each word.

"And what will you do with it?"

The logic of the question interrupted my rage over this unexpected news, which only added to my miseries. What would I do? Was it my love for the woman, my own curiosity or pure anger, which motivated the demand?

"The paper must be signed," I finally declared.

Christiansen's expression did not alter, mine did.

"Please," I implored.

He turned his seat from me, looked out the window, and kicked at something, hard.

"Damn it, Ernest, how could you both be so stupid!"

It was the first, and the only time, I've ever seen my godfather lose his temper.

I wanted to offer further challenge but recoiled, the fight left me.

"Please," I repeated softly.

He did not react, and I sat in meek silence. Finally, he rose and left the room for the outer office. He was gone for so long that I began to fear he'd simply left. When he returned, he shoved a piece of paper into my hands, walked back to the window, and clasped his hands behind his back.

"Get out."

I looked down at the paper and the name, scrawled in Justine's hand. With a grim sense of determination, I began to leave.

"Ernest."

I paused.

"I will hear of any incidents regarding this matter," this threat was uttered without him ever turning to face me. I left the office without comment.

Upon returning to the house, I turned Justine's room upside down, until I uncovered the hidden responses to her inquires regarding her husband's whereabouts. I had resisted the reality of the situation until I read the letters, but as I scanned through them, the mysteries of her behavior these past months began to become clear. It all seemed to be as Christiansen described: this husband was a cousin, son to an aunt she'd never before mentioned. The marriage began near the time of her mother's death, and the two had apparently not spoken since Madame Moritz's demise. But why had they not dissolved the unwelcome union upon Justine's mother's death? My clamorous search eventually drew Elizabeth from her room. I'd seen little of her since the night of Justine's arrest.

"Ernest, what are you …?"

She barely saw the letters in my hand before I thrust them into a pocket, and pushed past her. She followed me to my room, where I'd already assembled a bag of personal effects for my journey. I now added the purloined letters to the menagerie.

"I'll return before the trial," I stated, then rapidly quit the house before any additional inquiries into my actions could be made.

Further study of the letters revealed that this aunt lived in Basel, a town located in a region across the lake, which I had rarely visited. I boarded a modest-sized boat, bound for Laussane, which lay upon the northeastern shore of Lake Geneva, before nightfall, and began to map out my route. As I withdrew from the environs of Geneva, my misgivings wavered as I attempted to replace them with the cold reassurance of reason. The trial would begin in eleven days, and the letters provided conflicting information as to where this man could be. The more I read, the more I became convinced that this cousin, was in fact, younger than Justine, which might account for the lack of action taken to dissolve the union previously. Depending upon how much younger he was, perhaps legal action had been impractical, due to either his age or finances. Justine also could not have foreseen our current relationship immediately following her mother's death and, therefore, may have been content to leave her marital status unaddressed. Comforted by these thoughts, I began my search; it would last for nearly six days, and my return journey would last three.

I decided, in this particular case, that a lie was more beneficial than the truth. Were I to introduce myself as Justine's secret lover, intended fiancée or as a direct relation of the victim Justine was accused of killing, I could easily predict how long it would take for doors to be slammed in my face. So I decided to pose as a legal clerk, one who worked for Christiansen. In this guise, I hoped that my inquiries would not seem remarkable, and my errand would be viewed as a rational one.

Upon reaching Basel, I had little trouble locating Justine's aunt, who turned out to be a boorish gossip. Her voice also possessed the unfortunate tendency to rise slightly with each syllable spoken. It did not take long for me to understand why Justine's benevolent aunt in Chene was easily her favorite.

"Oh, I got those letters from miss high and mighty. Musta forgotten that her poor, dear aunt can't read a word of the scratch," the woman huffed.

I ignored this lie for the moment. The letters I'd located in Justine's room disproved her claim. Unless, of course, someone else had read Justine's letter to her and crafted her response.

"Yes, well, be that as it may, madam, my office does need to speak with your son."

"Which one?" she challenged aggressively.

I momentarily struggled to recall the name and had to scan quickly through the letters.

"Erik," I stammered.

The woman nodded but said nothing. Then her eyes narrowed shrewdly.

"You say this firm of yours is in Geneva?"

"Yes."

"Word's reached us here of some great sadness in that city."

Perhaps she'd heard of the accusations against Justine. Whatever the reason for this new line of conversation, I decided it was best to avoid it. I focused on the role I was playing. A legal clerk, at least a career minded one, would not engage in gossip or hearsay.

"There was an unfortunate incident, but the matter is being dealt with by authorities. Please, madam, where is your son, Erik?"

"And why should I tell you? Methinks you've come to abolish my dearly departed sister's final request." She grew somewhat misty eyed as she said this.

Or at least she tried to; she wasn't the best actress. I had no doubt that a certain financial arrangement lay at the heart of this matter. Few other motives could be behind her coy behavior. At one point, in order to maintain her evasiveness, she went so far as to serve me tea and explain the history of her family's serving set.

Our strained conversation ended nearly an hour later with little real information obtained. The best I managed to get from her was an offhand remark about his profession. Apparently, he worked as a type of migrant laborer on farms. This profession took him to numerous locations. In short, if this information was to be believed, he could be nearly anywhere along the Swiss, French, Germanic boarder region.

As I sat down in a local pub for a late lunch or early dinner, I briefly entertained the notion of abandoning the search. It seemed impossible that I could find this man in such a short period of time. Ingolstadt was not terribly far away from here, and I began to toy with the notion of going there and retrieving Victor. As I mulled my unhappy options, help unexpectedly arrived in a most unlikely form. The bartender struck up a conversation with this glum stranger, and upon explaining my purpose in Basel, he perked up at the mention of the name I sought.

"You're lookin' for Erik? Why, I just saw him not more than a week ago. Boy usually comes by every couple of months when he's between jobs."

I nearly choked on my food.

"Did he say where he was going?"

The bartender screwed up his face in concentration.

"I think he said the next job was north of the border, in the Baden-Wurttemberg region, tending cows or something like that."

I pressed for more information, but he couldn't recall any additional details. He suggested several other places, mostly pubs, which Erik might have stopped by before leaving town.

"Nice boy, but a little too free with his coins when he has some in his pocket. Not that I'm complainin'," the bartender laughed, and we continued our conversation as I finished my meal. I made certain that I was equally generous with my coins when I left.

The change of fortune that resulted from my banter with the bartender felt like the first thing that had gone right in months. With renewed energies, I set out in search of Erik. It would take several more days and numerous stops at various pubs, farms, and inns, but finally one sun-soaked afternoon, I managed to locate him on a farm in the southern Germanic provinces.

When his work for the day was completed, I took him to a nearby local establishment and bought him a drink. I quickly discovered that the bartender in Basel was not exaggerating when he'd observed that Erik was free with his money. Fortunately, he also was equally free with his conversation, and in a short time, the basic story of his marriage came to light.

It turned out that he was actually Justine's second cousin, and not the biological child of her aunt in Basel, but under her legal guardianship. When Justine's mother realized she was dying, she'd appealed to her sister to have Erik marry her daughter. She hoped that the union would ensure that Justine would be cared for after her death. This sudden charity wasn't motivated by any real love or concern for her only remaining child; rather, it had been provoked by her fear of the God she would soon meet. And there were other, even more malignant reasons, for her to propose the marriage.

By marrying Justine off to a family member, the dark secrets of abuse might remain hidden, and as a final slight to her daughter, she wanted to make certain that the family's land (meager though the parcel was) did not pass to Justine. Erik was nearly the same age as I, so at the time of the union, he would have had little say in the matter. His aunt stood to profit from the land, though she'd apparently told Erik it would remain his, as long as he stayed married.

His aunt's true designs were revealed as soon as Justine's mother passed. She evicted Justine from her home and offered her a simple choice: embrace her unhappy union or return to our household. The choice had been a simple one for all parties involved. Neither Justine nor Erik truly wanted the marriage, but both were either legally or financially encumbered, and could, therefore, do little to absolve it. She'd returned to us, and eventually he'd abandoned his traitorous aunt and begun to work toward a future of his own.

To add another level of complications to the whole affair, it turned out that Erik was, unlike his aunt, illiterate. This undoubtedly had made his aunt's manipulation of him, to gain Justine's land, a relatively simple matter. Though he spoke several languages, he could read none of them, and I had to explain what the documents I'd brought meant, and why it was important that he sign them. It was extremely difficult to keep emotion from my voice. He was reluctant to sign, not because he loved Justine, at least not as a wife, but due to his aunt's deceptions; he was now, understandably wary of signing legal papers of any kind. I pressured him, but he resisted.

"Why do you care so much if I sign?" he finally demanded.

I struggled to conceive of a way to get what I wanted, what I needed. No, the truth would still not do. But a portion of it just might. This would be extremely difficult, and I prayed for William to forgive me.

"She's trying to protect you," I said.

He lowered his mug, his third by this time, and listened.

"Have you not heard of the murder in Geneva? Of the child who was killed?"

He shook his head.

"Your wife has been accused of his murder."

His jaw dropped in shock. I did not give him long to recover.

"If you don't sign these papers, you could be brought in before her judges and questioned."

"My cousin is a killer?" he stammered, not even bothering to claim her as his wife.

I said nothing. After several tense moments, I tapped the papers.

"Sign this and you're free."

He took a last, long draught from his mug, and with my assistance, he finally signed the paper and ended his marriage. My task was complete. After buying the stunned man a fourth ale, I quickly made my escape.

The trip back to Geneva seemed all too brief. My own actions now sickened me, as did the knowledge of what awaited there. How could I believe so ardently in the woman accused of murdering my brother? How could I not? I'd longed for a reason to escape Geneva and these soul-crushing questions, but my errand, though successful, brought me no peace. Some questions were now answered, but others had only just begun.

The whole truth concerning Justine's marriage both reassured and disturbed me greatly. To what lengths had she gone to in order to hide it? Is this what William had discovered several days before his death? On the other hand, I could easily understand her desire to handle this privately. But, at the same time, her lack of openness regarding an issue which impacted our mutual futures disturbed me. I loved her one moment and hated her the next.

There were so many factors to question or that created doubt, her history of abuse among them. Father had once noted that among the criminal class, it was not unheard of that those once abused could turn into abusers themselves. I refused to believe this about my dear Justine, but I could not totally dismiss the possibility either.

She'd kept the marriage a secret. What else might she be hiding? What had she meant to tell me in the Haute's barn the night of William's murder? Why had she not been there? I knew the miniature found among her clothing would be used in the trial, and try as I might, I could find no way to explain its presence among her possessions if she were truly innocent. But she must be. She loved my family. She'd loved William. She loved me.

Upon my return to the city, I promptly visited Christiansen's office to deliver the papers. He took them without comment and examined the signatures.

"This signature was not coerced, I trust?"

"No," I replied automatically.

He studied my face a moment before his gaze returned to the documents on his desk.

"Very well, I'll show them to her later today."

I began to leave, but found myself unable to do so.

"Did you tell my father about Justine and me?"

At this, Christiansen stopped writing and looked up at me, the harshness was gone from both his gaze and body language.

"I'm not your judge, Ernest. This is a matter you must address with him. Not me."

I drew in a breath and nodded.

"Nothing new regarding her case?"

His eyes and mustache drooped visibly.

"I fear what the powers of justice will do with this case."

It was a sentiment I shared. I thanked him and left.

My homecoming was not a happy one, my abrupt disappearance only deepening the rift between my father and myself. Of my errand, I said nothing. Even if I'd thought it was a good idea, the notion of telling him about my secret relationship with Justine seemed impossible to explain under the circumstances. Elizabeth said little to me when I passed her in the upstairs hallway. She welcomed me home and told me that they expected Victor's return before the trial. I shut myself away in my room.

By eve of the following day, I'd still interacted very little with my family. My eldest brother, now my only brother, failed to arrive as promised, and the weight of what lie ahead tomorrow held my soul aghast. When it became evident that Victor would not be arriving, Father turned in early. I descended from my room and discovered myself drawn to the portrait of my mother above the fireplace in his study, the portrait Justine had prayed so furiously to the day she and William had fought. I studied my mother's face. What would she think of all of this? Gazing upon the portrait, I was suddenly struck by how little I'd really known her. Was she happy that William was safe with her in heaven? What would Justine's fate be? What would it be?

Lost in sadness, fear, and doubt, sleep did not overtake me until very late that night, and not long after it finally gripped my fevered mind, I was stirred to consciousness by a violent storm. The thunder shook the house and rattled the glass in the windows. Soon wind and angry bands of rain assaulted them further. My last thought before the blackness claimed me for good was to thank heaven that William need not fear the fury of storms anymore.

When I awoke, he was there. He stood before the fireplace, studying the same portraits I had before falling asleep the previous night. I'd not heard him enter, and when we spoke, it was clear that he'd failed to notice me asleep on the sofa. It was the soft sobs, which escaped him, that roused me from my slumber. It didn't seem possible, but he was here. I rose and greeted him.

"Welcome, my dearest Victor."

His clothing was damp, his presence a mixture of grief and brooding, and tears flowed freely from his eyes, as he beheld the small portrait of William, which graced the mantle piece. We embraced as brothers and consoled each other as best as possible.

"How are Father and Elizabeth?" he finally asked.

"We are all wretched," I confessed, grateful for his presence, "Elizabeth has blamed herself …."

"I saw the beast last night. He was loose in the storm. We must find him."

These words were rapidly and vehemently uttered, much to my astonishment. I was baffled as to their meaning.

"He? But Justine has been arrested and accused of William's death," I said searching Victor's face for answers.

"Impossible … impossible," he muttered as he walked away from me.

I followed him to the window, and in as concise a fashion as possible, I laid bare the arguments for Justine's guilt, at least the arguments that the court would likely pose.

"But she is innocent," he raved.

His outbursts caused me sufficient reason for pause, but before I could question him further, Father arrived. I tried to interject Victor's claims that he seemed to be aware of an alternate fiend, one capable of William's vicious murder, but Father glossed over the contention before it began.

"If she is innocent, our laws will protect her," he declared setting harsh eyes upon me. Shortly thereafter, Elizabeth arrived, and a tearful reunion between her and my brother ensued. She also advocated Justine's innocence and Victor seemed to sympathize with her sentiments. He made no further comment regarding the individual, whom it seemed, he'd initially felt was responsible for William's death.

The court proceedings would not begin until eleven in the morning, and Elizabeth and Victor quickly isolated themselves from Father and me. We were all to go and serve as witnesses, and I would be forced to offer testimony about my brother's final hour.

It was not until we prepared to leave for court that I was again able to speak with Victor alone. Father decided that he and Elizabeth would be driven to court by our neighbor, and that Victor and I should bring our carriage. This decision gave me some much needed time alone with my older brother. He seemed more serious and sullen than I remembered him, but I'm sure, given the circumstances, I seemed no less so. I began the short trip with some half-hearted attempts at casual banter, but quickly abandoned them. Time was short.

"Brother, it has been many years, but I once trusted you implicitly. I must now ask you something, which puts that trust to the test early in our reunion. Do you know something about William's murder which you have not shared?"

There followed only the briefest pause, but he did not look at me when he answered.

"Have I given you reason to believe so?"

"You said you saw 'him' last night."

"Forgive me, dear Ernest. I slept in the storm last night, and fear that the stress of my homecoming and a night poorly spent, overwhelmed my imagination."

I leaned back in my seat as I studied him.

"I do believe, as you and Elizabeth do, that Justine is guiltless," he declared passionately. Victor's emotion heartened me. He believed in her innocence.

"Then we all must speak on her behalf," I affirmed.

Victor shifted uncomfortably in his seat.

"That would not be practical for me. I was absent when the crime was committed and do not know her as well as you and Elizabeth."

And suddenly, in a rush, the great secret I'd kept from all the other members of my family came forth: my sole omission, my recent errand to annul her previous marriage. Victor was so astonished, he nearly drove our carriage in the river.

"You cannot speak for her," he stammered as he halted the carriage.

"I must. I love her."

"No, you can't!" he shouted.

A strange passion burned in his eyes as he frantically continued.

"Father doesn't know. Elizabeth doesn't know, and I just found out. No one will believe you. And if they do, it either makes her look even more guilty because you've kept this affair a secret all this time, or that you've lost your mind and will do anything to save her, your family be damned."

He was genuinely enraged at this information and squeezed my arm tightly as he spoke again.

"Only your silence can save her Ernest," his eyes bore into me.

I considered his words. Christiansen knew, but he would not be there today, he'd told me as much, but even if he were, I doubted that either he or Justine would say anything. His actions were motivated by his experiences with the law, and hers from years of keeping secrets as a matter of survival. What motivated my brother's advice?

"Say nothing. Protect her by keeping your secret," Victor counseled.

I should have realized in that moment that the Victor I'd known as a child was gone. The old Victor would have encouraged me, as Mother always had, to follow my heart, but this was far from the fearful sentiment he now shared. At the time, I could somewhat dismiss this behavior on the stresses he'd already mentioned, or the circumstances under which I so recklessly chose to reveal such a profound personal secret. But time was to prove otherwise.

In time, I realized, that the Victor Frankenstein I had known never returned from Ingolstadt. If only I'd recognized that fact then. Instead, I chose to act as my older sibling advised. I chose silence.

In truth, I remember little of the trial. I have long since repressed most of its grim proceedings, but a few moments do still linger in my mind. They are mostly images and thoughts. I remember Justine entering the courtroom, dressed in black, as a sign of mourning for William's loss. Of her eyes briefly touching mine in that surreal moment.

The case was laid out before the court, but much to my surprise, I was not called upon to add any additional details to the deposition I'd already given about the last time I'd seen William or the night spent searching for him. In fact, no member of my family was called upon. I recall Justine's brilliant, simple, logical, and above all, honest oratory. Surely this would move their hearts. But I also remember how no one, including her, could account for the miniature found on her possession. Her witnesses, frightened of reprisal, largely abandoned her when she called upon them, and as members of the victim's family the court deemed it improper for us to testify on her behalf. Still, Elizabeth stunned the entire proceeding, when she managed to give a spontaneous, impassioned speech in support of Justine's character, professing an unshakable faith in her innocence. Victor shrunk steadily during the proceedings as if he were going to be ill, and not long after Elizabeth's brilliant oratory, he fled the courtroom.

Her speech, at last, seemed to sway hearts and open minds to the possibility that Justine might be innocent. It also inspired me. I decided, whatever the consequences, I would also voice my support for Justine. But the adjudicators had other thoughts. Sensing the shift in momentum, they quickly cleared the courtroom, declaring a recess. Any chance I had to speak that day evaporated. Court was to begin again at eleven the following morning, but it proved to be unnecessary. Victor returned to the court early the next day and discovered there would be no continuation. None was needed. Justine had confessed during the night to the murder of my brother.

***

Geneva, June 1794

He waited until it was dark. He wanted her to feel the sense of calm reassurance that her brief, shining moment in court had granted her, before he came, to help her make the only choice left to her, even if she did not realize it.

This was his job. It was his passion, as it had been for those of past generations. To purify the souls of those, in the name of God and the Holy Church, who still could be saved, and cast out those who could not. She could still serve as an instrument of God, if she chose to. This was the path he must set her upon. She had strayed far from the Lord and from the guidance of the Catholic Church. The confessor was a master of his chosen art. He had the warmth and compassion a spider has for one who has become entangled in its web. He would study his victim, seek weakness, and then do as any creature must—embrace its nature.

The man began by interviewing Justine's guards. Who had come to visit her? How frequently? Had there been any correspondence? What did she seem to value in such a dismal place? What was known of her past? Did she cry out in the night? Was she a God-fearing soul? Had sins been confessed in casual conversation? And most importantly, where did she find hope?

She must hate him, yet ultimately, cling to him for salvation. He, and the Church, must come to symbolize hope. She suffered, the community cried out, and the dead sought justice. He could remedy all of this. It was a power God granted the righteous, not the wicked. The laws of God had been violated, and the laws of man were weak and ineffective. He said a final prayer before entering the cellblock, then crossed himself, and entered the domain of the lost and the damned.

He studied her before revealing himself. He'd seen her in court, of course, but this was different. She imagined herself to be alone or what passed for alone in prison. People's hearts were much easier to observe when they were alone. She seemed younger, somehow, than she had at court. The moon shone through the cell's small window, illuminating her actions more so than the torches, which burned on nearby walls. She was pacing and absentmindedly working something between her fingers. Could this be the necklace with the cross that guards had mentioned? It was apparently the one item she'd insisted upon bringing with her to the prison. He waited for her to reveal more. Several times she touched her abdomen and even smiled slightly once as she did so. The guards also mentioned that on two occasions she awoke in the night, screaming of something unrelated to her crimes, or at least to her current ones. Her family was dead. What did she cling to in this world?

He withdrew, silently to consider the most potent method of attack. He donned his finest ceremonial robes, making certain to affix a cross prominently across his chest to visually connect himself to her. Then, satisfied with his choice, he recruited two of the harshest guards on duty to accompany him with a large bucket filled with water. He also collected items to administer Communion. The sacrament would be his hook. So prepared, he finally entered Justine's cell near midnight.

*

It began simply as the priest arrived to offer her Communion. Before doing so, he inquired what crime brought her to this prison. She almost laughed at the question, it seemed so ridiculous.

"Father, I'm sure you must know. All of Geneva knows why I am here."

"Do you?" he asked thoughtfully.

Justine pondered the question a moment before responding.

"Because the guilty punish the innocent," she decided.

"Yes, yes. So it was for Christ, also. But what if he had not chosen to suffer for the sins of others? What if he had not embraced the role that God had destined him to play? Would there be redemption? Would I be here to offer you the blessings made possible by that sacrifice?"

Any trace of amusement in her was immediately suppressed.

"Do you think me guilty then, as so many others do?"

He leaned forward slightly.

"I do not know you well enough to know such things, but I can tell that your spirit suffers. At times, we have all walked the path of life alone, been changed by it, and then reminded that we are never truly alone. Confession can often bring us closer to the realization that God never abandons us, that only we can abandon Him. Perhaps, before Communion, you should offer Confession."

He smiled reassuringly. Justine had been raised in the Catholic faith as a child, but never shared her mother's near fanatical obsession with it. She knew the basics of the faith, but not the finer points, including the political nature of the Church. She saw the priest's offer of Confession as genuine concern for a soul in need. The first level of trust had been established.

Justine did not reveal all her sins, nor all the injustices visited upon her in this world, but it was enough for the priest to use. It was not a confession, so much as a cleverly manipulated interrogation. He learned of her family's history, some of her current relationships, and most importantly her fears. People only confessed the sins which catered specifically to their fears. The others were lost in the din of life or ignored as a natural part of human existence. Now, he could truly begin his work.

The hours wrapped around one another, as he wove his web of psychological manipulation and destruction. The shadows in the cell shifted, as the moon marched across the heavens. The onslaught was calculated, brutal, and exhausting. Where he had initially been mild, he became dogmatic and wholly unsympathetic. Then suddenly, his fire would seem to die, and again he would turn soothing and reach out to her. Her very soul was in danger.

At points, she began to believe she was some unholy monster. What else could explain all that had happened to her? She struggled to stay afloat in this shifting sea, but as time wore on, it became increasingly difficult. Her doubts and fears began to rise, as great swells in the sea, threatening to swamp her. Several times the guards even held her head in the bucket of water for prolonged periods. It was alternately explained to be a means of purification or else touted as a possible punishment she might suffer eternally, in the depths of Hell.

Justine was growing weaker, and still he pressed on without mercy. She still clung to hope, and this, too, he must destroy if he was to save her. She must be made to confess to the murder of the boy. Any number of appeals had been tried, and so far all had failed, but a sudden inspiration gripped his mind. He plucked the silver necklace with the small cross from around her neck; she issued a faint cry to its loss.

"This cross, why did you bring it?"

By now it was taking a long time for the exhausted girl to speak. She did not want to answer, but she also feared another simulated drowning might occur if she failed to do so.

"It was a gift," she breathed heavily.

"From who?"

"I told you hours ago," she wheezed.

"Tell me again," he commanded, mercilessly.

"Madame Frankenstein."

"Yes, your mistress. You were close?"

"Yes," she answered softly.

"You believe she walks with God in heaven?"

She paused.

"Yes."

He licked his lips before continuing.

"Now, now I believe you said at your trial that you would pledge your very salvation upon your innocence; is that not so?"

Her eyes became slightly unfocused as she tried to recall.

"I think so."

"You think you did or you did not?"

"Yes, I did," her voice trembled.

"Justine, you are not innocent."

She closed her eyes and shook her head.

"I am."

"So many would not have abandoned you if it were not so. Think. How would Madame Frankenstein feel right now?"

Her eyes opened, her mouth worked for a moment before he grabbed the back of her neck. She screamed.

"How would she feel?" he demanded as he pressed the cross back into her hand and forced her to stare at it.

"I don't know," she sobbed. "I don't know."

His hands cupped her face.

"You do! You do know. If she knew what you'd done. You do know!"

She cried harder. His voice softened.

"If you persist, you will cut yourself off from her soul forever. No comfort, no peace, she will have loved you for nothing."

"That's not true. It's not true."

"William has already perished for nothing. You will be found guilty. I promise you. And you will hang for this crime. That will be your legacy. Not love, not friendship, but guilt that will remain upon your soul, long after you've left this life. The gates of heaven will be eternally closed to you, and the person who loved you the most in this world, who comforted and protected you, she will be unable to reach you and forgive you for what you've done. You will wander in the darkness, an outcast soul, forever. And she will not be able to save you again."

This reached Justine as nothing else had. The hours of torment had led to this moment, but the powerful scars suffered in her life made his reality possible. She was dirty. She was a sinner, and she had failed Madame Frankenstein. She had died while under Justine's care. She released the talisman that had been wrought from around her neck, as her hand moved unconsciously, trying to sense the new life growing within her. She had failed her guardian who'd been lifted from this cruel world to a better place. Justine had always admired her, even in death. The thought of being forever separated from Caroline Frankenstein was unbearable.

"Justine. Are you with child?"

She didn't notice the question at first, but as it registered she slowly began to nod. The confessor had not failed to observe Justine's habit of placing a hand upon her mid-section when she was troubled and was pleased he'd surmised correctly. This must be hidden from the courts or the execution would be stayed, and he would fail. She was close. He knew it instinctively. He must act now.

"Will you also deny your offspring the love and salvation of God? If you die, excommunicated from the Church, you will."

And with that statement, the trap closed. Justine thought of Ernest at the trial. He'd said nothing. The man she loved, the man whose child she carried, had made no attempt to save her. He must also believe in her guilt. Why else had he not spoken? Elizabeth had. He would not love their child, and this baby would suffer, as she had, in this cold, thoughtless, hate-filled world. Could she bear to bring a child into such an existence? Ernest had abandoned her. Her guardian angel in this world had abandoned her. Would she now allow herself to be sacrificed needlessly and forever denied her guardian in heaven? The lie would set her free. And no one seemed to care about her or the truth. There was no escape.

"Serve His will child. Confess."

"I will serve God's will," she said at last.

**

After so many days in the cell, the brightness of the sun brought tears to her eyes. She'd vowed she could cry no more for herself, and wished for nothing more than to leave this world of eternal torment. Still, the tears traced silent paths over the curvature of her face. She was innocent, whatever else she may be; she was innocent of the crime for which she was to be executed.

As she was being led to the gallows, the mob, which had assembled to witness justice, assailed her with dehumanizing, hateful words. She was a beast for show, a wild hunted thing that would now be rendered forever harmless to mankind. She had never known hate could be so powerful. Some pulled her clothing, her hair, they scratched her, spat upon her; there was no dignity. It would be a hollow death, one perhaps she'd earned, through the hatred and cruelty of others. Where had this vaulted sense of justice been when her father had raped her, or when she'd been beaten by her mother and treated as a harlot? The only place she had ever known real love had been in the Frankenstein household and now, even that was gone. There was nothing left.

Though not exceedingly tall, the gallows platform and steps, shuddered and swayed alarmingly as she ascended them. Time was moving too fast; life was not supposed to reach this unnatural conclusion. How could one prepare adequately for this moment? She wanted a pure heart, a peaceful soul to accompany her from this life, but both were alive with fear.

Rough hands gripped her, and forced her body to a fixed location on the platform. The cries from the crowd were deafening. She was being asked something? She was being asked something by a priest, one of an order who had forced a false confession from her. One who, instead of serving as a champion for her innocence, had held her at sway with fear for her very soul—to die excommunicated.

What was the question? Last words? What had her first words been?

*

from the journal of Ernest Frankenstein

The question went unanswered, and suddenly she fell over, gasping for air. Our eyes met across a relatively short distance, but the gulf between us was vast. I stared into the eyes of the woman I loved. Into the eyes of the woman who had confessed to murdering my dear brother. Had they been the last sight he'd seen? I did not look away as they hauled her to her feet and applied the noose about her delicate neck. Apparently, I was to be the last thing she saw, for they did not bother to place a hood over her face. It was in this horrifying moment that a change settled upon her.

The stress, fear, and panic vanished, and she became Justine again, and in that instant, my suffering abated. The hopes and dreams we'd shared transported me from the nightmare life had become. Her lips began to part as words finally came. Would she ask for mercy, forgiveness, or offer one last prayer before the end? I will never know. The only sounds that reached me were those created by the shattering of her pitiful neck bones, followed shortly by the raucous cheers of the mob. Long after they'd gone, I wept alone before her body, as ceaseless rain fell.

But it did not end. The pain did not end. I fear that I am still beholden to the spirit of my lovely tormentor. Soon after her death, the nightmares began. William's and Justine's spirits began to live anew in them, and do to this day.

The dream is always the same. She comes from the mists, trying to tell me something, as William screams; his gaze transfixed upon something beyond me. And when I turn to see what he does, I realize that I am in a grave, buried alive. I am plagued by their loss.

Justine's legacy of love, mystery, and misery lives within me, but I have never learned to live with this unbreakable cycle of love and hate I feel towards her. Does heaven comfort them both, or does Hell clutch her? I alone have been left to try to understand.

And so they sleep, and so I die. I don't know what I'd expected to gain from witnessing that final brutal display: a last plea for pity, a detailed explanation of why, a relief from the emptiness growing within me. But when it was over, I felt nothing, and the emptiness remained. Each succeeding death, each monumental loss, would deepen this void within me, until it all but consumed me. I would lead a cursed life, until the day your mother reached out her blessed hand and lifted me from the abyss.

***

Geneva, 1797

Elizabeth was alone at the house in Belrive, when the woman arrived. Alphonso had not yet returned from Ireland with Victor, though recent letters indicated he soon would. His trial for the murder of Henry Clerval had concluded, and Elizabeth's doubts regarding her and Victor's future had never been more pronounced. It was into this atmosphere that a long silent voice from the past was awakened by this unexpected visitor's arrival.

The woman introduced herself and made her simple request. She misinterpreted Elizabeth's surprised reaction as one of revulsion and made apologies, as she quickly prepared to leave the house.

"No, please, Madame," Elizabeth entreated quietly as she reached out to halt the woman's flight. "It is I who should apologize to you. Forgive me, of course, you may."

The possibility of this moment had never occurred to Elizabeth until now. She'd had only the noblest, most heart-felt sentiments when she'd argued for the location of Justine's final resting place. She wrapped a shawl about her shoulders as she conducted her visitor to the gravesite.

Her father had steadfastly resisted the notion of burying Justine here, at first, but her earnest entreaties eventually softened his resolve and allowed him to reach beyond his pain and embrace the better qualities within his humanity. It had not been so with Ernest. He'd protested vehemently against the idea, and its acceptance had created yet another rift between him and his family. She and Victor, before his sudden departure for England, had tried again to explain Justine's actions to him by attempting to recount their final visit with her, but he would hear none of it.

He was the only member of the family to attend her execution, and it seemed for Ernest, that her professed betrayal would never be forgiven. At first, Elizabeth perceived his anger as a protective response to the tragic events they had suffered through, one that would lessen with time; however, it did not. He hated her now, as much as he had once loved her. Elizabeth suspected that their relationship had transcended mere friendship; this seemed evinced not only by his behavior but in details Victor hinted he'd revealed to him before Justine's trial. However, she had never directly confronted him about the true nature of their relationship.

There was a slight chill to the air, but the sun bathed the grounds in a pleasant light. Soon, spring would enliven the world again, but today its grasp was tentative. Elizabeth was uncertain if the woman wished to be accompanied all the way to Justine's grave or not. As it turned out, the visit was to be a relatively short one, and she did not seem to notice Elizabeth, once she'd been shown to the plot housed in the modest family cemetery. She prayed over the stone, which marked the final resting place of her niece, in silence. The winds of March, whistled softly through the nearby woods, making it seem as if Justine were using them to speak to her aunt. The deep ache Elizabeth carried inside for her poor "sister" awoke, and memories of the past wounded her anew.

Justine's aunt withdrew three roses from inside her cloak, then laid them between William's grave and Justine's. She kissed her hand and touched the stones. Then, with a final reverent bow of her greying head, she stepped away from those sleeping in the earth and approached Elizabeth.

"I must again thank you, Mademoiselle," the aged woman blinked tears from her eyes. "You are, indeed, most gracious to allow me to visit today, but the road to Chene is long. I thank you for every kindness you have ever shown my dear niece, and I am truly sorry for the loss of your brother. "

Touched, Elizabeth found it difficult to speak, but a final, kind smile from the woman, and a reassuring touch from her, made it clear that no words were needed. She began to depart.

"Madame, may I ask you a question before you leave?"

The older woman paused, and turned to face her.

"You need not answer, but I am curious; why have you laid three roses?"

The question elicited such a pained look upon the woman's face that Elizabeth immediately regretted asking. With great difficulty, Justine's aunt answered.

"One is for your unfortunate brother, one is for my lovely niece, and one is for the unborn child she carried when she died."

She slowly turned and left, leaving Elizabeth in a state of horrified wonder. Now she understood. Elizabeth wept. She never told Ernest about the visitor or the mysteries she'd helped to explain. In a brief four month's time, Elizabeth too rested beside Justine and William, murdered as her brother had been. Her loss would break Alphonso's heart, and soon, only Victor and Ernest would remain. But Ernest would never know that Justine's silent grave cradled not only the body of his first love, but also the body of his first child as well.

Chapter 12
Reconciliations

Villeneuve, 1794

Though it was near sunset, the air remained stagnant and oppressive, a rare thing in the mountains beyond Villeneuve, a town which lay upon the extreme eastern bank of Lake Geneva.

"How far to this campsite of yours, Ernie?" Jack asked.

Clearly suspicious, he'd wisely chosen to remain mostly silent during the trip from Belrive.

"We'll be there soon," Ernest promised, though he was not entirely certain of that himself. After all, he'd never actually been to their destination and was lying to Jack about the true purpose of this trip. How could he be truthful? None of it was rational; therefore, reason was not important. Ernest only knew that he needed release and hoped this act would grant it to him. He'd been planning this for weeks, ever since his father's astonishing announcement that Justine was to be buried in the family cemetery, next to William. Initially Ernest wanted to fly into a tirade, but instead, his anger found its voice as smoldering rage. But nothing he said convinced his father to retract his odious decision.

Finally, all Ernest could do was pressure him with questions.

"Why, Father, why? Must William never be at peace?" Alphonso Frankenstein said nothing, only leaned heavily for a moment against the doorframe before he re-entered his study.

"How can she have peace without William and Mother?" Elizabeth asked from behind Ernest.

His heart was ash. He glared at her before turning to leave.

"She was innocent," Elizabeth called after him. "You know it in your heart."

Elizabeth and he barely spoke after their father acceded to her request for Justine's interment in the family cemetery. In fact, it would not be until the final months leading up to her marriage to Victor and her own tragic death that the wounds from this confrontation would begin to heal. Justine's betrayal had consumed his dreams, changed his world, and corrupted Ernest's soul. She haunted him in his sleep; his emotions had become increasingly erratic. He would become angry or sad in an instant, then feel perfectly normal and calm the next. At home, Ernest was becoming increasingly invisible, a forgotten son to his father. And Victor was too self-absorbed to notice much of anything.

Upon returning to the house in Belrive, he'd taken to spending long hours in solitude: first out on the waters of the lake and then hiking alone in the mountains. Victor's moods were unpredictable, and by fall of that year, they would drive him away to the British Isles for some unknown purpose. He was a shadow, and it was not until after Elizabeth's death that he took note of his brother again. Death surrounded Ernest's life and touched all those who loved him to a varying degree. To escape such a grim and empty existence, he turned to the liveliest friend he had: Jack Clerval.

Henry had been everything that Jack was not: a poet, a dreamer, a romantic, a scholar, an obedient son, tall, gracious, quiet, and above all self-disciplined. Jack was the rambunctious, proud, direct, social climbing, money dropping, and brilliant but lazy son of Herrick Clerval. In point of truth, Henry and Jack were actually only half-brothers, but they'd been raised as full. Henry took more after his mother, while Jack embodied more of his father's traits.

He was stocky, a heavy drinker and gambler, who rarely observed social customs and who had no qualms about using his family's vast wealth to help him garner respectability. A perpetual cloud of cigar smoke swirled around him nearly every hour of the day and often heralded his arrival at social gatherings. During the early years of his life, he had lived abroad and often traveled with his father, who was an extremely prosperous merchant. His storytelling ability was the stuff of local legend and was unquestionably one of the reasons that, despite his scandalous ways, he remained a favorite in even the most respected of social circles. He was unique, and possessed more than enough favorable qualities to balance out the more crude or unsavory aspects of his nature.

Jack was the rarest of friends. He was charitable with his time, as well as money, and no man could have been so loyal to so many. He would quite literally stop whatever he was doing to listen to anyone who needed to be heard. His temper was quick, both to rise and fade.

To many, he seemed to take nothing seriously, while in fact, the opposite was true. He let others worry about judging, while he preferred to concentrate on living. The world was an adventure to Jack, and it was this kindred spirit that had first formed the bonds friendship with Ernest. Younger than Henry and Victor, but older than Ernest, he often referred to his friend as "little Ernie" just because he knew it annoyed him.

"Wish you'd learn to ride a horse. Wouldn't have to mess with this blasted cart then, would we?"

"We'll need the cart," was Ernest's sole comment to the chastisement.

Jack groaned.

"Don't tell me we're sleepin' on a pile of rocks again, Ern?"

Ernest smiled. He did have a knack for picking rotten places to sleep during their camping trips. Jack carelessly tossed his smoldering cigar into a passing ravine, and immediately began to ignite a fresh one without pause.

"Now, Ernie …," he said between puffs, "have I told you … the one about, the one about Portuguese Hannah?"

He reached into his other pocket and withdrew his flask. The thing cost more than Ernest's horse and cart combined. He held it out to his friend who downed whatever it contained.

"Have a care here. That stuff's not cheap, stole it right out of the old Bucell's cellar at a party two nights ago."

He downed a draught and winked.

"Not bad that, eh. But you'll never guess how I got down there."

"You seduced the maid," Ernest said mockingly.

Jack looked wounded for a moment, before waving a hand dismissively.

"The maid? It was the cook's lovely assistant, I'll have you know."

His friend rolled his eyes.

"You're truly a man of standards, Jack."

"Damn straight." He hoisted the flask and took one more tug from it before putting it away and slapping Ernest on the back.

"That's why I love ya, Ern. You know me so well. What are we stoppin' for?"

Struck by a sudden inspiration Ernest pulled onto a side road with a barn, one well-separated from the owner's house. He jumped down from the cart as Jack searched the area looking for as reasonable excuse as to why they'd stopped. Ernest walked towards the barn; curious, Jack followed.

"What are we doin'?"

"Relax, Jack. You like to steal," Ernest noted, as he quietly drew back the door latch.

"Yeah, what of it. Wait, you aren't thinkin' of pullin' some lame cow stealin' bit are ya?"

Ernest finished opening the door and smiled in satisfaction. The barn contained exactly what he'd hoped. Jack shook his head.

"No, I was wrong. This is lamer."

"You wanna sleep comfortably tonight or on a pile of rocks?"

Jack theatrically drew in a deep breath and adjusted his belt.

"Yeah, stealin' straw works," he nodded.

Six quick armloads later, and they were back on the road.

"I must be rubbin' off on you. Never seen you do that before."

Ernest smiled tightly but said nothing. A short time later, they passed the road mark he sought. He'd visited Villeneuve about a week earlier and posed some innocent questions in a local tavern. Three beers later, he had all the information necessary to fulfill his plans tonight.

The road they turned onto climbed steeply, and for a short time, Ernest feared the horse would not be able to surmount it. To be safe, they stopped about half way up to allow the horse to rest, but eventually, they made it. By now dusk was becoming a memory and night a reality. Ernest pulled off into the first clearing he could locate, certain that his goal was not too far distant. As he descended from the cart, Jack surveyed the area as best he could in the gathering gloom.

"Ah, damn it Ernie. There are rocks everywhere."

"Good thing we stopped for straw then," he commented dryly as he also surveyed the area, trying to gain his bearings.

"Yeah, good thing. Straw's gonna be blasted useless if it rains later," Jack complained. "Could swear I just heard thunder."

"Listen, why don't you start to get us set-up. I wanna check on something."

Without waiting for the inevitable protest, Ernest regained the road and ventured further ahead. Not more than a fourth of a mile from their impromptu campsite, he found it. As he studied the house, Ernest reached for a dead tree branch and twisted it absentmindedly in his hands. It appeared to be vacant, but he would have to make certain before he dare proceed with his plan. He moved through the humid air, senses alert, the sounds of his breath and rushing pulse were magnified by his nerves.

He peered, tentatively, through a grime speckled pane, and quickly realized his fears of occupancy were groundless. It actually made sense, he reflected, continuing on to the front door, only to discover it was securely locked. Part of him was pleased with this discovery; it meant he'd have to break in.

Ernest found a sizeable rock and heaved it at the pane he'd looked through; it shattered into countless shards. He could have simply proceeded in through the window frame, but fear now turned to anger as he gazed upon the house. He hurtled rock after rock into the windows and pounded them against the door, until it was pitted and parts of it were near crumbling. He didn't think, just embraced his rage and emptiness. He beat at the lock with his heel and forced the door in. Winded, Ernest at last entered Justine's childhood home.

He perceived this as the place that had created her, shaped her negative qualities, while he fancied his home had nurtured her positive ones. The house must have been locked since the day her vile aunt from Basel evicted Justine from it. He was probably the first person to set foot inside it in years.

It was relatively small, so the stale air was highly concentrated. The meager possessions within were coated in dust. Soon this was what Justine and William would become: pitiful dust. Their lives unfulfilled. Ernest began to grab objects at random and destroy them. This was where she had suffered. This was where he'd failed her. This place had created the fiend within the angel, and now it must be destroyed.

Eventually a cloud of scented smoke intruded upon his ruinous chore.

"Stay out of this, Jack," he snapped without turning to look at his friend.

No protest was offered, and he finally turned to face the doorway.

"Haven't even put my foot across the threshold, Ern," Jack noted coolly.

Ernest was practically panting by now.

"How long have … no, I don't care," he waved him away as he staggered back a step. A flash briefly illuminated the world beyond the doorframe.

"Might care 'bout that," Jack observed.

The leaves and branches of the trees outside were chattering excitedly in the winds that heralded the approaching tempest. He'd been so engrossed in his task that Ernest had failed to notice any signs of the incoming storm. He swore.

"How long do you think?"

"What? Until it rains? It's already blowing drops," Jack informed him.

Ernest was out of time.

"A question, if I may. You plannin' to finish this tonight or to come back?" Jack asked.

Their gazes met evenly.

"I'm not a total idiot, Ern," Jack grinned roguishly, "you want this place down, so let's be done with it."

Ernest nodded. His eyes made a hasty survey of the main room.

"I don't think it'll go up like this," he shook his head.

"Well, not if you're plannin' anything conventional," Jack scoffed.

Ernest considered this for a moment.

"The straw?" he asked blinking sweat from his eyes.

"Half of it flew down the mountainside. If you'd told me what it was actually for, I'd 'ave made more of an effort to save the stuff. Come on. We haven't got long."

Ernest followed him out into the surprisingly strong winds and echoing thunder. Jack had brought the wagon and unhitched the horse, which now neighed discordantly as it stood tied beneath a nearby tree. He wanted to leave.

Jack had affixed his bedroll over the straw on the cart. When they reached it, he stretched his arms beneath the covering and withdrew two glass oil lamps. His friend stared at him quizzically then suddenly remembered how he'd left Jack behind to close up the barn.

"What? You stole straw; I helped myself to some lamps. Never know when they'll come in handy." In his best patronizing tone, he remarked, "If it makes you feel any better, I left some money beneath the barn door when I locked up."

Ernest shook his head. Say what you would about him, but Jack always seemed to come prepared. Even if he had no idea what he needed to be prepared for. He studied the lamp in his hand.

"Don't be simple'bout lightin' it. Just throw the damn thing, Ern."

Seconds later it shattered against the wooden siding by the front door.

"Beautiful shot," Jack beamed, as he began dumping oil from the other lamp over his bed roll.

Rain was now coming at them sideways.

"Put out that damn cigar," Ernest admonished as Jack finished pouring the fluid from the lamp. He casually withdrew it and drove the glowing tip into the oil-soaked bedroll. With a brilliant flash, the lamp oil ignited. Jack cursed as the heat caught his hand. The straw began to smoke within seconds, and the cart glowed through the seams of its boards. Jack was still studying his slightly burnt hand, when Ernest began to shove the cart.

It should have been nearly impossible for one man to move, given the terrain and the wind, but he managed. A mad energy had seized him. He was dimly aware that Jack was yelling for him to stop. Ernest ignored him. He'd completely forgotten that the cart was on a small rise. Suddenly, the ground dipped, gravity took over, and trailing smoke and flame, the wagon careened swiftly into the house, igniting the fluid Ernest's shattered lamp had christened it with. The force of the cart's impact smashed in a portion of the front wall, and the roof sagged under the stress. And that was it. The tortured house lay aflame and utterly ruined.

As he watched it, Ernest tried to imagine that he'd done a cathartic, purifying thing, but suddenly the loneliness of the place consumed him. The wind-driven flames began to aggressively reduce the former structure to ashes. Who had he done this for? Not for her. And as Ernest stood there, another part of him quietly vanished. He could not tell if tears or raindrops now stung his eyes. He heard the sound of a horse and rider approaching from behind.

"Time to go, Ernest," Jack stated flatly. He pointed to a glowing column of lanterns and torches coming up the roadway.

"Folks probably think lightening hit it, but that cart's still plenty obvious. Best not be here when they arrive."

Ernest favored the burning hulk with one last glance, and then climbed up onto the horse behind Jack, who promptly stole his hat.

"Hey."

The hard rain began pelting off Ernest's skull.

"Hey, mine went up with your house. I kept tellin' ya to stop so I could get it."

"Left it on the seat, huh?"

"Shut up, Ernie."

Jack kicked the steed's sides, and they shot up the short hill and down the road, away from the approaching neighbors. Both were so worried about pursuers that they forgot about the steep hill, which led to the main road below. Whether it was Jack's skills or the horse's instincts that saved them, Ernest kept his eyes shut until well after they'd nearly tumbled to the bottom, saying a silent prayer of gratitude.

"How's your hand?" he cried out over the storm once they were safe.

"Been better, been worse. Nothin' scotch won't solve," he stated philosophically. "Figure we'd bunk in some inn with a tavern in Villeneuve, unless you still want to go camping?"

"The tavern sounds fine," Ernest agreed shaking his drenched head.

"Good. First round's on you. New cart's on me."

"No, Jack …"

"Shut up, Ernie."

He offered no further protests. What would be the point? When Jack made up his mind to spend money, it was useless to argue. Besides, Ernest hadn't even considered how he'd explain the loss of the cart to Father, let alone replace it.

"All right, I'll buy you a new hat," he offered.

"What like this gem?" Jack flicked the brim of his purloined hat.

"Fine, I'll give you money for a new hat."

"Got something better you can do."

"What?"

"Tell me why we just burned down a house."

Their return trip to Geneva two days later was also a quiet one, but this time it was for new reasons.

**

from the journal of Ernest Frankenstein

October 1809

Today, I am closer to returning home. I have slept little, but I've managed to locate some of the journals my tormentor from the cave bid me to seek. I finally remembered that I never properly searched the family safe, the whereabouts of which I will not mention, as I believe the secret of its location remains a mystery. Should this paper be read by my enemies, it will afford them no clues as to the status of that portion of my inheritance.

I've used my knowledge of the property to harass and confuse my ever-present gypsy spies during the night. They have made their presence known on several occasions since my arrival back at my house in Belrive; however, every time I've attempted to intercept or track them, they have eluded me. But after so many days in a fixed location, they have become less alert and habitual. I discovered one of their primary observation posts and used it to locate a portion of their contingent. They must speak some type of hybrid trade language, for their conversation was a blend of numerous tongues, and all but impossible to comprehend.

When they discovered that I had slipped away from the house unobserved, they began to hunt me, and as they did so, I infiltrated their camp and stole or destroyed their few comforts. Their bedrolls, I hid among the sundry items in the outer storage buildings, and then returned to the house. And in the darkness, I waited for endless hours by the window and watched for them. When at last the three shadows crept alternately to and from the storage buildings, I headed for the safe. There I found two, badly burnt journals, which contained writings in Victor's hand.

I stepped out into the grey dawn and held the books aloft, as I stood in front of the main entry. If this is truly why they watched me, I figured they would be eager to take them into their possession. But no one approached to take them or question me. I left them outside during the day, while I attempted to sleep, fully anticipating that they would be claimed. In the evening, much to my surprise, they remained undisturbed upon the stoop. I decided that I would take one back inside and leave the other for the gypsies. The journal I selected was nearly useless. Victor had apparently meant to destroy them both, but must have changed his mind after they'd gone into the fire. Pages were burnt, missing, torn, the ink had bled, and the sheer age of the yellow, cheap paper made reading difficult. The strange subject matter of the journal made it even more miraculous that I was able to decipher anything.

From the topics discussed in the surviving entries, and by one of the few remaining dates, it was obvious that this journal was written during Victor's university days in Ingolstadt. The first entry I read was fairly boring, and discussed papers, projects, and lectures. He seemed particularly taken with a professor of his named Waldman and with certain subjects of study. But as I progressed, the entries became increasingly incomprehensible and finally fanatical. His mood and thoughts would shift radically, mathematical and chemical formulas would be scrawled into the middle of sentences along with nonsensical statements. For example, one badly burnt, undated entry began, "I will pioneer a new way, explore unknown powers, and unfold to the world the deepest mysteries of cre ..."

Parts of several entries even seemed to be written in some type of code. At points, he expressed doubts or disgust with his mysterious pursuits; at others, he fancied himself rising above the mundane dreams of mortals. But none of the remaining entries revealed what he was doing. I traded the first journal for the second, which turned out to be even less useful. It contained only two legible entries and no dates.

"... cast among mankind and endowed with the will and power to my own spirit let loose from the grave and forced to destroy all dear to me."

And the final entry, of which, only five words remained, "... the wickedness of my promise."

*

Ernest felt ill as he turned the charred journal between his hands. What did the man in the cave wish him to see? Why was this of value to him? What flawed, fatal pursuit had so inspired and corrupted his brilliant brother? That Victor had been insane no longer seemed to be in question, but had it driven him to murder? Could the man in the cave be a victim, and if so, what was the nature of the crime against him? It made no sense. If one had been so wronged that they would go to such great lengths to force Ernest into understanding ... unless they meant to avenge that wrong upon Ernest, the last Frankenstein; no, not the last, not anymore. The image of Ailis, alone and pregnant caused his soul to shudder. What if all of this was nothing more than a diversion? What if others were meant to suffer for Victor's crimes, while Ernest continued to live with their legacy?

"Ernest, we must involve the authorities," Christiansen declared. "Kidnapping, extortion, stalking …"

The younger man held his bowed head.

"They can't do anything," he asserted, sitting back on the sofa in Christiansen's study. "I can barely track these people, and I never saw their leader. Have you any word from Ailis?"

Christiansen frowned slightly and then withdrew an open envelope from his jacket pocket.

"I received something from Ireland addressed to you."

Ernest glanced at the small, torn A marked across the envelope's former seal.

"When did it arrive?"

Christiansen rubbed his balding head a moment in thought.

"Say, maybe two evenings ago. Forgive my intrusion in opening it, but if your wife's health was worse … well, I didn't know what to make of it, so I kept it on me at all times … just in case."

The communiqué was from Abrielle. Ernest selected a pattern of important words imbedded in the correspondence, most of which was intentional gibberish.

Ag teacht du lettoyag. Maison go luath. Sœur más gá.

She was safely in Ireland, having eluded her pursuers. She promised to send word after she saw Ailis if there were any problems. Though treasured news, Ernest immediately destroyed it in the fire then gripped Christiansen's hand firmly, squeezing it in gratitude.

"Should I expect more letters from this person?"

"Hopefully not, but hide them if you do. Do you have a safe?"

Christiansen nodded as Ernest handed him Victor's second journal. After reading it, he'd abandoned any notion of giving either journal to the gypsies. They were the key to Victor and their loss might bring about the destruction of those Ernest loved with alacrity. The charred journal now felt like some holy relic he was charged to protect on his quest.

His godfather made no comment when he was finished reading, only leaned back in his chair and stared into the fire.

"I'm not sure where this leaves us," he said at last.

It was a sentiment the younger man agreed with wholeheartedly. Christiansen tugged at his moustache, as his brow creased in thought.

"You're certain there are no other journals in the house? Just this one and the other you described?"

"He could have hidden more of them any number of places," Ernest conceded, "but these were all I could find."

Christiansen nodded in a distracted manner.

"Well," he pronounced at last, "let's retire and give it more thought."

Ernest wanted to argue for action, but with no idea what an effective course of action might be, he settled for pursuing inspiration in his dreams.

*

"Best get dressed, my boy," Christiansen advised as he roughly roused Ernest awake several hours later.

"What? Why?" Ernest asked groggily. "You have a plan?"

"Yes, you leave town as quickly as possible. Old LaShall's dead," he exclaimed as he drew back the narrow curtains.

"What?"

"I'd asked him to check up on your place, until I could hire some proper guards. Never imagined you'd be back so soon." Christiansen was literally stuffing items into Ernest's bags.

"Do you think I had something to do with this?"

Christiansen paused.

"I wouldn't be helping you pack if I did," he asserted.

"How'd he die?"

Christiansen shook his head.

"The account was vague. Someone found him on a side road near your place late yesterday. His wife mentioned to the authorities that they'd recently been visited by someone claiming to be Ernest Frankenstein."

"Couldn't his death be natural?"

"Quite a coincidence if it is; there were marks found on his neck."

Ernest's heart began to race.

"Victor?"

"Or your man from the cave or these gypsies, who knows, but with your family's history I wouldn't advise staying. Besides, I have an idea I'd like you to consider."

Ernest listened to Christiansen's plan with mixed emotions.

"I don't know if he'll help," he conceded at last.

"But if Victor left something with Henry, this is the way to find out. Remember, Henry and he were in Ingolstadt together for sometime. Who knows what he may have seen or overheard …"

"I know."

"And he was with him in England too, until …"

"I know," the words sounded harsher than he'd meant them to, "Sorry. It's still thin. Besides, I thought you said the Clervals moved to Salzburg?"

"They did. All but Jack."

"That figures."

"When I saw him the other day, he mentioned to me that he'd be leaving for Salzburg this morning. He came to see me regarding a small family matter that …"

"Did you mention seeing me?"

"Certainly not"

Ernest frowned. With few options and LaShall's untimely passing, it did seem to put an end to his time in Geneva.

"Listen, I wrote two letters last night," he stated, handing them over without further preamble, "put these in your safe. If you don't hear from me in a month send the first to Ailis."

"And the second?"

"It's for you, directions on how to access my family's safe at the house. Send all but ten percent of what's inside to Ailis. Keep the rest. Does Jack still live at his family's old place?"

"Yes."

Ernest donned his coat.

"I'm willing you my horse. Sell it or keep it, I'm fine either way."

Christiansen touched his arm.

"What am I to do if your family contacts you?"

Ernest paused.

“Memorize it. Then burn it. Don’t try to contact me and don’t reply to them.”

They parted, uncertain if they’d ever meet again.

*

The smoke was there, as he knew it would be, and so was Jack, holding a pistol on him, and trying hard not to act surprised that some lunatic had just jumped into his moving carriage. Ernest made no motion until he felt fairly certain his old friend wasn’t about to shoot.

“You didn’t used to be so jumpy, Jack.”

It took several moments, but recognition slowly began to alter his scowl.

“Jesus, Ernest, I nearly blew your damn head off.”

He began to breathe again.

“No you didn’t,” Ernest asserted, pointing to the hammer, which had not even been cocked back into firing position.

“So I was sloppy this time,” Jack muttered as he lowered the weapon, “Didn’t figure I‘d see you again so soon.”

“Jack, it’s been ten years.”

“Huh? Well, seemed a bit shorter just now,” he noted retrieving the smoldering cigar he’d dropped. “So just back in town to hitch a ride or what?” he asked before tapping the roof of the carriage, which began to lurch forward again.

“Something like that.”

“So fallin’ in my carriage wasn’t just some grand accident?”

“I need your help, Jack.”

Rhythmic hoof beats filled the void until Jack slowly turned his eyes back to the living phantom.

“Ten years … ten years without a word and then … ‘I need your help, Jack’?”

Ernest shifted slightly in his seat.

“I didn’t have a choice. Victor …”

Jack’s eyes flashed.

“And where is Victor?” he growled, keeping his the pistol close at hand.

Victor had been put on trial for the murder of Jack's brother, Henry, in Ireland. Once acquitted of this crime, and with no other reasonable suspects, the case had been left unsolved. Henry's death and the trial greatly strained Ernest and Jack's friendship, which was further eroded by the Elizabeth's unexplained death. With his family dead, Ernest had adhered to Victor's advice that no one but Christiansen know of their fates.

"I honestly don't know."

"What is it … some kinda secret? The Frankensteins always loved their secrets," he scoffed.

"No less than the Clervals," Ernest countered.

Jack glared a moment, then let out a deep, knowing laugh, one that proved infectious.

"Ah, ya got me there, Ern," he admitted wiping a tear from his eye. "So what's this favor involve?"

"It's simple. Christiansen mentioned you were headed to Salzburg. I just want to come along."

"That's it, huh? Got business there?"

"That depends on you."

Jack's amusement was rapidly fading.

"How's that?" he asked warily.

"I need to see if Henry had any of Victor's old school journals," Ernest said bluntly.

"So much for simple," Jack mumbled and looked away.

"I'd assumed your parents took Henry's possessions when they moved …"

"'Course they did, that's not the point," he snapped.

Ernest knew it wasn't. His reappearance was bound to awaken past heartaches they'd just as soon forget. Henry's loss had devastated the Clervals, and they'd left Geneva because it reminded them too much of happier days when he had lived. They'd been preparing to move around the time the surviving Frankensteins' had fled. All these years, he'd assumed that Jack had gone with them. Privately, he wondered why his friend hadn't. Jack fired his still lit cigar out the carriage window and began to light another. For a moment Ernest wondered how many people had been hit by his flying cigars over the years.

"I don't know, Ern. I don't know," he repeated as he lit the new cigar, "you're askin' a lot."

Silently his friend agreed but said nothing. Jack ran a hand over his head.

"You know I never blamed you for the whole thing, 'cept the duel."

"You'd have killed Victor."

"Yeah, that was the point," Jack growled.

"Then I'd have lost my brother and my best friend."

Jack snorted but didn't protest further as he studied the city passing by. Finally, he spoke.

"Seems if you don't know where he is, then you have lost him."

He belched thick smoke. As they slowed at an intersection, Ernest opened the door to leave.

"Sorry, Jack," he said beginning to step out of the carriage.

"Shut up, Ernie. I'll take you to Salzburg," Jack vowed pulling him back inside. "But I can't promise you a warm reception."

"Of course," Ernest nodded. "Thanks, Jack."

"What are friends for?"

*

The next four days were a blending of the past and the present. Jack spoke with the same bravado he always had, but underneath, he seemed older, sadder. The breakneck pace of his lifestyle was beginning to wear upon him. He'd largely assumed the daily operation of his father's merchant business and remained in Geneva, partially for his commerce associations there.

By now, Jack was onto his third wife, whom he was going to see in Salzburg, having separated or divorced from the other two. He couldn't remember which.

"Actually I really hoped the third one would be the charm but …," he threw up his hands. Ernest raised his eyebrows.

"Mistresses?"

Jack nodded guiltily.

"Anymore, we really only see each other two or three times a year; she stays with my folks. I stay in Geneva. She's rich, I'm free; it's been a good system, but I think she's ready to move on."

A deep sadness touched these final words. Ernest had always mutually pitied and admired Jack at once. His fears of commitment ran deep, and

Henry's death had furthered those feelings. His father had lived a similar lifestyle, though his transgressions had largely been kept quiet in public circles. With such a model for romantic relationships, it was no wonder that true love eluded Jack.

Though he found it difficult to be open and loyal to one, he had little problem doing so with many. He still looked out for his friends and inspired others to do so by example. Jack's greatest flaw was though he recognized his shortcomings readily enough, he did little to address them. Unwilling or unable to change, to meet the commitments of a relationship, one party or the other lost interest, and he remained alone. Knowing personally the joys a true, committed union could bring only made Ernest feel worse for Jack.

"How long have you been married?"

"Ah, huh? Well, let's see … 'bout, ah … hhhumm."

It was too painful to watch him think.

"Never mind."

Ernest still couldn't always tell when Jack was acting and when he was serious.

"No, I'll get it. How's 'bout you, Ern?"

"What? Married?"

He nodded.

"Yes."

"Kids?'

"Not yet."

"Four years," Jack beamed.

"What?"

"Been married four years, give or take. Don't be a pain and ask me when my anniversary is."

They chuckled.

"So where is this mystery wife? Didn't come on your little trip?"

"No," Ernest answered quietly as his gaze drifted out the window.

"Ern, I know it's been awhile, but conversations that don't have only one or two word answers are a lot more interestin'."

"I know it's just … part of the reason I need the journals is to make sure Ailis is safe."

"From Victor?"

"Perhaps."

*

Omitting details regarding his fears about Ailis' pregnancy and Abrielle's secret involvement as a caretaker, Ernest provided Jack with the basic reasons for his visit.

"So some hobgoblin in a cave sends you across Europe lookin' for big brother's chronicles of life, and hires a bunch of lazy gypsies to follow you 'round for what?"

"He says he knows where Victor is."

"Bull."

Jack withdrew a small knife from his jacket pocket.

"What about the letter written in his hand?"

"Forgery."

"Christiansen and I checked. It was perfect," Ernest pointed out.

"Little reality check, Ernie. I keep a guy on the company payroll for just that type of job, and he'd better do it perfect for what I pay him. Don't tell anyone. I can't believe Christiansen swallowed the whole Victor note thing so easy. Maybe I'd better get another lawyer for this divorce?"

"That's just it. He doesn't fall for these things."

Jack gave a noncommittal noise to his friend's affirmation as he began to whittle a small stick he'd removed from another pocket. After a few minutes of silence, Jack cleared his throat.

"So ... where ya been for ten years, Ern? Finally join up did ya?"

*

from the journal of Ernest Frankenstein

November 1809

Jack, like Elizabeth and my father, never understood my desire for military service. Father was understandably upset and suspicious when I returned from Villeneuve with a different cart than the one I'd left in. When word of the fire at Justine's former home and news of the probable cause reached him, he completely reversed his stance on my desire to join the Foreign Service. He used his own official contacts to enlist me, for he feared I was becoming an unstable degenerate. He also viewed Jack as an increasingly negative influence, and worked to limit our time together. Before my training regimen was even half complete, Victor left the Continent with Henry and headed for the British Isles; he remained there in isolation for nearly three years.

Again during this time, my father used his influence to keep me posted to a detachment near Geneva rather than one stationed abroad. I resented his interference greatly, but also embraced any measure of freedom the posting could afford me. In the military, I learned basic combat skills: sword fighting, the fundamentals of horseback riding (though I was often an observer, rather than a rider), survival techniques, topography, maritime skills, navigation, and above all, discipline. Near what was to become the end of my service, I began to train as a spy. I never told anyone, and the training was still in its earliest stages when Victor and Elizabeth announced their final wedding plans. After her and Father's deaths, I was forced to suspend my service and tend to our property, as well as to Victor, who took quite ill.

His state of mind so deteriorated after their losses that he spent several months locked away in an asylum for his own protection. He said little to me when I visited, but wept openly for all those we'd lost. Later, as the time of his release drew near, he began to warn me that we were in mortal danger, that the Devil stalked us. I tried to ignore these disquieting warnings, but also began to feel that I was being watched. Several suggestive incidents during this time further unsettled me. I discovered doors mysteriously unlocked or opened in the house (now all but devoid of servants), objects were moved at random, noises of lamenting in the night, and once, I fancied, even laughter from one who knows they are free to act with impunity. Upon Victor's release, he became obsessed with catching and punishing the one who he felt was responsible for our miseries. And so we had planned our escape.

It has taken me nearly three days of the trip to relate the full details of my travels to Jack. But now that I've finished, even Jack is speechless, aware, that the Ernest Frankenstein who left Geneva ten years ago will never truly return.

**

Ireland, 1809

"If you please, Madame, I wish to see Ailis Tier … Frankenstein," Abrielle rose from her curtsey, and looked patiently into the eyes of the old woman. Could she sense how nervous Abrielle was? Actually, at first, she seemed slightly aghast, as though no one had ever shown her such manners; however, this soon altered to suspicion and curiosity. Why did this obviously, foreign stranger, now stand on the doorstep?

"On what matter, may I ask?" Her tone made the question sound regal.

Abrielle considered her response. She had escaped her pursuers, traveled across France, the Channel, and a good portion of Ireland to reach this place, but in truth, the distance she had traversed was far greater than all of that. She'd journeyed a lifetime to reach this moment, and now that it was here, she was terrified.

Her sister's face, that day at the orphan convent, the only day they'd ever beheld each other, flashed before her eyes; it bore the expression of confusion and pain she'd worn the moment when Abrielle struck their father. Would she ever understand why she could not forgive him? What if Ailis did not truly want her here? What might she have told other people about her? What would she think of her sister when she saw her? Ernest seemed to hold a favorable opinion of Abrielle, but then again, by his own admission, he'd been desperate for her help. She tried to set her doubts aside.

"I'm … I … I have come on behalf of her husband," Abrielle admitted awkwardly.

The old woman shifted slightly in the doorway, but gave no indication that she was ready to accept Abrielle into the house.

"Thiocfaidh mé chun mo dheirfiúr," Abrielle said in Gaelic.

A child-like light graced the old woman's eyes as one hand covered her mouth, and one reached down to take Abrielle's wrist.

"Bless me, her sister. Oh, my, yes, come, come," she bid, all traces of the stern guardian were lost, as she pulled the young woman into the house.

"I'm Mrs. Shaw. Ailis is in the back."

Abrielle was hurriedly led through the kitchen to the back door, but the old woman made no motion to follow her through.

"She needs you." She smiled, and nodded toward the figure of a woman, whose back was turned to the house.

The afternoon sun having escaped the blanket of clouds to a degree, now highlighted the tumbling waves with towering beams of light. In the distance, a rocky island stood in shadow, and seemed to be the focus of the woman. Heavily scented winds blew steadily at the dress and blonde hair of the girl, who stood bearing silent witness to the eternally changing sea. No, not silent. She was muttering words, and caressing her generously portioned abdomen.

Abrielle's heart was in her throat as she approached the woman, and though her nerves shook when she spoke, her voice sounded calm.

"Ailis?"

The girl jumped slightly, apparently unaware that anyone had approached her, until that moment. Abrielle reached out a hand to steady her. As their hands clasped, their eyes met. Even the roar of the waves did not penetrate their senses, as they slowly, delicately reached for one another.

"Abrielle," Ailis embraced her older sister, repeating her name over and over as disbelief changed into joy. Both held the other, as if fearing that, when the embrace was broken, the other would not be there. But as they hugged one another, the doubts and fears each had built over the long, lonely years faded to memory.

"My sister, my beautiful sister," Ailis said gently into Abrielle's ear. The love, gratitude, and relief in her younger sister's voice rendered her older sibling speechless. She'd never felt this happy. Abrielle tenderly kissed her cheek.

*

CHAPTER 13
THE LIES OF TRUTH

Hungary, 1809

Baseria sat nervously before her grandmother. What was happening to her? The only thing more frightening than the dream was the look of wretchedness in the old Seer's eyes.

"Forget this name," Nasi pleaded clasping her granddaughter's hands, "You must forget it, Sunflower. I beg you." She almost never used the nickname Mayte had given her youngest child.

"I cannot Nagyanya.[12] I have tried, but it plagues me."

The memory of the waking dream stirred within Baseria. The images and emotions entwined with it had become more intense and disturbing every time it came. She took the woman's wrinkled hand and drew it to the tears on her cheeks. Nasi shut her eyes for a long time, an anguished look etched on her features. She muttered something unintelligible, as if bidding the powers of fate to step aside. Then, reluctantly, she spoke.

"Tell me then, my child. Tell me what you have seen."

Baseria swallowed.

"It is always the same: a misty graveyard, the searching man, and the shadow that stalks him. I try to warn the man but the shadow stops me … glares at me with inhuman eyes … and then the name." Baseria clutched her chest. "I can no longer control it. The vision now comes to me when I am awake."

Nasi's eyes slowly drew open, burning with emotion.

"Your brother has heard you speak it?"

"Yes, while we prepared the morning meal."

"But Jal has not?"

"No."

The old woman became silent.

"Your father must not know this vision was yours," her voice finally cracked. Baseria nodded fervently. "Bring him to me."

---

12 (Hungarian) Grandmother.

She hesitated only a moment before departing the tent. She trusted her grandmother not to reveal the truth. As Baseria left her, Nasi stood, and after uncovering a small, ancient chest, she unlocked it to review the contents of the hallowed document inside.

*

Translated from the Ancient Scrolls of the Seer
Wild Rose Clan
Existence and Judgment

... all of nature is balance. And so the dawn of our kind brought the twilight of another; a failed race — known to us now only as the Old Ones. Immortal, they existed across countless eons, learning to understand the vast untold secrets of creation and the mysteries both of this world and those beyond this existence. Some of their kind aided our survival, while others sought our annihilation. But always we were separate until a member of our clan fell in love with one of their race.

Their union brought death into the world, and a plague was unleashed upon that powerful, once immortal race, until all but one, ceased to exist. The last of their kind sought out our people to offer up a final cursed blessing upon humanity. Our fates united, a vow was made to reveal the secrets of life and death to a member of our clan at the proper time — then the Old Ones were seen no more.

It is foretold that the First Light shall serve as a herald for the Old Ones' return and summon the Seer to restore the balance between humanity and the Old Ones which has been lost; lest they fail, the Second Light shall rise, for all shall suffer until balance is restored.

*

"Your father is most eager to find this man," Nasi explained that night when Baseria returned to her tent. "He fears the powers will reveal this vision to your aunt as well and the Moon Shadows will obtain him first."

"But I don't know where he is."

"There are ways," Nasi assured her.

She threw an assortment of herbs into the small fire that burned between them.

"The visions you have are a gift of the winds. But it is the water that will lead us to him. The currents of the unseen world will lead you to his energy."

Suddenly Baseria was afraid. Elemental Water was an erratic, unpredictable energy, even to touch. Her few training sessions with it always left her disoriented and badly shaken. It was far too simple a matter to become lost. The tides of time and emotion, which rippled through it, might lead her anywhere, and although she desired to serve her people, something within her deeply feared the shadow from her dream.

"Why does this man matter so much?" Baseria questioned apprehensively.

Nasi's answer surprised her.

"I don't know … but I think your mother did."

They rarely spoke of Baseria's mother. For both, the grief for her loss was too profound.

"Do I share my mother's vision?" Baseria breathlessly wondered.

Nasi paused and sighed deeply.

"You share one I once had … before the apoplexy. Your mother told me of it before my powers of speech had healed, before she was taken." The old woman seemed to shrink, as she spoke these words, with great difficulty.

Baseria's head swam.

"It is the name, child … this Frankenstein, it is the same."

Nasi had never before spoken of the onset of her apoplexy. Baseria knew she'd been meditating with her daughters, Mayte and Tasaria when it happened, but nothing more. Could this Frankenstein somehow be responsible for her affliction?

"Your mother questioned me most urgently about it, shortly before her enslavement in Romania. She said that I called this name out, over and over again, when the seizure came. Many times since my recovery, during my limited meditations into the unseen world, I have searched for meaning in this only to discover nothing."

"But Nagyanya, how does this name connect to the prophecy?"

Nasi covered her eyes with a shaking gnarled hand. "I have always wished my bones would be dust, long before this day came."

"But our destiny …"

"The prophecy can bring only sorrow before it brings peace. It is a curse, child, not a blessing. It is a curse upon us all."

Although aspects of the prophecy had become known over time, traditionally, only the Seer, and eventually her successor, knew the full contents. It was not until the onset of Nasi's fateful illness that the existence of a conflicting interpretation of the ancient prophecy became general knowledge among the people. This knowledge created an imbalance within the clan, one which had led them into an ideological war that might never end. What price would seeking this Frankenstein cost them?

"What is the connection between my vision and the prophecy?" Baseria persisted. All her life the prophecy had dominated her existence. She would not be denied its secrets now. Nasi refused to look at her when she continued.

"There are two," she poked at the fire. "It is said that when two Seers share a vision, the dawn of the prophecy is near."

Her granddaughter struggled through her confusion.

"But we have not shared a vision," Baseria protested, "and I am not yet a Seer."

Nasi pursed her lips and looked down into the fire without comment. Apparently she did not think much of these perceived distinctions. Baseria pressed her.

"What is the other?"

The old woman resumed placing herbs into the flames.

"That secret lay with your mother … and father. I cannot speak of it."

Baseria's breath caught in her throat. "Is that what you discussed with him?"

She nodded slowly.

"He claims that if we can find this man from your vision then he will retrieve evidence your parents obtained during my illness. If the vision and the evidence are true then … then it means that the Old Ones have returned."

Baseria gasped—the Old Ones. For several tense moments, the sound of flames, beating against the unseen air currents, was the lone noise in the tent. Only in the most ancient of their myths were there references to the Old Ones. A cold, shiftless, energy seemed to taunt her from the darkness, as did the memory of the shadow's vile laugh in her vision.

Could there be more of them hidden in the mist?

"Baseria? Baseria."

She jumped at the sound of her own name.

"I will attempt to guide you through the water, but it is your vision. It is you who must find this man."

"I'm afraid," Baseria admitted.

Nasi moved closer and leaned her granddaughter's head against her.

"So am I, child. So am I."

*

Intent, misguided or righteous, had to be pure when one sought to use Elemental energy of any kind, but Baseria felt only doubt. If she should find this man and all they feared turned out to be true, what would become of those she loved? She'd already caused so much damage. But if she failed to find him and her failure resulted in success for the Moon Shadow clan, what then? Preservation of the future, if not her people, demanded action, but what kind of future would her choices in this moment beckon forth?

Despite Nasi's confidence in her abilities, she was not yet a true Seer. She acted more on instinct, while trying to understand the deeper mysteries she touched. But she was not wise or powerful. Baseria was a poor substitution for her once commanding grandmother, her insightful mother, and promising sister.

She'd never sought this reality. There were other things she might do with her life. Secretly she longed to leave the clan and its war, and establish her own destiny. For Baseria, the old ways were meant to guide one's life, not bind it. Ultimately, only the love she felt for her grandmother and brother prevented her departure. Would serving them in this moment, forever sever her from that long-held dream of personal freedom?

"You ask much of me," she finally said.

Nasi made no remark. How could she? This choice lie with Baseria, and she would honor her granddaughter's decision, regardless of whether or not she agreed with it. She owed the girl everything.

"What should I do?" Baseria whispered.

"Honor your heart and you will know what to do," she held her grandchild.

Baseria drew in a deep breath.

"I will get Espen," she said, as she sat up, "and I'll meet you at the river."

She left the tent in haste.

*

With the last of the ash rubbed into his sister's flesh, Espen cracked the thin layer of ice encasing a portion of the river. All three were certain that the darkness, remote location, and lonely hour of the night kept prying eyes and minds far distant. Baseria sweated, despite the bone chilling temperature. Though fears worked to break her mind, her spirit was ready. It was time. She stepped down from the bank and into the frigid water of the river. She feared the water, physically, since the loss of her sister and cousin, and spiritually, since her troubling experiences with its turbulent energies as an apprentice to the Seer.

Hopefully the ash would protect her. It connected her to Elemental Earth and to Nasi. The old woman, also coated in ash, sat on a nearby rock, enshrouded in robes, which held the bitterly cold air at bay. Espen looked distinctly uncomfortable, but Baseria knew it was not the cold that bothered him. He feared for his sister's safety and paced restlessly along the shore, ready to save her at a moment's notice. Only his deep trust in Nasi permitted him to allow this in the first place.

The water numbed her feet instantly and sent an unpleasant shock up her spine. Her fingers prickled with the sensation, and her mind demanded that she remove her body at once from the source responsible for this disagreeable condition. All of this, she tried to ignore. Elemental Water did not require physical contact, but Baseria felt she'd be unable to complete her task without it. She relied on the tactile experience.

As she'd been taught, she opened her mind to a more meditative state, to levels of consciousness often set aside in this waking life. When her spirit was attuned to the rhythm of the water, her energies seemed to seep into the currents around her. The tranquility of the water was not to last. Suddenly she was rushing and darting, her breath stolen from her by the onslaught of motion. It was like swimming up a waterfall, backwards. For a time, she felt a presence moving with her, then it dimmed, and she passed on alone. And Baseria knew, she'd moved beyond Nasi's ability to protect her.

A host of new energies swiftly rose around her. As they were guided by unseen currents, some seemed to notice her, while others did not. Emotions, like musical notes, touched her from these energies. Time, bereft of its clockwork perfection, wove itself through the currents, adding to the sense of disorientation. Baseria fought against this maelstrom as best she could, but began to despair in finding the energy she sought. It was too much. Sympathetic energies heard her and drew near. They flooded her with conflicting emotions and offers of aid. Some stayed, others drifted off, in an attempt to help her. Angry or destructive energies were also drawn toward her, and threatened to pull her further from her body and the present. She encountered sudden shifts, and new energies would swirl about her, and then disappear as a new current caught them.

Without warning, an energy abruptly seized her from behind. If either of them had possessed hands, they would have been clasped together, as they fell through time. Baseria suddenly found herself in a new place. She was being dragged roughly to her feet, surrounded by hostility. She was in pain. She touched her head and discovered a deep, gushing wound there. A rope now hung about her neck and with it came a sense of tranquility. How could peace exist is such a horrific place? No, the peace did not come from the knowledge of death. A sensation of approval graced her consciousness. The energy, which was responsible for bringing her here, spoke into her mind.

"There," a voice whispered.

Baseria knew where "there" was instinctively. The vicious crowd vanished and only the stricken face of the man she sought remained; his energy now glowed like a beacon. Hope flooded her spirit. She'd found him.

"Thank you," she said to her guide, but the energy had vanished.

Baseria awoke to the sensation of Espen hauling her upward. Her spirit had drawn her body down into the icy water, and it now shuddered with the after-effects of hypothermic shock. Nasi lit a fire by the river. With the ritual over, they no longer need worry about attracting unwanted attention. Together, Nasi and Espen, worked to revive her.

In the morning when her senses were fully restored, she asked for a map. Closing her eyes, Baseria allowed her hand to move of its own volition. It felt unnaturally light as it hovered over the lines, seeking Frankenstein's energy. In the end, it indicated several points vibrant with the stranger's energy.

"You can recognize him now?" Espen asked skeptically.

Baseria nodded. Her body was heavy with exhaustion.

"Then we will leave with the others tomorrow," Nasi decided. "Baseria will be our guide."

"The others can't know," Espen asserted.

Nasi nodded in agreement.

"For now, they must believe that I lead them. But dangers may soon reveal the truth. We must be ready for this."

Her warning given, the old woman left the tent.

"I'd rather die than let Father know," Baseria told Espen as she slipped away into unconsciousness, "I'd rather die."

*

Salzburg, 1809

By late into the afternoon of the fifth day, the environs of Salzburg lay before them. Throughout his travels, Ernest never had ventured into (former) Austrian territory. The unyielding grasp of Napoleon's Empire now extended into this region and rendered the impressive fortifications of the Hohnsalzburg Fortress useless. The ancient bastion, which dominated the left bank of the Salzach River that bisected the city, had been taken by his forces without a single shot being exchanged.

Salzburg was a city renowned for its architectural grandeur, its religious heritage, and as a developing center of musical culture. Its unique alpine setting soothed the senses and painted an idyllic scene. It made his hateful pilgrimage here seem all the more intrusive.

By the time they reached the Clerval residence, the sun had long since dimmed to shadow. Jack and Ernest both arrived feeling nervous but for different reasons. The acumen of Ernest's decision to seek out the Clervals no longer felt like a wise one, and Jack agonized endlessly over his reunion with his estranged wife, Constanza. Though they'd traveled for days, Jack had actually spoken very little about her, masterfully manipulating the conversation away from the subject when pressed by his old friend for further information regarding their relationship. Upon their arrival, only servants greeted them. The Clervals themselves had gone to one of Salzburg's concert halls, owned by a wealthy and influential family. Jack, ever the spontaneous spirit, turned on his heel and headed back out the door. Ernest would have preferred to rest after nearly five days of travel, but knew Jack wouldn't wait to discuss the matter.

The performance turned out to be both concert and social gathering. The performance hall was lushly decorated, encased within tiered balconies emblazoned with highly polished wood and brass trim. Dark red curtains seemed to be draped everywhere. Though he had no idea what the hall was called or the occasion being observed, Ernest dutifully took a seat in one of the balcony boxes when the performances began. They featured a colorful variety of talents and instruments: pianists, harpsichords, violins, harps, cellos, and operatic performances. During the first intermission, Jack finally spotted his mother and father.

After a lengthy delay, he waved Ernest over to them. It was a cool reception, one which made him remember why these people had always made him uncomfortable in their presence. Jack's mother's aloof nature and his father's judgmental statements did little to alleviate Ernest's misgivings. After some verbal maneuvering, they agreed to Jack's repeated request that Ernest stay at the house for a day or so. He did not elaborate on the purpose for the visit, and both promoted the notion that he was simply passing through. The less said about Henry the better.

Late into the second round of performances, Jack began to fidget. He twisted his wedding ring endlessly around his finger, until Ernest became convinced he'd saw through his bone if he didn't stop. Finally he touched Jack's arm.

"What?" Jack asked, snapping out of his trance.

Ernest merely looked down at the ring he still touched, then back to his eyes. Wordlessly, Jack returned his attention to the performer on stage and crossed his hands beneath his arms. He also crossed his leg, set one atop his knee, and began to vibrate it furiously, hitting Ernest's in the process.

"Knock it off."

"Sorry."

Jack ceased his motions, but barely drew his eyes away from the stage. The woman who was currently singing, some operatic work, seemed a fairly average performer to Ernest, but Jack was enthralled. Near the end of the piece, he grabbed his friend's arm.

"This is the best part. I love when she does this."

A soaring note was struck, and her voice scaled and pitched in a unique and impressive manner as she carried it. She held it and when it seemed there could be no breath left within her, she continued to hold it. With subtle grace, the accompanying musicians rejoined her and helped to close with a stirring finish. The crowd seemed equally taken, and she blew kisses of recognition, and gratitude to them. Jack was whistling and clapping like mad.

"Ain't my 'Stanza great?!"

"Wait. Your wife is an opera singer?"

Jack ignored the question and waved madly trying to get his wife's attention. She continued to bow and gush modestly onstage. When it became clear that Jack's efforts were yielding no result, he collected himself and attempted to groom his hair.

"How do I look?"

"Desperate."

"Shut up, Ernie. Seriously, now."

"Desperate," he repeated.

Jack waved a disgusted hand at him as he exited the box. Ernest couldn't help but chuckle in amusement.

He studied the crowds below with idle curiosity. The floor was packed. Resolving to relax as best he could in the theater box while Jack sought his wife, Ernest couldn't help but idly wonder how their reunion might play out. Part of him wished it would play out onstage so he could witness it for himself. Amused by the thought, he relaxed and focused his attentions on the distant people still lingering on the stage.

"Frankenstein," a voice, deep and dry as the autumn leaves, whispered harshly through the curtain of the adjoining box.

Ernest's heart raced as anger and fear fought to control it.

"What do you want?" he challenged.

"You try my patience."

"And you have abused mine," he shot back.

Silence.

"I found your damn journals. Be gone."

"Yes, but apparently they told you nothing. And now you waste time, here, in Salzburg."

"It is mine to waste."

"I will end that illusion."

Ernest shuddered, remembering the physical power of this man and knew it was not an empty threat.

"I don't even know what I'm looking for," he finally admitted.

"Tell me what you have found."

"My brother was unbalanced and unhappy. But I knew these things before …"

"And what drove him to such a state?"

He resented the question.

"The loss of loved ones, a mental sickness which …"

An unnatural laughter from the other side of the curtain annihilated the thought.

"I will help you understand."

A sudden insight possessed Ernest's passions.

"Did you help LaShall understand?" he asked bitterly.

"Your neighbor's death was an accident, nothing more."

So this monster had followed him back to Geneva. What all had he witnessed there?

"If his death is so trivial, then explain how he died."

There was only the briefest of pauses.

"Fear," was the solitary answer.

Ernest's breath was now escaping in short bursts, and a cold sweat clung to his skin.

"Of what?"

"Of what you are seeing, right now."

He felt it, before he saw it. A hand had reached through the curtain to clasp Ernest's wrist. No, it was not such a commonplace sight which beset his eyes; it was anything but.

At least twice the size of a normal man's hand, it encompassed not only Ernest's wrist, but a portion of his arm as well. It was shriveled and mummified, the skin of a nearly translucent nature, which made visible the networks of veins and muscles throughout. The cruel nature inherent of the claw-like fingers, capped by blackened nails, was re-enforced by the strength of the grip. It felt as if Death itself clutched Ernest. Were it not for the visible movement of blood and the controlled beat of the pulse, he would have claimed that he was restrained by a corpse.

"What you seek awaits you in Ingolstadt," the voice wheezed, "Find the clues, Uncle, so our destinies can be fulfilled."

The pressure from the fingers increased. Ernest wanted to scream, but found himself too frightened to utter a sound. Into this void of reality, he heard a gasp, followed immediately by a woman's scream. He looked for the source of the sound, and saw Jack and his wife framed in the box's entryway. The expression of stunned disbelief was already disappearing from Jack's face as he began to withdraw his concealed pistol from his jacket. His wife dropped like a lead weight to the floor.

Ernest's tormentor must have either seen or heard what was about to happen because the hand disappeared behind the curtain seconds before Jack shot into it. The report echoed through the still crowded theater and elicited a wave of surprised shouts and a general panic. The gun had been close enough to Ernest's head to temporarily suspend his ability to hear. He just stared at the spot where the hand had been, and also at the smoking hole the shot had blasted through the curtain.

"… you all right? Ern, are you all right?" Jack asked shaking him. Ernest nodded. Jack fled through the entryway. He returned several minutes later, a troubled expression etched onto his features.

"No one there," he pointed towards the curtain, "no blood either."

Ernest started to rub his wrist, unable to purge the vile sensation left by the ghastly grip. Jack misinterpreted his friend's pained expression.

"Honestly, Ern, I'm not that bad of a shot."

"Did anyone see anything?"

Jack shook his head.

"Just some huge robed figure that vanished out the window."

Ernest had failed to notice that Jack had maneuvered his estranged wife into one of the box seats. She was still unconscious.

"Is she all right?" he asked.

Jack gathered her up in his arms and began to move toward the entry.

"It's just shock mostly. Don't think she was hurt by the fall. We'd probably …"

"What's going on here?" A very agitated official demanded from the door.

How could they begin to explain this?

"Is this how you protect your patrons and performers?" Jack huffed.

The theater official was momentarily taken aback.

"I demand to know who shot …"

"It was some gigantic lunatic, took a shot at my wife. Must be some crazed admirer; best get her home to safety. 'cuse us."

Jack attempted to force his way past the man. He stood his ground.

"Now I know for a fact that this woman is not married," the official bristled as he blocked Jack, who glared at him icily.

"And I know for a fact that she lives at the Clerval residence with her husband, me," Jack retorted, thumping his chest.

The man's eyes bulged.

"I tell you, you will never leave with …"

Stanza moaned slightly as she began to come to and looked up into Jack's face.

"Stanza?" both men said at the same time, then glared at each other.

In a thick Austrian accent, she asked, "Don't you have any normal friends, Jack?"

"Guess that means you're fine," Jack commented dryly.

"Air, you fools, I need air," she threw a harsh, woozy look at both men as Jack set her down, and she collapsed into a seat.

"Freulein?"

"Away, Fritz. Away," she swatted the air around her as if she was attacking some pestering insect. She breathed deeply. Jack made shooing motions at Fritz, who shot him a heated look of resentment. Jack smiled smugly in return, but his mood darkened the instant the other man vanished out the door.

"So it's on to Fritz now is it?"

"Please, darling, please," she held up a hand, her eyes were shut as she fanned her face and ignored Jack's jealousy.

Ernest thought Jack was going to challenge her further, but to his surprise, he merely took out a new cigar and began to light it.

"What in the name of Hell was that?" he demanded.

"What I need to protect my family from," was the best Ernest could manage.

"Some smelling salts would be helpful," Stanza interjected.

"Yeah, I can see that, but what was it? I mean nothin' in nature that I know of looks or moves like that."

"Jack your smoke. This is murder on my vocal chords," Stanza was furiously whipping the swirls of cigar smoke out of the air.

"Revived ya, didn't it. Ah," Jack thoughtlessly threw the cigar over the edge of the balcony. "Let's go."

*

That first night in Salzburg, upon returning from the concert, Ernest discovered that Victor's burnt journal from Geneva had been stolen from his rooms. A search of the house revealed no intruders. As he bedded down, he tried not to think of the hideous hand and prayed it would not find him in the darkness. Needless to say, he slept poorly.

Fortunately, the Clervals themselves spent little time at their luxurious residence. They rarely spent much time together, even back when Ernest was younger, and even less after Henry's death. He should not have been surprised that Jack's own marriage would mirror that of his parents' so closely.

Unlike Jack's parents, Stanza was present constantly. She was beautiful, intelligent, inquisitive, boorish, judgmental, off-putting, direct, spoiled, loud, outrageous, and demanding, just to name a few of her qualities. At first, Ernest couldn't fathom how she and Jack had ever agreed to marriage, but the more time he spent around them, both together and separately, he began to realize that beneath it all, these two really did love one another. It seemed that the more they fought and snipped, the closer to the surface their true feelings for one another came. Though there was love, the path they took to express it, or discover it, was a destructive one, as each said and did things to wound the other. It was as if they were both performers for an exclusive audience. In the course of a single afternoon, he must have heard the idea of divorce raised no less than six times. But the next moment, they'd be cooing reassuringly to each other.

All the drama, however, did hamper Ernest's work. Jack, who when he wasn't dealing with marital issues or running out to meet a different parent, at various locations, kindly volunteered to spend long hours with his friend in the attic examining Henry's possessions. Henry had loved learning and language, so there were literally volumes of journals to review. Some contained stories of romance and heroism, others sundry notes on assorted topics of interest, while still others were crammed with personal reflections, intellectual recordings and drawings. None of the numerous volumes of captured thought was in any type of order. They had simply been packaged up in crates and boxes and moved here hurriedly from Geneva, left alone in the quiet memory chamber of the Clerval's attic.

By evening of the second day, the long hours were beginning to tell. Stanza spent a great portion of the day, practicing the same three songs over and over downstairs, with varying degrees of success. It rained steadily, and the drafty attic became quite uncomfortable. Jack was absent nearly the entire day. More frustrating than all of this was the lack of progress.

Ernest gave up hopes of finding anything of Victor's, and instead, concentrated his efforts on pouring through Henry's journals looking for the "clues" his aggressive phantom had hinted at. He was rapidly losing interest in being shackled to the past, wanting nothing more than to feel Ailis' soft, loving touch, in the safety and security of their home. By now, not a single hour passed when he did not think of her. What if he failed to find anything here or chose not to go to Ingolstadt? Would it really matter?

"Hey, Ern," Jack's voice suddenly beckoned from below, "let's go get drunk."

This was Jack's normal solution after a day spent too long in the company of his parents. Ernest wasn't particularly in the mood, but the knot in his neck and shoulders convinced him that Jack's suggestion might be the ideal distraction. As Ernest finally descended the stairwell, he overheard the end of yet another argument between Jack and Stanza.

"Well, I'm only waitin' ten minutes, then," Jack yelled at her retreating form.

"She's coming?" Ernest asked dryly.

"Looks that way," Jack huffed.

They waited an hour and a half before leaving, and then Stanza slipped into the role of tour guide for their guest. Her knowledge of Salzburg and its history were actually quite impressive, and Ernest might have enjoyed the tour, if Jack hadn't kept complaining throughout it. They ended up at a party thrown by one of her wealthy patrons. She split off to revel with the crowd as her companions retired to an obscure table in a dimly lit corner.

"Sorry 'bout all that," Jack stated as he downed some type of drink in a single slug. "But if you couldn't tell, she's quite proud of her hometown."

"No problem, actually it was rather interesting. Wish the rain would have let up though."

Jack downed another drink and nodded.

"So, what were you up to all day?" Ernest asked nonchalantly.

"Oh, parents, mostly lecturing me 'bout the state of my union like they've got room to talk," he snorted.

"Still thinking about that divorce?"

"Well, I already divorced and remarried her once. Probably can't afford to do it again."

Ernest choked slightly on his drink. Jack didn't seem to notice.

"Been givin' some thought to your own situation as well," he continued, "'bout the other night and all."

Jack studied his empty glass.

"Victor was studyin' medicine or the like, right?"

"That was my impression; we never really discussed it much."

"Yeah, big shock there, Ern. Anyway, what if our big, ugly friend was involved in some experimental treatment that went wrong?"

Ernest paused to consider the idea.

"Did Henry ever write you and mention much about Victor?" he finally asked.

Jack made a face as he downed the drink he'd nabbed from a passing tray.

"Ah. Why didn't I think of that? I bet I sent some of his letters off with my folks when they moved. Couldn't bring myself to read them again at the time, wasn't certain how long I was gonna stay in Geneva and all. We should look for those in the morning, might be down in the study."

"But how could this experimental treatment of others affect Victor?" Ernest mused.

Jack played with a box of matches before lighting yet another cigar.

"Well," he paused thoughtfully, "suppose that fellow the other night was a leper or got burned or something, would explain the skin. And say Victor tried to be some hero and was creating some new medicine, and tried it on both himself and his patient."

"And you think something like that drove him mad?" Ernest asked, his curiosity now piqued.

"Now we're just guessin' here, but you have to admit, it would explain a lot. Maybe he got hooked on the stuff and it caused him to commit other crimes, and sometimes he'd remember and others …"

"He'd forget," Ernest finished the thought.

He leaned back in his seat awed by this new idea. Jack was right. It could explain so much: the mood swings, the hysteria, even the decrepit physical and mental state Henry had discovered Victor to be in when he'd arrived in Ingolstadt. Even the ravings in the burnt journals suddenly seemed to make sense. Only the wretch's address of Ernest as "uncle" lingered as a point of doubt, though one that could be dismissed as a result of madness.

"That's brilliant, Jack."

"Looks and brains, that's why she loves me."

Jack beamed and toasted his friend as the slightly off-key sounds of his wife's singing filtered in from another room.

"So you married her twice?"

*

"M. Waldman. Henry refers to being introduced to this professor on two separate occasions. Name sound familiar, Ern?"

It had taken more than an hour of searching the Clerval's immense study before locating the letters they sought. Jack squinted at his brother's writing.

"According to Henry, this guy's visits really agitated Victor."

Ernest lay down the stack of papers he'd been reviewing as Jack handed him the letter.

"I think Victor mentioned a Waldman in the journal that was stolen," Ernest commented as he began to read. Henry's impression was that this man had served as a mentor or source of inspiration for Victor's studies but offered no additional insights.

The greatest revelation, however, was found an hour later in one of Henry's final letters from Ingolstadt.

"What? I don't get it?" said Jack as Ernest tapped excitedly at several lines.

Ernest fumbled for one of the earlier letters they'd reviewed.

"See. Here. Henry mentions leaving some of Victor's effects with Waldman. Once when Victor was still recovering from his prolonged illness and here when my brother left for Geneva. It makes sense."

"Good. I'm glad the guy's a junk collector …"

"No. Victor left Ingolstadt in haste after William's death, and to the best of my knowledge, he never returned to the university. Henry planned to, but instead chose to accompany Victor to the British Isles. So no one ever returned for whatever items Henry left with Waldman."

"So?"

"What if Henry left some of Victor's journals with Waldman?"

For the first time since his unwilling encounter with the man in the cavern, Ernest felt genuinely closer to accomplishing his task.

"Bit of a stretch, Ern," Jack noted as he lit a cigar. "No guarantee this M. Waldman still resides in Ingolstadt, to say nothing about him keeping Victor's possessions."

Ernest nodded. After a decade, it did seem unlikely, but his tormentor had already guided Ernest's steps towards Ingolstadt. Now Waldman seemed to be the key to understanding the great mystery. And if Waldman did retain the missing journals, hopefully it meant Ernest could go home to Ireland in a week or so. If nothing else, at least Ingolstadt was in the right direction.

"I'll leave tomorrow morning," Ernest decided looking out the window at the pouring rain.

"Fine. I'll handle the transportation arrangements."

*

Jack rolled up to the front door in a cabriolet early the next day.

"Tie up the luggage, and let's get goin' before it starts rainin' again," he beckoned.

"You're not coming with me, Jack."

"How ya gonna get to Ingolstadt without me?"

"I'll buy a horse. You need to stay here with your wife," Ernest said.

"Not a problem, this was her idea. Practically insisted I go with you."

Was that good or not?

"Stanza's quite taken with ya, Ern," Jack continued, "doesn't want anything bad to happen, and she wants me to watch out for ya."

"That's … very generous … of you both," Ernest added, "but …"

"Hey, maybe I'm not doin' this just for you, all right," Jack snapped. "Henry deserved better. If solving the hobgoblin's mystery accomplishes that, so be it."

Conviction burned in his friend's eyes. Jack was right. If this trip did uncover the secrets of Victor's elusive past, it might also begin to heal the Clervals' wounds as well. Ernest offered no further protests as he climbed abroad.

"Besides, mountain roads through Bavaria aren't always safe this time of year. A shame if you survived all that other stuff at sea just to end up under an avalanche or somethin'."

"Thanks for the cheery thought, Jack," Ernest remarked as he settled into his seat. "So Stanza really likes me?"

"Yeah, this has been one of our best visits ever. Normally she's never this nice."

*

Ingolstadt, 1809

The search for M. Waldman turned out to be exceedingly brief and ended in a most unexpected location: an asylum. His former colleagues were reticent to reveal this information at first, but after Ernest mentioned Victor's name, one finally relented.

"Whatever became of Victor?" the aging scholar asked. "We always assumed he'd come back here to teach or perform research."

Jack and Ernest exchanged an uncomfortable look.

"His passions took him … elsewhere," Ernest said truthfully.

The man smiled politely, unwilling to press the matter any further.

"I see. Do you need directions to the asylum from here?"

"Yes, but could you tell us why M. Waldman is there? No one will talk to us about him."

The short, gruff-voiced professor shook his head.

"Not surprising. Poor fellow simply lost touch with reason about six years ago, quite a shock really. He was one of the most grounded, disciplined, academicians I ever knew."

"What, did he hurt someone?" Jack asked.

"Fortunately no, but he began to become obsessed with some personal experiments he was conducting, away from the university, and eventually, his paranoia over them took control."

Ernest tried his best to mask his eager fascination with the professor's intriguing tale.

"Did he ever say what types of experiments?" he casually asked.

The man frowned and his lower lip jutted slightly in concentration.

"Nothing of merit. Towards the end, he claimed they would re-invent humanity itself. But I've heard the same thing from poets," he laughed wistfully before continuing. "I took it to be some advancement in his field of specialty, chemistry, but I suppose it could have been something else. We'll never know though."

"Why?"

"Well, everything was destroyed in the fire, of course, including his mind."

And with this statement, Ernest's hopes seemed to wither and perish in flames.

"Was there anything left?" he inquired, but the academician only shook his head. So Victor's intangible journals, if they had ever existed, must have also been consumed by the fire. They'd come here for nothing. But Jack was intrigued by this tale and pressed on.

"The fire was six years ago, too?"

The professor nodded.

"Roughly, quite a massive one, burned down his lodgings and the two on either side as well. Everyone assumed he'd set it, and between the fire and his bizarre behavior before and after … though come to think of it, he was calmer in some ways after."

"Any family we could talk to?" Ernest asked.

The professor pursed his lips.

"No, he was a pure scholar. He lived for the pursuit of knowledge. Only worked with one assistant after Victor's departure, and that poor young man's body was found in the professor's house after the fire. Tragic."

"They rebuild the place?" Jack queried as he fumbled to light a new cigar.

"Oh, yes. You'd never know by the look of the block today that there'd ever been such a calamity."

The scholar kindly gave them the promised directions and made to leave.

"Forgive me, gentlemen, but I'm going to be late for lecture."

"Yes, well thank you very much Professor …?"

"Krempe, good bye, good luck." He shook hands briefly and departed.

"Well, this just keeps gettin' better," Jack commented several moments later through a cloud of cigar smoke.

Ernest paced, hoping that the movement would either relax or inspire his thoughts.

"Coincidence?" he said at last, while rubbing his hands together against the cold.

"What your ugly friend, insane brother, and his cracked professor?" Jack asked sarcastically. "Not likely."

"The journals do link all three," Ernest agreed.

"True," Jack conceded, "but that's assumin' that Waldman kept 'em, and that there was somethin' a value in them to begin with."

"True," Ernest muttered dejectedly.

"Too bad that assistant didn't survive. Probably could have cleared everything up," Jack noted as the droning, peal of church bells called out the hour.

"Well, how ya want to play it, Ern?" Jack shifted the cigar in his mouth. "Day's gettin' on."

By now they'd wandered back out onto the campus proper. Ernest's hand rubbed through his hair as he looked up towards a white steeple.

"We're close to something. I can feel it," he declared turning back upon his friend suddenly.

"Ya know, whatever we find, it's not gonna be pretty," Jack observed seriously.

Ernest sighed.

"Why don't we get some lunch and then find the asylum."

Jack smiled mischievously.

"Food and a show. Sounds like my kinda afternoon."

*

The only other asylum Ernest had ever visited was the one in Geneva where Victor stayed after Elizabeth's and his father's deaths. The facility where Waldman lived revived those memories and made them seem cozy by comparison. Here there was only chaos.

Insane ravings blended with desperate cries, and all around, the cacophony of unrestrained minds rent the air with their unique and terrifying symphony. There were rooms, some filled with those experiencing violent fits, while others held galleries of people restrained in any number of horrifying and undignified manners. It was stifling: the air smelled of sweat and urine, and the misery of it all threatened to overwhelm the senses. The faces within swirled past: insanity knows no boundaries of age or class, the visages of the hopeless, the hollow, and the tormented burned into Ernest's and Jack's eyes. It was in this living nightmare that they met with Victor's former tutor.

Waldman's hair, or what he hadn't torn out, was shock white. He was not screaming or abusive, but self-contained and distant, lost within the confines of his own mind. He sat, wrapped in blankets in a small, plaster-white alcove on the second floor. Over time, he had scratched chemical and mathematical formulas on the surrounding walls. Those who worked here still called him "the professor," but primarily for the sake of mockery. He bore scars upon his hands and neck, reminders of the fire M. Krempe had told them of. He paid little attention to Ernest's repeated summons, and instead focused on a cricket, which had somehow managed to survive this late into early winter. Jack finally threw up his hands.

"We're wastin' our time here, Ern. Ya'd get more outta his wall scratchin' than you will outta 'im," he noted in annoyance.

It did seem that Waldman now dwelt beyond their ability to reach him, but Ernest wasn't willing to give up so easily.

"Why don't you wait outside, Jack?"

"'Cause it's cold, Ern," Jack stated testily as he studied the writings on the wall.

"Well, wait downstairs, then."

"Why, what are you gonna do? Some South Pacific witch doctorin'?"

Ernest smiled.

"Perhaps."

"Ah, I could use a smoke anyway. It stinks in here." He shrugged and wondered off.

Waldman had still not drawn his eyes away from the cricket, which now sat close to edging outside of a barred window. Without thinking, Ernest kept it from escaping, and then placed it gingerly into Waldman's hand who stared at it as it ran across his palm, then stopped and perched upon a knuckle. It was then Ernest noticed the manacles, which anchored the lunatic to the wall. They'd been hidden beneath the mass of filthy blankets he was enshrouded in.

"Bio-chemical stimulus, respiration, and variant structure," Waldman noted as he studied the insect. He seemed oddly amused by it.

"Professor?"

His face darkened before he snapped at Ernest.

"Erroneous that. Was Zeus so plagued by mortals?"

At least it was a response.

"Professor," he said more forcefully.

The man's face twitched.

"Fidget elsewhere, lest your elements shatter, dear bug." He turned away, casting the cricket off his hand before trying to cover his ears, muttering all the while to himself. Ernest leaned forward.

"Sir, you taught my brother once. His friend left some of his possessions with you years ago. Do you remember Victor Frankenstein?"

With a suddenness Ernest was unprepared for and motions only madness can give grace, he seized the younger man's head nearly pulling him over. Waldman seemed to examine Ernest's cranium, and then to a lesser extent, his eyes.

"Shocking," he muttered when he finally released him, "Shocking lack of resemblance. He's too common to understand, too common."

The lunatic itched at the bug bites under his chin as he pronounced his observation.

"My brother was too common or I am?" Ernest asked in confusion.

Waldman's right hand swatted at him.

"To waste my time with such questions. Of course not, the second one proceeds the first in all things. They took it," he roared pointing accusingly towards Ernest. "Collapsed the cornerstone. HE caused the temple to fall … reduced all meaning to so much dust."

The man's decrepit visage grew bitterly sad with remorse, then mild.

"What sadness found you, hence?" he suddenly inquired. This final question was spoken as if he'd just realized he was actually speaking to someone. Could his previous ranting have been nothing more than scenes playing through his destroyed mind? Ernest swallowed.

"Please, professor. Can you tell me if you kept any of Victor Frankenstein's journals?"

The old man actually cackled at this question, raw madness carved onto his face.

"Seek you death or knowledge?"

He continued before Ernest could answer.

"You will find both in the charnel houses. If you wish to understand, go to them as your brother did. Seek what he sought, beyond the common, only then will you know the secrets he learned."

He shook with another round of hysteria as he tried again to clutch at Ernest, hissing and crying out, but the chains restrained him.

"Frankenstein!! Frankenstein!!!!"

Ernest backed away from the lunatic, as his outburst brought unwanted attention from nearby inmates and sanitarium personnel.

"Believe in the end to know the beginning," were the last words he heard Waldman scream, as Ernest rapidly descended the stairs.

*

The moon rode into the heavens, veiled and terrible that night. Those hallowed, lonely hours would never know the brilliance of that traveling candle, as fast-moving mountains of smoking darkness denied all but the faintest trace of light from the sky. Winds made unwelcome demands upon empty branches, which in turn excited the air with their chattering. Lurking specters of the mind gave life to shadow and sound. A swirling shroud of mist fought the winds for control of the graveyard. It hung, low and thick, among the stones and monuments, adding an unearthly veil between the living and the dead.

The realities of a madman had driven Ernest here. What did he seek in such a place? What had Victor sought? Waldman claimed the charnel houses were bastions of not just death but knowledge. Across untold civilizations and countless centuries, humankind had searched for meaning in mortality. What knowledge could come from death? Great philosophies and religions had established themselves, by providing answers and hope to this most basic yet essential question of existence. What hope did Ernest have in answering it by tracing the steps of a lunatic? Believe in the end to know the beginning.

Jack had begrudgingly acquiesced to following the insights of the insane after they'd left the asylum. There was little choice. They'd spent the remaining daylight hours in search of Victor's former residence but been denied entry by its current occupant. A visit to Waldman's former habitation also yielded precious little. It was, as Krempe said, a revitalized area, and their investigations proved fruitless. Consequently, only the cemeteries remained as a possible avenue to pursue the elusive mysteries of a dark and troubled past. Ernest probed the shadows with his eyes. What had his brother sought here? Would the clues present themselves as etchings upon the nearly indecipherable tombstones? Could Victor, himself, be buried in one of the cemeteries of Ingolstadt? Were there more victims, as Jack had postulated, of Victor's medical experiments? What was the relationship between M. Waldman and Victor's insanity?

Darkness reigned for several hours before they'd decided on this course of action.

"I'll take these two, you try this one," Jack commanded as they huddled over a map of Ingolstadt.

"But those are both in town," Ernest protested.

"Yeah, what of it?" Jack asked indifferently.

"You could get caught by the authorities and arrested for trespassing or something."

Though daylight might have aided their efforts, they'd mutually decided that stealth and time were more valuable.

"I doubt it," Jack said derisively. "Besides, who's the better liar here?"

"Good point."

They folded the map and separated, with Ernest striking out for the furthest, most isolated cemetery they'd been able to locate. The winds made lighting a candle or torch impractical and should have dissipated the fog, which persisted over the low-land cemetery he was investigating, but it hadn't. In fact, it seemed even more substantive since he'd entered the graveyard.

For over an hour now, he'd cast about looking at headstones and entering mausoleums, rich with the scent of decay and niter, heavy in the stale air. Here the inequalities of life were cast aside, as all were devoured by time and the elements, as they returned to the dusts of nature's imagination.

It was upon exiting the third charnel house that two things happened: the winds subsided and the first torch appeared. It hovered up on the ridge where the road bordered the cemetery. Ernest cursed. The last thing he wanted was a caretaker asking questions or to be brought up on charges of grave robbing or some other such nonsense. Still there was no reason to assume that the torch bearer knew he was here. The mists persisted, and he carried no light to betray his location. With any luck this visitor would disappear shortly, and he could complete his task unencumbered. He waited among the dead for the living to remove themselves. But it was not to be.

A second torch ignited in the cemetery proper, much closer to him than the first. A cold shock began to course through his veins. Was someone searching for him down here? Had Jack been caught? A lone visitor he could handle, but two might be difficult. A third torch sprang to life in the dark, obscuring mist, followed shortly by a fourth, then a fifth, then sixth. There was no more time to think; every second brought a newly awakened, point of ominous light. They were all around him and closing in.

Ernest reached for his gun, but quickly realized the futility of doing so. He was surrounded, and even a wild shot through the fog no longer guaranteed him an escape route, for the torches were too numerous and close together. Someone had known he was here; someone knew exactly how to ambush him. Figures now appeared, some with torches, others without, faces, obscured by shadow and flame. He spun, searching desperately for any means of escape, finally taking refuge behind a large headstone. The lights continued their steady march. Ernest clutched the pistol in his hand. If he could surprise them, he still might be able to escape. A great shadow, backlit by the oncoming torches, suddenly loomed above him, and swatted the gun away as he turned to fire. Ernest was still concentrating on the towering shadow when the blow came from behind and the world tumbled out of existence.

Chapter 14
Among the Mystics

Wisps of blonde hair beat at the stiff wind; a sense of agonizing loneliness, and profound despair was etched on her precious face. She was watching, waiting, pleading for him to return from across the tumbling sea. Her voice seemed to reach beyond the roar of the deep or was it something else? He wanted to answer her cries, even more to touch her. But he couldn't. Soon, he promised, soon and hoped that she'd heard him, as she began to slip away. And though his eyes were now open, the disturbing image of Ailis was only slowly replaced by the surprised look of a young stranger. Oddly he felt no fear in her presence. It all seemed perfectly natural somehow. There was an exotic quality to her. Had he seen her before? His eyes and mind could not seem to focus. No, it was more of a quiet insightfulness, he now saw in her eyes. No, that felt wrong, too. He shook his head and suddenly the questions tumbled in quick succession through his mind: where was he, who was she, why had he been taken from …?

He felt dizzy, sick. The world felt wrong. The details of his surroundings were slow to reveal themselves to his senses. Was the world moving? He must be in some type of wagon. At least the motion made it feel that way. Ernest tried to listen to sounds, but they all echoed and blended with one another resulting in an unpleasant din. His head refused to clear, and it was only made worse when the girl leaned over him, holding some type of burning mixture beneath his nose. Several seconds later, she blew its heavily scented smoke over his face. She veiled herself immediately as Ernest unwillingly inhaled the concoction. It must be some type of drug. He wanted to argue or fight back, but the smoke, rich with the scents of honey and herb, soothed him too quickly. His euphoric sense returned. Yes, this was fine. His muscles relaxed and his surroundings again grew distant. Life continued around him, but he had no sense of time or any desire to join in it. Everything tingled.

The girl's face flowed in and out of his consciousness, as he did. When she spoke, he understood nothing. Sometimes it was light, and other times it was dark. Dreams passed and then returned. Ailis. He wept that he'd lost his body and could not get back to her. Would she understand? The pleas of her soul touched him again. No, this was wrong. He had to get back. He had to. His mind searched for his body and fought to reconnect to it.

The first sensation he remembered clearly was fresh, cold air being drawn into his lungs. Breathing felt new. It felt wonderful, and for an unknown length of time, that's all there was. Sounds descended upon him next, followed quickly by blurred, shifting shapes, which finally coalesced into people. No one seemed to be paying any attention to him. He was surprised to discover at least thirty people, most sitting around a series of small cooking fires, laughing and talking as if everything were normal. Ernest's mind now cleared rapidly, though parts of his body still felt as if they were asleep. The disagreeable sensation in his muscles hinted that he'd been in the same position for sometime, and he tried to shift in order to return feeling to his entire body. His small motions drew no attention, so he watched this bizarre pageant unfold.

If this was a raiding party that had captured him, it was comprised of a most unusual mix. The group did seem to primarily consist of men, but there was a wide variety of ages scattered throughout: some with beards hoary with age, while others appeared no older than eight. A few women darted among the fray, performing an assortment of tasks: serving, sewing, talking, cleaning, scolding, hugging, laughing, and even several who were dancing. All were dressed in colorful, unique styles, and all bore weapons upon their person, even the children. His first thought was that the gypsies, who'd shadowed him since his initial encounter with them in southern France, had again taken him hostage. But the language these people spoke seemed different, familiar, yet wholly unknown to Ernest. Was it an Eastern European dialect or some type of pidgin language offshoot, perhaps?

He was now, more or less, fully cognizant of his surroundings. He was tied beneath a large tree, which seemed to be near the center of the encampment, not close to an edge as he'd previously thought. Over his left shoulder, he could see wagons, carts, and horses dimly lit by the moonlight. Turning to his right, he was startled to find the girl who'd drugged him, perched silently upon a barrel, scrutinizing him as he watched the others.

She was dressed in an outfit of dark reds, purples, pink accents and greens. Parts of the fabric shimmered in the light. Her earrings glinted and stood out against her straight black hair, which was partially covered by a green bandana. She could have been any nationality or background. Her slightly oval eyes were dark colored, her height was difficult to discern with her legs crossed beneath her, and she appeared to be in her late teens. They regarded each other silently for a long moment. Ernest fervently hoped she wouldn't try another potion on him. Hopefully the breeze would prevent it, but she still might have other means of rendering him incapacitated.

Without uttering a word, she held out the half-eaten plate of food she'd been devouring and gestured for him to take some. Ernest wasn't certain his bonds would allow him enough slack to reach it, and at the moment, the thought of food was none too appealing. He shook his head; she persisted with words he could not comprehend.

"Very kind but, no, thank you," he politely protested.

The girl's expression changed, first to shock, and then to one of unreserved distaste. In a smooth motion, she lowered herself from atop the barrel and knelt close to face him. She quickly rattled off angry words and tossed the plate of food roughly to the ground next to him and stalked off. Ernest was still attempting to understand her strange response when a soft chuckle attracted his attention.

"You must forgive my child," a deep, voice boomed in broken, halting English, "but you have used the forbidden tongue. Great offense was taken."

A massive man, whose face was nearly hidden by an equally substantial black beard, appeared from the far side of the tree. He stank of horse, alcohol, and tobacco. A rifle was affixed to his back by a sash that navigated his great bulk. His face was largely hidden by a combination of beard, a worn hat, and the night's shadow, but his voice sounded slightly amused.

"Forbidden tongue?" Ernest wondered aloud.

"Your French, is bad here. Best use this English now, unless you're blessed with knowing Magyar … ah … your country, say, Hungarian," he explained to Ernest's bewildered look.

"You're Hungarian?"

"No! I am Wild Rose clan," he said by means of explanation and thumped a spot on his chest for emphasis, "as are we all." He drew out this last word as if it were to offer some comfort to Ernest, who paused before asking his next question, hoping it would bear more fruit.

"Why have you brought me here?"

The massive man slapped him on the back and laughed as if Ernest had just finished telling an elaborate joke.

"Eat," he ordered, continuing to laugh as he walked away towards the campfires.

"But …"

"Later. Later, perhaps," the man shouted back without turning, as he joined his comrades by one of the fires. He was either very popular or the group's leader, for as soon as he sat down a crowd assembled near him offering food, drink, and an eager audience. Ernest studied the scene for further clues, but after awhile, his interest waned. Though by the time his attention began to drift, he'd deciphered that the black-bearded man appeared to be named Jal.

Truly alone, Ernest tried to assess his situation. So far there seemed to be no evidence that Jack had also been taken prisoner, so apparently they'd only been interested in him. Why? Had the large man guessed that Ernest would be able to understand English or had he known? It seemed strange that a gypsy from Hungary would choose to converse in English, but the significance of this, if there were any, eluded Ernest. The issue of speaking French proved even more perplexing. Why would speaking French cause such a vehement reaction from the girl?

The contours of the land were difficult to discern in the darkness, as was the hour. The combination of moonlight and bare tree branches made ascertaining his direction from the constellations nearly impossible. Was he already in Hungary? Could these people work for Victor's vengeful leper as well? As he pondered these questions, he began to eat the discarded food, hesitantly at first, but was surprised to discover how hungry he actually was. If he'd learned one lesson of survival during his travels, it was to eat when you could, since you never knew when the next meal might come.

In spite of his bonds, he managed to finish eating without most of the meal covering him. He leaned back against the tree fighting his own fatigue. She hadn't drugged the food had she? Ernest dismissed the idea. No, she'd been eating it, so it seemed unlikely. He must be suffering the after-effects of whatever they'd been using to keep him under. He needed to escape these people … but where should he go then: Ireland, Geneva, Ingolstadt, Salzburg?

He was exhausted and longed to be reunited with his family. Lost in thought, Ernest failed, at first, to notice the commotion at the far end of the camp. It was only when the shouts and screams began that he became fully aware that something was wrong.

The scene played out quickly. Two men, obviously injured, bore the body of a third and presented it to Jal. He must be the leader. One knelt over the body, stunned or saddened, while his friend related information to Jal. He pointed repeatedly off in one direction, as a woman tried to bandage his wounds. Jal issued a rapid series of directives, and all but three men left. He then took out a map of some type and they studied it, pausing unconsciously to look in the direction the wounded man had indicated. Was someone coming for them? Perhaps Jack had been able to track these bandits and brought the authorities in pursuit.

Ernest brightened at the thought. He strained at his restraints in anticipation. If he could escape now, the distraction might prevent the gypsies from leaving in time, and the authorities might capture them. Sadly, the knots were tied in such a manner that any pressure only increased their clasp. If he continued his efforts, his circulation could be cut off. With no real option, Ernest relaxed and waited. Then he heard the sound. It was an ancient call that came from the wild, empty, lonely places of the world.

Primitive emotions and fears were awakened by it, and he renewed his struggle against his bonds. Everyone in the camp paused for a moment when the sad wail from the darkness was heard. It primarily emanated from the same direction the injured man had indicated. The sound repeated, closer this time, and Jal's hastily convened conference abruptly ended. One of the men came towards Ernest and roughly helped him to his feet. A third cry, again closer, rent the night, and the man leaned down and sliced through the bonds which held his feet. He could walk, and they hurriedly proceeded through the camp toward the wagons.

The girl and another man met them by one of the wagons, and all but Ernest's escort clambered quickly into the back. The campfires still glowed softly in the moonlight, but all were now abandoned. The camp was in chaos, as the group prepared to both fight and escape. The escort called the girl to the front, leaving Ernest with the guard, who was rapidly retying his ankle bonds. With a jolt, the wagon suddenly sprang forward, and the guard reached out to extinguish the lamp, which still burned within. With Ernest secured, the man pushed his prisoner toward the front and took up a musket position in the back.

Ernest strained to listen over the clamor created by the horse and wagon wheels. He was grateful his head was finally clear, though the tight, high speed turns the driver was making kept turning his stomach. Through the rear canvas flaps, he could see the guard intensely watching the cliff-face to the wagon's left. It must not have been very high for his attention was divided between the road and the top of the cliff. Obviously, he expected trouble from above. He did not have long to wait.

Suddenly he jerked upright and fired back down the road at something, swearing as he did so. He grabbed the pistol tied to his waist and fired again. A new and creative curse was uttered. The shifting wagon was undoubtedly affecting his aim. He called out to the girl, Baseria, who parted the front flaps and listened to his instructions. Holding on for dear life, she nodded, made her way into the back and began to help him load weapons. The guard fired two more shots before his end came. On the second, he leaned out to take aim, and as he did so, the attack from above finally came.

Ernest couldn't have guessed how much the wolf weighed, but with the gypsy's uneven balance, it knocked both of them from the wagon. If the fall hadn't killed him, the animal certainly would. Baseria gasped as she stared at the spot where the man had vanished seconds before. She crossed herself, and then turned to resume her seat next to the driver, when a cry of agony was heard from him, followed by the snarls of another wolf. Blood spurted through the canvas, as the unseen, merciless mauling continued. Suddenly the wagon careened dangerously to the right and began to turn over on its side.

No longer controlled by the reins, the frightened horses broke free, and the unanticipated shift threw the rapidly disintegrating wagon in the opposite direction. With his hands bound, Ernest had little chance of securing himself. His weight flung him hard against the wooden supports for the canvas. Baseria's body hit his, the impact of which dislodged the canvas completely from the cart; splinters of wood bit harshly into their skins as they rolled in the entwining canvas.

Their hearts were racing by the time they finally stopped moving, and the heavy, wound canvas prevented more than a narrow shaft of air from flowing in to them. Panting within the dark mass, they struggled to free themselves. The girl was crying, either from duress or frustration, as she fought to grasp the knife around her waist. Ernest realized what she was attempting to do and managed to purchase it first. For an instant, she froze as their hands touched.

"Give me the knife or I'll kill you," Baseria threatened in the Germanic tongue.

"Cut me loose!"

She struggled unsuccessfully to free the blade from his grasp.

"You'll murder me, if I release you," she affirmed, catching her breath.

"We'll both die when the wolves get here."

The statement had a sobering effect on them both. He handed her the blade, and in four swift cuts, Ernest's hands were free. During the fall, however, his shoulder had become dislodged, and he fought now against the searing pain. If he cried out, the wolves would only find them faster.

"We should stay here; they won't be able to tear the fabric."

"No, we can't. They'll come down the ends and rip out our throats," Ernest decided.

Baseria considered this, but did not stir.

"I can't move, I'm pinned," she admitted.

Ernest studied the narrow space they had to work with.

"Not even to your left?"

Her body struggled uselessly.

"No."

Then only one option remained. He could still wiggle forward towards the opening if he moved on his dislodged shoulder. The thought made him queasy. The pain that shot through his back, spine, and neck, when he actually moved, made him sick. The heat and musty stench from the canvas was becoming unbearable.

"What is it?" Baseria demanded as he cried out.

"My shoulder's out its socket," Ernest wheezed through the pain.

"You can't move?"

The best he could manage was to shake his head.

Baseria began a frantic attempt to cut through the layers of canvas and wood, but the confined space made manipulating the knife almost impossible. She screamed as a great weight suddenly landed upon the canvas. The wolves had found them.

Without really knowing why, Ernest barked out an order.

"Roll towards me!"

With the energy of blind panic, Baseria obeyed, though it took several agonizing attempts to actually move anywhere; when they did their canvas cocoon rolled down an unseen incline, careening wildly as they hit numerous stones and glanced off the sides of tree trunks. Suddenly they were floating over nothing, and then just as quickly, they smacked into solid ground, hard.

Ernest's shoulder burned with pain, and during their rapid, unexpected escape, Baseria managed to slice her palm on the knife. However, the desperate flight also produced a positive result: the canvas was loose. In spite of their injures, they both surged toward the opening and drew lusty breaths of fresh air. As he gasped for breath, Ernest was surprised to discover that they'd landed back on the road.

He froze at the sight of a pack of wolves that were swarming around the body of one of the gypsies, their snouts glistened with blood. They stared back at the living humans, bloodlust burning in their eyes, anticipation clear, as they began to stalk towards them.

"Back in! Back in!" he cried as the wolves sprang forward.

With seconds to spare, Ernest rolled the canvas over the entry and tried to shield Baseria as best he could. His injured shoulder made accomplishing this a nearly miraculous task, and his strength began to waver under the onslaught of the animal's aggressive attack. Baseria stretched herself over him and grabbed the canvas, desperate to keep the wolves out.

Others now began to dig and claw at the sides of the abused canvas shelter. A set of vicious teeth found Baseria's feet and tore at her ankles. Encouraged, another animal attacked the same area and savagely clawed the backs of her outstretched legs. She screamed in terror and agony. Ernest tried to kick at the beasts, but the motion only made it more difficult for Baseria to maintain her tenuous grip on canvas protecting the entry. Teeth suddenly ripped into Ernest's wounded shoulder. He could feel the warm blood cascading down his back and chest from the gash. Still he held onto the canvas. They'd be dead in seconds if he didn't.

Baseria continued to shriek in unmitigated pain as the vicious animals tore freely into her flesh from above. She couldn't last much longer. When the wolves forced their way in, he'd try to protect her with his body. Perhaps his sacrifice could save her. But in his heart, he knew she was just as dead. His fingers slipped on blood pouring from his clawed knuckles. It would not be long now.

An inhuman cry suddenly broke the night, followed quickly by two more. A dead weight hit the outside and did not stir. A series of snarls and growls, some of protest, others of determination, were mixed with yelps of pain and distress. The slaughter of several of their companions split up the pack; some of them turned upon their attackers, while others disappeared into the night. More shots rang out, along with angry voices, howls, and hoof beats. Ernest and Baseria finally succumbed to heat, fear, and their appalling injuries, and in unison, they dropped the canvas. Baseria sobbed in pain, relief, and gratitude. She clung to Ernest and wept.

"Can you move?"

"I'm sorry, I'm sorry, I'm sorry," she chanted over and over between tears.

"Baseria, I need to know if you can move."

They were still in great danger. He had to get her under control.

"I'm sorry, I'm …"

He grabbed her head and forced her to look into his eyes.

"We can't stay here. If they return they'll kill us. Can you move?"

She blinked for a moment, and then shrieked from the blinding pain when she attempted to move her legs.

"I'm sorry, Baseria. It's okay, it'll be okay." Right now he needed to believe this as much as she did. He twisted his head towards the road as hers collapsed upon his chest. His view was obstructed by several wolf carcasses. Who had killed them?

A face suddenly hovered above them.

"Baseria! Baseria!"

The man vanished and, a moment later, a sword bisected the canvas to their left. The remainder of the sheltering canvas was cast off them. Ignoring Ernest completely, the young man knelt beside the girl and examined the brutal wounds to her legs. He tried to speak to her in Hungarian, but she'd completely lost consciousness. He shrieked something angrily at Ernest, as he hauled the poor girl off of him. As he removed her, Ernest got his first real glimpse of what the wolves had done to the young woman.

The skin, what was left of it, on the back of her legs was in tatters and bleeding freely. Her left ankle had been punctured numerous times, and bone was visible through several of the serrated cuts. She was bleeding to death.

Ernest struggled to get to his feet. It was obvious that the young man had no idea what was happening to the girl. Ernest tried to explain their situation to him in German, but the gypsy only yelled back in Hungarian, as he positioned Baseria in a manner that ensured she'd only bleed out more rapidly. Ernest again tried to protest this; the gypsy lobbed a backhand at him.

Fortunately years of conditioned responses seized Ernest, and he easily dodged the intended blow, while managing to steal the man's sword. Upon realizing that he'd lost it, the gypsy spun and brought a pistol to bear on Ernest, but he wasn't paying attention. Ignoring the drawn weapon completely, Ernest stepped back towards the ruined canvas, and begun to slice off large sections of it. Confused the man held his fire. When he was done, Ernest dropped the sword and staggered back to the gypsy. He motioned what he needed to be done then dropped to the ground, exhausted.

The gypsy didn't move.

"She's dying you idiot!" Ernest finally screamed in English. "Help her!"

The man divided his attentions, as he wrestled to decide his next course of action: remove his eyes from the prisoner or help the girl. Finally he met Ernest's gaze.

"Wolves," he barked in English, then tossed the pistol to Ernest and began to wrap Baseria's wounds.

They'd reached an understanding, for now. Silently Ernest breathed an inward sigh of relief that the gun hadn't accidentally gone off when the gypsy tossed it to him. His gaze wandered across the murky landscape as he watched for wolves. Occasionally he would note the gypsy's progress out of the corner of his eye. There was so much blood. Ernest set his useless, injured arm at an odd angle across his lap. Still alert, he allowed his mind to drift for a moment.

Obviously this young man knew Baseria; his initial reaction spoke of a very personal relationship between them. Could he be her husband, a suitor, a life-long friend? Where had he come from? Hadn't he heard multiple shots? Where were the other shooters now? Without warning he was suddenly pitched backward by his arm, which was twisted until a sickening crack from the friction of bone and tendon was heard. Colors and pain shot through his senses, as it slowly dawned upon him what had happened. The gypsy, surmising that his adversary was wounded, had set the shoulder in the most painful way possible. In the process of doing so, he'd also regained his weapon. As Ernest gasped in pain, he decided that maybe the young man wasn't as stupid as he'd appeared.

Apparently the stranger was beginning to have similar feelings for he helped Ernest back to his feet. To Ernest's great surprise, he also handed the pistol back to him.

"Wolves," he winked, and then bent back down to pick up the prone form of Baseria, who was still unconscious. Ernest hoped the man's comprehension of the English language extended beyond one word.

"How are we getting out of here?"

The man said nothing, only indicated with a nod of his head which direction they were going. Fortunately, it wasn't far, and the horses he'd tied up hadn't been killed by the wolves. It turned out that the young man's English was actually quite good. Ernest made a mental note that he must stop rushing to judgments about him.

"We are still in great danger. The others I came with have distracted them for now, but if they catch your scent again, they will come. Take off your clothes."

"Why?"

"You wish to live, yes? We must try to mask your scent."

"I don't think riding the horse naked will help," Ernest affirmed.

"No, put on his clothes."

The man pointed to the body of a dead gypsy nearby. Ernest was about to protest when the young gypsy interjected, "He gave his life trying to save yours. It is his mount you will ride. Hurry, we have little time."

Repulsed, but determined, Ernest extracted the articles of clothing from the bloody corpse and put them on. By now he was covered in so much blood, it hardly mattered.

“Make certain you take his weapon too,” the gypsy commanded from atop his own horse where he’d managed to secure Baseria in front of him.

“Why would they focus on me?” Ernest demanded as he took up the dead man’s pistol.

“They’ve been trained to. Though, as you can see, they have no problem killing us as well,” he gestured to the body.

“Trained by whom?” Ernest asked as he assumed his own mount.

“The Moon Shadow clan, our enemies,” the gypsy added darkly as he paused to shift Baseria’s weight slightly. Ernest was dubious that the man could keep her secure, especially if she awoke. The pain she’d be in would be overwhelming.

“You’ll ride slightly behind me, to the right. Do not waste your shot unless you have to. It’s best if we just out run them.”

Ernest nodded in agreement.

“We’ll have to stop soon. Your wife will bleed to death even faster with her legs hanging down like that.”

The young gypsy began to nod, then paused and grinned at Ernest while shaking his head.

“Keep up.”

With that he shot off into the night with Ernest in pursuit. They only came across two wolves that apparently hadn’t heard the approaching horses. Ernest steered his horse directly at them at a full gallop. The wolves initially fled, but after the horses had passed, they attempted to follow for a mile or so, nipping frantically at their prey, but eventually, they disappeared behind the riders into the night. By the time the men stopped in a wooded area, both felt fairly certain that they’d slipped away from the pack and were relatively safe.

The richly-toned glow of the rising sun illuminated the horizon. Ernest practically collapsed after lowering himself to the ground. The wound in his shoulder burned and was bleeding more than he’d realized. Fortunately, the gypsy was able to lower Baseria to the ground on his own. She issued a faint moan then jerked awake, eyes frantic, as she began to cry out something in Hungarian. The gypsy clasped her neck in an instant and applied his thumb and finger to two specific locations, with a third applying pressure to her temple. Her body seized then sagged, her head lulled, and she again slept. Ernest stared, dumbfounded. He’d only seen something similar to this once before, but that had been on the other side of the world, under much different circumstances.

"The pain is too much, she must sleep," the man explained simply when he noticed Ernest's slightly haunted look.

"Of course," Ernest stammered as he shook the dark memory from his mind.

The gypsy stood and surveyed the area.

"Where are we?" his wounded companion coughed.

"Where we need to be," was the cryptic response.

"How did you know where to find us?"

The young gypsy smirked.

"We left ten minutes after you. The camp was already under attack. We came across Stiv's body on the road and found the wolves attacking you a few minutes later."

Ernest smiled weakly.

"You saved my life. I want to thank you."

A look of reproach greeted Ernest's expression of gratitude.

"The price of your life is too high," the gypsy observed in a bitter tone, as he looked away. What could Ernest say? A simple apology for what had happened to Baseria seemed hollow.

"I don't understand any of this," he admitted.

The gypsy studied the landscape.

"You should rest," he advised.

"I don't understand," Ernest repeated more forcefully. He was tired of his life being placed in jeopardy, of mysteries, and chaos, of being controlled by others.

"What is there to understand?" the gypsy wondered irritably as he rounded on him. "You serve each moment of existence, and then the moment changes. That is life. It does not require understanding, only an acceptance of what is."

"Why am I here?" Ernest persisted. And why would an entire clan of people want him dead?

"I don't know. I wish you weren't," the other man declared.

This was too much. If every inch of him wasn't bruised, bleeding, or throbbing with pain, his response would have been a much different response than the one that came: he laughed. The gypsy's incredulous expression crumbled, and he also began to laugh. It felt like a long forgotten luxury.

"This is insane," Ernest finally stated, as their mutual amusement faded.

The man nodded his head in agreement.

"So neither one of us knows why I'm here?"

A haunted, troubled expression crossed the gypsy's brow as he caressed the unconscious girl's hair.

"She does."

Baseria's breaths were so shallow that her chest barely seemed to move. If she survived to see the sunset, it would be a miracle.

"I'm here because of her?" Ernest's voice trembled in amazement; his mind struggled to process the idea.

"She led us to you."

Ernest was certain he'd never seen the young woman before. How could she possibly know who he was? Could there be a connection between this young woman and his unnatural tormentor? Or was there a link between the girl and Victor? The gypsy regained his feet and began to wander a short distance away. He continued to talk as he searched for, and gathered up, assorted items from the ground.

"My sister knows much through the arts of the unseen world. She is quite gifted."

His sister? Well, that explained the man's earlier amusement to Ernest's wife comment. He was not a jealous lover, but a protective brother. In spite of this new information, Ernest could find nothing of relevance in it. What "unseen arts" could the young gypsy be referring to? What possible reason could this girl have to order his capture? Had she somehow learned that the clan's enemies were planning to annihilate him? If so, why should it matter to her or any of these people? His musings were interrupted by the scent of burning wood as the gypsy started a fire.

"We're not leaving?" It was as much a question as a statement.

"You may as well rest," the gypsy shrugged.

How could this man be so calm? His sister was dying. He should be seeking help. Was he really going to sacrifice her so that Ernest could remain in his clan's custody, for some purpose only Baseria seemed to understand? Ernest's heart pounded in his chest.

"You can't let her die. Leave me here. Say I was killed."

The other man shook his head in remorse.

"Her fate is already decided. I cannot change it."

Ernest's anger rose. "You're her brother!"

He calmly rose and faced him. "I have lost a sister before."

Memories of his own dead momentarily rose before Ernest's eyes.

"But she's not lost yet. Save her," he urged frantically.

While Ernest made his impassioned pleas, the gypsy began to distribute the rocks he'd gathered into some type of pattern around Baseria. When his task was complete, he added more wood to the nearby fire and then settled his back against a nearby pine tree, apparently content to wait. He stared at nothing for several moments then returned his attention to Ernest.

"You really should rest. It may be some time. There is no way of knowing how far the others were scattered."

Ernest studied the patterns the man had created with the stones: small and large piles, mixed with single stones of all sizes and colors, alternating in shapes and spaces between them. He could decipher no meaning to the arrangement nor form any conclusions as to why the man had taken the time to create it. And there didn't seem to be anything particularly unusual about the place, certainly nothing that warranted remaining here. Still there must be a purpose.

"How will the stones help her?"

It was a long time before the young gypsy was able to answer the question.

"I'm not sure they can," he conceded.

Ernest certainly couldn't see how they could.

"If we continue to ride, she'll bleed to death," the gypsy explained. "I can't leave her with you, and if the Moon Shadows regain you … here she has a chance."

So the gypsies he'd encountered in France, who had shadowed him in Geneva, Salzburg, and likely Ingolstadt were members of this Moon Shadow clan. Strange that groups so distant should engage in such a bizarre conflict.

"Only the unseen world can save her now," the man concluded.

This was the second time he'd used this phrase.

"Do you practice witchcraft?" Ernest asked with a degree of hesitation. A part of him feared to hear the answer.

The other man snorted derisively.

"Is that a convenient label for something you must judge in order to understand, eh? Will this judgment give you understanding? I think not."

"I want to understand the moment," Ernest said evenly. Perhaps using the language of the gypsy's own beliefs would get him somewhere.

The gypsy considered this flawed statement. Trying to enlighten this stranger only seemed to result in a circular argument, though his curiosity might be taken as a positive sign. He decided to take a chance.

"She is a Seer among my people, a rare and honorable position. Their arts study and connect them to the earth, in all its forms: elemental and spiritual. She is a living connection to the unseen world, and to that which has been and that which must be."

He waited for another ignorant response from the prisoner, but when none was forthcoming he continued.

"My sister must heal. The rocks will help channel the earth's energies into her and help her to summon Nagyanya—our Grandmother. The earth will heal her or bid her to rejoin it. Only time will tell."

Ernest listened with rapt interest. This was not, as the gypsy presupposed, a ridiculous or completely unheard of notion to him. His travels to the savage and serene places of the world had exposed him to countless beliefs, customs, and views, many of which were quite different from his own. Some were even so outlandish that they seemed born from beyond imagination, but he had learned not to discount them out of hand. The power of one's belief, regardless of how it was interpreted or accepted by others, could be a formidable force for good or ill, and right now, if belief bore Baseria past this terrible moment and into the next, it was not Ernest's place to question it.

Besides, her brother was right, no flight by horse would save her for her body would shut down from blood loss. Ernest was not familiar with the land, which would make his seeking help alone time-consuming. The fact that the gypsy had so readily stopped here might also hint at other, unseen dangers in the nearby countryside. If Baseria's brother left them, Ernest might succumb to his own injuries or be again located by the wolves and have to fight them alone. He relented with a heavy sigh.

"How did you learn English?"

"The war has taken us many places," Espen shrugged.

"You are not a Seer?" Ernest observed after several minutes of silence.

The young man shook his head.

"How did you know the proper formation to arrange the rocks in then?"

"I am of the lineage. I was taught as a child."

"So your mother was a Seer too?"

"I will not speak of her," he closed his eyes.

Ernest pressed on. "Is there anything else we can do?"

"Be at peace, Frankenstein."

Though the gypsy now appeared very close to sleep, Ernest doubted that it would take the man more than a handful of seconds to bring the weapon he clutched in his lap to bear, should anything happen. He might doze, but he would not sleep. He would protect them. The fire would be tended and the injured looked after until help arrived or Baseria died, whichever came first. If all of this had come to pass at her bidding, Ernest did not want to think what would become of him if she should die.

He fell into a dreamless sleep, until his senses alerted him to a muted conversation taking place nearby. As he opened his eyes, the last rays of the dying day fought to maintain their hold on an unseen horizon. Lazy flurries of snow drifted on invisible currents of air. Ernest looked up to see the massive gypsy, Jal, talking to Baseria's brother. He watched them, dimly for a time, until something in the gypsy's conversation caused the younger one to gesture towards him. It was then that they noticed he was awake. Jal knelt down.

"My son says you saved my daughter," Jal intoned in halting English.

"No," Ernest worked to get moisture back into his mouth, "no, he saved us. I couldn't have kept the wolves out if it hadn't been for Baseria. I owe them my life."

A rapid exchange in either Hungarian or the gypsies' pidgin language ensued, concluding with another sour look upon the young man's face. Suddenly both men knelt and helped Ernest to his feet. It felt strange to be vertical again, and Ernest felt uneasy with his sense of balance. His entire body pulsed with pain.

The gypsies walked him a short distance to a boxy, wooden wagon, which was fully enclosed. Inside Baseria lay, pale, and covered by a large quilt. Her skin seemed to be covered with some sort of paste, richly scented with herb and mint. An ancient, wizened figure, completely covered in assorted robes, draped with clothes, attended her. The face of the woman, for the shape of the hands, gnarled by age, identified the figure as being such, was largely hidden by decorative bangles. Ernest hoped this was the Nagyanya.

She would not meet his Ernest's eye as Jal helped her descend from the wagon. She reacted as if she was frightened of him. She ceaselessly muttered words, in a hush, tranquil tone. When she was no longer in danger of meeting the stranger's eye, she gave instructions to Jal, and then was escorted to the front of the wagon by the younger gypsy.

"Inside," Jal said shortly.

Ernest obeyed and lay gratefully down upon the bench, on the opposite side of the small wagon from Baseria. Jal reached into a storage area above and pulled down a red stool. He placed it between the benches then grabbed his daughter's left arm. Ernest's right was set upon the stool in a similar fashion; Jal tied the two together then made ready to leave.

"It is balance," he rumbled, unprompted, "my child saved you, you will now save her. You were injured together, now you shall heal together, is balance." He nodded stiffly then shut the wagon doors.

Two lamps illuminated the relatively warm wagon interior and bathed it in soft, shifting shadows. Ernest's fears dissipated as the rhythmic sway of the wagon lulled him back to sleep. This time he did dream. He was alone on a beach. The stars and sand stretched beyond sight. He had just completed …? Fire burned his hand. It burned quickly up his arm, and then the flames pulled him into an even greater fire. And suddenly he was awake, his body awkwardly bent, his hand felt as if it were on fire. He could sense the intense heat of fever through Baseria's hand. Her breathing was frighteningly rapid, then ceased altogether.

Ernest crawled beside her and squeezed the fingers of their bound hands together, but there was no reaction. She was gone.

With a deep sense of regret, he released her fingers and sighed. A spasm abruptly shook her body, and her fingers locked onto his in an unnaturally strong grip. Baseria's eyes shot open, desperate, pleading, and alive with fear.

"Return, return to me," she cried in abject sadness. "Return to me," she again pleaded. "The sea is lonely. The stars are silent. Our child. Our child."

Ernest's heart shuddered.

"Baseria?"

"Our child," she repeated as she wept.

The rope connecting them disappeared. She locked herself around his neck, nearly cutting off his air with her intense, possessive grasp. Her erratic breathing returned.

"Always remember me," she whispered lovingly in his ear then collapsed, dead.

He felt light-headed, and a fresh sense of loss washed over him, but it was not for Baseria. He did not even know the girl, really. Still, everything within him burned with the knowledge that he had not been speaking to her just now. He placed his head in his hands in misery.

"She will sleep now," a familiar voice suddenly assured him.

Ernest looked up to find the clan's ancient "Grandmother" and Baseria's brother sitting nearby, watching him. Unsettling as all of this was, he was additionally startled to discover that he was no longer in the wagon but was, in fact, in a large tent.

He studied the cluttered, seemingly familiar surroundings. How long had he been in this place? A quick survey of his person revealed that the numerous bruises and cuts he'd suffered were mostly healed; even the deep gash in his shoulder was closed. Now that he studied her, Baseria too showed astonishing progress in healing her own nearly fatal wounds. This realization only made her death moments earlier even more tragic.

"It has been six days," the young gypsy answered the unspoken question when Ernest looked to him. Six days! He studied the wound to his shoulder again. It alone should have taken a month to heal this well. His gaze returned to Baseria.

"Was she hallucinating?" he asked in bewilderment.

Her brother blinked.

"Who, my sister?"

"Yes."

"When?"

"Just now," Ernest responded in astonishment.

How could these two people have just witnessed Baseria's final heartbreaking demise and have no reaction to the girl's death? But she wasn't dead. She was sleeping peacefully with no indication that she'd recently been awake.

"She stirred slightly when you were screaming, but otherwise no, she has been resting. You have healed each other."

The gypsy actually grinned as he reached out and clasped Ernest on the shoulder—the formally injured shoulder.

"But she was dying …," Ernest asserted.

The old woman stirred and spoke in low tones to the man, shaking her head and making direct, pointed gestures with her hands. Then she was silent. Again she never looked at Ernest.

"What is it, what did she say?"

The young gypsy shook his head.

"Do you doubt what you have seen?"

Ernest knew what he'd seen; it just didn't make any sense. She had died. It was a dream, but also a reality at the same time. His soul felt naked.

"Yes," he finally answered.

"Good. Only with doubt can there be true understanding. When the time is right, you will know the truth of what you have seen," the young gypsy promised.

"Is that what she said?" Ernest nodded toward the shrouded figure of the old woman. The other man was more hesitant to respond this time.

"She said the union of your energies has made you as one—to heal. It is difficult to say how long the bond will continue."

Ernest looked at the aged figure, but she revealed nothing.

"There was nothing more?" he prompted.

The gypsy seemed to consider the wisdom of revealing more to him. Finally, he nodded.

"The connection may become more intense or lessen in time," Espen explained. "There is no way to tell which. It is possible that the bond you now share may never sever, that the power used to heal you will reside inside you both forever."

Ernest weighed the thought. Had the dream been some sort of a vision, and if, as the gypsies said, they shared some connection beyond his comprehension, whose future had he seen, his or Baseria's? Or was it the past? Was he to be now plagued with such disturbing, enticing, and confusing insights? Again he looked to the silent mystic who avoided his gaze.

"Why do I frighten the old woman so?"

The young gypsy translated the question, and the Grandmother clicked her teeth before answering. The response was surprisingly short, but when the gypsy translated it into English, even he looked troubled.

"She fears what must be."

Chapter 15
Anamnesis

Romanian Territories, 1800

Baseria shook her head and opened her eyes, seeking the furry attacker. Only several weeks old, the kitten loved to pounce and run as she explored the world. Seeing her prey awake, the animal meowed before running out through a gap along the bottom of the tent. She smiled. The kitten had made a habit of seeking out only Baseria's bedroll early in the morning and snuggling up to her, purring deeply as they dozed. Apparently she was feistier in the evenings. Baseria loved the animal because, unlike many people, it wanted to be with her.

She blinked, realizing she'd fallen asleep after dinner, not an uncommon occurrence, especially for a ten-year-old who'd been doing the work of at least two people the last few days. Her parents were speaking in low tones outside.

"You know I hate it."

"He is almost fifteen, Mayte," Jal countered. "If he is to follow in my footsteps and become the leader of this clan one day then he must go out on patrols at night just as I always have."

"If there's still a clan for him to lead," his wife observed before sighing heavily. "Sometimes I feel we are losing our children trying to hold it together."

"That is your sister's fault," Jal asserted. "She and Nicabar have used every opportunity since the beginning of your mother's illness to sow division among our people."

"I fear more and more of them are listening," Mayte said. "The people are losing faith in our great destiny. If Nasi does not awaken soon, I'm afraid they will have enough support to follow through on their threat."

Jal snorted.

"Even they are not foolish enough to leave."

Though Jal tried to conceal it, he knew times were desperate. For generations, the line of the Seer had been maintained among the people of the Wild Rose clan, but with Nasi's children, that line was in peril. In the eight years since the onset of the old woman's devastating apoplexy, neither Mayte nor her older sister, Tasaria, had been able to heal the Seer. Despite their mother's unprecedented measure of training them both in the ancient teachings, each seemed to lack many of the abilities traditionally inherent to their lineage.

Baseria's thoughts tended upon Nagyanya. Despite her young age at the time of her grandmother's stroke, Baseria still remembered feeling loved and accepted by the invalid as no one else ever had. She was closer to her mother and brother, who had always cared for her, unlike her father and older sister, though this lack of acceptance from them did not keep the inquisitive girl from reaching out. She felt certain that, in time, they too would find value in her, just as her other family members did.

"There are whispers of them moving far to the west," Mayte remarked.

"Impossible."

"The wars have made trade there favorable."

"They have not made our people favorable," Jal said bitterly. "Survival there would be difficult."

"They will go because they share Tasaria's beliefs," Mayte sighed. "If they are not concerned about the dangers of following them, then they will have little concern for the ethnic hatreds there. Maybe it is wise to consider moving the clan, at least back into Hungary."

"My wife, we are safe here high in the mountains," Jal decided after a moment. "The Romanians need us for their trade and their endless wars with the Ottomans and Russians consume much of their time."

It grew quiet outside. They rarely discussed these issues in front of their youngest child; in spite of this, Baseria already knew her parents' sadness all too well. Without a true Seer to guide them, the very foundation of the Wild Rose clan was splintering, as was their family. She rolled over and stared at the ceiling of her family's tent.

"I'll heal you, Nagyanya," Baseria quietly vowed to herself.

*

"Baseria. What are you doing?"

Her father's authoritative voice startled her, and she dropped the rock, fumbled for it seconds later, before quickly concealing it in her satchel.

"I was just looking for more berries," she innocently informed Jal.

"You're supposed to be feeding your colt," he sternly reminded her. "I don't want you to be late relieving your brother."

"I won't be," she promised as she ran past him towards the black-coated foal he was allowing her to raise. She loved coming to the high mountain meadow her clan used for a pasture; only her secret place overlooking the waterfall could rival its beauty.

"Don't forget to brush him, Baseria, like I showed you," Jal instructed as she hooked the feedbag onto her horse. As if she would forget. Baseria pulled out her brush and pulled it across the animal's coarse coat and looked to her father. He'd already busied himself with tending to another mount.

It was all right, she thought. He didn't seem to fully understand what his willingness to allow her to care for this horse meant to Baseria. After Espen's birth, he'd hoped for another strong boy, and the disappointment he felt at Baseria's birth did not seem to be waning with time.

Her father frequently ignored her as a child and delegated much of her upbringing to her siblings and mother. She was Mayte's youngest and held a special place in her mother's heart for this reason, but she was not extraordinary. Her elder brother, Espen, seemed destined to become a leader and held value for Jal as his sole male heir. Baseria simply was. She was not to be trained for anything vital as Patia was, and her role in both the clan and her family was limited by her gender.

Tending the horses with her father was finally creating a bond between them, one she hoped in time would only deepen. She loved her demanding father, gruff exterior and all; on occasion even Jal revealed, despite his coolness towards her, that he loved his youngest child, too. Unfortunately, as she worked to become closer to her father, the distance between her and Patia was expanding.

As Jal's favorite child, Patia had long ago adopted her father's attitude toward Baseria, treating her as inferior, a fact not aided by an eight-year difference in their ages. However, the recent public revelation that Mayte had broken with tradition and all but completed training Patia in the arts of the Seer only made Baseria's sister more arrogant. The announcement blessed a society increasingly frightened and fragmented with hope, but training one so young violated traditions long-established for the sacred position, a fact that raised doubts in a time which could ill afford them.

Jal towered over her.

"It's time, Baseria."

She took a moment to free the accumulated hair from the brush before stowing it in her satchel. She kissed her horse.

"Have you decided on a name yet?" her father asked.

"Pur,"[13]she proudly stated.

A deep laugh escaped him.

"Is good name," he agreed. "Go. Your brother is waiting."

"Father." She smiled to herself as she left, savoring his approval.

Baseria only made one stop on her way to Nasi's tent. She withdrew the rock from her satchel and placed it in the hidden bucket with the others, patting the cover she placed over them before continuing on.

"You're late," Tasaria stated as Baseria entered her grandmother's tent.

"Apologies, my aunt," she managed, recovering from her surprise. "Where is Espen?"

"He was required elsewhere," she answered, rolling up a piece of parchment.

Mayte might have been more gifted when it came to directly utilizing the arts of the Seer, but she could not hope to rival Tasaria's advanced study of the extensive writings in the ancient scrolls of the Seer. It was partially her study of this vast chronicle which had plunged the clan into years of discord. The prophecy itself remained locked in an ancient language, but Tasaria had come to understand that as the grand destiny foretold in the prophecy transcended generation after generation, it was interpreted in different ways by various Seers, until now two contradictory interpretations of the original prophecy existed, a fact which had been concealed by her mother.

Nasi's daughters each accepted opposing viewpoints based on their limited knowledge of the prophecy. One, which Mayte believed, foretold fulfillment of the prophecy would destroy humanity. Tasaria, however, adhered to the belief that the realization of the prophecy would bring

13 (Romanian) Pure.

peace and a new understanding to all humankind.

"Do you wish me to stay until your uncle arrives to watch over your grandmother?" Tasaria asked.

"No, my aunt."

"I will see that he brings you some food," she assured her niece as she departed.

*

How many times had Baseria and her siblings witnessed their mother and aunt's attempts to employ this technique to heal Nasi? Alone, Baseria studied her work. It had taken her weeks to collect these particular stones, taking only the ones she felt summoned to.

Hoping to one day connect with her older sister, and intrigued by stories her mother told her about past Seers, she'd often taken to spying on Patia and Mayte's secret training sessions, memorizing philosophies, motions, and words as best she could. Several of the lessons dealt with the use of Elemental energies. One taught how the power of the earth could be summoned through stones and used to convey healing powers to one in need.

"I know you're in there," Baseria whispered to her grandmother's crippled form as she stroked the grey hairs on her head. Since suffering the apoplexy, Nasi was unable to speak, her crippled body aged prematurely from the stress, but perhaps her mind remained intact, trapped within.

Baseria lay there, listening to the earth. Something didn't feel right to her. Instinctively she stood and removed several of the stones, her hands shifting their configuration until it felt right. Nothing happened.

She leaned forward and kissed the old woman's forehead.

"Please, Nagyanya, we need you." The forces which threatened to tear the clan asunder could be managed, guided by her spirit, and wisdom. If only someone could reach her. An hour later, her uncle Nicabar ended Baseria's silent vigil; mournfully, she returned to her family's tent.

*

The next day, much to the entire clan's astonishment, the old woman began to show signs of healing. A vitriolic argument immediately ensued between Mayte and Tasaria as to who had placed the stones. This so frightened Baseria that she told no one what she'd done—no one except Patia.

Knowledge of her accomplishment frightened the young girl, and she longed to tell someone who might understand and guide her.

"How dare you," Patia glared down at her sister. "Interfering in what you don't understand. How could you possibly have healed her?"

"I'm, I'm sorry," Baseria stammered.

"You're a liar, Baseria. How do you think father will react when I tell him?"

"No! Please, don't tell him. Please!"

"You're nothing but a child. Mother never spent a minute of her life training you." Patia was becoming increasingly irate. She struck Baseria across the face.

Stunned, Baseria stood stock-still for a moment, as her eyes slowly welled with tears. A wild look filled Patia's eyes; was it jealousy, anger, fear? Her sister backed away.

"I watched you!" Baseria screamed. "I learned everything you did, and I saved Nagyanya. Maybe you're nothing!"

Confused and anguished, Baseria fled the family's tent.

She sought solace in a special, secret place in the rocks beside a great waterfall, high above the nearby river, which she and her six year old cousin, Jucika, had discovered several months earlier.

For a time she wept. How could this have happened? Nasi's salvation was supposed to unite them again; instead, all it seemed to be doing was destroying her family. Would Patia follow through on her threat to tell their father what Baseria had done? Maybe she'd simply decide to take credit for the act.

"I don't care what she does," she told the kitten she'd brought with her. "We'll just make this our new home."

Yes, they would be quite happy there, she decided. The kitten purred softly to her. Baseria basked in this gentle acceptance and enjoyed a few quiet hours alone with her pet, wistfully contemplating the picturesque spot, until the shadows of the setting sun lengthened against the towering cliffs.

"Baseria. Baseria."

The familiar voice sounded as if she'd been saying it for awhile. Baseria leaned over and looked down at her younger cousin, Jucika.

"Go away."

"Everyone wants you to come home."

"You shouldn't be up her by yourself," Baseria scolded.

"She's not," Patia asserted. "Climb down Baseria or I will tell father about what you've done."

With little choice, she acceded.

What happened next would forever remain a jumble of half-remembered images and emotions. The years of blame inflicted upon Baseria by herself and others made it so.

She remembered arguing with her cousin over the kitten and screaming at her for bringing Patia. She could recall yelling at Patia for striking her. A struggle ensued among them and then … the screams, the blood-curdling, nightmarish screams as Jucika and Patia fell from the cliff and into the river's rushing waters below.

What had happened to make them fall? Baseria could never remember. Had one been attempting to save the other? Had she pushed them? The trauma of the moment stole all but the numbing sounds of their screams as they descended, wingless angels into the abyss. She remembered seeing their bodies, as they were consumed by the white-capped waters far below, and then nothing else.

**

<u>Hungary, 1809</u>

Jal's eyes traced the damage inflicted upon his daughter's body. As one hand replaced the blanket over her legs, he ran the other over his mouth and beard. He closed his fist, resting his face upon it for several moments as he regarded Baseria's sleeping form before he stood and left Nasi's tent.

It was cold this morning.

"I trust you have come to tell me you are leaving," Nasi said.

Jal nodded down to the old woman, who sat by a small cooking fire.

"Espen will be in charge in my absence."

"It was kind of you to take a moment to see your daughter before leaving, especially as you have not done so these past eight days."

"Forgive me for thinking that protecting the encampment was a valuable use of my time."

Nasi offered no quarter.

"Espen has also been protecting the encampment, but he has visited Baseria … and so has Kelv …"

"They are not the leader of this clan. We are at war. The Moon Shadows will come; we must be ready for them and if that means leaving my daughter to the care of others, then it is a small sacrifice."

"Does she really mean so little to you?"

Nasi asked as she stirred the contents of a small pot.

He smiled bitterly.

"Without her, this war would not exist," Jal affirmed.

Many, including her own father, still blamed Baseria for the war and for the all the sufferings of the clan. He refused to believe Patia's death was an accident, and her aunt and uncle would never absolve her for the loss of their only child. For many, the clan's future had ended with the death of Jal's first born.

Nasi's recovery was slow, and, though she healed physically, it became apparent she could no longer connect to the unseen world as she once had. Without Patia, who many believed had successfully employed the powers of the unseen world in the salvation of her grandmother, it seemed, that after untold centuries, the powers and knowledge of the Seer would soon be forever lost to her people.

The old Seer stood and faced Jal.

"You shame us all with such hateful words. She is no more to blame than we for our suffering. If not for your battle in England or my refusal to continue Tasaria's training, this war might not exist."

Two years after the Moon Shadow's departure from the Romanian territories for the unfamiliar domains of Western Europe, a truce permitted them to discuss the resumption of Tasaria's role as Nasi's student, and possibly a reunification of the clans. Though her powers had never fully developed, Tasaria was plagued by visions, which she felt validated all she'd done; the negotiations failed, and a permanent shadow fell between mother and daughter, driving the clans further apart. Two years later, the clans met again, this time in a short battle, which resulted in the burning of a building at the British Admiralty. The Moon Shadow clan was now forged into such a separate society that little remained to bind the groups, except for a legacy of hate and their mutual, though differing, beliefs in the prophecy.

Jal took a deep breath.

"Mayte's enslavement gave me no choice but to fight in England."

Several weeks after Patia's death and the departure of the Moon Shadows, he and Mayte left the Wild Rose clan encampment in search of their daughter's body, which unlike her cousin's had not been recovered. They were captured by a powerful Romanian lord, Mayte taken as a slave. After Jal's release, the Wild Rose clan had returned to Hungary.

Five years ago the Romanian Boier[14] had contacted Jal and offered a trade: Mayte's life in exchange for the record of a British exhibition to the Arctic. But the Moon Shadows ambushed him at the British Admiralty, forcing Jal to return empty-handed, forfeiting Mayte's life. However, his wife's death had secured several powerful assets, ones he must now retrieve from their hidden location in Slovenia.

"I would never have needed to attempt her rescue were it not for Baseria."

"One day you must tell me more about Mayte's fate," Nasi said calmly after a long silence between them.

"When I return," Jal said, "perhaps you will understand."

*

"How many days has it been?"

Espen held up four fingers in response to Ernest's question about when he'd first awoken from the healing trance.

"Baseria is still asleep?"

The gypsy nodded as he blew air over a bowl of soup. This was the first day of his convalescence in the Nalie tent when Ernest felt his need for rest did not exceed his curiosity regarding the people of the Wild Rose clan. He slowly sat up. Espen motioned for him to eat. They'd spoken sparely these last few days; however, Ernest did recall learning a little more about the Moon Shadows.

They'd managed to settle in France during the chaos of the French Revolution. As various governments rose and fell, each was too preoc-

14 (Romanian) Title of nobility; a lord.

cupied to deal with the modest gypsy invasion, until eventually, even Napoleon had seemingly lost track of their existence. Perhaps it was the Moon Shadows' struggle to survive, in such a hostile social climate, which had compelled them to train vicious wolves for protection.

As he ate, Ernest's eyes returned to Baseria's bedroll where he'd been sleeping.

"You have a question, I think?" Espen prompted.

Since first awakening in Nasi's tent, feelings and images he could not explain continued to plague Ernest, especially when he slept.

"My dream, I saw the face of a girl. She was falling into … water, a river perhaps … God, her scream …"

He trembled at the memory.

Espen's own face grew pained as he slowly nodded.

"It is Baseria's past which plagues you. It is either my cousin or elder sister you have dreamt of."

"Dead?"

"Yes, for many years now," the young gypsy said quietly.

"And Baseria saw them die."

"Yes." It was more difficult for Espen to answer this time. "She has never healed from those wounds … inside."

A silence fell between them. Ernest wondered if she could sense his own inner wounds.

"How long does this bond last?"

"I cannot explain the specifics for it is old magic, but the joining, the healing, continues. I have not experienced it myself; as far as I know, no one living here has, but the forces that join you do not stop with the mending tissue or bone, they delve … deeper."

Ernest shook his head ruefully.

"Why would you ever heal people this way?"

The gypsy looked confused by the question.

"To contribute to life, in any way, is to honor it."

Ernest wished he could ask Baseria how she felt about this honor they'd achieved, but she slept. His questions for her would have to wait.

"How little you truly understand about life, Frankenstein," Espen admonished.

"And what makes you think you do?" Ernest retorted.

"Many things," the gypsy crowed with a smirk, "your being here is but a small example of that."

"Espen, why am I here? And don't answer me with another riddle. My wife is pregnant with our first child. She was ill when I left. They need me, and holding me captive here is putting them in danger."

"We are protecting you, not holding you," he asserted immediately.

"Protecting me from what? Wolves? This clan war of yours?"

"Worse than that," Espen poked at the fire.

"Then you still don't know why I'm here?"

Espen's eyes narrowed.

"Too often our enemies have been one step ahead. You will change that."

Though Ernest could not fathom how, he knew Espen's feelings were true. His presence would bring change—though for which of them, he could not say.

*

The world had enfolded her into itself and changed her a dozen times. Its presence was reassuring, calming. Baseria had moved beyond her senses and out of time. An intimacy existed here, one which surpassed all of her previous experiences. She knew things she should not, could not know, anywhere else. Understanding was simple. It was peaceful. As she slowly regained an awareness of the world, aspects of this knowledge began to take shape in her mind and emotions. Nature's embrace seemed to dim and sadden. She fought to regain her connection to peace, but the answers now were slipping away, to be replaced with thoughts and images, which were confusing and contradictory. A face would appear, and an emotion would accompany it, followed by questions she could not answer. They came faster and faster, with clear insights being confused by thoughts that were not her own. There was someone else here. Whose emotions was she feeling?

Baseria awoke trembling and terrified. The presence would not leave her. She felt invaded, unnatural. Where was she? What had happened to her? She worked to extract herself from the blankets, and the cold air raced across her skin. Half-naked, she huddled against the nearby familiar form, who reached down and stroked her hair.

Slowly time reestablished its possession of her senses. She knew where she was, and she wept as the memories of the wolves returned. Her body remembered, too. She could feel the merciless teeth, the claws, ripping, biting, tearing into her flesh. Her life, as it had drained quietly from her form. It also reawakened the guilt she lived with daily. She clutched the filthy robes of the old woman as she sobbed, but the memories returned.

Baseria's body quivered in her grandmother's loving embrace. Deep within, a part of her, long consumed by guilt, wished that the wolves had killed her. But she was stronger than that. The tears began to abate. Her grandmother softly hummed a familiar, treasured melody, as she stroked the girl's black hair. Baseria reached down and pulled the blanket over her shivering body. She did not want to speak yet—the questions were too painful to ask. And so, for a long time, the near silence remained between them.

"Forgive me, Sunflower," the old woman finally said, "I put you in mortal danger."

Though there was truth in this, Baseria could not bring herself to condemn her grandmother. She should have been dead. Her fingers traced the delicate, healing tissues on her feet, ankles, and the backs of her legs. There would be scars upon them for the rest of her life, but that they'd healed at all was miraculous. Still, she did not feel gratitude or relief. She felt wrong.

Swathed in the blanket, she stood and stooped to look outside the tent. Towering rows of pine trees framed the field of the encampment, which stretched down towards the river and up the rolling hills. The sun had just finished burning off the last remnants of the thick morning fog. If summer had held lease here, the fields would have been creatively adorned with an assortment of wildflowers and dancing grasses. The mild air would have carried birdsong and the lively hum of pastoral insects. But winter's claim upon the land banished these simple delights. Even the sun was now denied long, idle hours in the sky. Baseria blinked at the bright light outside. She wrestled with emotions, uncertain which were hers.

"Who?"

"Frankenstein. You have taken what you needed from another in order to heal. It is only natural that this should connect you."

Baseria felt violated. The world was no longer hers alone. It was altered, corrupted by feelings and understandings that were not her own. What knowledge and thoughts had been taken from her by him? The intimacy frightened her.

"Connect me," Baseria scoffed. "You should have let me die."

Nasi pressed a warm mug of something into Baseria's hands.

"It was not my decision. You both gave freely to the other in need. Had you not, one or both of you would be dead. To save one another was a mutual choice. Your energies are now bound."

"Then break it, shatter this bond," she demanded, the hot water burned her slightly as it flew from her mug.

The old woman said nothing, as she patiently ladled another cup of tea to replace the one Baseria had just sloshed upon the ground. She handed it to the girl who sipped quietly at it. The tea soothed her more so than it normally did. Nasi must have snuck some rum root and honey into it. When she was again calm, her grandmother spoke.

"Time may break it or destiny may bind it forever, as it does all things."

Chapter 16
The Darkness Visible

"You are mistaken, old woman!" Jal roared behind her as Baseria fled the tent.

For the moment, she didn't care where she went. It was over. It was all over. And the news was spreading faster than she could outrun it. On all sides, the gazes that fell upon her were a blend of awe, fear, and anger; the whispers only added to her dark sense of confusion and turmoil. Tears began to sting her hot face, as she desperately sought a way out of the camp. She was too angry and embarrassed to think clearly. The moment she'd dreaded for nine years had come. Unbidden, undesired, change had come.

Her breath sounded unnatural, even to her own ears, labored in a manner she wasn't used to. Then she realized part of the reason for this was that her unconscious path of flight was taking her uphill. Baseria's still healing legs protested against the tortuous exertion, but she embraced the pain. Should she flee into the pine forest? She studied the trees only for an instant. No, the darkness there felt too lonely. But she desired solitude, didn't she? In the end, a rocky outcropping, above the winding river provided the seclusion she sought.

A stiff, cold wind teased the tears across her face. If she possessed the strength to move any of the sizeable rocks readily available, she'd gladly have strained to push one over the ledge and into the river. Something to do, anything was better than this … this helplessness. As it was, Baseria ended up hunched down behind the rocks. The fear and rage came to her in alternating waves. She could find no purpose in any of this. And now her father knew, even if he could not accept it, he knew. He knew because of Frankenstein!

Again as conflicting emotions fought for control, her surroundings dimmed for a moment. By now she knew what this meant. The waking dream was upon her. That woman's face was threatening to appear again, as it had everyday since she'd awoken from her healing trance. Those sad, haunted grey eyes, the desperate plea, the longing … her soul wept, but Baseria could not help her.

She raised her eyes towards the cold fires of the heavens, hoping to drive the pervading phantom from her mind. Countless tranquil sentinels burned dispassionately in the void. Was the answer there? Had it always been? She often wished Nasi's vision, which had been damaged by the apoplexy, was better so that their training could have included the ancient Seer arts of celestial reading. What could they tell her now?

What would it feel like to float, forever beyond the reach of humanity, while bearing silent witness to its uncounted triumphs and tragedies? Had these same stars guided the Old Ones? Flurries began to mix with and even obscure the lights from eternity.

"What do you see?" A familiar voice asked.

Baseria lowered her gaze from the heavens.

"Go away, Etolie."

"You should know that line doesn't work by now," Etolie chastised as she lowered herself next to Baseria.

Etolie was actually closer in age to Espen, which is how Baseria first met her. Her family had followed a series of successful trading contacts and left the Wild Rose clan to travel to western portions of the Continent, something extremely rare before the departure of the Moon Shadow members. A year after Patia and Jucika perished, the death of her father prompted Etolie and her mother to return to the clan, just in time to witness its final descent into war. For a time, Espen pursued Etolie romantically, but ultimately the two discovered that their relationship worked best if they simply remained friends.

Despite this, Etolie had practically been adopted by Jal and Baseria. Etolie fascinated her, for many reasons, not the least of which was that she was one of the few friends Baseria could actually claim. Etolie's knowledge of other countries and cultures was remarkable and had opened Baseria's eyes to a world beyond the clan. She told her friend stories about great cities, of art and architecture, wars and romance, exploration, new sciences, enticing landscapes, and powerful rulers. She spoke of an alien world, one that transcended guarding ancient secrets and nomadic survival.

It was Etolie who'd encouraged Baseria to consider a life beyond the Wild Rose clan. Though she secretly longed for such freedom, Baseria always told Etolie it was impossible for her to leave, though she'd never explained the true reason to her friend. Before tonight, it'd been easy for Baseria to convince herself that maintaining her secret training from Etolie kept them both safe. But now it only added to her misery.

"So what do you see up there?" Etolie repeated.

"Stars. What else?"

Etolie abandoned her attempts to tease Baseria.

"Is what they're saying true?"

Her young friend's troubled expression only deepened.

"About which rumor?"

"The one that has you cowering up here, alone, behind a rock."

Baseria's anger suddenly faded.

"I … I wanted to tell you …," she trailed off unable to complete the thought.

An awkward silence hovered between them. So it was true; Baseria's own words confirmed the worst. Baseria's mind went numb, and then she began to weep again. Etolie reached out and rubbed her back soothingly.

How could she be imbued with such powers and be so helpless, loathed by so many? Far from comforting her, the power and the knowledge her training brought served only to further isolate and sadden Baseria.

"I don't understand any of this," she finally sobbed. "I don't even know what I'm doing. This … this was supposed to be Patia's life, not mine," she suddenly looked up, stricken, "Oh God, Etolie, am I being punished?"

Etolie held her friend, the girl she saw as her younger sister. Etolie had prayed the rumor was false for it could only bring them all more misery. The existence of a new Seer could have but one result: the war between the clans would continue, perhaps even escalate, and her friend would suffer anew, unless Baseria chose to embrace her free will and reject this calling that had been imposed on her by others.

"I'm sorry," Etolie said, echoing the sentiment in her friend's heart.

Growing up largely removed from the clan granted Etolie with a unique perspective, one that many of the others lacked. Baseria's lowly status among her people provided her with a more open, compassionate, and worldly view, one which Etolie had helped to shape and nurture. Her friend deserved a better life than this. For the past several years, she'd often expressed a desire to leave the clan, and that long-dreamt of destiny was one Etolie had always expected her to embrace, sooner or later. Could all this Seer nonsense be a final attempt to gain the clan's acceptance? Etolie doubted it; this was her family's doing. She'd never seen Baseria so despondent.

"Oh, Ba," Etolie sighed. "What's happened tonight?"

***

Ernest wasn't surprised to find the by now familiar faces arrayed inside Nasi's tent; what amazed him was the variety of moods each radiated. Jal was pacing like some powerful caged beast, hardly able to contain himself, impatience expressed in every motion. Espen stared dully into the fire, but his features were dressed in pensive thoughts. Nasi, as always, refused to look at Ernest, but was too occupied in some ritual to spare him much attention anyway. And then there was Baseria.

She pulsed with more conflicting emotions than he'd ever felt from another human being. He'd only really been near her twice since moving out of the Nalie family tent and into a small, cramped wagon of his own; she'd been harsh and distant during both brief exchanges. Tonight, she seemed shy, embarrassed, angry, fearful, and … it was this last, unidentifiable emotion that worried him. Or did it intrigue him?

It had been growing steadily with each encounter. Their mystical bond had not faded; the strange dreams and flashes of insight continued. Before leaving the Nalie tent, he'd suddenly felt it important to shuffle the bedroll into a certain position. He knew, on some intimate level, that this was the location she preferred to sleep in, and after availing himself of its use for several days, it seemed the least he could do to repay her. When she entered the tent and witnessed his actions, she'd quickly averted her eyes from his, but not before Ernest saw their haunted look. She knew why he was doing it.

"Get out," she ordered in German. He'd left without protest.

The second encounter had occurred only that morning when he crossed over the river into an area he'd never previously visited. Sleep often eluded him now, and he'd taken to wandering the gypsy camp at all hours in an attempt to calm his vexed spirit. He discovered the pasture where the clan's horses grazed on the meager grasses offered by a winter's field. The morning sun was still burning off the mists of dawn when he heard the steady beat of hooves approaching. Again, without understanding how, he knew who the rider would be and much more.

She loved to ride. It was the one passion she and her father shared. Ernest knew when she appeared she'd ride atop a handsome, black steed, her favorite, the only one she'd ever been permitted, by Jal, to raise from a colt to an adult. He'd never discussed these things with any member of the Nalie family; still when she appeared out of the mists, she was mounted on an impressive, black-coated horse, one who appeared much at ease with the rider on its back. Ernest hadn't seen her appear this strong and relaxed since the night at that first camp before the wolves had come.

At first, she didn't see him. Her eyes were half-closed; her body moved in union with the horse. Her hands barely touched the animal, and he observed no saddle securing her to the powerful steed. It was a delicate balance of trust and grace, which maintained their symbiosis. Even sudden shifts in speed or orientation did not endanger Baseria. Her colorful attire sparkled as the sunlight danced behind the pair.

As he watched her in fascination, his mind drifted back home. Images and emotions flooded his senses. A memory of him and Ailis riding together through the Irish countryside formed in his mind. The trip had been mere weeks before they'd learned of her pregnancy. He desperately needed to talk to Baseria, to leave this place.

Without warning, the delicate balance between rider and mount was broken, and she hit the ground, hard. Ernest raced across the field at a dead sprint. Fortunately, by the time he reached her, she was already sitting up, and though obviously dazed, did not appear to be seriously injured.

"What happened? Are you all right?"

Coughing and noticeably shaken, she looked up toward the voice, as if just becoming aware of her surroundings again, before recoiling at the sight of him.

"I'm … fine," she stammered as she got to her feet, shaking off Ernest's efforts to help her up. Ernest studied her as she gazed across the field in search of her horse and did all she could to ignore his presence. Despite his efforts, she would not meet his eye. The horse began to circle back around the field toward its mysteriously errant rider. Baseria moved to walk away from Ernest.

"We need to talk," he asserted, lightly reaching out to touch her arm.

"I told you, I'm fine," she snapped defensively, again avoiding his touch. A sudden suspicion entered his mind, the certainty of it burning like a flame. His eyes narrowed.

"What made you fall?"

Baseria could not conceal the look of guilt that crossed her face.

"What? I don't know," she aggressively retorted, but Ernest was not deceived. She was terrified of him, and if this healing union was responsible, it would be better for both of them to confront it.

"I knew it would be you riding even before I saw you, and you were amazing until I thought about …."

"Enough!" she huffed before he could finish. Baseria began marching away towards her waiting horse.

"It was me, wasn't it?" he called out after her. "I was thinking about my family, about home."

She halted and turned to face him.

"No!" Baseria passionately denied. "Maybe … maybe the horse saw you and shifted, how should I know?" She flung her arms out in frustration. But he now began to recognize that her anger was a shield. Whatever this connection was doing troubled both of them deeply.

"It was me," Ernest affirmed.

His certainty upset her. Baseria's lips moved to deny his accusation again, but as soon as she met his eye, she turned and resumed putting distance between them. But Ernest was in no mood to be ignored any longer.

"Look at me!" he pleaded in distress as he caught up to her, but she would not face him. Desperate, he spun her around by her shoulders.

"Your brother says I'm here because of you. I need to know why. Why am I here, Baseria?"

Her eyes were daggers as they looked down at his hands then rose to meet his.

"Take your hands off me," her steely voice commanded.

He'd get nothing from her by making her angry. Ernest gently released his grip while attempting to regain his composure as she remounted her horse.

"Please Baseria, I have to return to my family. You know that."

For a moment she wore a stricken expression as if she were struggling with something inside.

"You love them?" she finally asked, her voice cracking.

The question took him by surprise.

"More than anything."

"Then you should never have left them," her emotion-laden voice declared a moment before she rode away.

*

They separated, both wounded by the exchange. Baseria left him alone in the pasture and spent most of the morning riding in isolation. She wanted to forget what she'd said, even more what she felt, but today she could find no peace and the emotional pain consumed her.

What was happening to her? He would keep demanding answers of her, and she had few to offer. Bringing him here had been a mistake. It must be.

Why had she fallen? Accidents such as this were nearly unheard of for her. Still, she could not deny; his presence troubled her, greatly.

Upon returning to camp, she was surprised to find that Nasi was also in a highly agitated state. A week after leaving without word of his destination, Jal and his small scouting force had returned.

"He came to my tent the moment he reached camp, demanding we meet in a few hours, after he informed the families of those who have not returned and he's rested," her grandmother hurriedly stated. Baseria was confused.

"I don't understand, Nagyanya. What are we to meet about?"

The old woman drew in a raspy breath before speaking.

"Your father's errand, Frankenstein, and the prophecy are united. Our enemies gather strength, and the time for understanding grows short. The time of prophecy has come." Her words had a chilling effect.

"I will need your help tonight, Granddaughter, more than ever. We must be prepared for anything."

"Of course."

The girl had always given of herself so freely, but she did not understand what Nasi was trying to warn her of. How could she?

A vast reservoir of talent and power flowed through Baseria. The girl's willingness to learn, her natural aptitude, and open spirit were undeniable assets, but many of the mysteries of Baseria's calling remained—including understanding the true origins of her power. Without it, controlling her abilities remained problematic. If only there was more time. Their training had been limited by Nasi's own depleted condition, time, and the need for secrecy. Fearing the pressures Jal might inflict upon their studies if he should learn of his youngest child's unsuspected gifts, they'd gone to great lengths to keep her training hidden.

And tonight she would participate in a moment the world had awaited for countless ages. No Seer had ever related the prophecy to the First Light—the one meant to hear it since the dawn of time. To do so could summon humanity's ultimate salvation or destruction, and it certainly threatened to expose Baseria's secret to the others. But there was no time left to consider delicate problems. Regardless of her lack of faith in her own abilities, Baseria had been chosen for this moment. She must serve its purpose. Nasi's faith and the destiny of their clan now rested solely on Baseria, and though she wanted to say more, her love of the girl held her words back. The knowledge of what was to come could only upset her.

*

Baseria's fears only deepened as she gathered those the old Seer meant to attend tonight's meeting, though she made Espen tell Frankenstein. She couldn't face him now, not yet. She managed, with great difficulty, to find a few relatively peaceful hours for quiet meditation before returning to help Nasi with the final preparations.

And now all was in place. Baseria's remaining family, the clan elders, Frankenstein, and the old Seer were gathered around the fire. Though this initial meeting was intended for only these select few, she knew that the unseen masses were gathered outside the tent, waiting. Baseria's nerves danced. Well before the meeting concluded, the particulars of what had been discussed would certainly have spread across the encampment. Jal had placed guards outside the tent to prevent this, but Baseria was dubious his efforts would prove successful.

There was a palpable energy on this ageless night, both inside and outside the tent. Though the subject matter of this unprecedented meeting was supposed to be a secret, one of the elders, unable to contain his excitement and fear, had broken his silence. All now knew that for the first time ever, the Seer of the Wild Rose clan would openly relate the entire content of the prophecy generations had guarded for untold centuries.

A strange blend of scented smoke hung heavy within the crowded tent as Nasi concluded reciting a series of incantations. To Ernest, her hands felt as dry and delicate as burnt paper; his heart began to race, though he did not understand why. Perhaps it was simply the anticipation of long-awaited answers. Espen had been silent about the purpose of this meeting, other than to tell him that the truths he sought would be provided tonight.

Though the old woman still refused to look at him, she'd been most insistent that Ernest sit beside her. Baseria sat to her left, handing Nasi various items: bones, incense, herbs, and parchments. The language the old woman now spoke was not Hungarian; it was something totally foreign to him, though he did manage to catch a few words in Latin and Greek.

For a long time after completing her incantations, Nasi clutched his hands and remained silent. His skin tingled slightly under her touch. Though he could see little of her face through the shroud, Ernest could tell her features were fixed in deep concentration. She was turned inward, as if she'd encountered some unexpected problem and was uncertain how to overcome it. Finally, she nodded to Espen, who gave a curt, formal response.

"I will translate for her," he said.

The old woman, suddenly, forcefully, tightened her grip on Ernest's hands and spoke.

"All of nature, even creation, is balance," Espen translated. "Without it, all suffer until balance is restored. Only you can help the Seer restore the balance which has been lost for you are the herald."

Ernest remained silent. Nasi continued.

"My words are the words of the Ancients passed down from generation to generation. Only with an open heart can you accept them. Only a valiant soul can understand them. Hear them for they have always been meant for you."

She paused. No one noticed Baseria, suddenly holding her head in pain.

"The true history of our world has been corrupted and lost to the arrogance and fear of humanity. Our true past lay in the myth of the Old Ones, the ones who ruled the Earth before man—the failed race. They existed eons before the dawn of our kind, and some alternately aided our early survival, while others worked to annihilate us. Their power lay in their profound understanding of the great mysteries of existence."

"We were separate, apart, our realities forever divided, until a member of our clan fell in love with one of their race. Our fates were sealed when their union brought death into the world. A plague was unleashed upon that powerful, once immortal race, until all but one ceased to exist. The last of their kind sought out our people to offer up a final cursed blessing. A vow was made to reveal the secrets of life and death to a member of our clan at the proper time—then the Old Ones were seen no more."

Ernest was sweating; his throat burned. A living silence gripped all of those gathered around the flames. It was a story that challenged everything humanity believed about itself, and everyone fought to reconcile these words with reality. Could there be any truth in this?

"The voice from the cave, the echo in the darkness," Baseria said.

Everyone jumped at the sound of her strained and unnatural sounding voice. Her words seemed to jolt Jal, who suddenly stood up, towering above Ernest like a great angry god.

"And now because of you, the Old Ones have returned," he growled. "You will bring about the prophecy, destroy humanity. You will unmake existence!"

"How?"

The question, spoken in French, did not come from Ernest, but rather from Baseria, who sat with an abnormal stiffness, her eyes unfocused.

Jal shot her an evil glare, but she didn't seem to notice. In fact, she didn't appear to be looking at anything. But her father took little note of his troublesome daughter as he withdrew two journals from a satchel. Obviously, he'd expected more of a reaction from Ernest than the confused expression he wore at the sight of the journals. Jal's eyes flashed with resentment, as he flung the books down at him. They detailed Ernest's crimes and Jal would not allow him to claim ignorance of them.

"What crimes?" Baseria asked before either Jal completed his thought or Ernest opened the journals. She was making a mockery of the proceedings.

"Shut up, girl, or get out!" he snapped.

"No," Nasi's voice seared the word upon the air.

Jal faltered momentarily and slowly sat back down. Ernest gazed at the journals Jal had flung into his lap, and with a trembling hand, opened one.

"The man in the cave … justice," he heard Baseria say and suck in a breath, but he did not take his eyes away from the aged and worn pages of the journal.

He began to flip the pages, unable to comprehend exactly what he was seeing. Page after page was filled with calculations, mathematical and chemical formulas, mad passages of scribbled notes, a few grotesque sketches, what looked like inventory lists, but all of these things—with the notable exceptions of the sketches—were clearly laid out in some type of indecipherable code. But he recognized the handwriting. He knew he would the moment Jal produced the journals.

"But … these are not mine?" Baseria said with a look of puzzlement, "They belong to my brother."

Shocked, Nasi's head snapped up as she released Ernest's hands and turned to Baseria in ghastly alarm.

"And who is your brother?" she demanded of the girl in broken French.

"Victor."

After uttering the name, Baseria slumped back, exhausted, gasping for air.

For a moment, everyone was silent, then very slowly, Nasi turned, and for the first time, looked into the eyes of Ernest Frankenstein. She studied him across an impossible moment then closed her eyes; her features sagging as she did so.

"The Second Light," she muttered woefully to herself again in French, "she found the Second Light."

A chorus of hushed voices rose and fell inside the tent, as they sought meaning in her words. But Nasi only shook her head as profound sorrows overcame her. She'd been wrong. What consequences must now unfold?

"This is preposterous!" Jal thundered as he gestured wildly at Ernest. "You are Frankenstein. The Seer led us to you. And the Seer is never wrong."

Ernest's mind felt fractured. Out of the corner of his eye, he noticed that Baseria was regaining her senses, trembling as if she'd been immersed in icy water. As he looked at her, Ernest realized something terrible was about to happen, but he was powerless to stop it.

"Tell him, Nasi. Tell him, your vision of the Old One's return," Jal persisted.

Nasi slowly, dejectedly shook her head in defeat.

"I cannot."

It took a moment for Jal to realize what she'd said. He turned to her.

"What?"

"It was not my vision," she explained. "It was the Seer's."

"Wretched liar! You're the Seer!"

"I am a liar," the old woman calmly agreed, "but I am no longer the Seer. That power has passed to another."

Jal wavered between rage and confusion to this profound revelation. Every face in the tent searched the others for answers, except for Espen and Baseria, her pallor gone deftly pale.

"Then who brought him here?" Jal demanded as he pointed an accusatory finger at Ernest. Many had died to secure this man and these journals, now it seemed for nothing. He would not be denied the truth. Nasi's gaze met Jal's evenly.

"The vision belongs to the new Seer, your daughter, Baseria."

A strangled gasp escaped Baseria an instant before she fled the tent.

"You are mistaken, old woman!" Jal roared as his youngest child sought refuge.

He was livid. Aided by Espen, Nasi, with a degree of difficulty, rose and glared at Jal.

"You have just witnessed her power. Do not blame me for your blindness."

"She has no power …"

"Baseria took the words from this man's mind, as well as your own, before they could be spoken. It is the will of the unseen world that she do so. Her bravery has given their powers a voice again. She is responsible for healing me, not Patia."

Nasi barely paused now that she had the initiative.

"Her power has burnt around you for years, but you would rather cling to the false potential of the dead than honor the sacrifice and achievement of the living."

Jal sneered.

"And what is her achievement, eh, the resurrection of your mind, having us waste our time protecting the unworthy?" He gestured a hand hastily in Ernest's direction. "Do not be deceived by your love for her."

Nasi's voice grew soft.

"You are weak, Jal. I know there is purpose in what she has done."

"Then you are a fool," he countered. "If she is the Seer, then she has failed us."

"No," Nasi said gently. "I've failed her, as have you."

Jal's final eruption never came; he left without a word. Espen nodded to the assembled, and they, too, silently wondered out into the night. When the others had gone, Nasi issued a brief command to Espen who left shortly thereafter.

"What did you tell him?"

"To watch his father," Nasi replied in French, as she stirred at the fire absently.

But she said no more as she lit a pipe and began to smoke it.

"Nagyanya, I don't understand. How do my brother and I connect to your prophecy?"

She fixed him with her eye, but said nothing as the smoke swirled in lazy patterns. Finally she relented, her tone thoughtful.

"Where is your brother?"

Ernest leaned back and sighed.

"I don't know. I assumed dead or that maybe you knew. I thought that might be why I was brought here," he shrugged.

Nasi chuckled softly.

"And I'd assumed you were he—a host of bad assumptions between us. Forgive me."

A sudden realization flashed into his mind.

"Is that why you wouldn't look at me? Because you thought I was Victor?"

She slowly nodded as if this were a painfully difficult admission. Ernest stared in wonderment.

"Then you knew him?"

Nasi closed her eyes, her lower lip pursed as if to ward off a dark memory.

"In a way, I suppose, I did. It was he who crippled me."

When her eyes opened, they held no resentment towards Ernest. In fact, she looked apologetic for the pain the accusation brought to her guest's face.

"How did he do that?"

Her hand moved slowly across her brow.

"In her arts, a Seer may inhabit many realms of this world, some of which our senses perceive, and others that remain largely mystery, but all of these connect to one another. Many years ago, a disruption to nature, unlike any I have ever known, nearly destroyed my mind and spirit. And my prolonged illness fragmented our people."

Again she paused and waited for Ernest to draw his conclusions. It was important that he be allowed to do so. When he did the words came slowly.

"Then, you believe that Victor did something to cause your apoplexy?"

"Yes," she replied sorrowfully.

Ernest shook his head.

"But I don't understand how. My brother had many secrets but if you've mistaken me for him, you couldn't have met, so why would you think he is responsible?"

She sighed.

"The answers you seek lay inside his journals. When you are ready to understand, the truth will reveal itself through them."

Ernest hefted the bound volumes.

"And how did Jal get these if Victor was never here?" Ernest challenged. Nasi drew one last time upon the pipe.

"He traded his soul, child. He traded his soul."

With this statement, she knocked the ash into the glowing embers of the dying fire and began to stand. Ernest moved to help her up.

"Nasi, you said I was the Second Light?"

She drew a deep breath as she attempted to straighten her back.

"You are. Though Baseria's summoning of you puzzles me greatly. I must ponder this for a time before I say anymore."

She drifted into sleep soon after, and though the stars danced in the heavens as he left Nasi's tent, Ernest could see only the darkness.

Chapter 17
Red Night of the Moon Shadows

"What?" Baseria sputtered.

"I said, don't drown."

The gentle waters of the hot spring ran relaxing, pulsating bubbles across her skin, and Baseria blinked and laughed as she sat up. She'd almost forgotten what clean felt like. Her toes floated to the surface, and she playfully kicked a spray of water at Etolie's face.

"Knew I shouldn't have snuck that bottle down here this early," Etolie laughed as she sent her own fountain of water towards Baseria, who ignored the spray and sank blissfully back into the waters.

"Where'd you get that wine from anyway?" she asked when she again surfaced.

Etolie sighed indifferently as she lazily waved a dripping hand at the question.

"Leftover from the wedding, trading with locals, who knows, who cares?"

Baseria silently agreed. Her body hummed, as all the problems of the past several days dissolved in the gently rocking waters. She felt invigorated as she closed her eyes and floated peacefully.

"Speaking of trading, Kelv and I will probably be leaving in a week or so for Budapest and then the area around Prague. You should come with us, Ba."

Baseria half-opened her eyes and looked into the clear sky suspended high above.

"How long do you think you'll be gone?"

Etolie's eyes remained closed, but a slight smile crept across her face.

"There was some bad flooding up there last month. Come spring, everyone will want to work on rebuilding, but Kelv figures if we go now, we'll have our pick of carpentry jobs. No one works in the winter, so we could be gone awhile."

Baseria allowed her body to float freely in the water as she considered what Etolie was really asking. Was she ready to leave the Wild Rose clan?

The last few years had been extremely difficult, the last two days, though, nearly unbearable. Nasi's revelation of the prophecy and her admission that Baseria was now the true Seer had left her people in a highly emotional state.

Jal had banished both she and Espen from his tent. He viewed their mutual deception of him as nothing less than treasonous, even though he still refused to believe Baseria was the Seer. It was actually a sentiment Baseria herself partially agreed with. She may have the power, but it was her grandmother who possessed most of the knowledge. Nasi had conferred little with her since learning that Ernest was not the First Light. She was consumed in meditation, offering Baseria no real guidance about what they were to do next.

Baseria's status as an outcast had never been more palpable: people felt betrayed, confused, and fearful of her. Many simply could not accept that Nasi's powers were largely faded or that the most unworthy among them should be bestowed with such power. That Baseria's first public act as Seer, bringing Frankenstein here, seemed to be in contradiction to the prophecy only seemed to confirm the fears of most. She remained a curse.

"You don't have to think about it that hard, Ba. A simple yes or no will do," Etolie teased.

"I know," Baseria smiled. "Afraid you'll have nothing to listen to but your husband's hunting stories for the next few months?"

Etolie groaned.

"I just hope we don't come across something he hasn't hunted yet. We'll never hear the end of it. At least he's smart enough not to expect me to clean up his mess anymore."

Baseria laughed lightly as she continued to ponder her choice. The only truly compelling reasons for Baseria to stay now were Nasi and Espen. Her brother had been, and always would be, capable of taking care of himself. Unquestionably, if she left, he would care for Nasi. She sat up fully in the water, wafts of steam trailing off her skin.

"I just worry about leaving them," she admitted.

"Or do you want to stay with Frankenstein?" Etolie asked playfully.

It was Baseria's turn to groan. She wished Ernest would just leave, as he'd pushed to do for weeks; however, since the revelation of the prophecy, he'd made no further mention of it. He just sat in solitude, studying his brother's journals, which her father had somehow mysteriously obtained.

Etolie could tease her, but she did feel something for Ernest, though she did not fully comprehend it. Such complex emotions would take time to understand. In many ways, his situation made him the person most likely to understand her actions. They'd been drawn together for some, as yet, unknown purpose, which remained as intangible to him as it did to her.

Actually, over the past two days, there'd almost been a sense of peace between them. She hadn't even experienced a waking dream with the woman, and the few times she'd been near him since that night had been pleasant enough. Perhaps their disquieting healing connection was finally fading. Knowing that it was the brother, not Ernest, who represented the danger made her feel much more at ease with him. Still, he was no reason to stay.

"I'll go with you," she decided.

Etolie smiled.

"Good, then let's celebrate. I've got another bottle hidden under that blue blanket back in the tent."

Baseria volunteered to retrieve it. She toweled off and redressed—though she was annoyed that she couldn't locate her favorite headscarf—and began the long trek back toward the encampment in high spirits.

*

She felt liberated. The choice, now that it was finally made, seemed a simple one. This was what she wanted, a chance to start a life of her own. If things went well, she might even travel far beyond Prague. What would she experience out there? What would it be like to finally live in peace? The notion excited her, as did the possibility of leaving her primary obligation behind. People only seemed to resent her actions on their behalf, so why continue this struggle? Nasi's powers may have diminished, but she still had some limited ones, certainly enough to …

It claimed her without warning. A rush of overlapping, whispering voices suddenly filled her ears. It was deafening. Her breath left her.

The joints and muscles in her arms, legs, and chest throbbed with blinding pain. She wanted to breathe, but it felt as if some great weight beset her chest. Her body burned with fever. An old woman hovered over her offering words of comfort, but her mind was turned inward. She would end alone. No, not alone. Their child would die with her. Would he ever know how hard she'd fought? What could have happened to him? The young woman's despair for all that had been lost and all that could now never be, filled Baseria with an echoing sense of wretchedness. In her mind, Baseria began to shout over and over, "Yes. I hear you. Yes! He's coming."

Across the impossible distance between them, Baseria wanted to tell her to hold on, that it would be all right. With every part of her essence, she struggled for the woman to hear her. She had to hear her.

And then she was back on the cold, hard ground of the trail to the encampment, her clothes soaked in sweat, her eyes tearing in pain. She gulped in the sweet, cool air all around her, grateful to all the powers of Creation that she could breathe again.

"Baseria! Baseria!"

Still dizzy from her experience, it took a moment for her to recognize where Etolie's hysterical voice was coming from. She was running full speed, up the trail, only partially clothed. Her eyes were bright with alarm. She flung herself to the ground next to Baseria, grabbing her arm, as her eyes frantically probed the landscape all around them.

"Did you escape him, too?" Etolie breathed heavily.

"What?"

"The man! From the woods, did you see him? Oh God his face …"

Baseria's head was finally beginning to clear. Etolie clasped her in abject terror.

"We can't stay here. He tried to grab me, Ba!"

"Etolie?" Baseria asked as if she finally realized that she was being spoken to.

"Baseria, what's wrong with you?"

The constriction in her chest lingered, but the image of the suffering woman had faded.

"Help me home," she pleaded.

*

Ernest stared down at the journals. He couldn't bring himself to look through their pages of code or the bizarre renderings anymore. His dreams had been dark, and his sleep even more restless, these past few nights. When he closed his eyes, the nightmare involving William and Justine assailed him or a decrepit hand wrapped around his throat.

Unpleasant, unimaginable thoughts pulled at his mind and emotions. What was it that he truly held in his hands? Were these merely more artifacts of his brother's madness or something too odious to comprehend? Over and over, he kept reminding himself that if his family's safety didn't rest in the balance, he'd have put them to the fire days ago. He should.

But he was tantalizingly close to something tangible; he was sure of it, now more than ever. If only he could decipher the truth. Or had he already done so and was unable to accept it?

The night the prophecy was revealed, Baseria had cried out for him to remember the voice in the cave, the one belonging to the diseased man who'd followed him across half of Western Europe in his twisted pursuit of justice. She seemed to know so much about his life just as he did of hers, but both lacked context for their information. Still, he wondered if she could use her abilities to tell him more about his brother — to solve the mystery which had determined so much of his life. Perhaps her insights could end this madness.

A loud knock rapped the door of his small wagon. Espen whipped it open seconds later.

"Come on and bring those," the gypsy added, pointing to the journals.

Ernest quietly obeyed and immediately followed him to Nasi's tent. Jal was inside, pensive as ever.

"She needs you, and then I do," Jal stated gruffly.

Puzzled, Ernest looked to both for an answer.

"What's going on?"

Jal made to leave, but paused in the doorway and glared at Ernest.

"You will guard my daughter—fail me and I will kill you."

He left without another word.

"Someone tried to grab Baseria's friend this morning," Espen explained. We've begun searching the area, but it's got everyone pretty shaken." By his expression, this seemed to include Espen himself.

"Are they all right?"

The young gypsy nodded as he ran fingers through his hair.

"What are you thinking?" Ernest asked, as he studied the stressed features of the man. He shrugged.

"Could be a local criminal, a slaver, a scout from the Moon Shadows … it's not good."

Distracted by his own thoughts, Espen began to leave before the other man clasped his arm.

"Wait. I can help scout," Ernest offered. If his tormentor had discovered them, he must make certain no one else suffered the fiend.

"No, Baseria asked for you," Espen said simply, a wry grin on his face, and then he vanished through the door.

"Sit, Frankenstein," Nasi requested.

Ernest was so engrossed in the assortment of orders and explanations that he'd nearly forgotten about the old woman sitting on the ground behind him. He wanted to ask if this would take long, but managed to stifle the disrespectful words before they came out. They would not help. But if there was danger close by, then sitting here talking about prophecies and mysterious titles wouldn't help anyone. Nasi did not seem to share such concerns as she calmly poured Ernest some type of uniquely scented tea.

"My grandson tells me that you have been as deep in meditation as I," she smiled.

Ernest's eyes flickered briefly to the journals he'd absentmindedly laid next to him as he reached for the proffered cup.

"Yes, but I still don't have any answers," he confessed.

"No answers or none you wish to embrace?" Nasi asked, as she stirred sugar into her cup. Ernest took his time sipping the tea.

"Have you read these?"

Nasi shook her head as she blew the steam from her drink.

"Then why are you so convinced that there are answers in them? Because Jal thinks they do? Because a man you say you never met, but blame for your apoplexy, supposedly wrote them?"

She took a sip then said gently, "Not all answers are found in books, Frankenstein, most real answers are found in the heart, even the disquieting ones."

Yes, Ernest's heart was full of appalling conclusions.

"I've been searching mine for what to do next," Nasi admitted as she continued, "and the heart can often be a troubling place."

Ernest nodded in silent agreement as a question reoccurred to him.

"I need to know, Nasi, what is the Second Light?"

She sighed as she set her cup aside.

"There is little said of it in the ancient writings other than it exists, and, therefore, has a purpose."

"It? I thought you said I was the Second Light."

"There can be many parts to a whole," she pointed out. "They may work differently and not always in unison; however, they will create the whole. I believe you will balance the First Light. I believe your search for answers will serve to unite the whole."

She nodded as if agreeing with herself, then leaned back to retrieve an object from the ground behind her.

"Before we part, I offer you this gift."

The gift was a wooden box, sealed shut, though no locking mechanism was evident. It was not large or heavy, and Ernest sensed it was of great antiquity. The most significant quality about its appearance was the decorative carvings intricately hewn into the wood. He studied the box with his eyes and his hands before looking to the old woman questioningly. She did not appear amused by his puzzlement.

"It contains what you will most need during a dark hour yet to come. Keep it with you and do not open it until then."

Ernest scrutinized the impenetrable wood again.

"How will I know …?"

She waved a hand dismissively as she touched his.

"As long as your heart is true, you will know the proper moment," Nasi assured him.

Her words filled him with foreboding and hope. He nodded in gratitude and placed the box and its hidden contents within his jacket pocket.

"Before you leave, I would ask one final favor of you," the old woman stated. "I can entrust no one else here with it."

Ernest was skeptical.

"What is it?"

She outstretched her arms and turned subtlety, her fingers expansively pointing to stacks of paper all around her.

"You must destroy all the sacred written knowledge of the Seer."

*

Baseria paced the inside of Etolie's tent. She'd been living in it since her father had exiled her from his. She could have stayed with Nasi, but she was still extremely upset with her for admitting to Jal what Baseria truly was. Though she knew her grandmother wasn't fully to blame, she held onto her anger. Too many things in her life were changing too rapidly and without her anger she felt defenseless. It had certainly made her decision to leave a few hours earlier simpler, but the vision on the trail once again cast her future into uncertainty.

She understood now who the woman was, vividly aware of the great pain she was causing her. What was taking Frankenstein so long? When Espen and Kelv left, her brother had promised to bring Ernest to her, but that was several hours ago. She leaned low and looked outside, the sun would sink into the earth soon, and then finding him would be more difficult.

But she could not leave her friend. Etolie had reverted to a nearly silent state, able to provide only a few details to the search parties. They sought a gigantic, cloaked man who'd come from the woods as she dressed and attacked her. Mercifully, he only succeeded in obtaining one of her socks, but the incident had shaken her to the core.

"He came out of no where. If he'd caught me …"

She must have repeated this twenty times in the past few hours. If he'd caught her, both women knew what could have happened: rape, slavery, death, perhaps all of them. Her life erased in an instant, Baseria's mother's fate. Baseria kept attempting to calm her friend, but Etolie still jumped at every noise or shadow outside the tent, convinced that her attacker would reappear.

"You should have seen him," she said hauntingly, but refused to say more. The memory was too disturbing.

Still, Baseria needed to find Ernest, but was afraid to leave her friend in such a delicate state. Several times she stepped outside and asked anyone passing by if they'd seen him. Many people simply ignored her, but a few did stop to talk. Finally, she spoke to Isyll, who claimed to have seen him several hours earlier going into Nasi's tent with Espen.

Baseria's dilemma was solved by Etolie herself who'd been watching her friend grow steadily more agitated as the hours passed. Whatever was going on between Baseria and the stranger, it obviously deeply troubled her that she'd been unable to speak with him. Etolie made her decision. Besides, if the man from the hot spring did reappear, she doubted there was much either woman could do to stop him.

"We'll need to make dinner soon," Etolie remarked quietly when Baseria came back inside the tent after talking to Isyll. "Why don't you see if Nasi can spare some ginger root?"

Baseria studied her friend for a long moment.

"Don't worry about me. I'm sure they'll be back soon," Etolie said, though the reassurance she hoped to inspire sounded hollow, even to her own ears, "Go."

"I'll be right back," Baseria promised.

She came across few men in the encampment, but asked one of the older teens she encountered to go and stay with Etolie until she returned. Somewhat begrudgingly, he did so.

Baseria's trepidation grew as she approached her grandmother's tent.

Her heart could find only one answer. She must go with Frankenstein and attempt to heal his wife. Though she feared her skills were vastly inadequate, it seemed the only way to atone for her mistake in bringing him here. She took a deep breath before stepping into Nasi's tent. When she did, she immediately dropped her pretense for the visit. Why did it look so bare?

"Where's Ernest?"

Her grandmother pulled back her head scarf, her eyes searching her granddaughter's, but she said nothing. Baseria's breath caught in her chest as realization dawned. She was too late.

"You sent him away. Didn't you?"

"Not yet. But soon he will embrace his future, as will you," Nasi attested as she stared into the fire.

"He must leave now," Baseria passionately declared as the memory of her excruciating vision made her nerves dance. Her grandmother ceased poking at the fire and looked directly at her.

"Then you must tell him," Nasi commanded, her face impassive.

"Where has he gone?" Baseria demanded.

"Up by the northwestern bluffs, over the river," her grandmother gestured.

Baseria made to leave but Nasi's next statement drew her steps to a halt, "Do not stop him from completing his task, Sunflower."

Suddenly she realized why the tent looked so different, and she spun to face her mentor, aghast at her betrayal.

"No."

It was unthinkable. How could she?

"It must be done," the ancient woman said.

Baseria staggered from the tent and immediately spotted the trail of smoke rising beyond the pines near the northern cliffs. It was over a mile distant, and the sun was just setting. Time was her enemy. Too horrified for rational thought, she frantically began her uphill assault, away from the camp, and soon vanished into the gloom of the forest and the chill dusk.

*

Nicabar swore silently to himself as the thin trail of smoke steadily grew on the northern horizon, beyond the encampment. He twisted a stick mercilessly, as he weighed his options. His Moon Shadow fighters had successfully snuck across the river and climbed the imposing cliffs, no small task. One of the Wild Rose clan's search parties had already stumbled across the last of his men, as he'd been about to cross the river. They'd been dealt with, but if their absence raised the alarm, then all the Moon Shadows' hard work would be for nothing.

Originally, he'd planned to wait until late into the night, and then set the diversionary fires out in the horse pasture. This was to have kept the Wild Rose warriors busy, and knowing where Jal's men were was essential to the plan. Enough of them had to be kept away from the camp in order for the mission to succeed. Was the smoke he was seeing now some sort of signal to the others? Was the Wild Rose clan planning an ambush? If so, then delay could be fatal.

"I say we do it now," Pias urged though clenched teeth into Nicabar's left ear. "We're too vulnerable here."

It was true enough. The Moon Shadows' position in the eastern pine forest caught them between the river and the encampment. If Jal already knew they were here, it would be a simple matter for him to sneak a force across the river downstream, then launch an attack from the encampment and drive Nicabar's people into the rear force across the river. Indeed, Nicabar had survived enough battles with his former brother-in-law to expect such a tactic, which is why he discounted it now. Jal was not one to repeat surprises.

Pias, though competent—in point of fact he was a rather brilliant tactician—was too young and rash to consider his options fully when faced with such an opponent. He'd proven this recently by trying to eliminate Jal as he returned from some errand in Slovenia. Instead of waiting for his support forces to arrive, Pias handled the matter impulsively, a choice which had cost Nicabar several good men and even a few of their valuable attack wolves. The loss of both still angered the Moon Shadows' leader.

Nicabar passed his hands over his bald head, surprised to find that despite the cold, he was sweating. Impatient Pias might be, and undoubtedly he was anxious to make amends for the debacle in Slovenia, but in this case, Nicabar agreed. Their position was too precarious to risk delay. But the situation did merit a change in tactics. Jal's search parties had all but disappeared, their whereabouts now unknown, and with the mysterious smoke in the sky to the north a potential signal to them, it made igniting the diversionary fires they'd planned to set too dangerous. And there were others factors, within his own force, to consider.

Getting Pias' trained wolves up the rock face and into the forest silently had been a miraculous accomplishment. They would use them now to their fullest advantage. But the longer they delayed, the greater the chance became that one of the aggressive animals might give them away.

Besides, the twilight would render it a relatively simple matter to sneak a few men at a time down into the encampment. Once they were positioned, the wolves could be given the appropriate scents to track and the mission completed quickly. In order to stave off a counter-attack, Nicabar's force would have to retreat immediately. With any luck, it would all be over, long before Jal and his men returned.

He turned to Pias and explained the adjustments to the plan.

"Remember, securing the Seer is your responsibility. I'll set the wolves tracking at your signal."

Pias nodded and turned to relate the orders to his underlings. "What's the signal?" one of them asked. Pias smirked devilishly.

"Don't worry. You'll recognize it."

Nicabar's hand clamped onto Pias' shoulder like a vice.

"I want her alive," he commanded. "All of this will be futile if she dies. Never forget, you serve the will of the Master."

"As do we all, Nicabar," Pias solemnly asserted.

The two men regarded each other a moment.

"Then do not fail him tonight."

Pias issued a curt nod.

*

Fortunately for Pias, the Seer's tent was not far from the tree line. As he made his way through the dark, he slipped a ring onto his finger—one which bore the emblem of his true identity—he then picked up his burden, and began to make his way down toward the Wild Rose encampment.

This ring, this symbol of his family's honor, which he now wore into battle, was the only distinguishing feature about him. There was nothing significant about his height, weight, age, physical features or manner. He assumed roles as needed and had done so for as long as he could remember. His father's brutal lessons ensured this now flawless ability became an integral part of his son's life.

Even though these were not his people, this was his battle. He'd worked tirelessly to ensure that it was so; though, of course, his companions remained ignorant of his true heritage and intentions. Pias was content knowing that Nicabar relied on a completely false impression of him. The deliberately botched Slovenian raid only helped Pias to further solidify this false image into Nicabar's mind.

Nicabar's erroneous assumptions gave Pias freedom, leverage, and most importantly, power; just as they did for the Moon Shadows' perceived Master. However, absent Pias' furtive manipulations, the Moon Shadows would never have encountered their dark and odious Master, whom they now devoutly served. Ultimately, though unaware, they secretly served to fulfill Pias' desires and plans. The leader of the Moon Shadows, his people, and their precious "Master" would all underestimate Pias until it was too late, and then his true work could begin at last: the resurrection of his nation, his wife's mind, and his dreams of conquest.

Pias smiled tightly to himself, knowing that his current assignment was further proof that his plan was working. If the attack on Jal in Slovenia had been deemed successful, Pias would have been stuck overseeing the deployment of his wolves, rather than being the first to infiltrate the encampment and confront the old woman. This was his punishment, this was his chance to redeem himself in the eyes of the others, but Pias did not care about such things.

Securing the Seer, though important in the minds of the gypsies, was not Pias' goal. He did not want the Seer; he wanted the knowledge she was said to possess. It was the information that really mattered, and he was confident that the other small issue that needed to be resolved tonight could be handled without him.

The Moon Shadows Master had his own goals to achieve, and for now, those benefited Pias; however, the time would soon come when this was no longer true. Both knew what must follow. Until then his servant's power and influence, though useful, must remain controlled. And to serve that purpose, Pias had decided that the Seer must die for she alone could invalidate Tasaria's visions, the ones which so firmly connected the Master to his subjects; her power could change what must be.

It was not the first time Pias had worked to circumvent the fiend's plans, nor was it likely to be the last. He placed the shrouded package outside the Seer's tent, lit a cigarette, and then entered.

*

"Hello, Nagyanya."

Nasi turned to the entryway of the tent and beheld the man who stood there studying her coolly. Though the words he'd spoken were in Hungarian, the man was a stranger among her people.

"You're older looking than I'd imagined, but I can see the resemblance," he commented dryly as he sat down across from her.

The old woman said nothing as he sniffed at her teapot. As he did, Nasi noticed his ring and realized exactly who it was that sat before her. So, the rumors of a son's existence were true.

"What, no questions? Or let me guess, you already know who I am and what I want?" he laughed mockingly, as his eyes surveyed the interior of the meager tent.

"I've lived long enough to recognize Death in all its forms," she retorted.

He smiled and set the pot aside. Pias was pleased she'd seen the ring. He relished the utter repugnance in her voice as she recognized it. If only there were time to tell her everything about the true source of his power, his insight. How the knowledge would pain her before she died. But the others were waiting.

"You need not meet your daughter's fate. No one need die tonight; I simply need you to give me your scrolls. Or tell me a story, preferably a prophetic one, and then I'll leave."

Her expression did not alter. The man sighed.

"Nicabar would have me offer you a chance to join us, to teach Tasaria again. He expects it for they must be certain if they serve the forces of light or darkness."

"Then he is a fool, especially if he has not recognized what you are."

This time the man flashed a genuine grin.

"I begin to like you, Nagyanya, but time is short and so is my patience. Let's see if we can't speed things along."

He emitted two sharp whistles then returned the smoldering cigarette to his lips. From beneath the blankets outside, the wolf he'd carried down from the woods emerged and entered the tent. Its ears flattened, and a low growl escaped the animal when it spotted Nasi. Still she said nothing, as he stroked the menacing wolf's fur. Neither man nor beast was prepared to acquiesce.

"If I die, you still gain nothing," Nasi declared coldly. "The information you seek will be lost."

"Come now, with everything that's been going on here the past few days, I doubt it," the man calmly replied. "Maybe one of the others will prove more helpful, Jal, perhaps, or your grandchildren. You may think you're protecting them with your silence, but as we've spoken, they met their fates. Soon there will be no one left to protect. Why prolong what already is happening?"

"You said no one need die?"

He leaned forward.

"I did. Give me what I want and we'll leave."

The old woman reclined and serenely prodded the fire.

"Why do you seek to understand what you will never be able to, my Boier…?"[15]

Pias' temper flared for a moment as the ancient gypsy woman mockingly addressed him by his Romanian honorific; then he subsided into another self-assured smirk. He shook his head in self-admonishment.

"That I should fear the words of a crippled, old mystic; you underestimate me." His eyes searched for any last information he might gather before departing.

"You're a butcher," she charged.

"Butcher? It was Jal who agreed to his wife's enslavement … service to my family in trade for the journals. No, no. I'm simply a lover of nature, as are you."

With reluctance, he stood to leave.

"I'm just more of a realist about its darker side. As I said, no one need die, but that is not my choice to make. I will not kill you, Nagyanya, but the fire probably will. The choice is yours."

Pias paused, and with a kind smile, bowed his head minutely, as he ushered the protesting wolf from the tent.

"I'll wait for you out here, just in case," he added as he sealed the flaps on the tent, then he used the stub of his cigarette to set alight the matches in his pocket. In moments, the dry brush around Nasi's tent was ablaze with the greedy flames leaping up the sides of the tent. Satisfied with his work, Pias retrieved his pistol and lit another cigarette as he waited for the others to arrive.

*

Baseria's lungs ached with fatigue and burned from the cold air she was relentlessly forcing into them, but she continued through the richly scented forest of pine, as quickly as she could. Only dim rays remained to guide her to the smoke now, and she was determined to reach it before the rapidly fading daylight succumbed to the stars. Besides, her physical discomfort kept the tempest raging in her mind and emotions at bay. The incline increased sharply, and she was forced to dig her hands into the gritty earth and rock. And then suddenly, she was there.

Ernest stood over the fire, his face hauntingly lit by the unnatural

---

15 (Romanian) Title of nobility; a lord.

glow of the oddly colored flames. He seemed dazed and didn't even notice her arrival at first. One look, though, told her it was already too late.

The fire had been ignited in one of Nasi's chests filled with parchments, the last of which, now twisted in flame. Countless centuries of knowledge were now lost forever. The magnitude of the crime was impossible to comprehend. Gateways to insights and powers, the answers to so many mysteries were now ash and dust. Her people's identity, Nasi's legacy, Baseria's heritage smoldered in ruin at the feet of Ernest Frankenstein.

Anguish swirled through her. It was impossible to contain all the feelings at once: fear of what this meant, anger that choices had been made for her, relief that they had, rage, love, regret. She staggered slightly as something close to a laugh escaped her, the sound of which finally alerted Ernest to her presence.

"What are you waiting for?" she challenged as she looked at the items in his hands, which held him so transfixed. Then she recognized them—his brother's journals. That these should be the last thing to remain, the selfishness of the act enraged her. Baseria charged him and unleashed both her fists and an assortment of insults upon him.

"I mean nothing to you! How could you do this? How could you do this to me?!"

Ernest kept backing up and pushing the infuriated young woman away from him. Finally, her rage abated, and she sank before the burning remnants of knowledge, shattered by the loss.

"I did it to save you …," Ernest said quietly from behind her.

Baseria held out a hand.

"Please, stop."

She didn't want to hear this. Nasi may have convinced him this was true, but she knew differently. She'd failed, and now the archives would not be needed for there would be no more Seers. The line was truly broken.

*

"I'll wait for you out here, just in case," the vile man promised as he sealed the flaps of the tent. Nasi made no move towards them. Instead, she reached for a small pouch around her neck. As the smoke from the burning brush outside began to seep in, she uttered a few words and sprinkled the contents of the bag into the fire before her.

This life was drawing to a close, but she could allow herself a few moments to reflect before departing. Would they understand in the end? She smiled at the memory of Ernest struggling with the all of the papers in the massive chest. The sacred writings were safe. They'd returned to the earth, as she now must. The walls of the tent ignited. The flames burned with a brilliant white-orange splendor, but they would not reach her.

Nasi looked down at her own fire, the flames of which now burned a blue-green hue: the cold fire had been summoned. It was the same fire she'd commanded Ernest call forth to transform the writings of the Seer, and now it would transform her. It was time.

She discarded her robe as she stood, and stepped into the cold fire. A part of her always hated to leave the physical behind, even though this form was now painfully crippled. Nasi relaxed as the flames began to take hold. Her last thoughts were of Baseria. She wondered if she would still be able to guide her. Then Nasi's concerns left her as she joined the earth, and her powers spread out into the unseen expanses. But it had always been this way.

*

Baseria pushed the black strands of hair from her moist cheeks.

"You need to leave," she muttered to Ernest, without looking back at him.

"I'm sorry," he said. "She said no one else would do it. She said it was the only way to protect you."

Baseria turned her head.

"And you believed her?" The bitter accusation hung in the air. "You have no idea what you've done do you?"

She looked away from his wounded expression in despair. Only the wind intruded upon the silence.

"You need to go home, Ernest," Baseria finally said in a toneless voice. Could she still bring herself to go with him? The destruction of the scrolls left her bereft of any guide for healing Ernest's wife, other than her own instinctive use of Elemental energy, the powers and scope of which she was only beginning to understand.

Suddenly the world seemed to collapse in on itself. Another vision of the woman was coming.

"Baseria?"

No, this felt different. And then something passed through the Earth and into her. It was like receiving an electrical charge. Her senses overloaded completely, the nerves in her body all seemed to fire at once, and her mind grew dull with shock. She knew, with unshakeable certainty, that Nasi was gone. A new and powerful awareness flooded her being as she collapsed, senseless, against Ernest.

The still smoldering fire was in front of her, and the treacherous edge of the cliff was close by. Ernest leaned down when she began to seize and tried to restrain her as best he could. He'd never seen anything like this before.

"It's all right," he kept whispering to her though she didn't seem to hear him as she gasped uncontrollably. She began to sink further toward the ground; then without warning, a convulsing hand reached out and grabbed the back of his head. Her adrenaline-empowered grip strained his neck terribly, but Ernest barely noticed the pain. All he suddenly saw was Ailis, and all he knew was her devastating pain and sorrow.

"Save them." Did the command come from his own heart or was it Baseria's?

Consciousness returned to him in stages. His body was soaked in sweat. Baseria had stopped convulsing and now lay unconscious in his lap. He wiped his hands over his eyes as a burning guilt took hold of his heart. He gently lowered Baseria's head to the ground. He knew what he had to do now. It was an effort to stand, but once on his feet, he staggered toward the accursed objects on the ground. Before he could go home, these must be destroyed.

He was about to head for the fire when a harsh voice admonished, "No, Uncle."

Still shaking, Ernest peered over the fire and into the darkness of the nearby pine forest where the voice had come from. An enormous shadow detached itself from one of the trees and came forward. The huge being was hidden under a large, black-hooded cloak, and at his side, stalked a coal black wolf. Both of their eyes sparkled with a yellow menace.

"You will not destroy Victor's journals."

*

Pias casually rubbed the apple against his sleeve. He'd found a basket of them outside a tent near the Seer's. He hadn't realized how hungry he was until he devoured the first apple in only a few greedy bites. By the time he finished it, Nasi's tent was all but reduced to a mound of ash and soot.

The wolves rushed in quickly and located their targets. Screams now rent the night. The stolen items of clothing taken over the past several days made locating the women to be taken a fairly simple task. Still, several fled, and at least one had been killed by the wolf tracking her. If only she'd had the good sense not to run.

Nicabar uttered some curse at him when he passed by, following his own wolf off in the direction of the mysterious fire to the northwest. Pias sighed. The man was certain to berate him for killing the Seer, but would he ever recognize the great service Pias had performed?

If the Seer's knowledge gave the Wild Rose clan any type of tactical advantage, it was now gone. If it mattered at all, the prophecy could be forced from another member of the clan much more easily. And most importantly, her death would be a devastating blow to her people, one they might never recover from.

As he tossed the apple core into the smoldering ash, he smiled in self-reflection. This night possessed distinct parallels to his destruction of M.Waldman's estate. If only his grandfather had not opposed him, then Waldman would be here witnessing Pias at the threshold of achieving his dream. *Se poate dovedi aceasta noapte la fel de util.*[16] Old habits died hard, he mused to himself over the screams and chaos ringing out through the night. In another ten minutes, it would all be over.

He began to raise another apple to his mouth, but never bit into it. Instead, an arrow blasted through his forearm. This was followed closely by a chorus of others, which whizzed all around him. Pias tried to roll for cover, but was slowed by another arrow that embedded itself in his right ankle. It tore and ground against bone and flesh. He managed to find scant shelter behind a wagon, while he cursed himself for being caught off guard.

---

16 (Romanian) You can prove this night as useful.

He peered through the wheels seeking the source of the arrows, which turned out to be the western pine forest. He was surprised to discover a line of torches there. No, not torches, flaming points of light suddenly sprang through the night as fire tipped arrows sailed to their targets. Though it was a tactic he'd employed, Pias was astonished they'd fire so carelessly into their own camp. But instead the arrows sang over the encampment and into the grassy area in front of the eastern pine forest, which suddenly exploded into a towering wall of flame. It was a truly brilliant display, the force of which, knocked people to the ground and illuminated the entire area. Anyone in the encampment was now trapped between Jal's forces and a wall of flame. There would be no re-enforcement and no escape. This would be a fight to the death.

Pias could feel their vibrations before he heard them. Mounted cavalry streamed out of the western forest and down into the encampment. The men and trained wolves of the Moon Shadow clan were suddenly the hunted.

Some were crushed beneath the relentless, pounding hooves of the horses. Others were shot dead, either by those on horseback or from the Wild Rose clan musket teams, which eagerly joined the hunt. As Pias worked desperately to pry the intransigent arrow from his ankle, several men, now ablaze, nearly caught both him and the wagon he'd been using for cover, on fire.

One man succumbed to the flames and collapsed. Pias delicately reached over to the charred body and retrieved his sword, which burned his skin when he grabbed its hilt. Oddly, this encouraged him. It was perfect.

Quickly, Pias dug the relatively cool blade into this ankle finally freeing the offending arrow from his flesh. Then he reversed the sword and seared the gapping wound closed with the smoking hilt. The excruciating process took less than thirty seconds, but as he spit out a stress-fractured tooth, he wished he'd taken a few more to find something to clamp his jaw down on.

*

Nicabar's mind raced as he beheld the smoking inferno below. How could this be happening? The report caused by the ignition of the fire had halted his uphill progress, and he stood silently bearing witness to the melee. He assessed the disaster.

Damn, Pias. His forces in the camp were trapped; only the river at the far end of the meadow or a trip to the end of the fire line and around it offered possible means of escape. But by now Jal was undoubtedly positioning his forces to block both routes.

He needed to create a third option and quickly. He shoved the green bandana the wolf was using for tracking purposes into this pocket, then gave the all clear hand signal in an attempt to calm the animal, who puzzled as to why his master had stopped following his lead.

Nicabar closed his eyes and forced himself to relax and think. The key was Jal. If Jal feared the camp might be attacked, he'd have prepared for as many contingencies as possible. That was his great weakness, his tendency to over prepare. But how could Nicabar use that to his advantage and save his men?

A stray shot ricocheted off a nearby rock forcing him to bend down for cover. The wolf, however, was intrigued by the noise and went to investigate the flattened projectile. It sniffed it thoroughly, then to Nicabar's surprise, it trotted eight meters away, and began to paw at the ground and whine. Could there be a weapons cache buried up here?

Nicabar surveyed the area quickly and realized the answer to his problem had already been, albeit inadvertently, provided by Jal. The leader of the Wild Rose clan had not only created a fire line by the eastern forest, but along the north, and Nicabar was willing to bet, along the western forest line, as well. It seemed to be a mixture of tar and gunpowder, which explained the ferocity of the flames below, as well as his wolf's ability to detect this line.

A brief flicker of hope touched Nicabar's mind. Depending on where the northern line stopped, and if he could gather some of the men he'd held in reserve to ignite it, they might be able to open a defendable escape route for those currently trapped in the encampment. In a matter of minutes, he and the wolf located the end of the line. It was a race now. One Nicabar intended to win.

*

Ernest hesitated only a moment after the cloaked figure spoke. The edge of the cliff and the fire were equidistant. He decided the fire, rather than the river below, would guarantee the destruction of the journals. He was dizzy but need take only three long steps to ensure that they reached the greedy flames, and the man was at least ten steps away. Ernest lunged toward the fire but was hauled off his feet by his second step. He had no time to marvel at the unnatural speed by which the man intercepted him, for he was moving backward and upwards, as the attacker gripped him savagely by the throat.

By the dim light of night and the dancing shadows of the fire, he glimpsed a momentary flash of the living nightmare under the hood. The mummified hand flung him with incredible force into the nearby rock face. He could feel the blood throbbing out through the gash in his head and was stunned by the ringing in his ears. Between this and Baseria's earlier blows combined with the aftereffects of their shared vision, he was fortunate to be conscious at all or perhaps not.

In double vision, the great black shadow towered silently over him, the half-light of the fire etching his silhouette against the sky.

"You used me," Ernest finally gasped. "You used me to get those. Did you kill my brother for them?"

"You disappoint me," the shadow's vile voice said, "to have come this far, to have read these, to know the Seer, to hold life and death in your hands, and yet not to understand."

The journals disappeared into the cloak as the looming menace silently regarded him.

"You doubt me, believe I will betray you in the same manner your brother did me, when I have witnessed how hatred and mistrust destroyed him? You have no faith in me, Uncle, when you above all others know what it is to be treated as less than human. I see now you must be taught trust before you will be ready to accept all you have seen and heard, before our great purpose can be fulfilled, our destinies made one."

The figure retreated beyond the fire to retrieve something. Ernest struggled to regain his feet, still seeing double. As he shook his head clear, he realized what it was the man sought.

"NO! You will not harm her!"

He began to reach for his pistol, but paused in mid-motion. He'd forgotten. It had been lost in the graveyard outside of Ingolstadt weeks earlier. Still he needed a weapon. With limited options, he stooped to pick up one of the large rocks at his feet, but stopped when he heard a low snarl next to his ear.

The man's nightshade-colored wolf had silently approached and now stood less than a foot from Ernest, ready to pounce, ready to kill. A distant rumble momentarily distracted both man and beast before an object suddenly clattered onto the dirt in front of Ernest.

"Pick it up," the shadow commanded.

Astonished, Ernest did not move. This had to be a trick.

"Pick it up," the voice repeated more forcefully.

As he struggled to remain conscious, Ernest slowly reached down and retrieved the pistol the man had inexplicably given him. It contained one shot. He pulled back the hammer, as the wolf issued another threatening growl.

The cloaked man flung the still unconscious Baseria over one massive shoulder. Her arms hung limply, her head dangled near his waist; her hair blended with the dark cloak. The man's sickening eyes never left Ernest's as he positioned himself near the edge of the cliff, right next to where the sheer rock face continued alternately to climb into the heavens and to plunge down to the river. He placed a lone, decaying hand on Baseria to steady her and applied the other to the rock face. Then he whistled, and the wolf backed several feet away and sat. It too never removed its eyes from Ernest, who was now trapped between the two.

"You trust these heathens but see me as a monster, not as a savior who can heal your pain. So I offer you a choice, Uncle. Which beast do you slay? Do you shoot me, the girl, the wolf, or yourself? Whose nature do you trust? In whom do you have faith?"

If he hadn't been holding Baseria, Ernest's choice in that moment would have been simple. He'd gladly have shot dead whatever this thing was. The wolf would then most likely kill him, and maybe even the unconscious girl, but it would be over. If he shot the wolf, the man could easily escape and resume his reign of terror later, but what would become of Baseria? Would he keep her alive, abandon her there on the edge, or drop her to her death? If Ernest chose to die by his own hand, then nothing mattered, but it would mean that this fiend had won and that Ernest had again failed those he loved.

If only he could reason some way to get Baseria free. What did he trust? Who did he trust? Why give him the weapon at all? Had he offered

Victor the same choice? It was then that he noticed, the slight movement in one of Baseria's hands, indicating that she was beginning to come around. He must delay the great being long enough for Baseria to awaken. Then, he might have a chance, if he could even manage to shoot straight in his current physical state.

"Why do you call me 'Uncle'?"

Glimmering teeth suddenly stood out from the shadows of the hood, as unseen black lips curled into a sneer.

"Although he would never claim me as such, I am the offspring of Victor Frankenstein. We are of a kind, Uncle. We are family."

Ernest could feel only the pounding of his heart. There were no words. The cloaked man seemed to relish the expression of astonishment frozen on Ernest's face. And then he was gone. There was no more time. The choice must be made.

Ernest turned his head to check on the wolf. He'd expected it to already be at his throat, but the animal had not moved with the disappearance of its master. There was no aggression in its stance, no snarls; it simply regarded the man with the pistol as the man regarded him. One was just as capable of destroying the other if they so chose, but neither invited death, neither moved. The wolf wanted to live, as did Ernest.

Without ever breaking his gaze, he backed slowly towards the cliff's ledge to the spot where the man had disappeared. Still, the wolf remained statuesque in its stillness. Ernest decided to take the risk. His eyes stole from the wolf and rapidly searched up and down the cliff's sheer walls, but he could find no trace of Baseria or the monster who'd taken her. They'd vanished. When he turned to check on the wolf, it too had mysteriously evaporated into the relentless depths of night.

*

There was no dawn to speak of; even the birds remained silent. First fog and smoke obscured the sun before a cold, ceaseless rain hid it. Ernest hoped to find some trace of Baseria, but the barren rocks kept their secrets, and the rain soon obscured any trail left by the wolf. She was gone; their bond was silent; still, he was more aware than ever that some of the power they shared resided in him. Perhaps there was some way he could use it to save Ailis, just as he and Baseria had healed one another. Unable to continue, he sat to rest for a time. His soul felt stained by Ailis' pain, Baseria's kidnapping, and the repulsive, burgeoning belief that her captor's final words to him were true.

As he descended into the meadow an hour later, he could barely recognize the encampment. Smoking, charred tents, unburied bodies, dead horse and wolf carcasses littered the ground, as did evidence of smoldering fire lines which scarred the landscape. Here the living and the dead mingled: loved ones were mourned, bodies were burned, and the interrogation of enemy fighters had begun. Ernest could hear their cries down by the river. All about him exhausted, frightened, wounded people shuffled or sat silently, their eyes focused on nothing. Such was the case when he found Espen standing over the remains of Nasi's tent.

His face was black with soot; his right arm bore a deep, angry-looking gash. Ernest stood next to him, but Espen said nothing, only stared blankly, at the heartbreaking scene of ruin before him.

"Dead?" Ernest finally asked, though he already knew the answer.

Espen nodded, but remained silent, as he replayed events in his mind. Why had his father held them back? They'd begun to assemble in the western forest before the mysterious smoke signal appeared, but Jal had waited. Why?

"We're not all in position yet, boy, can't give ourselves away now."

Then his grandmother's tent had ignited, and still his father held them back. But Espen could no longer wait. He'd charged from the woods on his horse, ahead of the arrows. He put at least two into the murderous gypsy who'd done this, but still the man escaped.

When the northern fire line ignited, the resulting wind and force of the explosion knocked Espen from his horse just as he cornered the man against the eastern fire line. In the confusion that followed, the man vanished, Espen could only assume through some temporary gap in the line, created by the downdraft. But he remembered the man's face, the unmitigated cruelty in his eyes, and he silently vowed that Espen's eyes would be the last thing the murderer ever saw.

"Baseria?" he numbly asked.

"Taken," Ernest's voice shook with emotion.

Espen walked away and headed toward the river without another word. Ernest followed.

*

Jal finished the interrogation of one of the Moon Shadow prisoners. The man was now dead, but Jal always started with the injured and dying prisoners first. Most men wanted to die with a clean conscience, but so far, this was proving to be a most stubborn group. These men seemed to be dying almost willingly. Of course, if the Seer were still alive, none of this would have been necessary. He wiped blood from the dead man onto his pants as a rider approached. From his expression, the news he brought was not good. The weary man dismounted.

"Well, Kelv?"

"They scattered, too many trails to follow. I need more scouts," Etolie's husband urgently explained. Jal considered the request, finally shaking his head.

"We must prepare to leave this place. We are too vulnerable here."

He placed a reassuring hand on Kelv's shoulder before the younger man could mount a full protest.

"We will find your wife and the others. I swear it."

As he completed his vow, Espen appeared over the rise.

"What is it?" Jal growled, still infuriated with the boy for disobeying his order to hold.

"Frankenstein's returned," Espen called back as he continued down the hill toward them. "He says he destroyed the scrolls of the Seer."

Jal began to push past him in anger, but Espen restrained him.

"Grandmother told him to do so." His father's eyes narrowed.

"Baseria?" Jal asked, her name echoing down the expanse of the river.

"Taken," Espen answered as he joined in conference with the others.

"That's five then," Kelv noted angrily. "Baseria, Etolie, Vochallet, Sebbi, and Isyll."

"And they were after more," Espen reminded them. "Two died trying to escape wolves that were tracking them early in the battle. At least I've heard that from several people now. We'll have to confirm it."

Kelv nodded.

"Where is he?" Jal harshly demanded of Espen just as Ernest appeared.

When he reached them, he grimly withdrew a pistol loaded with a single shot and handed it to Jal. The two silently regarded one another.

"My daughter is taken?"

"She's alive," Ernest stated simply.

"And this?" Jal hefted the pistol.

"A weapon, given to me by the one who took her."

Jal grabbed Ernest and pushed him viciously against a tree, then smashed the pistol against his temple. He pulled back the hammer.

"And you did not kill him with it?"

What would Ernest have killed if he had shot: a diseased lunatic, a monster, his brother's son?

"If I'd used it, Baseria would be dead."

Jal ignored this claim as he dug the barrel into the younger man's skull. Ernest waited for the shot.

"She … she cannot die now," a pitiful voice said.

Everyone slowly turned their eyes down to one of the dying Moon Shadow prisoners. He was a boy, really. The wound in his chest oozed when he spoke, but he continued.

"The Old One, our Master, will take her to the north and await you, Frankenstein."

The boy's eyes slipped in and out of focus as Walton's warning words coursed through Ernest's mind. Jal released his grip on Ernest as Espen knelt and leaned over the dying child.

Victor's self-proclaimed son — the Old One?

"Why were the women taken?" Espen asked softly.

This time the child struggled to speak. "They have … been …chosen … for the Master's great purpose."

His eyelids fluttered. He was sinking into death.

Espen leaned close.

"Tell me. What is this great purpose, boy?"

The word escaped him, as his life did.

"Immortality."

After a moment, Espen closed the boy's eyes; then he stood and slowly walked away from the prisoners. Bewildered Jal, Kelv, and Ernest joined him. It was Kelv who broke the silence.

"Nasi was right then. The Old Ones have returned."

"Baseria was right about Frankenstein," Espen's eyes bore into his father. But Jal did not notice his son's reproach.

"They have the Seer," he muttered to himself.

"Do you think they know?" Kelv asked the assembled.

"It doesn't matter," Espen declared. "We have to get her back. We have to get all of them back."

"No," Ernest said, "I have to get Baseria back."

The others considered this silently for a time, as their gazes fell to the body of the dead boy.

"It is balance, you lost her, you will restore her," Espen finally stated, Kelv reluctantly nodded in agreement. "But we will help. Father, we must track down Nicabar and those he's taken. We can't waste any more time."

Jal turned to his son, stone-faced.

"We need more information. Continue the interrogations and the preparations to move camp. We leave at sundown."

Espen hesitated for a long moment, then nodded and left unhappily with Kelv. Jal regarded Frankenstein.

"Is there truth to any of this?"

Ernest considered his words carefully. He could not bring himself to divulge the legacy of Victor's unparalleled sin. "Baseria was not taken by a man. And it also mentioned some great purpose to be realized."

Jal held up the pistol Ernest had given him.

"Until my daughter is restored to me, I claim your life. That is balance. I will save this shot for you should you fail to recover her alive."

He stuffed the pistol in his belt.

"You destroyed the knowledge of the Seer?"

"Yes."

"Why would Nagyanya ask this of you?"

Ernest shook his head.

"I'm not sure. She said the scrolls had become dangerous, that their destruction was vital."

"Your brother's journals are also destroyed then?"

Ernest hesitated before looking Jal in the eye.

"Yes."

Jal silently studied him before turning away.

"I have to leave, Jal," Ernest called after him. "My wife and first child's lives are in danger."

"How do you know this?" Jal snapped over his shoulder.

"Baseria showed me," Ernest answered truthfully.

The imposing gypsy paused, clearly reluctant to allow his departure.

"When all is ready, you will meet us to save her," Jal commanded as he turned to face Ernest fully.

"Your word you will do this."

"I will."

CHAPTER 18
A LIFE BEYOND

The trick was in the breathing, she reminded herself. To control one's breath was to control one's emotions, and by extension, the movements of one's own body. In the chaos of life, it was often all too easy to forget, the clarity provided when one focused only on the basic, the essential.

Her mind relaxed, the tension in her neck muscles eased. She visualized what needed to happen and tuned her body's actions to the measured pulse of her breathing. And then she was motion.

Her body flowed into a series of graceful, but potentially deadly movements. It spun almost with a will of its own, as she moved to minimize both her exposure and time as a target. Abrielle dropped from the beam, hurtled the throwing knife at its intended target, and reached the spot she'd selected for cover within seconds. It was a maneuver so well-rehearsed that she should have been able to perform it with her eyes closed, and often had. But for the sixth time tonight, the knife failed to find its mark. Instead, it glanced off the distant, now well-gouged pole, spun wildly, and then clattered uselessly to the ground.

By now the muscles in her arms and legs burned with fatigue. She'd been at this drill now for far longer than she should have been. Her hair, though tied back, glistened with sweat.

Even without conducting her practice exercises, she would have been exhausted. Maybe that was really the problem, she reflected as she walked across the barn to retrieve the blade. Her body was so exhausted that it was distracting her mind. Well, that was certainly part of it. The real problems she knew went much deeper. How could she hope to focus? It was all slipping away so fast.

Abrielle picked up the knife, folded it, and then opened the barn door. Of course it was raining; during the nearly two months she'd spent in Ireland, it always seemed to be raining. The damp earthy scent wafted in, to mix with the honey sweet smell of decaying hay. She stepped out into gentle, steady drops. Abrielle's mouth opened as her head lolled back and forth, letting the cool water cascade down her neck. Stepping back inside, she pushed the remaining drops from her face, blowing those near her lips away in a fine mist.

Abrielle blinked. What time was it? Anymore the days and nights blended with little distinction from one to the next, and despite her best efforts, she could not seem to fully adjust to the early evenings and late dawns this climate offered. She sighed in self-disgust. It didn't matter. Whatever the time, Abrielle was sure she should return to the house.

She blew out the candles she'd scattered around the barn then took up the lamp. Yes, time was the problem, she thought, as she worked to keep her normally tightly controlled emotions balanced. She wiped a tear from her eye, but it was quickly followed by another. She shook her head in an effort to make them cease. Who was she crying for: her dying sister, the unborn child, or herself? Abrielle knew she had to stop. It was her job to be strong; she could not let the others see this moment of weakness. Her fingers fumbled with the knot holding her wet hair. She tore at the implacable mass, eventually resorting to ripping the ribbon from her head. She abandoned it on the barn floor.

Abrielle was halfway to the chicken coop before she remembered that the birds had been moved to the Shaws. As Ailis' condition continued to deteriorate, caring for the animals had become increasingly problematic. They'd finally decided that Mr. Shaw could care for them while Abrielle, Mrs. Shaw, and Dr. Martin cared for Ailis. Still, the trips to the coop had become such a habit that she'd headed there without thinking.

Her own thoughtless actions disturbed her. How could she serve as an effective guardian like this? The rain beat at the flame in her lamp, which flickered and smoked in protest. She allowed it to ebb from existence, as she realized that the first hints of dawn were now firmly establishing themselves. Ignoring the rain, she wandered into the backyard and stood where the waters met the stone, at the place where she had, at long last, embraced her dear sister for the first time.

Alone in the rain, Abrielle again looked out over the sea. She wondered how many times Ailis had stood here, dreaming and intermingling her thoughts with the eternal waves. As she drew in a deep breath, Abrielle realized that she felt as if she'd known this place her whole life. Her sister's passions for it had brought it to life in Abrielle's mind, long before she'd ever seen this beautiful setting herself. It was only fitting that one whose heart was so lovely should draw her strength from here.

Since her arrival, Ailis often commented on how pretty her sister was but seemed almost to dismiss the inestimable gifts she herself possessed. The debilitating forces at work within her body drained her energy, crippled her physically, and exhausted her emotionally. And yet the unconditional love she'd shown her sin-stained sister, the good she inspired in all those around her, the courage she displayed by her choices, in the face of all that was happening to her, awed Abrielle. The tears returned. This time she knew whom they were for.

"Abrielle!"

She blinked as she turned to see Mrs. Shaw motioning to her from the kitchen doorway.

"Get in here, girl."

Abrielle rushed to the house.

"What is it? What's wrong?" she demanded as the old woman closed the door behind her.

"Sit there," Mrs. Shaw commanded, as she pointed to a chair by the fire.

"Ailis? She's …"

"The doctor's checking her now."

Mrs. Shaw shook her head in irritation at Abrielle's state. "Honestly, girl, you'd think you had some strange aversion to being dry."

Before Abrielle could offer any defense, she was covered with a blanket; then some type of hot drink was forced into her hands.

"And you'll not be seein' her until you've eaten and put on some dry clothes," Mrs. Shaw declared as she stirred a pot of something she was cooking over the fire. Abrielle smiled a little as she sipped at the odd concoction in the mug. Under normal circumstances the two women would have made unlikely companions, but in their own way, both had grown fond of the other. The weeks of physical and emotional hardships now bound them, as did their love for Ailis. Still two primary sources of tension, beyond caring for Ailis, continued to create moments of animosity between them.

One was Abrielle's absolute refusal to divulge Ernest's whereabouts. She would not even say exactly where or when the two had met. It was not that she did not trust Mrs. Shaw, but she was in a situation awash with questions but bereft of answers. It was safer for all of them if she remained guarded in her responses.

Upon arriving in Ireland, she'd shed her identity as a French national as rapidly as possible, revealing it now, only to a choice few. It would have been impractical to try and hide it from the Shaws or Dr. Martin, but on the exceptionally rare occasions when she left her sister's farm, she kept her true origins well-concealed. If other locals did not see her as a foreigner, it would make it harder for gypsies, or anyone else who might be looking, to find her. And she knew that Ernest's gypsies, the threat she'd been sent to protect her sister against, were quite real.

If Mrs. Shaw learned of them, the knowledge could only trouble the aged caretaker more than she already was. Worse still, she might slip and let Ailis know, and that was a risk too great for Abrielle to allow. In her sister's current state, any additional stress, such as the knowledge that her husband and unborn child were in danger, would be too much for her too handle. And so Abrielle did whatever was necessary to keep this knowledge of an outside threat from both her sister and Mrs. Shaw.

The second, albeit linked, issue between Mrs. Shaw and her were Abrielle's disappearances. In order to protect her sister when she'd first arrived, Abrielle needed to gain a more detailed understanding of the area: routes enemies might exploit, defensible positions, and should the need arise, means of escape. Early on the scouting work was relatively simple to conceal as she took fairly short trips. But Abrielle soon realized that she would need to conduct regular patrols. Once familiar with the land, she assumed the wearying and time-consuming task of scouring it for threats, both day and night.

She also had, with some difficulty, managed to more or less maintain her regular training regime. The barn provided a relatively private location for her exercises, which she practiced but only when time permitted. All of this had to be done while still caring for Ailis, preparing for the arrival of the baby, and managing her sister's farm and property.

Unfortunately, due to the incessant winter rains, she often returned from her sentry patrols soaking wet, much to Mrs. Shaw's chagrin. What if this continuous exposure led to Abrielle taking ill as well? Ailis was far too weak for the elderly woman to tend to alone, and she certainly could not afford to take care of both of them. However, despite numerous arguments on the subject, Abrielle continued to disappear, and she refused to tell Mrs. Shaw the truth about what she was doing. But by now, she'd simply run out of false pretexts to explain her behavior.

"Fine, keep your secrets, but if you catch pneumonia, you'll have to leave. Can't chance your sister or the babe gettin' it," Mrs. Shaw finally declared.

The tension between them eased marginally after this agreement, but now as Mrs. Shaw dished up bowls of soup for them, Abrielle realized that the old woman had already wordlessly assumed the burden of guarding Abrielle's health, as well as Ailis'. The two sat and ate a silent meal, each lost in reflection.

Three weeks ago Ailis' condition had worsened significantly. Privately, each of the women now wondered how long they could collectively struggle against the inevitable.

**

from the journal of Ailis Tierney Frankenstein

Until Mother's death, I never really questioned Father's explanation for his trips to France. He'd told me that he was "searching for a lost treasure," and I'd accepted that. Occasionally when he would return from those trips, I would ask if he had found this treasure. Sometimes he would answer directly that he had not, sometimes he would only shake his head, and sometimes he was too pained to provide any answer.

The day after Mother's burial, as we crossed the Channel, I watched the waves march and slap against the hull of the ship.

"Am I going to help you find treasure?" I asked naively.

He did not answer me but reached down and took my hand. His eyes never left the sea.

After a rough crossing, we stopped to eat lunch in a café near the shore. Towards the end of this meal, Father broke his silence.

"Ailis, you have been a brave and true child, and I will need your help a great deal in the weeks ahead."

I was so startled by this statement that the bread I'd just bit into nearly fell out of my mouth. Father had asked for my help before, but never like this.

"I have been seeking a great treasure for a long while, and that is why we are here but …," he frowned momentarily in concentration before continuing. "Your mother was a unique treasure, yes?"

I clumsily nodded in agreement.

"Good. I feel the same. Before I met your mother, I lived here in France for a time."

"Did you meet Mother here?" I eagerly inquired.

"No, we met after, but I did meet someone for whom I cared for a great deal, and I was married to her for a time." The words came awkwardly.

"You cared about someone more than Mother?" I could feel the tears welling. I felt ill. How could he?

"No, not more," he continued unabated, "but yes, I cared for her very much; unfortunately, she drowned. I met your mother after all of this when I returned to Ireland."

I was in no mood to hear more but another question burned within me.

"Why are we here?" I scowled. His expression never changed.

"To find the great treasure lost to us, to find your half-sister, Abrielle."

It has taken me a long time to realize all the confusing emotions I felt in that moment: the betrayal perpetrated by my parents, uncertainty about my place in the world, embarrassment, but also a curiosity to learn more.

I refused to speak to my father for several days as we traveled by coach through the French countryside and, to his credit, he did not try to make conversation. It was 1798, and France was a tinderbox of social problems and revolution. This rich and charged atmosphere was my first exposure to a foreign culture, and I eagerly devoted my energies to observing as much of it as I could.

I burned with a thousand questions I secretly yearned to ask Father, but my emotions choked them off. As it turned out, I would have plenty of time to ask them.

Paris was the largest city I had ever seen. It seemed to stretch endlessly in all directions. It was here that I first began to develop an awareness of social class. Clothes, tones of conversation, habitation and even dietary choices marked people. As an outsider looking into another culture, I became more aware of how my own country's class system worked. Most of our time, at least early on, was spent in musty public record buildings. During our fifth trip to one such place, I finally relented and asked my father a question.

"What are we looking for?"

He peered over the reams of papers he was studying and considered me for a moment, as if he'd forgotten I was with him.

"We have already discussed that. As I recall, you were disinclined to help."

I blew out a huff of air and crossed my arms. This seemed to please him as a hint of welcome amusement touched his face. He finally stopped pretending to read and leaned forward in his seat.

"Well, Miss Ailis Tierney, if you're offering me your assistance, we are looking for two things: a marriage certificate and contact information for a certain French priest."

Uncertain of what to do with this information, I leafed through some of the papers on the table.

"Why can't they just write in English?"

"Because they're French," he replied, his tone matter-of-fact.

"Well, we speak English, but we aren't."

"That's true," he nodded, "and when we go home I'll teach you our proper language, Gaelic. But right now we are in France, so if you want to help me, you must learn French."

It took another day or so, but eventually boredom and curiosity eroded my remaining resistance, and my father began to instruct me in French.

Unfortunately, this unexpected adventure afforded me few opportunities to indulge my curiosities about the French people. Instead most of our time was spent relentlessly pursuing Father's quest, with me trailing along after him. The daily chore of searching through endless stacks of records became so repetitive that the language lessons became an anticipated outlet.

In fact, I grew so persistent that one night Father left our lodgings and disappeared for an hour. He returned with a French language primer and a novel by an author named Perrault, which turned out to be a collection of stories. I was to learn the language by translating the book, while he continued his work.

This may sound strange, but it was actually a very effective arrangement. For the first time since my mother's death, I had a definitive purpose. If I learned the language, not only might we hope to locate Abrielle faster, but, as Father noted, if I so chose, I'd also be able to communicate with her. The knowledge lifted my spirit and strengthened my resolve to succeed. Some days I would accompany him in his travels, and others, I would stay in our rooms reading and translating the additional books he brought me. Gradually, we began to have more and more of our conversations in French.

One day Father returned from his travels in a state of great excitement. He had located the old priest who had married him to his French wife (I never wanted to know her name). I'd rarely seen my father so exhilarated, and for a moment, it was as if the sad, troubling weeks and strange environment faded away. Nothing mattered aside from the fact that he was happy, so I was happy. We could leave Paris and begin the next leg of our journey. This realization made the prospect of meeting my sister more tangible, and for the first time since leaving Ireland, I shared his sense of urgency in finding her. My curiosity regarding both her and my father's mysterious past rose, and I became increasingly impatient for answers.

We awoke early, and by mid-morning, we were traveling through the sun-soaked fields of the French countryside. Our driver paused in a small town where we purchased fresh mushrooms, bread, apples and cheeses for a picnic lunch. Father also took the opportunity to post several letters back to Ireland.

We settled in a quiet spot near a pine forest on the outskirts of town to enjoy both our lunch and the pleasant summer day. It was idyllic to be outside after so many months cooped up in confining lodgings and noisy cities. I eagerly recharged my soul in that sunny, pine-scented oasis of calm. But that peace was troubled by a question I'd longed to ask him. I pursed my lips, uncertain of how I should broach the subject.

"What's on your mind, girl?" he asked casually as he cored an apple.

"Why did you abandon Abrielle?"

He raised an eyebrow.

"Ah … is that what I did?"

I was uncertain, but it seemed to be the only explanation. "Then why didn't she come to Ireland with you after her mother died?"

A shadow crossed his face as he wrestled with something inside himself before he looked up at me.

"My marriage was what you might call a bit of a secret. I came to

France as a sailor aboard a merchant ship. When I met Abrielle's mother, I abandoned my shipmates and pursued my heart. As a sailor and a foreigner, I was not considered respectable by her family so I was denied her hand in marriage."

My father had been a sailor? I was captivated. What other secrets had my parents kept from me? The first revelations of my father's younger days had made me angry; now I was fascinated. I urged him to continue.

"We were married in secrecy by the holy man we are on our way to see now. He helped us when no one else would."

"Why did he help you?" I asked, suspicion creeping into my voice.

"He was related to my wife, and we promised him a portion of her dowry, if we could obtain it, as a means of compensation. He promised to file the paperwork necessary to legitimize our marriage once we did. My wife had obtained a portion of it when she died, but I haven't been able to find out if he ever fulfilled his promise. Without the document, I have no legal claim over Abrielle; nor does she to her own inheritance, if any still exists since the Revolution," he muttered before taking a bite of his apple.

"But why didn't you take her back to Ireland with you after her mother died?" I persisted.

He chewed another slice of apple as he pondered his response.

"She was an unexpected blessing," he said at last, "one I wasn't aware of … for some time. I went back to sea for a period soon after we wed. My own inheritance had not been secured then, and we needed the money if we were going to start a life of our own. The voyage took me very far from her for a long time. When I returned, I learned that my poor wife was dead but that she had borne a child; however, I could learn little else, aside from the name she'd given our daughter. Abrielle's family didn't want her, but they didn't want me to have her either."

He turned away; his voice shook slightly when next he spoke.

"I always suspected that my wife had turned to the priest we're going to see for help, but he vanished soon after her death and remained hidden throughout the Revolution. Most of the rest of her family left France or were killed."

I was horrified.

"Killed?"

"They were aristocrats, Ailis," he said bitterly. "Part of the reason for the Revolution was because most aristocrats treated everyone else as inferiors, not much different than the way the British view us, really. They could be quite cruel and there was rarely justice for their crimes. Before I returned from my voyage, I'm certain my wife's family probably suspected Abrielle was mine and wanted no part of her. Then her mother died, and I couldn't locate her. Our best hope is that the Church took her in."

I twisted a pine needle between my fingers as I considered what all of this might mean. My sister was a foundling abandoned to the Church? I had heard stories of such things — none of them good. For some reason, this knowledge made me more fearful about whom I would meet if we at last found Abrielle.

"I see. Well, how old is my sister?"

"Nearly 17 by now," he sighed.

"Will she come home with us?"

My father's voice grew very soft, and he could not meet my eyes when he answered.

"Hopefully, hopefully."

*

We found the priest the next day. He towered over me and when he spoke, his voice was rich with deep tones. In his younger days, the man would have been quite a formidable presence, but now, hobbled with age, he seemed but a frail wisp of the man my father had known. At least that was our first impression.

As it turned out, he was still a formidable presence. He repeatedly claimed not to remember my father or his unfortunate wife and attempted to slam his door shut. But Father's perseverance, a Tierney trait I'm certain you will possess, was quite effective with Bishop Duphrix, who finally relented and reluctantly sat us down in his parlor.

"For all the misery you've afforded me, I was hoping never to see you again," he grumbled as he indicated where we should sit.

"I'm sure," Father rejoined. "So, tell me, how long ago did you change your name?"

The older man smirked. This expression did not sit well with Father. He was not known for keeping his opinions to himself, and soon the two were embroiled in a boisterous argument. Though my fluency was improving, my skills with the French language were far from complete. I understood small portions of their intense discussion, but most of what I could comprehend was conveyed in their body language rather than the actual words they exchanged. Both repeatedly became either flushed or silent during different moments in their terse conversation.

Father later explained that this bishop was, in fact, an elder brother of Abrielle's mother. I never learned the specific details, only that he had been compelled by his family to become a member of the clergy. In performing the secret nuptials for my father, he deliberately placed himself in direct opposition to his powerful, aristocratic family, not out of love for his younger sister, but out of spite for his family and the promise of personal financial gain.

When she returned with only a portion of the dowry and told him of her pregnancy, he panicked and fled, fearing he would be forced from his post or even imprisoned, a fate my father actually suffered for a short time at the behest of his wife's family. The priest destroyed the marriage papers the night he fled France. In an effort to elude his family, my father, and the dangers of the Revolution, he had changed his name at least twice and remained largely abroad. He claimed to have no knowledge of Abrielle's whereabouts and refused to help us any further.

The visit devastated my father. Whatever hopes he'd clung to seemed to evaporate in an instant. He was silent during the return to our lodgings, and not long after posting a letter, he took to his bed. He did not have a fever or illness that I could detect, but he was distant and silent. He'd failed a daughter and both his wives, and had never really properly taken the time to grieve for the loss of my mother. Looking back now, I can understand his feelings, but at the time his complete sense of despair was very frightening. I worried he might remain in that state forever. He'd used his quest for Abrielle to keep him going after my mother's death. Now he realized he would never hold my mother's hand, feel the warmth of her presence, or be at peace. And it seemed he would never know his first born.

For four days he wrestled with his demons. Then a post arrived from Ireland. He would not tell me what it contained, but when I awoke on the fifth day, Father was missing. He left a brief note promising to return by nightfall and bid me to keep working at translating the novel he'd bought me. In truth, I was onto my third novel by now, but I hadn't told him. I'd begged or stolen others from the various carriage houses and inns where we had stopped during our travels. The translating practice was helpful, but after four days in the room I was restless. I was also eager to put my skills to use with someone other than my father, though I was wary of strangers. I solved my various dilemmas in a rather bizarre manner—I left our room that day and went to the local cemetery.

It was quiet, I could interact with strangers for brief periods if I chose, and I was out in the open air rather than cooped up at the inn. I spent hours reading chiseled epitaphs (Father's note had suggested I keep up on my translating work), climbing trees, and hiding from any locals who tried to chase me off.

Though the cemetery was lonely and a bit morbid, it also served to remind me of how much I missed Mother and how far away from home I truly was. I remember spending a lot of time staring at a monument with a moss-coated stone angel collapsed and weeping atop a grave. Mother was with the angels now, but we had not mourned her. Father had abandoned her and forced me to do the same. As I left the cemetery at dusk, I decided I'd had enough of France. If it was no longer possible to find Abrielle, then it was time to return to Ireland.

I decided to wait for Father in the inn's small sitting room by the main door. I used the money he'd left me to order a huge meal, which I devoured as I read by the fire. During the week we were housed in these lodgings, the pinch-faced innkeeper and his wife had taken to watching my activities. This wasn't the first time Father had left me alone at the inn, and I'm sure they were curious about our business. While the wife seemed genuinely concerned for my well-being, her husband seemed more worried that I'd either steal something or be abandoned there.

Over the course of the evening, they visited the room several times to check up on me, both made a point to inquire when my father would return. I really didn't mind because at least someone was paying attention to me. Eventually I fell asleep, and I have a dim memory of being carried up to my room either by the innkeeper or by my father.

"I want to go home," were my first words to him the next morning.

"Get up and pack your things, Ailis."

I kept my eyes shut. I would force him to acknowledge my wishes. I felt Father's weight as he sat on the bed next to me. Slowly, I opened my eyes and met his grey ones.

"We're going home," he smiled reassuringly.

I blinked. I hadn't expected my simple plea to be this effective.

"What about Abrielle?"

"I think I've found where she was sent to. It's on our way back."

The second statement turned out to be rather exaggerated, but at the time, it barely registered. I was much more interested in the first. He'd found her? I was certainly awake now.

"How?" I puzzled, swatting at unruly strands of my blonde hair.

"I went back to see the bishop."

I shook my head. "But he said he didn't know anything and that he hated you …"

"Yes, but I reminded him that he'd once shown me some measure of kindness in the past and managed to plead my case. This time he listened."

He turned and began packing. Even at that young age, I doubted obtaining the information had been as simple as Father's tone made it seem.

"And he just told you?" I blurted out.

Father grimaced.

"I traded him bank notes for the information. I told him to take them in trade for the remainder of the dowry money he never received."

A memory stirred.

"The bank notes were in that letter from home? Weren't they?"

He nodded approvingly and continued his explanation.

"Apparently for a short time after he fled, he corresponded with another of my wife's siblings. It seems the subject of one of these letters concerned the issue of inheritance and informed him where your sister was taken. Since the Revolution, there is no longer an inheritance to argue over, but he still wants nothing to do with Abrielle."

I was shocked that anyone would value money more than family; however, wealth—or the loss of it—makes people do unnatural things. In his desire to find his daughter, my father actually signed away a significant portion of our land, some of which your father and I have managed to reacquire.

By now the summer was spent. As it turned out, the convent we sought was located in a town on the southwestern coast of France, which sits astride the Atlantic Ocean and the Pyrenees Mountains. Abrielle's mother's family had hidden her there in an effort to put as much distance between themselves and the offending, unwanted offspring.

Our journey there took many weeks, and we faced a host of challenges along the way: demonstrations by peasants, some of which were harshly crushed by the military, transportation problems, food shortages, highway robbers, personal illness, storms, and the general weariness of our transient life. Finally, one evening in late October, we arrived in the town of Bayonne, exhausted but nevertheless committed to finding Abrielle.

During this trying time, I became more proficient in French and more interested in what life with an older sister would be like. I'd formed an entire image of what my long-absent sibling would be like and how she would change our lives. We would be friends, and she would eagerly embrace her new identity as a Tierney in Ireland. I could imagine the look of joy that would spread across her face as Father introduced us. The wounds of the past would disappear as all of us began new lives together in County Mayo. Our trials would be over tomorrow.

When I slept that night, I dreamt of Mother for the first time in many months. I took this to be a positive omen. Maybe her spirit knew that we would soon be back in Ireland with her. With so many days spent on the road, our clothing and appearance left much to be desired. As anxious as we both were, we decided to clean up for our meeting with Abrielle. We did not buy fancy or expensive clothes, but at least these weren't patched or splattered with mud. Father was tense but calm as we crossed town to our destination. I put my hand in his and ignored the cold air of late autumn. It was a glorious day.

When we arrived at the convent, we discovered that it also functioned as both a home and school for a number of orphans. It did not seem to be a hellish or unhappy place. The nuns and other adults seemed quite friendly and helpful when we visited that afternoon. A Sister Annette and my father held a brief but rapid exchange, and her pleasant smile and demeanor silently assuaged my fears. My sister had been well treated and loved, probably so much so that she wouldn't even want to leave with us. The sister left to find Abrielle while Father and I feigned patience.

It was an awkward and exhilarating moment when the door swung open to reveal my sister. I had always imagined she would be pretty; I hadn't imagined she'd be beautiful. She was tall, with soft brown eyes and long brown hair which was full and a bit curly. Her clothes were simple, and she walked with the slightest hint of a limp, as she favored her right leg. I glanced to my father whose face had transformed into an unreadable mask. What the moment meant to him I could not even begin to comprehend; however, I look back on that moment as the calm before the storm.

Whatever pretense she arrived under melted when Father introduced himself. It must have been a devastating moment. I'd had months to prepare for this; she'd simply been summoned to Sister Annette's office. For seventeen years she had been here, no family had claimed her, no parents or siblings had marked or shared her birthdays, holidays; instead, she'd often chosen to experience these events in isolation, beset by doubts. Now, a man and his young daughter sat before her presenting her with an image of the life she'd never known, a family that for years had left her to languish in obscurity and uncertainty.

I'll never forget the rapid succession of emotions that tore across Abrielle's face as our father explained who we were. After he finished, she strode boldly across the room and slapped him across the face. She stared at me a moment, then without a word, she fled the room and left three stunned people in her wake. How could this have happened? She was supposed to be delighted that her family had overcome so many difficulties to find her. She was supposed to shed tears of joy and embrace us as kin.

She fled. With no viable information to pursue and dwindling funds, we were compelled to abandon our search for her. This was the end.

Our trip home was uneventful, and not long after landing in Kinsale, I found myself, with Father, beside Mother's grave. We laid flowers, and as we stood in the falling snow, the grief and stress finally overwhelmed him. He crumbled upon her grave.

"I've failed," he told her as silent tears flowed.

After all that had happened, part of me could have been happy to see him reduced to this state. He did not want pity—that was not who my father was—but I think, in his own way, he needed to be forgiven, and who better than my mother. But she was gone, as was his first wife, and now, his first child. I made no motion to comfort him. This was not a moment of weakness I was witnessing, and I was beginning to realize that our journey together had taken something from him but given something to me—a future.

**

Abrielle screamed then began to collect herself, as she slowly realized where she was. Her body was still tense from the nightmare she'd been having. She sat up and was trying to wipe the sleep from her eyes when she heard a knock at the front door. From the rhythm and harshness of it, the knock either heralded bad news or had already been repeated several times. Oh well, they could wait a moment longer.

She stretched her jaw and back, and was alarmed at how dark it already was outside. She must have slept through the entire afternoon. The summons was angrily repeated. She sighed and fixed her glare which stopped the man on the stoop in mid-motion when she swung the door open. He opened his mouth to speak, but she cut him off.

"There is a sick woman in this house trying to sleep," she bit out each word.

"Then don't leave me drownin' out here," the unfazed man whined, as held up a letter, which he drew back upon seeing her interest.

"What's your name then?" he asked as Abrielle tried to study the marks on the envelope.

"Catharine Shaw," she lied, "I'm visiting my grandmother."

Abrielle had been using this identity for cover ever since learning that some of the Shaw's children moved between Ireland and the Continent. It helped to explain Abrielle's accent and provided a creditable reason for her to be staying here. She just hoped Mrs. Shaw didn't find out that she was passing herself off as one of her grandchildren.

"Shaw?"

The man studied her, with an expression of incredulity as his eyes passed appraisingly up and down Abrielle.

"Don't look like a Shaw to me. Hey, haven't I seen you at the post counter?"

"Probably," Abrielle snatched the letter from his hand.

Actually, he'd taken quite an interest in her the last time she'd visited the store. His curiosity regarding her, though not alarming, was also not welcome as it could only raise more questions.

"Hhhmm," he huffed at her reluctance to join in his banter.

"Don't normally go through this type of trouble, 'cept I know there's a woman indisposed at this farm. That's for 'er husband."

He grabbed the rain-soaked brim of his hat, sloshed a bit of water off onto Abrielle's feet then left. She resisted the temptation to slam the door shut.

Ernest Frankenstein. His very name elicited more emotions within her than she was capable of processing at once. Why had he failed to respond to any of the three letters she'd sent him? Granted, the initial letter was sent before she'd actually seen Ailis; the second two, however, had informed him of her sister's deteriorating condition and urgently pleaded for his immediate return. Still he sent no word.

What could have happened to him since they'd parted? His silence was ominous. The tempest of emotions raged. She could suppress it for a time by embracing annoyance or anger, but underneath both lay fear. She set the damp letter by the fire in the parlor, where she'd been sleeping, to begin drying it out, and then headed for the kitchen.

In many ways, Ailis was nearly as good an actress as her sister when she needed to be. Ailis had been so convincing those first few days after Abrielle's arrival that she'd almost begun to accept her younger sibling's quiet assurances that she was merely tired from the pregnancy. They'd spent hours talking and learning more about each others' lives, or in Abrielle's case, aspects of her life. But the illusion her younger sister worked to maintain was one that could not last for long; Ailis was desperately ill.

A part of Abrielle could, begrudgingly, forgive Ernest's ignorance of Ailis's true condition, but another part refused to. The emotional toll his continued absence placed upon Ailis was unforgivable. The poor girl spent hours outside in the cold, by the sea, praying for his return. Around Christmas, the doctor confined her to bed, but she insisted that they turn it so that she could still look out to the sea. The sea had brought him to her once, it would do so again.

But this was not an unshakeable faith. She suffered many dark hours filled with loss and despair when she feared that he was already dead, and that she would never see him again. And there was little Abrielle could offer beyond paltry assurances.

Stepping into the kitchen, Abrielle considered the clock, which was approaching eight. Should she take some food upstairs? No, best wait for Mrs. Shaw to finish her shift then ask her when Ailis had last eaten. She herself was not hungry, but she was sore. She must have pulled some muscles during her morning exercises. Or could it be the result of her restless sleep? She sat and sipped a glass of water, continuing her dark musings.

A disturbing incident had taken place two days after Ailis was put on bed rest. It continued to distress Abrielle greatly. Restricting Ailis to her bed initially did very little to reduce the stress on her. She'd slept exceptionally poorly those first two days, her body a mass of pain.

The normal stresses of pregnancy were horrendously augmented by strange tumors, which had spread throughout her body. As they grew, the masses created throbbing pressure on her joints and bones. They taxed her vital systems, making it difficult for her even to breathe at times. When the baby became active and kicked, the internal pressures were unbearable. Worst of all, there seemed to be little the doctor could do, other than to try and make her more comfortable. Ailis' body was dying and if she did not give birth soon, her child might die with her.

"I just can't fathom it," Dr. Martin had muttered to himself as he packed up his bag downstairs.

"What's that?" Mrs. Shaw asked.

"If she has what I think she does then … well, she's known about her true condition for some time and said nothing. There was a time when I might have been able to do more to help her. Why would anyone chose to endure such pain in silence?"

***

"There was no choice," Ailis said numbly.

Her hand felt very warm in Abrielle's. Why hadn't Ailis told her husband the truth about her condition?

"Maybe you believe that …," Abrielle began.

"There was no choice," her sister repeated. "I know you understand this but … above all, love requires sacrifice. My mother understood this. That is why in her darkest hours, she never kept Father at home with her, but let him go in search of his missing child, for you. He never stopped looking for you."

Abrielle leaned back and listened to the rain. Ailis cringed as another wave of pain suddenly dug sharply into her side. Her vision momentarily wavered. The doctor had explained that if she did not deliver soon, the baby could be damaged, or even crushed, from the pressures shifting inside her, but surgery might kill them both. As the pain mercifully subsided, Ailis realized the appalling truth of what she'd done. The words escaped her in a whisper, but Abrielle heard them.

"I've killed my family."

Ailis had encouraged Ernest to leave, sent him into danger, and betrayed his trust. Despite what the others kept telling her, regardless of reassuring murmurs in her dreams, Ernest was gone. The thought that she would never see him again was more than she could bear, but her tears brought no comfort. She'd fought so hard, but she would die without him. Their child would die. The pain from her body faded to be replaced by the emptiness of her soul. She was such a horrible person.

"Oh God, Abrielle, I killed my family."

Her sister was next to her, holding her hand, as tears began to fall freely from Ailis' bloodshot eyes. For a moment she lost herself to sorrow, but only for a moment. Abrielle squeezed Ailis' fingers.

"No, honey, no you didn't. You're just tired, Ailis."

"No, it's my fault, it's my fault," Ailis sobbed uncontrollably.

Abrielle held her as she wept; their hands never parted. When Ailis began to regain some measure of control over her emotions once more, she studied them. The long delicate fingers, the slender yet strong palm—they were the same. Her sister's hands were the same as hers. She could feel the rhythmic percussion of Abrielle's heart next to her ear. As a child, Ailis could remember listening to her mother's heart in the same manner. Her mother had died of this disease, but her courage and sacrifice now made this moment possible for her daughter. For Ailis was here with her father's long-sought treasure, with her sister, her family.

Abrielle began to hum gently as she stroked her younger sister's hair. She silently berated herself. She should never have confronted Ailis like this in her current state. But the emotional release did seem to be having a soporific effect. Ailis was finally beginning to drift into sleep.

"Will you promise me something, Abrielle?" she asked sedately.

Abrielle kissed the top of her head.

"Anything."

Ailis smiled faintly.

"Promise me that when I die, you'll raise my child."

**

Abrielle stared vacantly into the parlor's fireplace. She'd retrieved the letter from its drying spot on the hearth and now fingered the paper absentmindedly. Was it even possible for her to fulfill her sister's request?

By now, Abrielle's mysterious flight and prolonged absence from the Imperial Intelligence Service was bound to be viewed as traitorous. For months now there had been a steady, growing paranoia that aspects of Imperial Intelligence and the military were actively conspiring against the Emperor. Evidence remained elusive but the fear remained consistent. What action would they take when they located her? It was not improbable that they could eventually track her here. Her presence then would endanger the baby, not protect it. If only she could explain to Ailis what her sister truly was.

Abrielle held her head. She had never known the true love of family until now, but she was no mother. How could she be? She'd never had one. But if Ernest was dead, Abrielle might be the child's only living family member. She could not simply abandon her sister's child to some other family, or condemn the infant to an orphan's existence. She knew that life all too well. And what if Ernest lived? Did she remain here with them or return to France, and attempt to resume her life as best she could? Could the dangers from his past threaten the baby? It was all such a bitter irony, as her heart struggled to decide what kind of life she should choose, while her sister lost hers.

The edge of the envelope cut into her finger. It was not a deep cut, but it bled generously. She sighed, knowing she might as well open the letter before her blood obscured the writing within. Actually, she'd been opening the mail for weeks now in an effort to keep abreast of the Frankenstein's property dealings and obligations. The gritty paper bore an English international postmark, but no date, she noted as she extracted the letter inside.

She had to read it three times to understand it. The letter was written, in what could best be described as an attempt at English. The handwriting did not help, as it was almost illegible. What she could make out meant little to her:

Frankenstein,
Now, the promise. 942 Gulley, Portsmouthe.
Jal

Abrielle shook her head and folded the letter back over. If Ernest returned, it would be waiting for him to decipher.

The clock began to chime softly; it was time to go upstairs to her sister. Already having selected something to read to her from the parlor library she casually slid the letter among the pages to use as a bookmark, and then gathered up her blanket to take with her; the upstairs could be disagreeably drafty. She ascended the steps and exchanged a few brief words with Mrs. Shaw.

Ailis had eaten little during the afternoon, but the soup from this morning was still being kept warm on the kitchen fire. When the doctor returned in the morning, they needed to ask if he had an extra pillow he could bring during his next trip. She seemed to be more comfortable, at the moment, when propped up. Abrielle bade Mrs. Shaw good night then continued to Ailis' room.

She was not surprised to discover the room's window open, but was glad that the rain finally appeared to have stopped. Abrielle set the book she'd brought on the nightstand. As she sat to brush Ailis' hair, she took a moment to wrap a blanket around her. This had become their ritual. Ailis seemed to be dozing, but that didn't matter. She always smiled when Abrielle began to pull the brush through the strands of her blonde hair.

Only a faint breeze accompanied the dull sound of the breakers outside.

"Maybe we could actually close the window tonight," Abrielle suggested as she began to brush her sister's hair.

"Did you read my journal? The entries about me and Da' when we were trying to find you?"

Abrielle was silent a moment, her emotions too conflicted for speech. For weeks now, she'd resisted Ailis' repeated attempts to discuss their father but her reluctance was dimming in the face of grim reality. How could she continue to selfishly deny her sister's request?

"Yes," her voice stated unsteadily.

They paused in silent union with the moment. There was so much Abrielle wanted to say, so much she felt from seeing Quinn Tierney through her sister's eyes. So much of her own life she needed Ailis to know and understand.

Ailis' eyes suddenly came fully open in stunned trepidation. It took her a moment to speak. This was it.

"Abrielle … get the doctor."

Ailis' voice shook as she fought against the rising surge of both thrill and terror.

"Why? What's wrong?" Abrielle demanded.

"My water just broke."

*

She was barely prepared for it when it came. She was still gasping for air from the last contraction when someone tried to pour water down her rasping throat. As they patted her back in an effort to stop her coughing, Ailis noticed that the first glimmers of sunlight were streaming through the mist outside. Abrielle gently laid her back against the pillows.

"Sorry," she hastily muttered.

Abrielle began to towel sweat and excess water off of Ailis as best she could. Too exhausted to really speak, Ailis merely tapped her sister's arm reassuringly. Everyone was tired. Her labor had lasted through the night, but the time between contractions was now very brief.

An ashen-colored Mrs. Shaw sat in the corner behind the doctor. She'd tended Ailis for the first two hours, while Abrielle sought Dr. Martin. Mr. Shaw departed the room again to fetch more water and to prepare some food for everyone. The elderly man readily offered jokes or words of encouragement as he left, anything that would help to see them through the ordeal.

The constant pressure weighing on Ailis' spine all but numbed her legs. Every joint burnt with pain, and several times she'd either momentarily fallen asleep or passed out. But she was still here. She must deliver this baby before her body failed her.

"All right, Ailis, you're doin' great. On the next one I need you to bear down," Dr. Martin instructed struggling to keep his voice even. He knew she could not hold on much longer.

They all could sense Ailis was losing this battle for life, and every hour the labor continued severely weakened her fragile body further. If the baby did not arrive soon the strain would kill them both.

Something felt wrong to Ailis as she attempted to bear down.

"What?"

"Push," Abrielle ordered, as she again took up her sibling's hand.

The contraction came just as Ailis' breath gave out. A sharp pain wrenched her nerves. She fought to force air back into her lungs. She could hear the others urging her to push, but right now all she wanted was to breathe again.

"The doctor shook his head. "I think the baby might be breeched."

"I don't … think I can push," Ailis cried as the pain finally released her.

"You've got to try honey," Abrielle pleaded.

The doctor probed Ailis' abdomen.

"If we can get one foot out I think we'll be all right," he decided. "We haven't got long. Abrielle, I need you down here."

Hearing nothing from her, he looked up, but Abrielle's attention wasn't focused on him, or for the moment, her sister whose hand she still clasped. Her expression was unreadable as she stared at the doorway. There stood the gaunt, bruised, and silent figure of Ernest Frankenstein.

Ailis, still dizzy from her last efforts, had not noticed him. He got down on his knees and took his wife's other hand. Ailis slowly turned her head to face him, and as she beheld him, her eyes filled with tears. Abrielle released her other hand, which now reached out to touch the phantom of her husband. But he was not a ghost. He was real.

"Ernest," she whispered as he took her hand into his. He tenderly kissed her forehead.

"Hold on, Ailis."

"I'm so scared. You were gone so long … I thought …"

He held her frail form. If he truly possessed any power from Baseria, he willed it be given to Ailis now with all of his heart.

"Abrielle, now!" Dr. Martin barked.

Abrielle's face blanched as she stood.

"During the next contraction, I want you to push very gently against the bulge, here," the doctor explained to her in hushed tones. "We've got to get the other foot out, understand? Okay. Watch me."

Nearly breathless with fear, Abrielle placed her hands were the doctor had indicated. The seconds faded like thunderous years.

"Now," the doctor calmly instructed.

Abrielle pressed.

"Stop," he ordered without looking up.

Again they waited. Ernest was with her once more; Ailis could feel a new strength building within her. Before it faded she must save her baby, regardless of the price. The doctor continued giving orders.

"Go. Wait. Good. Stop. I've got it."

Abrielle stood upright; her sister was looking anxiously down at the doctor.

"I'm just checking that the cord isn't … push, Ailis."

With love in her heart, she looked to Ernest as another contraction gripped her, and this time she did push; one final prayer in her heart, one last great effort to give life to the baby within her. Ailis' face squinted with exertion then relaxed, as she began to draw in deep, even breaths. She began to laugh when the doctor's efforts yielded a new cry, one the world had never heard, from one who had just drawn first breath. It was over.

As the doctor finished cutting the cord and performed a careful, initial examination, Ailis hugged Ernest, then Mrs. Shaw. Abrielle recovered a clean blanket from the room next door then returned to cover her shaking sister, who kissed her.

"What is it?" Ailis asked expectantly.

Dr. Martin beamed down at the tiny life, wrapped in a blanket in his arms.

"A girl, Ailis. She's a beautiful girl."

Ailis hugged her old friend and mentor, as he handed the child to her.

"Thank you," she whispered to him.

Then she and Ernest beheld the miracle they'd created.

"She's beautiful," Ernest said, before kissing his wife warmly.

For the first time in months, Ailis felt no pain, only a joyful euphoria. Silent tears glistened down her cheeks, as her baby tried to open her eyes for the first time.

“Oh, she’s an angel, Ailis. Do you have a name picked out?” Mrs. Shaw asked.

Ernest looked to his wife, whose gentle smile danced in the warm glow of the sunlit room.

“Tara,” she said. “Tara Tierney Frankenstein.”

Chapter 19
Eternity

The release was subtle. She had been sleeping next to Ernest. She was sleeping next to him. She would never sleep next to him again. All were true. Time and eternity blended; they were the same but different. She existed without limit and not at all. Like a whisper from an old companion, the grey light shone to reveal this to her. Ailis was as she had always been and would never be again. She basked in the warm, happy knowledge that all was as it should be. Prayers of thanks were given to her and gratitude was offered in return.

But he would awaken in the dark, she remembered of that light best loved, the one who had always been poetry to her. She could not leave him in the dark. She could leave none of them in darkness. She hadn't. She knew she hadn't. They would all still guide one another to beautiful truths, beyond creation or destruction. Such was love.

CHAPTER 20
THE PROMISE-KEEPERS

The rain pinged off the lid of the heavy metal pail. As Abrielle paused at the end of the Shaws drive, trails of her breath, twirled away into the black night. Though she needed to get home, she could no longer ignore her protesting neck muscles. She set the pail on the ground then sat down upon a sturdy log by the side of the road. Mr. Shaw had offered repeatedly to drive her back home, but at the moment, she craved only solitude. This was the first time she'd been truly alone for days. She needed silence.

Abrielle hunched over, crossing her arms and legs. Right now, she just wanted to believe pretty lies. She wanted someone to hold her and reassure her that everything would be all right. But how could it be? She had lost her, forever. Ailis was dead.

She had lived only a single day after Tara's birth, her spirit flown during the night. Abrielle discovered her near dawn. No, she'd found them. Tara and Ernest had been sleeping in the room with her. It was Tara's crying that awoke Abrielle. It was as if the child knew that her mother had been taken from them, stolen. There she found Ernest, holding Ailis; his gaze lost to eternity, her eyes closed. The endless pain no longer marred her sister's lovely features. A single tear graced both of their faces, as though one was mourning the loss of the other. How long had he held her in the darkness? Abrielle reflected on the fact that she'd not seen him cry since that day. It was as if the shock and appalling pain in his soul prevented it.

Abrielle could not allow herself the luxury of grief these past twelve days, despite the burning anguish and emptiness within. Caring for Tara had become her life. It was difficult those first days, preparing for the funeral, while learning to care for her niece. Thank goodness for Mrs. Shaw's guidance in such matters. Ernest, however, was consumed by a numbing grief that had all but paralyzed him; though in the past two days, he'd shown some signs of improvement.

Despite this, Abrielle worried about the man. Tragedy seemed to stalk him, though how much of it was of his own creation, she still hadn't decided. Then again how much of her own misery was she responsible for? Each suffered silently in pain and uncertainty under the burden of their own dark secrets. Neither was comfortable talking openly to the other about their pasts or what they should do about the future. Though united by their love for Ailis, both concealed selfish truths first from her and now from one another.

Of his long absence, he'd said little. And other than stories told to her by Ailis and the Shaw's, she really knew almost nothing about him. Where would his grief drive him? Should she leave him? Would he abandon Tara to her? In some ways, Abrielle felt that he already had. Were they both meant to be a part of her life or only one of them? Would honesty provide answers or destroy them?

Shaken by these thoughts, she resumed her grip on handle of the covered milk pail and willed herself to walk again. She pulled her cloak closer. It had not stopped raining since the morning of the burial. Abrielle knew she needed to give him time to grieve, but her patience was beginning to wear. It would be a relief if Ernest would, at least, get the family cow back from the Shaws so she didn't have to make this trip twice a day.

At least these trips forced him to watch over his child. Abrielle and Mrs. Shaw had insisted upon this. He needed to bond with his daughter, but Ernest was reluctant to be near her.

The reasons, though, were no great mystery. Tara favored Ailis, in so many ways. For now, she served to remind him of all they had lost, but in time, he would come to know his daughter in her own right. At least, Abrielle hoped he would. Tara was also the last Frankenstein, and Ernest's recent trials and time in Geneva had undoubtedly reminded him of his earlier losses. Perhaps he was scared to love her.

As she trudged onward, Abrielle's mind was so lost in thought that she failed to notice the scent at first. It was muted by the rich odor of water-laden earth. Besides, the smell of smoke on a damp winter's night was nothing unusual. But as she rounded the bend the in the road, the scent and scene before her froze Abrielle's steps. An unholy glow illuminated the nearby horizon.

"Oh God. Tara!"

The pail was instantly abandoned, as she began to run toward the farm. What could have happened? She cursed herself. How could she have been so stupid? She should never have left them alone. Her rain-soaked clothing and the mud taxed her so that by the time she reached the trees near the end of the driveway, her lungs burned. But her mind was fully alert. For an instant, a flicker of relief touched her heart. It was not the house, but the barn, which burned in the relentless downpour. Then she saw them. Old reflexes took over and quickly carried her out of sight. Had they seen her? She peered around the tree at the two men, clad in gypsy garb, who stood outside the barn watching it burn.

Her mind raced. Should she confront them now or try to slip past them and into the house? She could probably reach it without being noticed, unless of course, there were others she could not see, who might raise the alarm. Then again, what if the fire had simply been set to draw Ernest out? She studied the men a moment. No, their stances were more defensive, they were guarding the barn, which could mean only one thing.

She withdrew her knife then tried to move, with stealth and speed, to within a few feet of the pair. It was difficult. Her boots repeatedly sank into the soggy grip of the earth, and she prayed they did not hear the alternating slosh and sucking sounds, issued by her harried passage. When she reached her destination, she paused for only an instant. Though she strained to hear them over the sounds of steady rain and the roar of flames, Abrielle was unable to discern much of anything. The language was wholly unfamiliar to her. But, as she prepared to strike, there was one word, repeated twice, which triggered her memory and focused her attention: Jal.

*

Ernest looked away from the fire to the tiny life beside him. The life he and Ailis had created, the life she'd sacrificed her own to bring into this world. Tara shifted subtly in her sleep, issuing soft sounds as she did so. Her mouth worked to form a yawn. He rocked the cradle he'd built for her before leaving for Geneva, hoping to keep her asleep until Abrielle returned. She would be hungry when she woke. He whispered soothingly to her.

Her lids fluttered momentarily, revealing her grey eyes, her mother's eyes, and then she slid back into a light slumber. Ernest closed his own eyes, as the deep shame and guilt over Ailis' death burned within his soul.

"The disease progressed very rapidly, Ernest. There was nothing anyone could have done," Dr. Martin had told him after the funeral.

But there was. He should have been here with her, with them, not chasing ghosts across Europe. If he'd stayed, things could have been different. Instead, he had failed his beloved, and in doing so, robbed Tara of her mother, her beautiful, gentle mother, forever. Ailis had suffered here alone; the memory of Baseria's vision haunted him, and now death had taken her to a shore he could not reach. Why hadn't he been able to save her?

He listened to the dull sound of pelting raindrops against the window panes.

"The fact that Tara is here at all is a miracle, one she died to give you," Martin had asserted.

He held his head in his hands. Why hadn't Ailis told him how sick she truly was? His emotions surged wildly whenever the thought entered his mind: anger became anguish, then guilt, love, sorrow, regret and then it all began anew. The painful phantoms of his past were also reborn in this familiar pattern. How could he help but feel betrayed, abandoned again? Ernest's jaw squeezed tautly and his eyes closed momentarily as the images of Justine returned. But Ailis had given her life for their child …

Numbly, he stood; his halting steps took him to the kitchen. The cooking fire was still burning, but he added more wood just to be sure. The milk would need to be heated as soon as Abrielle returned. This chore was unfair to her, especially after all she'd done. He really should move the cow back to the barn. Tomorrow, he promised himself, he would do so tomorrow. A cold gust of wind suddenly beat the flames of the cooking fire as the front door was opened and then closed.

"Abrielle?" Ernest called.

There was no answer. Tara began to cry. She must have stopped to check on her. He wiped a hand over his eyes, as he walked toward the front room.

Time stopped.

Four gypsies, one of whom was a woman, stood in the room. He barely noticed their presence, though, for all his attention was focused on Jal Nalie. Tara was crying in his arms, the pistol given to Ernest by Victor's son, pointed at her chest.

"You have betrayed me, Frankenstein. Your word is dust," he spit at the ground. "I claim your daughter, until you fulfill your oath and return mine to me, as promised."

Ernest never heard the gypsies who entered through the kitchen. Only the crushing blow to the back of his head alerted him to their presence. Tara's screams echoed in his rapidly dimming mind.

*

The gypsy woman vanished with Tara out the backdoor. Jal motioned for two of his men to pick up Ernest.

"What of the mother?" one asked.

Jal waved his hand dismissively and then nodded to the front door. They hauled Ernest into the rain, depositing him roughly onto the hay covered floor of the barn. Jal shuttered the doors.

"Light it in two minutes," he instructed, "we should be away by then. Follow when you can. If anyone interferes, kill them."

"I thought he was to find the Seer?" one of the men stammered.

"If he lives; I now have other means to save my daughter," Jal sneered before disappearing into the darkness.

*

Ernest awoke gasping for air. It took him several moments to realize where he was and what was happening. Was escape possible? Despite the smoke and ruinous flames surrounding him, he made no motion to get up. He calmly studied the embers burning above him as his vision faded. It could end here. All he most feared had come to pass. His wife and now his child had been taken from him; there was no one left to lose. He hadn't been strong enough to save them.

Everyone he'd ever loved was gone: Tara, Ailis, Justine, Elizabeth, William, Victor, his parents. He'd failed them all, and he held no hope that Baseria lived. There was nothing more to understand, no dreams left. His soul could suffer no more losses, endure no more pain. He wanted it to be over. He closed his eyes and welcomed oblivion.

*

The moment had come. Abrielle divorced herself from emotion as she engaged the first man. She raced from the woods; her knife sliced his forearm as she passed, slowing his reaction time and dividing his attention. They were fast. The second man was already tracking her with a pistol. She lunged at him but was forced to duck the sweeping blade of the sword unsheathed in his other hand.

He recovered quickly, and the blade hummed through the air a second time before it was inadvertently driven deeply into a log of firewood piled near Abrielle's head. She seized the opportunity to kick the neglected pistol from his hand as his momentum slammed his body into the woodpile. He momentarily tried to free his sword, but was unable to immediately do so; he pounced on her. Their struggle was brief. Despite his greater physical strength, he challenged most of his energies and efforts into re-obtaining his pistol. She had one chance.

"Where are they?"

He viciously stabbed her in the ribs, with his sharp elbow. She released her hold on him, and he dove forward and greedily snatched up the pistol. He spun to take aim at his target, but never completed the motion. Abrielle snapped his neck clean.

Before she could move to pick up the weapon, a wild shot tore into the dead man. The other gypsy had recovered, though; she'd correctly surmised that he was left-handed. Her initial attack had served the tendons in that hand, rendering it almost useless. Forcing him to rely on his weaker hand had probably just saved her life. But she needed to immobilize him before he could mount another attack.

She also needed this one alive, but the look in his eyes made it clear this man was prepared to die fighting. The gleam of the dead gypsy's blade hovered two feet away. Gambling that her living enemy didn't have a second pistol at the ready, she lunged forward and began to pull at the sword's hilt with all her strength. To her great surprise, it released easily. The dead man's frantic efforts to free it must have been closer to succeeding than either of them had realized.

The first gypsy groped for his sword, as she stood and charged him.

Unfortunately, it too was attached to favor his now-crippled left hand. The injury cost valuable seconds. He pivoted his body and was just withdrawing the blade from the scabbard with his right hand when she struck. He gasped in shock and pain. Only dimly, did he perceive that she was forcing him backward. The pain and pressure increased; then his body reeled under a new impact. His own sword clattered uselessly to the ground. She kicked it away.

Abrielle's strategy had worked. She'd stabbed the gypsy directly beneath the collar bone, and forced the blade through his back. Using her own momentum, she'd managed to stagger him back to the tree line. The sword now pinned him solidly to a trunk.

"Where's Frankenstein?" she yelled, brutally twisting the imbedded blade. The man screamed in agony, then heaved lusty breaths, as she released the pressure. He spit blood on the ground then glared into her eyes.

"You just gonna let them burn?" he asked in French and began to laugh.

Without pause, Abrielle ran towards the conflagration.

*

Her head came gently to rest against his chest, and he bathed in her warm essence. Tara's third feeding had gone well, and she was now fast asleep. She rested in the cradle where Ernest had set her for now. Her breaths were short and heavy, as her new lungs adjusted to a different way of operating. Ailis nuzzled him affectionately, her hair catching slightly on the stubble of his chin. He smiled bitterly. They'd had so little time together.

A dull roar momentarily erupted in his ears, but neither his wife nor child stirred. All was peaceful again as he bathed in the scent of her skin.

"I missed you," she sighed sleepily.

His embrace tightened. He could feel the muted pattern of her heart-beat.

"I love you."

He could sense her smile. He'd saved her. His vision flickered with a dazzling light. He would never leave her again. The light grew stronger. He needed to tell her now.

"Did you find Victor?"

His eyes opened, and smoke mercilessly stung them. He blinked to clear the tears from his eyes and saw her hovering over him. Her lips were moving, saying something to him. Words began to echo in his mind.

"Not yet, not yet."

And then Ailis was gone. He choked violently on soot as he became aware that Abrielle was dragging him from the barn.

"Not yet, you're not dying yet," she screamed hysterically as they finally broke into the clean, cold rain. They both coughed uncontrollably, their clothes belching smoke as she continued to drag him away from the burning barn.

When she decided that they were at a safe enough distance, she collapsed next to him for a moment. Her chest was heaving but she knew she could not rest. She rose to her knees and grabbed him.

"Where's Tara?! Where is she?!"

Ernest blinked and tried to work moisture back into his mouth. After a brief fit of coughing he answered.

"They took her," he wheezed.

Suddenly something flew by them. Wisps of water splayed off the tips of Abrielle's hair, as she turned to see the gypsy, who'd been pinned to the tree, run past her and into the burning barn. She swore vehemently as she stood to give chase. As she did, her progress was arrested, instantly, and she fell to the ground, hard. Had she slipped? No, something was holding her. She looked back. Ernest clung to her shoe.

"Wait…."

Infuriated by his actions, she kicked him viciously in the face. His grip released immediately, and she scrambled madly to her feet. She did not look back.

By now, the barn's structure was moments from collapse, yet the heat and smoke did not seem as prevalent as they'd been a few minutes ago when she'd rescued Ernest. As she pivoted in search of her prey, the answer became obvious. He'd forced the back door and escaped through the far side of the barn. She charged through the opening seconds before the barn's roof collapsed.

Flames licked Abrielle's heels as she ran, but she didn't stop. Hopefully, the fires smoldering on the hem of her dress would perish in the rain, and though they stung her, she paid them little mind. Her focus was on the trail that the panicked gypsy had left: the tale was told in mud, on rock, by branch, and blood. If he escaped, she might never learn Tara's fate, or he might reach reinforcements. Her dress entangled on all manner of obstacles as she pursued her foe. Bare branches bit her flesh, and her sweat froze in the clammy rain, but she pressed on, following the man up a short rise.

Her heart sank as they broke into the open ground of a pasture; though injured, the gypsy was gaining a respectable lead over her. Abrielle had been slowed, first by Ernest, then her search in the barn, her clothing, and now her own fatigue. Her muscles burned and her lungs' passionate pleas for air were beginning to slow her steps. If she was going to catch him, it must be now.

She summoned the last resources of her remaining strength; sustaining herself now on raw emotion alone. She couldn't fail Ailis. Anger drove her legs; the appertaining rage she felt over her niece's abduction silenced her fears. She would not fail Tara. She would catch this monster, no matter what. Her limbs felt light as the oxygen-starved muscles within them began to cramp, but she was closing the distance. Each painful step brought her closer to her prey.

The edge of the pasture dipped where a natural channel formed to drain runoff. The gypsy hesitated only a moment before he hurtled down the embankment. He was just coming up the other side when Abrielle launched herself from the opposite one. Her body smashed into his. She managed to grab his legs, but viciously twisted her own ankle in the effort. The combination of the sloping landscape and the unexpected force of her impact proved fatal to the man.

His weight and her momentum forced his head to be carried into the trunk of a nearby tree. The repulsive sound of his neck bones shattering pierced the night. Heaving breaths, Abrielle crawled up the rise to where he'd landed. The man would be dead in seconds.

"How were you going to escape with the baby?" she shouted.

His dull eyes became unfocused. She shook him harshly, reviving him for only a moment.

"…the sea," he breathed. Then he was no more.

Abrielle rolled away shaking, fighting to regain control of her exhausted body and tumultuous emotions. She was freezing, and her muscles were cramping terribly now. Three times she attempted to stand on her injured ankle, only to fall to the ground, panting with pain, and a growing sense of unfathomable loss. All of her love, all of her skills had not been enough to save her sister or her niece. The last time she fell, she struck the dead man's body, causing it to roll further down the embankment. She stared in bitter anguish at the form of the man who had so successfully lured her away from Tara. The rain began to fall harder.

*

"What would you have me say, then?"

"The truth, Mr. Frankenstein, the truth, indeed such a thing would be a most refreshing change."

"But I've already told you all I know," Ernest asserted again.

Magistrate Kendrick rustled his papers in frustration.

"You have provided this board of inquiry and investigation a series of facts, which do no' correlate and only hamper our efforts to locate your daughter, if she still lives."

Ernest's patience with these men was wearing thin. As he'd lain unconscious on the ground, neighbors had come to help extinguish the blaze, and so too had these representatives of the law. Tara's apparent murder or abduction by gypsies, the discovery of the dead men, the disappearance of a mysterious sister-in-law, who had masqueraded as Mrs. Shaw's granddaughter, and the fire raised any number of questions, which fascinated local gossips and the press alike.

"Which facts, sir?" Ernest requested without hesitation.

"What?"

"You say my facts are unhelpful to you. Would you have me invent new ones simply to fit your theories?"

Kendrick bristled.

"Sir, we are trying to help you, and we can no' help you if you continue to block our efforts to solve this deplorable crime."

Ernest chaffed at the notion that anyone here wanted to help him. For over a week now, they'd given him endless new justifications for his continued detention. In the tortuous, lonely hours spent in his cell, his dreams of late often returned to the weeks of William's murder trial. Selfish reasons drove this inquisition, just as it had driven the trial then.

Ernest knew firsthand that there were careers to be made from such a high profile affair as this. Truth and justice he knew had little to do with these proceedings.

"Now, let's discuss your wife's sister?" Kendrick began anew.

"She's dead," Ernest shrugged.

"So you claim. Yet you can offer us no proof of tha'." Kendrick noted as he wagged his finger.

Ernest sighed and shook his head. At least that motion no longer made him dizzy.

"I saw her run into the burning barn. She did not come out. And I've been locked up here ever since. How am I supposed to offer any additional proof beyond what I've already told you?"

Kendrick sniffed haughtily.

"And why would she go into tha' blaze?"

"I told you, because those men put my child inside," Ernest choked. "She tried to save her."

The official removed his glasses in aggravation and massaged the bridge of his nose.

"But you've previously testified that you cannot confirm that the child was in fact in the barn. So it's all supposition."

"It's true. I was unconscious for much of what happened. But I believe in my heart that she was inside. Besides, you can't confirm who was inside any better than I can," Ernest charged.

The fire had burned with such intensity that any trace of human remains would have been turned to ash. The mystery of who might have actually been inside was one that Ernest found useful.

"Besides, if my sister-in-law were alive, why would she disappear?"

"Well, perhaps she has more to hide, after all this is a woman who apparently went around for months claiming to be poor Mrs. Shaw's granddaughter. How honest is tha'? You yourself have stated repeatedly that you do not really know her. Perhaps she was in league with these men and stole your child. But I suppose you still refuse to believe tha', though?" he noted, as he perched the spectacles back on his nose.

Yes, Ernest thought to himself. There was a great deal Abrielle had kept hidden. The fact she was apparently responsible for murdering two strong, well-armed men made that abundantly clear. Still, he kept changing the details of his story just enough to confuse the investigators as to whether Tara and Abrielle had lived or perished. He'd labored to make the authorities believe that Abrielle was dead, and bore no accountability in the gypsy's deaths, though they hardly seemed to accept his theory that the gypsies must have turned on each other. Ignorance was his shield; it was the best way to remove the law's attention. Then he'd be free to act.

"Why would she have saved me then?" Ernest shot back.

"Ransom. Your inheritance in Switzerland is substantial, yes?"

Ernest appeared unmoved. Kendrick's fingers drummed the table. He decided to try a new line of questioning.

"You claim to have been in Geneva these last months, tying up your family's affairs?"

"Yes."

"But that you had no contact with these gypsies who attacked you during this time?"

"Correct."

"None?"

"If I had I would tell you," Ernest promised evenly.

Kendrick's voice rose.

"I find it impossible to believe that gypsies, foreign to Irish soil, would suddenly, and for no apparent reason, come here, attack you and harm your child, Mr. Frankenstein. Now why do you continue to obstruct this investigation? Are you in league with the woman? Does your daughter's life mean less to you than she does?"

Ernest held the man's acrimonious gaze. He must hold his tongue; the magistrate's patience was beginning to wither. He was grasping blindly now, trying to gain anything useful from this hostile witness. But there was nothing they could charge him with. He would be free soon. Ernest knew that the laws of nations could not help him. He must pursue justice alone; that his thoughts should so closely echo the sentiments of Victor's offspring ….

"Thank heavens, old Quinn Tierney did no' live to see this shameful day," Kendrick huffed, "or his daughter."

Ernest's heart smoldered, but he said nothing. To do so would only further delay his search for Tara.

"Now, let's begin again," Kendrick said calmly, "on the night in question you were waiting in the front room for your sister-in-law to return …"

*

He awoke with such a start that he almost tumbled from the cell's bench. The surroundings coalesced as Ernest blinked sleep from his eyes. His prayers had unknowingly become one with rest. What had he been dreaming? It felt so real. He could only recall an image of Baseria, then a sense of dread. She was surrounded by an army of the dead in a frozen wasteland. Were these thoughts merely a product of sleep or could their bond be returning? He'd felt nothing from her since Hungary. Could she still be alive?

He shook his head slightly in an effort to drive away his fatigue. As Ernest gazed up at the jail cell window searching for any indication of the telltale light of dawn, he beheld a sight which sent an icy shudder through his heart: a single red rose lay set among the steel bars.

*

Ernest bent down to examine the remnants of the small boat. The fragments of rough boards clattered harshly against the rocks. If not for the frayed rope anchoring it to the shore, he was certain that no trace of it would have remained. Its twin, which Jal had used to escape with Tara, was long since departed, leaving only a cut line and Ernest's numbing grief to testify to its phantom existence.

The morning sun lay somewhere beyond the walls of dense fog. He could stay and await further illumination, but he knew there was nothing more to be learned here when the fog dissipated. The sea had left no other traces of his daughter's fate.

He was free now, due largely to lack of any concrete evidence regarding his role in these mysterious matters, but at the moment, his freedom mattered little to him. Ernest studied the ground as he began to make his way toward the front of the house. He'd returned to it late last night, and just as it had been ten years earlier, a lifetime ago in Geneva, his home, once so alive with love and happiness, was dark and silent and he was alone.

Upon reaching the front of the house, Ernest turned his attention to the charred remains of the barn; only the stone walls and some twisted iron remained. All else was ash. He stared at the ruin and wondered if he would ever rebuild it. Quinn had managed to do so when he'd returned to this place. But it's true worth had been in the wealth of old family objects it had stored and the memories attached to them. Much of his wife's family's past now lain in cinders. Spying some object in the ash, he stooped to retrieve it.

As he did so, the click of a pistol being cocked emanated from behind him. He could sense that the barrel was pointed at his head.

"Turn, slowly," a familiar voice commanded.

He obeyed. As if she'd arisen fully reborn from the fire's ash, Abrielle stood before him, weapon in hand. No, actually she was leaning slightly on the remnant of the stone wall she'd been hiding behind. She looked pale and sick.

"Let's go inside," she suggested.

Ernest lowered his hands.

"I'd rather you just shot me here," he declared.

"Fine."

She pulled the trigger, but only the sound it produced was that of the spring releasing. Each of their bluffs had been called, some measure of trust established.

"Now let's go," she bid. "I'm cold."

Abrielle limped slightly as she walked away toward the house. Ernest released a breath he hadn't realized he'd been holding as he considered her retreating form, already vanishing into the fog. Who was this woman? A part of him feared to learn her secrets; that was, if he lived long enough to learn them. Still, he had to know the truth. He set off after her in determination.

"I need water," she said as they entered the house.

Ernest was still wary of turning his back on her but decided that it really didn't matter. She could have killed him several times by now and had not. It seemed unlikely she would suddenly do so. In fact, she had saved his life. Then again, what was there to stop her from changing her mind? He went to the kitchen and as he poured a glass of water, he heard her ascend and then quickly descend the staircase. Was she checking to make certain they were alone or had she retrieved something, another weapon she'd hidden perhaps?

When he nervously returned to the front room, she sat silently in the chair beside the empty cradle. She coughed slightly as her fingers caressed the blanket in the bottom, the blanket she and Ailis had spent hours creating, together for her beloved niece. A book, not a pistol, sat in her lap. She sipped from the glass Ernest handed to her then folded her hands and hung her head.

"I'm sorry."

These words were the last thing he'd expected. How could she be apologizing to him? Ernest had never seen Abrielle so unguarded, even her grief for her sister she'd kept mostly private. For some reason her sudden vulnerability awed him. He began to refute her.

"No, Abrielle, it's my fault ..."

Wordlessly she handed him the book. Confused Ernest studied it. It was one of Ailis' books of poetry, but beyond that fact there was nothing significant about it that he could perceive.

"I don't understand?"

"Who is Jal?" Abrielle asked, as she looked up, accusation and need burning in her eyes.

Ernest stared at her mystified.

"How do you know about Jal?"

"Look inside," she said quietly.

From among the well-worn pages, he retrieved a letter.

"That arrived … the night Ailis went into labor," Abrielle's voice shook, "I was going to read the book to her but with everything … I ...," she looked away unable to finish.

As he read the words, Jal's final declaration to him echoed in Ernest's mind:

"'You have betrayed me, Frankenstein. Your word is dust. I claim your daughter, until you fulfill your oath to return mine to me, as promised.'"

Ernest closed his eyes as the tragedy now lay bare before him. His return home had been delayed by heavy snows in the mountains and stormy seas. Jal's pursuit of Baseria must have taken him another route, and he'd arrived in Portsmouth, England, well ahead of Ernest's own arrival in Ireland.

When Ernest failed to come as promised, Jal had fulfilled his own vow: he'd acted on his claim back in Hungary. There he'd said Ernest's life was his; apparently he'd extended that declaration to Ernest's family. In the absence of his own child, he had taken Tara. No doubt he somehow viewed this as balance. And Ernest had led him to her by revealing the whereabouts of his family. If he tried to save her, without finding Baseria, Ernest held no illusion that Jal would not fail to use the fiend's pistol to kill Tara.

"If I hadn't knocked you out, we could have saved her that night," Abrielle's haunted voice trembled.

Ernest delicately reached for Abrielle's hand. She recoiled slightly at his unanticipated touch, but finally met his eyes.

"He thinks I betrayed him. If we had tried to rescue Tara, Jal would have killed her, then. You probably saved her life."

Abrielle looked bitterly towards the empty cradle as she bit her lip. It took some time before she could speak.

"Where is she?"

Ernest was unable to respond as he struggled with his own guilt and grief. Why hadn't he told Jal the truth about Victor's journals being taken when he knew the gypsy did not believe him?

"Hungary, perhaps," he finally managed. "I don't really know."

Abrielle nodded as if she'd just obtained a long sought answer. No wonder she'd been unable to decipher the blended languages used by the gypsies who had taken Tara. Her duties for the Empire had only taken her as far east as Austria. But why had the last gypsy spoken to her in French?

"What are you?" Ernest asked.

Abrielle lowered her eyes for a moment but there was no choice.

"I'm a spy for the Empire," she declared as her gaze returned to his. "Ailis never knew."

"Why didn't you tell her the truth?"

Abrielle looked down at her trembling hands, her eyes rich with shame.

"Because … I thought she would never trust me … never, love me, if she knew what I've ..."

She managed an awkward, tragic smile as she wiped a tear away.

A loud knock at the door startled both of them. From somewhere, Abrielle instantly produced a knife. Ernest peered out the window, into the depths of obscuring mist, as she crept toward the door. He was certain he'd seen something move.

"Wait. Don't open it."

"I don't think we'll have to," she commented as she returned from the hallway with an envelope bearing his name.

They wordlessly regarded one another for a moment.

"I'll check the back door," Abrielle decided. She disappeared into the kitchen.

Ernest withdrew a brief note from within the envelope. The words it contained both froze his soul with terror and offered him a perverse sense of pleasure:

Uncle,
I have learned of your sorrows. I will await you, for a week, on the northeastern shores of North Ronaldsay Island. Come alone.

Ernest's eyes danced with a disquieting light.

"What is it?" Abrielle asked when he handed her the note. Ernest rushed into the parlor to consult an atlas, tearing madly through its pages until he located the information he sought.

"What does this mean?" Abrielle demanded as she brandished the missive.

"The Orkneys. He's in the Orkneys."

Ernest paced rapidly about the room. Abrielle re-read the letter.

"Wait. Ailis said your family was all dead. Then who is this from?"

He stopped and looked directly into her brown eyes.

"A nightmare my brother summoned, a demon, who walks as a man, that thinks as one, who claims me as his family; he is the one who is responsible for all of this; he is the one I must confront in order to save my daughter."

*

Sunlight echoed through the racing clouds as they stood alone among the dead. Ernest's eyes focused on the Latin inscription that Abrielle had insisted be carved into the Celtic cross: *Alis votat propris* — She flies with her own wings.

Ernest knelt beside his wife's grave, lost in silent prayer and reflection. Ailis had always known his heart better than he. She had saved him, believed in him, loved him. When this was all over, Ernest could not conceive of a life without her. But first he must survive the dark days to come.

Abrielle and he had spent the past four days learning to accept impossible truths about one another. Guarded, many of their conversations had taken place at night in a small sailboat, far from the cold shore of Clew Bay. At moments Ernest could not help but fancy that Ailis drifted through the night with them.

He still didn't know if he fully accepted that his sister-in-law was a spy for Napoleon's Empire, just as she would have to come to terms with the knowledge that they must now involve themselves in another culture's war of faith in order to save Tara. However, Ernest did know that Abrielle would never stop searching for Tara. Both knew that only their openness, faith, and trust in one another could save all of them. Each needed the strength of the other.

Coming to the cemetery during the day was a risk but it was also necessary. When they left here, they would separate, their tasks divided, but their purpose united. Abrielle would return to the Continent. There she would use her skills and resources, to track down and infiltrate the gypsy clan and rescue Tara. Ernest's task would take him to the Orkney Islands of Scotland. There he must at last face Victor's self-proclaimed son—the Old One—and rescue Baseria and the other Wild Rose women he'd taken. Secretly, both feared they would never return, or worse, that they would fail.

Abrielle stood near her sister's grave pondering the daunting difficulties ahead. She could not decide if she should return to France immediately, or begin her search, as Ernest suggested, in Geneva. If she went home, she might be able to secure her own allies, or she might be imprisoned as a traitor. Ernest had already written Christiansen and informed him to expect her arrival in Geneva, though she held serious doubts as to how much help Ernest's godfather could be. He'd also offered to contact an old friend named Jack, though he seemed to have some reservations about her doing so. Regardless of where she began, Christiansen would again serve as their mutual contact.

Her own doubts were not helped by Ernest's revelation that he'd wanted to die the night she'd saved him. A part of her understood and another hated him for it. She insisted that an oath be taken between them, before they departed, the nature of which she had devised. He would have to prove his courage and loyalty to her before she would trust him fully.

As she waited for him to indicate he was ready, she tried to ignore the grave just beyond Ailis', the tomb of her father. This was her third trip to this cemetery, and she only permitted herself a fleeting glance of his final resting place. Still her anger toward him burned less bright thanks to Ailis. In time she might even allow herself to forgive him. How strange that her life should mirror his so closely; for now, she too must seek out family who had been unjustly taken.

They would not return to these shores, until the vow they were about to take, was fulfilled. The property in Ireland would be entrusted to the Shaws. If Ernest did not return in three years' time, the land would be theirs. Abrielle would miss the old couple, who still believed her dead, though Ernest had hinted otherwise to them.

Both Abrielle and Ernest had selected a few talismans from the house that would accompany them on their journeys. She'd taken only two items: the blanket from Tara's cradle and her sister's flute. Ernest chose one of Ailis' journals, and the small box, decorated with beautiful carvings, given to him by Nasi. During these dark days, it continued to defy his best efforts to open it; yet, instinctively, he knew it must accompany him.

"It's time," Abrielle said softly as she moved to one side of Ailis' grave.

Ernest nodded, kissed his hand, and laid it gently upon the earth before standing.

Abrielle had said nothing of what this vow would consist of, but somehow he was not too surprised when she drew her knife.

"Your right hand," she ordered simply.

Ernest extended it, and she sliced a deep gash into his hand, which bled freely, then did the same to her own. She then clasped their hands together so that the pressure of the grip dripped their mingled blood onto Ailis' grave. Their eyes met, and she spoke, using the Latin she'd learned from the nuns at the orphan's convent, translating her words for Ernest.

"*Cor unum a mari usque ad mare*—One heart, from sea to sea. *Dum vita est, spes est*—While there is life, there is hope. *Is nos spondee nostrum carus*—This we promise our beloved."

And from that thin place, from which hope emanates, for the first time, they embraced and recognized each other as family.

Chapter 21
The World to Come

They had been following him since his arrival in the Orkneys, but Ernest paid them little mind. It was not the Moon Shadow gypsies he sought, but their abhorrent Master. These men were simply here to help guide him into the trap. The coarse sands of North Ronaldsay's Linklet Bay glistened in the afternoon sun, which would not last. Leaden storm clouds hung threateningly on the eastern horizon, dull flashes of light pulsing intermittently between them. Further out in the bay, the white sails hung on the double masts of an impressive schooner-style vessel, weighed at anchor, which stood out against the gathering gloom.

He was approaching a small landing craft from the vessel, about which three sullen figures stood waiting in the waves. It was as if they feared to set foot upon the same shore where the ominous, wind-whipped, black-cloaked figure stood, waiting.

When Ernest reached him, the two regarded one another in silence for a moment, then the great being turned and began to stalk away. Ernest alone followed. Would their quests for justice unite them or destroy them?

"It has saddened me to learn of the losses you have suffered, Uncle," the mysterious being said gently.

Ernest walked beside him down the shore, but said nothing.

"I am sorry my people did not arrive in time to protect your family," the other continued.

"Protect us?"

Ernest halted, but only for a moment, as the man proceeded down the beach undeterred.

"That was always their purpose," the shadow explained when Ernest again walked by his side. "Just as their purpose shall now be to secure the child who was taken so unjustly from you by our treacherous enemy."

Lies, these must be lies, Ernest told himself, as they continued past the men near the boat.

"And those you've taken …"

"Are my concern."

They walked for a time before he continued.

"They will bring us justice, repair Father's damage."

"Their abduction caused my daughter's. They must be returned or Jal will kill her."

The creature rounded on him.

"Do not be deceived. He sees you as an enemy; he will not keep his word. He cares only to forestall what must be, just as your brother did."

Ernest swallowed hard.

"Is this why you've summoned me here?" he bitterly asked.

The other said nothing.

They proceeded up a small rise from the beach and came to stand before a ruined cottage. The grassy roof had all but collapsed, no door remained, but the stone walls and chimney stood firm against the relentless ocean's winds. Ernest wished he could see the hooded face, whose singular attention was rooted to this ruin.

"This," the other stated, "this was the site of your brother's most malicious crime against me. The place where I was to forever be denied happiness."

Ernest feared to speak or look toward his disquieting companion. But he also knew he must ask the question. He swallowed before addressing the vile shadow.

"What …what did he do?"

The figure slowly turned to him, yellow, inhuman orbs alight with loathing.

"He refused to free my beloved mate from death as he did me."

With these words, he drew back his hood, and Ernest gazed, with unspeakable horror, upon the hell-forged nightmare beneath. Every nerve was alive with fear, his mind screamed for him to avert his eyes, but he could not turn from the unholy specter, from living Death.

"I cannot allow you to suffer the same fate, Uncle," the creature said sympathetically as he resumed his hood. "You have already suffered too much for his crimes, been made as inhuman as I by your journeys. We are family. Father created us both. He abandoned you as he once did me, intent that we should never meet. He pursued me into the frozen wastelands of the North; there his body died, but his fate is linked to ours.

Now, thanks to your retrieval of his journals, I can at last re-claim my birth rite, heal my pain … and yours."

Finally, Ernest could understand Victor's madness.

As the creature turned to begin back towards the small boat upon the shore, Ernest shook with fear, as he fought to regain air in his lungs and against the disbelief in his heart. However Victor's creation had come to be, Ernest was now beholden to it. The deliverance of the Wild Rose prisoners, Tara's salvation, his soul, depended on Ernest embracing his brother's killer. There was no choice but to follow—he staggered after the ghastly being.

Upon reaching the boat where the gypsies and their Master awaited him, Ernest turned and fixed his eyes to the southwestern horizon, back toward Ireland, back to Ailis, to the life he must leave behind. He had come to realize that whatever strength he'd given her that final day, she'd used not to prolong her own life, but to give birth to their child. Ailis had sacrificed everything because she loved him and the tiny new life their love had created together. He could do no less for her or his child. He would honor her sacrifice by at last accepting Victor's great sin as family. It was the only way to save Tara.

"Come, Uncle," the Devil bid, extending his decrepit hand to Ernest. "In that direction lay only death. I offer you life. Join me and I will restore your family to you."

Slowly, mournfully, Ernest turned back toward the boat, accepting the proffered hand of Victor's 'son.' The gypsies freed the craft from the soft sands and began to row through the shifting tides, towards the distant ship, as the clouds from the gathering storm extinguished the sun.

Story continues in
Frankenstein Soul's Echo
Book 2 of 3
The Resurrection Trinity